# Hadassa

# Loves
# In The
# Shadows

**EDITORIAL CORRECTIONS**: Loves in the Shadows

Action should be spelt *Aktion* when referring to the assembly and deportion of Jews to the death camps.

Selection should be spelt *Selektion* when referring to the selection of inmates in a concentration or death camp for slave labor or to be put to death.

The title of Chapter 3 – Among The Jaws – should read: Into the jaws of danger
The title of Chapter 9 - The Delation – should read: Exposed.

p.334, line 17: the words "built by King Herod" should be erased.

Hadassa Mor

# Loves In The Shadows

Translated from Hebrew
by Aviva Perlmutter

 Mazo Publishers

Loves In The Shadows
ISBN: 978-1-936778-84-3

Copyright © 2012
Kochav Publishers and Hadassa Mor
kochavpublishers@gmail.com

*Published by:*
Mazo Publishers
PO Box 10474
Jacksonville, Florida USA 32247
Tel: 1-815-301-3559

PO Box 36084
Jerusalem, Israel 91360
Tel: +972-2-652-3877

mazopublishers@gmail.com
www.mazopublishers.com

First published in Hebrew, 2011
Kochav Publishers, Tel-Aviv

Editor: Ira Hollinger

Historical advisor: Evyatar Nur
Astrological advisor: Herzel Lifshits
Cover painter: Shimon Kahan

**All rights reserved.**
No part of this publication may be translated, reproduced, stored in a retrieval system, or transmitted in any form or by any means, electronic, mechanical, photocopying, recording or otherwise, without prior permission in writing from the publisher.

All the characters in this book could be
Each one of us.
We are the victims, we are the survivors.
We are the wretched, we are the heroes.

This is a fictional story based on
Extraordinarily true happenings and events.
This is true history of the dark days
Of the War and the Holocaust,
Interwoven with stunning personal experiences.

This is the story of the Jewish people
Struggling all along the History to overcome
The hate and discrimination and antagonism against them,
By means of strong Spirit, deep Faith, and sense of Justice.

As a school teacher and as a Jurist, this novel is
My gift to everyone in the world – who cares.

                                                    Hadassa Mor

# Contents

| | |
|---|---|
| 1 | The Imaginary Husband |
| 2 | The Biological Father |
| 3 | Among The Jaws |
| 4 | The Escape |
| 5 | The Uprising |
| 6 | With The Partisans |
| 7 | In The Anders Army |
| 8 | Majdanek |
| 9 | The Delation |
| 10 | On The Death March |
| 11 | Stirrings Of Freedom |
| 12 | Rape In Italy |
| 13 | The Collapse |
| 14 | The Kielce Pogrom |
| 15 | Traumatic Uprooting |
| 16 | Dramatic Encounters |
| 17 | With The Abandoned Child |
| 18 | Battles Of Independence |
| 19 | Wheel Of Fortune |
| 20 | Exposing The Truth |
| 21 | Monuments |

# 1
# The Imaginary Husband

Yuzhi was born without roots, and so he lived for most of his life, trying to clutch onto any branch, or grasp the remainder of a bough, though in vain. How a person, who is known as a tree of the field, does not achieve the status of a tree, how can such a person manage to live?

Yuzhi had grown up as a low, fainting bush with superficial roots, sweeping around, hovering up and down in the winds without the anchor of family lineage to secure himself; trying hard to convince all his surroundings, by pretending, that he indeed is a scion of a stable family.

Yuzhi knew who his mother was. As to his father, he had not the faintest idea who he was. His mother had, for decades, totally refused to discuss this delicate, loaded issue with him. She refused to give him even a scrap of information about the true identity of the man who had fathered him. Here and there she would throw him contradictory crumbs of information, mingled with false facts, which took over his thoughts and permeated deeply into his mind.

These fragments of knowledge left him up in the air. Was his biological father indeed his mother's Jewish husband, as she insisted, or was he another man entirely, one whose identity was hidden from him, like a heavy concrete stone blocking the opening to a burial cave? Yuzhi had, in fact, rolled this stone to the entrance of his conscience, regarding anything pertaining to his birth father.

Yuzhi did not ask, did not investigate, or scrabble in his family tree, like those who are afraid that if they fail to discover their roots, the tree of family connections might wither and die; like those who follow up every link about their ancestors, digging deep to excavate the roots of their origins, so that they can reveal and present them to the eyes and ears of the world, or at least to the descendants of their family so that they will not forget, will not inadvertently cut off the branch of continuity on which they sit.

For very many years, Yuzhi did not have even the slightest clue to start him off on his search for his father's family. The hermetic seal with which his mother had put over her mouth about everything connected with the true identity of his father, produced a constant state of severe anxiety in Yuzhi. This anxiety was so overpowering that it created a barrier to his natural desire to know who his birth father was. Better to let the matter rest, and live with what lay on the surface, he thought. He would have to be satisfied with his mother's lineage and with the facade of the account he chose to assume for himself.

Even as a youth, Yuzhi had begun to convince himself of the version he later adopted – as if it were really true – which he constructed from the scraps of information his mother threw in his direction, like sparks spluttering from the embers of a fire. His deep longings and creative imagination made him flutter his rendering of his origins in all directions.

Yuzhi's behavior became extravagantly extrovert, and a never-ending waterfall of words cascaded from his mouth; he made it impossible for any companion to carry on a conversation with him because of his overwhelming, almost compulsive, need to prove to anyone and everyone his deeply established lineage. Everyone who happened to come his way, whether grocer or vegetable seller, pharmacist or optician, cobbler or watchmaker, people he had never met in his life and who would vanish from it immediately, they were forced to listen to his life story. Yuzhi had convinced himself that there was nothing more interesting to anyone than the origins of his family and the story of his life. There were those who, unfortunate enough to bump into him and have to listen to his outpourings, would listen to him courteously, managing to maintain a pleasant demeanor; others, however, were exasperated to the point of bursting.

Yuzhi would enthusiastically relate to them the most expedient version of his story, having ironed out the wrinkles, smoothed the rough edges, rehearsing to himself the potential questions his audience might pose, together with plausible answers so that he would not be caught off guard. However, sometimes he was not quite so fortunate, and he was put on the spot by a skeptical listener.

When the truth was finally revealed, it cast a dark shadow over his life. He was already not a young man, and the scars on his mind, which with each year had multiplied, swelled and intensified and caused his whole, intricately constructed life to collapse into a heap of sadness and bitterness, creating a somewhat flawed personality.

Yuzhi's mother's name was Reizele Reznik. She was one of many children born to the Reznik family, who had lived for many generations in Zamosc, a small town in southeast Poland, which had the distinction of having been founded in 1580 by Emperor Jan Zamoyski.

More than twenty thousand Jews lived in Zamosc between the two world wars, and they comprised almost half of the population of the town. They earned their livings from small industry, in particular making clothing, shoes, and furniture, as well as from trade and services.

Zamosc boasted many professional Jewish associations, as well as Zionist political parties and youth movements. Jewish schools and kindergartens flourished and included a school in the *Tarbut* network and one in the *Yavne* network, where Hebrew was taught. A Yiddish-speaking elementary school was named for the well-known writer I. L. Peretz, who was born in Zamosc; there was also a gymnasium for Jews where

Polish was spoken. The Jews set up their own sports clubs and drama and literature groups. Yiddish journals were published, and there were many other cultural activities.

Reizele was different from the rest of her girlfriends. She was taller, and had a well-developed body with firm, prominent breasts which added several years to her chronological age. She had pleasant manners, a pretty face and she was sharp-eyed and without guile. She studied at the Jewish gymnasium in the town and also helped at home, doing the heavy housework; she stringently observed the Torah laws and Rabbinical demands, taking care to wear long sleeves and dresses, with the hem well below her knees.

The Reznik family was religious, like all the Jews who had lived for hundreds of years in Poland, until the decree of death fell on them.

Reizele's father, Yechiel Reznik, was the Rabbi of the Central Synagogue, which was the pride and joy of all the Jews in the town. This ornate synagogue had been built at the end of the seventeenth century. From the outside, it resembled a fortress. Inside, it was magnificent.

The impressive stage, centered amongst the seats of the worshippers and facing the niche for the holy Torahs, was decorated with wrought-iron intertwined leaves, branches, and geometric cones that formed into a Torah crown. The niche itself was decorated with motifs of the musical instruments used by the Levites in the holy Temple. A massive Chanukah menorah, with nine candle holders, stood in front of the stage. The walls of the synagogue were covered with illustrations from the Torah; paintings of animals set against a background of rich foliage, so as to not transgress the Torah prohibition, as written in the second commandment, not to make any sculpture or picture depicting human figures.

Outside, the gate to the entrance was supported by two pillars in the baroque style, whose stone cornices served as the bases for the two ends of an arch, over which was an inscription from the Torah: *How full of awe is this place! This is the house of God, and this is the gate of heaven.* In the center was an additional inscription, this time from the Psalms: *This is the gate of the Lord; the righteous shall enter into it.*

Rabbi Reznik served his community with devotion and was well respected. However, their esteem did not enable them to augment his meager salary, for this Jewish community was a poor one. For the Reznik family, it was enough for existence, but of necessity a frugal one.

From when she was a child, Reizele sensed how heavy the load was on this large family of eight children, all of whom lived together. Surrounding their large house was a vast courtyard, with enough space for their goats to bleat and the hens to lay their eggs, which were collected each day and were thrown straight to the frying pan.

Reizele always had a positive outlook, that is, until she became aware of the threatening and oppressive steps creeping towards their corner in Poland.

The violent outbursts and hatred towards Jews in Germany, on Kristallnacht, the night of the broken glass, when synagogues and Torahs were torched, and practically everything Jewish ransacked, windows of Jewish businesses smashed, all of this terrified Reizele. The slivers of broken glass which covered the wide sidewalks of distant Berlin seemed to dazzle and blind her eyes. The events of Kristallnacht upset her completely, and the lack of response from the Jewish community, with her father the Rabbi at their head, disturbed her deeply.

These events resounded in the ears of the Jews of Poland like an echo of far-off thunder which could have no direct effect upon them. Their placid lives continued as before. Here and there they heard of, and even knew, about some families who had requested entry certificates from British Mandate officials in Palestine, so that they could immigrate to Eretz Yisrael. These families felt that the earth was shifting under their feet because of the evil declarations emanating from the Reichstag, calling on the Jews to emigrate from Europe. So they decided to leave everything behind them and set out for the unknown land.

But Yechiel Reznik was not among them. His whole life was wrapped up in being Rabbi of the synagogue, his every minute lived in accordance with religious precepts and practices, known and esteemed by everyone in his community. He refused to hear of abandoning Poland, his country. Only those families who were not religious were leaving, the Socialists, he would say with a sneer. Rabbi Reznik had even heard of a few families who had left to live in Eretz Yisrael, but after short time came back to Poland. They just could not bear the burning Mediterranean heat, the poverty, the disease, the economic hardships. So, yes, there were families who returned from Palestine to their former lives in Poland, which at least were familiar to them and which seemed to them Utopian, relative to the hot winds and harsh conditions of their lives in Eretz Yisrael. These people had no inkling of what particular Hell awaited them, and on which stake they would be burned.

Reizele's good instincts sent warning signals to her brain about the strong, bad winds blowing closer and closer.

Because of her position in her family, as the eldest daughter, she was used to doing much of the daily work of running the large household. It was Reizele who went to the market to buy provisions for the family, and was also compelled to take care of her younger brothers, who hung onto her and depended on her, and she felt it was too hard to carry the weighty burden responsibility for them.

For all these reasons, Reizele longed to leave her parents' home and move far away. But where could she go, and how would she get there? Where could a Jewish girl, the daughter of a Rabbi, make her escape to? Perhaps her only means of escape would be to find herself a *chosson*, a bridegroom, who would take her away from here. For some time now, she was ripe for this step; she would soon be eighteen years old, so this was a wonderful idea – she would find a *chosson*.

From the way she behaved and talked at home, it was clear to her parents that she wanted to get married. They accepted her wish with mixed feelings. They knew that when Reizele left home they would be losing a valuable member of their household staff. But on the other hand, their way of life dictated that a young woman who had reached Reizele's age should be married – and this, in their eyes, took precedence.

So, this eldest daughter who had reached the age of almost eighteen, and lived in the house which was so chock-full with several generations of family that she hardly had room to breathe, she needed a husband who would remove her from all this, and take her into his care.

Therefore, bearing in mind the difficulties of the time and the social and economic factors, she began to busy herself with finding a *shidduch*, her matrimonial match. She needed to find someone who would take it upon himself to look after her and provide her with security and a good living.

My parents made me a match with a Jewish boy, a yeshiva student, Reizele would mumble to Yuzhi when he would ask her about his father and she would try to calm him down and extricate herself from his awkward questions. My parents made a match for me with a yeshiva boy, she would repeat, mumbling at him in an unconvincing tone of voice.

A *shidduch,* which is generally made to the mutual desire of both sets of parents, in order to reduce, one by one, the tribe of daughters still in the family home, as soon as each reaches the age of puberty. The parents call for the town's matchmaker, the *Shadchanit*, to come to the house, and she appears – a substantial lady, swathed in colorful scarves and a wide-brimmed hat with a plume of feathers heralding her arrival. The *Shadchanit* sits herself down in an armchair in the living room, or on a chair in the kitchen, spreading herself out expansively with the dignity expected of one in her position.

With a well-practiced air of self-importance, she pulls her notebook out of her bag, which contains her full list of young girls and boys eager to find themselves a good match.

She ponders each name on the list and then makes her offer: Here is someone for your daughter – Shuki the shoemaker. He is not an observant Jew? In that case, I can recommend Burka the butcher. I can see you are turning up your nose a bit, so what about Fischka? He is lame?

Well, if none of these young men fit the bill, and you want me to try to find a yeshiva student, you must understand that I do not have too many of them left of the right age. Ah, but I do have one I have not yet found a wife for. He has been turned down by each family I have suggested him to. He could definitely be a suitable *shidduch* for your daughter, if you are so keen to marry her off. Oh, it is not you who is pushing her out of the door, but she herself who is impatient to get married?

Maybe your daughter is right. After all, she is already eighteen. If she does not hurry up, she might end up on the shelf, Heaven forbid. So if I were you, I would take this yeshiva student. Basically he is all right; a bit hunched up, on the thin side, pale, not too strong. But he will be a good husband. He does not actually have any money, but thanks to the stipend the local community doles out to the yeshiva students, he can put food in his mouth. After the wedding, he will have to make a living somehow, as they all do. He will earn a few coins here, few coins there, so that he can support his wife and all the children that will come, with God's help. Nu, that's how it is with us. That is reality. So, that is all I have on my list to suggest to you.

It was not clear to Yuzhi if that was exactly the way things were handled between his grandfather and the matchmaker, or if there was, in fact, a matchmaker. The only fact that his brain registered was that his mother had married a Jew. Two facts, in fact. She married – and she married a Jew. He kept repeating the second fact, emphasizing that point to himself, for he did not look Jewish, and certainly did not look like a Polish Jew. His skin was quite dark, which suggested that his father could be from the East, perhaps Uzbeki or Kazakhi, who knows?

Yuzhi possessed few details about either the circumstances of his birth or the death of his father. He was left, therefore, with vast empty spaces in his mind, which he had an almost uncontrollable urge to fill with something – anything – of substance that he could cling to. He spun a story that he could live with, which he himself was not sure was truth or fiction. He thought, if I have no factual roots, I will create roots for myself, plant them firmly in the soil and tie them to a heavy weight so that a strong, upright, and stable plant will grow out of them.

Hence, Yuzhi's mother married Mottele, son of Berele the blacksmith, a yeshiva student who other young women had rejected. It was time for him too, since he had already reached the advanced age of twenty-one, and was still immersed, body and soul, in Torah study, in a world where time stands still, while his friends were all married, with babies in their arms!

Reizele agreed to marry Mottele without knowing anything about him. All she wanted was to get out of that cramped, crowded, noisy house, to distance herself from the place where she felt that the ground was shaking beneath her feet. She instinctively felt that wherever else she would be, everlasting contentment would be hers. So her imagination envisioned her life and this powerful, subconscious instinct to distance herself from her own house, in the end saved her life. That was why she was in need of a husband who could remove her from her parents' house and from the town of her birth. Yes, this would be the condition she would put in front of her prospective bridegroom, that he would take her away from Zamosc, and they would go together wherever they would go.

When Mottele's father told him the news, he could not believe his ears. Was it true that he, Mottele, was due to marry a girl he had never seen and the only thing he knew about her was that she was the daughter of the esteemed Rabbi Reznik? After all, from morning to night he sat in the study hall and studied Torah. He barely saw the light of day. From before dawn until nightfall, he would sit bent over the yellowed pages of the Talmud, hardly raising his head, the perfect Talmudic scholar. And now, he was being confronted with a challenge of frightening proportions: To prove his erudition outside the four walls of the study hall, to rise to the challenges of the everyday world unknown to him. It was astounding to him that from now on, he would need to earn a living, stand on his own feet, close his books, and be burned by the dazzling rays of the sun, and freeze when snowflakes melted on his clothes. He zigzagged between hope and dread. Reality was such that he would have to work to support himself and Reizele. He agreed to this. Whatever would be would be, he was getting married, doing what a man should do, according to the Torah commandments. He would leave the yeshiva, that warm and protective womb, and go out into a harsh world full of pitfalls for the unsuspecting. But he was not afraid. He was determined to make a living so that he could support his future family.

When the shy young couple was formally introduced to each other, they trembled like delicate leaves. Soon, however, all their uncertainties had left them. Reizele, the attractive one, found Mottele, so he would agree to the condition she imposed, to take her away from Zamosc.

The wedding was held in the courtyard of Rabbi Yechiel Reznik's house. It was a modest wedding, to which all the members of the extended family came – aunts and uncles, grandparents, nieces, nephews and cousins. Many prominent guests arrived, wearing their traditional attire, including the *streimel* and *kapote* and the magnificent *yarmulke*. Three klezmer musicians enlivened the proceedings with joyful Chassidic melodies and some men were even emboldened to break into song. Reizele's heart pounded wildly. Mottele stood under the wedding canopy, his hand holding the cup of wine, shaking as it neared his bride's lips. Through the thin veil, he could discern happiness and apprehension on her face, as she, though still distinct from him, hovered on the threshold of an unknown, mysterious world they would face together.

Reizele wondered to herself who this man was standing in front of her, with whom she would be sharing the rest of her life; how strange, she thought, fate was. After she had sipped the wine, Mottele took possession of the glass, and with a resolute movement of his foot, broke it to pieces, in accordance with the Jewish tradition to remember the destruction of the Temple. He felt proud to have fulfilled that traditional act, to have torn down the barrier and opened the way to a new, more complete life. Yes, he would find work, Mottele resolved to himself, no returning to the yeshiva anymore.

Berele the blacksmith could not understand his son's haste to leave his home and the town of his birth, and wander off in search of a new life in another town, though he was impressed by Mottele's resolve. Reizele's own eagerness to go forward with the proposed match, as long as the condition she imposed of leaving the town was fulfilled, left Berele no choice but to accept that he would have to part from his son.

It was fortunate that Berele had distant relatives living in the town of Belzec, not far from Zamosc. So, he thought, at least I'll be able to go and visit them from time to time there, and see all the grandchildren I'll have very soon, Amen. With that, he made up his mind to send them to his relatives in

Belzec, Adela and Chaimke, who sadly had not been blessed with children. Berele informed them that his son and his new wife would be coming to live with them, for a trial period, so that his son could look for work in Belzec. He even sent them money to cover the cost of their board.

The wedding night itself the couple spent separately, each in his parents' house. This was the condition, for as long as they did not have a place of their own. The marriage would begin in earnest only when they took their leave from their parents and left the town.

Thus, early on the morning of the day after the wedding, which was the first of September 1939, Reizele and Mottele climbed into the rented wagon, full of their possessions, which was standing in Rabbi Reznik's courtyard. All the members of the large family poured into the courtyard to say their goodbyes and wave them off. There was not a dry eye as they said their farewells to the newly-married couple, but in the back of their minds they could not help having a feeling of relief, when they thought about the extra room in the house the departure would give them. Reizele and Mottele, for their part, were both anxious and hopeful as they set off on their journey towards the unknown, with all the uncertainties that awaited them.

After a day of stops and starts on the road, they arrived after sunset, weary and hungry, at the home of Berele's relatives in Belzec, on the first of September 1939. In spite of their tiredness, Reizele's spirits brightened when they arrived: Joy flooded her thoughts when she looked forward to the pleasant life she and her husband would lead in a quiet and peaceful place. But her illusion was short-lived. Adela and Chaimke met them at the door, their smiles of welcome swiftly replaced by frowns of tension and anxiety.

We are delighted to see you, they said, but you've arrived at a very difficult time. War broke out today; the German

Army has invaded Poland. Do you know? The exhausted couple did not have the strength to take in the implications of this news. They unloaded their belongings in the room they had been given.

In the center of the room was a large bed, covered with a feather comforter. They had been warmly welcomed, in spite of the anxiety which had clouded their arrival, with a simple, tasty meal of bread, vegetables and barley soup, which seemed like a feast to them, and now retired early to their room. At last they could rest, together. This night would be their wedding night.

Trembling with emotion, they climbed into the big bed and under the cover of the comforter, they began, hesitantly, to stroke and explore each other's body, the first intimate touch for each of them. They were more tense than excited, extremes of unfamiliar emotions, swaying between revulsion to attraction, raced through their bodies. Gradually their embarrassment subsided in a long embrace in which passion overrode all else, and they became one.

Without any warning, in a lightning strike on the first of September 1939, the German Army invaded Poland and conquered the country in less than a month. Hitler must have chortled heartily when he drew his sword, as it were, and sliced the Munich Agreement into tiny pieces, which he had signed only the year before with the British. Based on this agreement, he would receive the Sudetenland from Czechoslovakia, in return for peace and non-aggression with Europe. Indeed, the French and the British had betrayed the defenseless Czechs and sacrificed the Sudetenland, which was an integral part of their country, to the Germans. But to what lengths would people go for the sake of peace? After all, what is that peanut called the Sudetenland, in comparison to the desirable idea of peace in the world?

Chamberlain, the British Prime Minister, returned to his country from Munich after he had signed the agreement with Hitler, as a winner. Who can forget the image of him, the great savior of his country and of the enlightened world, arriving at the airport, dressed in his customary Homburg hat, triumphantly waving that contemptible piece of paper he and Hitler had signed, and declaring: Peace in our Time!

What could he be thinking and feeling now, when he heard that Germany had invaded Poland, an act which would light the match to set off the flames of war? At least he had the grace to admit to his nation that he had been deceived and that his signature on the Munich Agreement was not worth the paper it was written on. And if it was the sword which sliced to pieces the Munich Agreement, it was also a cracked whip across the face of the Soviet Union, for only the week before, the Molotov-Ribbentrop Pact was signed between Russia and Germany, whose stated intention was to safeguard the independence of Poland for ten years! And now, within the space of a week, Poland fell under the heels of Nazi troops!

The Germans conquered Poland with astounding speed. Britain and France declared war immediately on Germany. However, the Soviet Union swallowed the bitter pill of dishonesty, having failed to see the deceit of the ally with whom they had signed the pact. They relied on the fact that Germany was still committed to not going to war against them, and on the territorial benefits agreed between them.

Next day at dawn, Reizele and Mottele awoke to the reality of war. Mottele went out early to search for any kind of work which would provide him with some money. He knocked at every door, even though he had no trade, and was turned away with a dismissive gesture by each and every one he approached. With each rejection he grew more and more despondent. Only a week later he found work in the warehouse of a shoe business where he looked after the stock, made the deliveries, and acted as a general gofer. His place of work was more than an hour's walk from his lodgings.

On his second day at work, the fifteenth of September 1939, Mottele heard a rumor which was spreading like wildfire: The German Army had reached Zamosc the day before and stormed the town, but even before that – on the ninth and again on the twelfth of September – they had bombed Zamosc, and 500 Jews had been killed. Among the dead were those Jews who had fled there from western Poland, and Jewish refugees who had escaped from Kielce and Chestochova. Unfortunately, as it turned out, they had been trapped; from the frying pan into the fire. When he returned home that evening, Mottele told Reizele, Adela and Chaimke the dreadful news. With worry and fear, they sat close together, holding hands to draw strength from each other. What was happening to their beloved family in Zamosc, what would the ruthless Nazis do to them? The Nazis' reputation for brutality had gone before them, and they feared the worst. At least, they comforted themselves, they were safe in Belzec, the Nazis would not reach this town. What a relief you came to us, just at the last minute, said Adela and Chaimke in unison.

It was the cruel irony of history that in the same period two leaders – albeit at opposite ends of the political spectrum – let loose their reign of terror and launched the Second World War: Stalin and Hitler, each one with his particular threat to the existence of his own nation and the huge numbers of subjugated people living under their rule in far-flung lands. Two leaders of two large states, who had concocted the most cynical and devious pact that had ever seen the light of day, signed by the Foreign Ministers of these states, the Russian Molotov and the German Ribbentrop on the twenty-third of August 1939, just one week before the outbreak of war.

The pact appeared to be innocuous. Neither side demanded

anything extravagant from the other. Each party to the pact undertook not to attack the other, and guaranteed to come to the aid of the other if it went to war against a third party, and not help that state if attacked. In other words, go ahead and kill, lay waste, conquer – we will not interfere. The two powers also agreed that neither of them would enter into any political or military alliance against the other. However, that was not all.

A confidential, secret protocol stated that if war broke out against Poland ... If? What unsurpassed conniving was this, when it was known to both sides that in another week war would break out and Poland would be attacked! And so, the deal was worked out that if Poland was conquered, it would quite logically be divided up between the two sides: the East under Soviet subjugation, the West under German rule. Russia would take Lithuania and Estonia, and Latvia and Finland in the north; this was in exchange for the Russians closing their eyes and not interfering with whatever Germany did in the parts of Western Europe it lusted after.

It is not difficult to imagine the expression on the faces of each of these Foreign Ministers, masters of cynicism both of them, during the negotiations leading up to the signing of this pact they each desired. The cake would be divided up between them, and to hell with personal morality. Let political expediency and ambition rule the day!

The negotiations were conducted with many a knowing wink. Uppermost in Molotov's mind was to keep the Germans as far away as possible from the Soviet Union. To the Germans, he said, if you keep to this, we are prepared to shut our eyes to your exploits in the West, and we will take the Baltic States for ourselves, as well as other areas in the East.

The talks were held in a magnificent palace in Moscow. At the end of the negotiations, Molotov shook hands with his counterpart, Ribbentrop. Two opposites: Molotov the immense Russian bear, whose behavior seemed naïve and unsophisticated, and Ribbentrop, the sleek, cunning German fox. They signed the eponymous pact, which they desired so fervently, each for his own reasons.

Barely one week after the signing of the pact, on the first of September 1939, Poland was attacked, and on the fourteenth of the month the Germans conquered Zamosc. They controlled the town for only two weeks after which, in accordance with the agreement with the Soviets, the Russians immediately took their place. But only for one week. At the end of that short period, the Soviets left Zamosc, because of a change in the boundaries between German-conquered Poland and those areas conquered by the Soviet Union.

The withdrawal of the Soviets from Zamosc after such a short time had the effect of leading thousands of Jews to join up with them and leave the town together with the Russian troops who returned to areas held by the Soviets. In retrospect, this step had saved those Jews' lives.

After this week, in which no one took charge, the Polish inhabitants of the town attacked the Jews, blaming them for collaborating with the Soviets. On the first of October 1939, the Germans returned to Zamosc and abuse against Jews began immediately and rapidly gathered momentum every moment of the day. Jews were forbidden to engage in business; their property was confiscated; their schools were closed down; they were forced to wear the yellow star as a badge of shame; they were forbidden to leave the town.

The mistreatment reached its peak with the expulsion of Jews from the picturesque part of the old city, where they had always lived, to Komarov, a neglected and poor neighborhood far from the center of the town. Komarov became an open ghetto without walls, where all the Jews were crammed. Even though it was not closed off, Jews were forbidden to leave it. In time came the forced labor, the murders, and the transports to the death camps. Only at this stage did Reizele come face to face with the horror.

Reizele did not have the mental strength to think anything different. To some extent, she was able to close her eyes to what was going on, for it quickly became clear to her that she was pregnant. Hence she closeted herself within her own four walls, barely going out of Adela and Chaimke's house. She spent her time helping them with the housework, and tending the small vegetable plot and the cow, which enabled them to be almost self-sufficient. In addition to milk from the cow, they occasionally ate meat from the last-born calf.

The months of Reizele's pregnancy were relatively uneventful. Mottele was delighted with the news of her pregnancy, and promised her that when the time came for her to give birth, he would be at her side and take her to the small hospital in town, where their child would be born, either a boy or a girl would be fine with him.

After most countries in Western Europe had been crushed under the heels of the Nazis – except for England, which would not give in – Hitler turned his face to the East, to conquer the Soviet Union. His addiction to conquest, subjugated by an uncontrollable urge, lodged in his bones and his twisted megalomaniac mind.

Hitler was impelled to occupy more and more countries and create a vast German Empire. This ambition would not be fulfilled without conquering the entire Soviet Union! Only this and nothing more, at least for the meantime! So, he, the Nazi leader, with one stride of his jackboots, had violated the Molotov-Ribbentrop Non-Aggression Treaty only two years after it was signed, when the guarantees were intended to be in force for a total of ten years. His powerful foot invaded, stamped on, trampled and crushed all the obstacles which stood in his way to conquering the Empire of Eastern Europe.

Stalin, naïve as an innocent and stupid sheep, did not believe until the very last moment that Hitler had duped him. Even with the previous evidence of the violated Munich Agreement before him, Stalin failed to realize that to the German snake, an agreement was worth about as much as last year's snow, which made him fall to the depths of disappointment, shock and humiliation. The Russians could not understand how they could have believed that the Germans would not honor their agreement. Only two years had passed and the treaty had been broken; now a frightening invasion was falling on their heads.

On the twenty-second of June 1941, after breaking the pact, German troops began to invade Soviet territory, and caught Stalin totally unprepared to meet the Barbarossa Operation. This time Stalin and Hitler faced each other, not as allies but as adversaries. What an irony!

During the morning of that fateful day, Mottele hurried Reizele to the maternity hospital, which was housed in an old building. Even though he knew that the birth of their child was imminent, he could not take the chance of missing a day's work; he could be dismissed. He promised his wife that he would come back to see her in the hospital in a few hours' time.

When Yuzhi came into the world, the cries of the newborn baby merged with the thunderous roar of the bombs which the Luftwaffe airmen began to rain down on Belzec with unexpected intensity. When the baby emerged from his mother's womb and Reizele's body was still shaking from the heroic struggle of childbirth, she felt the floor literally quaking under her bed and heard the shattering of glass from the windows blown out by the blasts from the bombings.

Many of the frightened hospital staff had fled in panic, deserting their patients when they heard the bombs falling all around them. The senior staff now made a swift decision to abandon the hospital before the walls collapsed on their heads. The wailing of the infants and their mothers' cries for help filled the delivery rooms.

Those members of the staff who had not run from the hospital began to help the mothers pack their sparse belongings and wrap up their babies in whatever came to hand. They urged them to make haste while they could, for they feared the hospital might take a direct hit from a bomb. Reizele, however, lingered and tried not to succumb to the panic which surrounded her. She prayed for a lull in the bombing, which indeed there was for a brief hour, and waited for her husband to come from work and take her home. Indeed, Mottele had heard the bombs falling, and had been delayed by them, for he was frightened to death to go out in the streets while bombs were falling; he could get crushed by the crumbling buildings. So Reizele stood fixed to the spot in tense anticipation, her gaze never leaving the door through which she hoped Mottele would enter at any moment. He must come to get me, she repeated to herself, over and over.

I cannot believe that after a whole pregnancy when nothing happened, more or less, just today war has broken out here. They must be out of their minds, Reizele thought. What about the agreement they signed with the Soviets? Bombs are flying through the air like vultures – landing on women and babies. I am not going to move until my husband comes to take me away from here.

Hours passed, her infant son cried in her arms, but still Reizele kept her eyes on the door facing the outside. Suddenly Mottele appeared, his face in a state of shock. His clothes hung loosely on his gaunt body, all covered in dust. Joy and apprehension intermingled when he looked at Reizele. There was no time to speak, neither about the birth nor about the sudden state of war they found themselves in. Another bomb fell on the adjacent wing of the hospital, and the clatter of falling walls sounded like the rumble of far-off thunder.

Their faces showed the extremes of their emotions; smiles

of happiness together with tears of anxiety. Swiftly they gathered up their few possessions. Mottele took Reizele's hand, even while she was nursing her baby, and the three of them managed to drag themselves out of the hospital.

Mottele walked a few meters in front of his wife and child as if to clear a path for them, between the hundreds of terrified people rushing in all directions. Their faces were contorted with fear, their steps slowed by the heavy bundles they carried. The gap grew between Reizele and her husband. She was clutching her baby, trying with all her strength to overcome the weakness of having given birth – thank the Lord it had been an easy delivery. Now the sound of the bombing seemed to be further away, and it seemed as if the air was calmer. They slowed their pace. But not for long.

The sound of airplanes flying nearer and nearer blasted their eardrums. The squadron had taken the fleeing crowds by surprise, and instantly their walk turned into a run, a race against time to run for cover – anywhere – from the airborne destruction of the fighter pilots. The thunderous noise reverberated in every direction, a precursor to the storm of bombs which fell all around; on roads, houses, fields, gardens, and trees, and on the multitude of people running away from the onslaught of bombs raining down on them from the skies and sowing destruction and death in their wake.

The three of them – the husband, the wife, and the infant – were thrown in different directions. Reizele was thrown by the blast to one side; her baby son was hurled from her arms and thrust to the other. The boom of the airplanes was deafening, while the screams of the injured rang in the air. When the airplanes finally withdrew overhead, the area looked like a battlefield. The moans and cries of the injured resounded everywhere. Reizele, who had fallen down on the ground by the force of the blast, lifted herself up and began cautiously touching herself all over her body, to see if she had any injuries. To her amazement, all her limbs were intact and miraculously, she seemed to have escaped injury, apart from a few surface scratches. A ghost of a smile settled on her face, although this immediately vanished as soon as she realized what was missing from her cradling arms.

Reizele jumped up as if she had been bitten by a snake, and began to run between the bodies, ignoring the pleas of the injured. She was eaten up with anxiety.

Where is my baby? Yuzhi! Yuzhi! My baby, where is my baby? Have you seen my baby? she yelled wildly, all the while running like a madwoman looking for him all around. Minutes, which seemed as long as eternity, passed, until she discerned, between the dead bodies and the injured, a blanket which looked familiar to her. She went over to it, afraid of what she would see. There was her baby, lying on the filthy ground, motionless. With trembling hands, she bent down over him and cradled his little body in her arms. Yes! He was breathing, uninjured, all his limbs were intact. What a miracle, he was untouched, he was alive!

There was not even any crying. The shock of being wrenched from his mother's arms must have rendered him unable to utter even a feeble cry. Silence and quietness in such traumatic circumstances, which at some future time would turn into a torrent of words streaming out of his mouth.

Reizele hugged her son to her breasts and laughed aloud and cried in turmoil, physically and emotionally. She was thrilled to the core, her heart overflowing with joy and thankfulness for the miracle which had occurred to her and her son.

When she had calmed down a little, suddenly a sense of disaster came over her. With her son safely in her arms again, she was shocked to realize that she had forgotten to search for her husband, to find where he had fallen. Had he been killed? Was Mottele, her husband, still alive? She tried to push through the river of people standing and lying on the ground. She hunted here and there, until the moment when she came upon him. She had no doubt that it was Mottele, lying still, with a dribble of blood trickling from his mouth.

Your father lay dead at my feet while I held you in my arms, Reizele would tell Yuzhi through clenched teeth, putting on a face of mourning. That is how your father was taken from me. I could not believe my eyes; I did not know what to do. It was terrible.

Reizele did not have to decide what to do at that stage, for immediately she was swept into the stream of people rushing forward to dodge another bomb which a pilot had released over their heads. Even had she wanted to, she could not have retraced her steps. To go against the hordes of panic-stricken people would have been impossible. In any case, she knew she could not help her husband in any way.
There was no time to waste. The threatening roar of planes overhead was deafening, and she rushed forward together with the hundreds of people struggling to escape from that hell. Whatever would be, would be. She had only herself to rely on. She would have to do whatever she could to save herself and her baby. If her husband was still alive, he would find them somehow. If he had been killed, which seemed more likely from what she had seen with her own eyes, there was nothing she could do for him. So she determined to make her escape with her baby son, as long as her strength lasted and she had breath in her body.

Reizele would often tell Yuzhi the story of her struggles. With my last ounce of strength, she would say, I stepped over the dead and wounded, and ran through streets and alleyways, clutching you in my arms, until I collapsed in front of the house when Adela and Chaimke carried us inside. They had been frantic with worry about us. They kissed you and stroked your cheeks tenderly, gazing at you with emotion, being Mottele's son, Mottele, may his soul rest in peace.

No, there was no doubt that he had been killed; Reizele had seen him lying on the ground, unmoving. It was too dangerous to go to search for his body, for there was no let-up in the bombing, so their only chance of surviving was to hide themselves as well.

And here come the questions: For how long of a time did Reizele hide in Adela and Chaimke's house? What happened to them all? How were things arranged for them as Jews under Nazi rule? How did they manage to survive in Belzec, which attained notoriety after the war?

With painful insight, Yuzhi saw that what his mother endured in the war was still an open wound to her. He did not want to probe too deeply for fear of hurting her. The conflicting, fragmentary versions his mother transmitted to him of those events did not disconcert him. Yuzhi preferred to let his imagination help him build up a more consistent account of his infancy, and he wove himself a story which was more pleasing to him. That is, until he discovered the truth; which shook him to the depths of his being, for he had covered himself for so many years with the clothes he had himself woven, and now he felt as if a razor-sharp knife had cut them off of his body, and he was exposed, in all his nakedness.

The version of the history of Yuzhi's early years which he had adopted for himself, and which he loved to relate to everyone, was that his father was killed on the very day of his birth and that he and his mother were saved from the bombing and hid themselves in a cellar for the duration of the war. This, of course, only scratched the surface of their saga. But in spite of the nightmarish situations they found themselves in, there was an element of adventure which Yuzhi relished. He loved the story of his birth and the simultaneous death of his father, and he felt no need to probe further.

So this, then, was the version which Reizele fed to her son, spoonful by spoonful, while he was growing up. It was sufficiently convincing, both to satisfy his curiosity and eliminate the need for her to reveal the real truth of her exploits, which was as different as night from day, from this more prosaic one. It was infinitely better, Reizele thought, to hide the truth in the deepest recesses of her brain, sealed and double-locked so that it could not be penetrated by her son or, later, by all her descendants and other relatives. Until, that is, she was forced to break the lock.

# 2
# The Biological Father

Reizele was born in Zamosc, as the eldest daughter of Rabbi Yechiel Reznik. She was the first-born in a succession of eight children, and had not even learned to talk when her first brother was born. This male infant commanded all the attention for himself, so she could not even protest against the blatant deprivation of love and attention due to her, still a baby herself, which left her feeling lonely, neglected and virtually abandoned, embittered, and eaten up with jealousy.

Within the year, another brother was born. The house began to become crowded, and with each additional child it was more and more crammed full of people and possessions, even though it was a big house with a spacious yard and even separate lodgings at the back for the household servant.

As the eldest of a troop of brothers and sisters, Reizele's lot in daily life became more and more difficult. She was expected to look after the babies, clean the house, wash the dishes, sweep the floors, run messages, and go to the market to buy food. The family was stringently religious, insisting on the strictest standards of modesty in appearance: long sleeves and the hem of dresses well below the knee. Her father, the Rabbi, sent her to study at the Jewish gymnasium in the city, while his sons learned reading and writing, *Torah* and *Gemara*, from him in his *Talmud Torah* school.

Reizele had a hard row to hoe. Her life consisted of either schoolwork or housework. No games, no outings, no friendships to lighten her load. She was so fed-up with this kind of living, under such joyless existence, that she started to wonder how long she could suffer this enforced seclusion, and came to the conclusion that she could not go on like this much longer. She put all her energy into finding a way to make her escape from the home she felt kept her imprisoned.

When she looked at herself in the mirror, the image reflected was very pleasant; a pretty young girl gazed back at her. No one could imagine that this young girl was only dreaming of the knight on a white horse who would appear in a flash and rescue her from her own house, which had become her prison. These thoughts troubled her. They were impure, she told herself. It is forbidden to think this way!

To quiet her conscience that was so disturbed by the sinful thoughts which kept coming into her mind, she devoted herself to taking care of her little brothers and sisters, doing the hard household tasks which the one servant woman had no time for. Confused by mixed emotions, she felt responsibility and deep loyalty towards her family, but on the other hand she felt bitter and rebellious, and longed to break out of the iron chains which enclosed her personality, as if she was entrapped in a cage.

With all her might she tried, hopelessly, to suppress these mutinous thoughts, acknowledging that the miserable reality of her life left her no chance of being able to free herself from her poor situation.

But that was not written in stone, an edict for all time.

*Historical events of tremendous importance explode into the fate of individuals, sweeping people up in a sudden surge of experiences which cannot be predicted, changing their lives extremely and forever – for better or for worse.*

Out of the blue, there had arrived in Poland, little by little, rumors of the Kristallnacht which had taken place in Germany on the ninth of November in the year 1938, when Torah books were burned in the streets, synagogues set on fire, Jewish-owned stores were looted and their windows smashed; innocent Jewish people were killed in the streets.

Terrible, frightening news, but still not to the Jews of distant Poland, who at that time found these scenes impossible to envision. Poland is not Germany, they reassured themselves.

While it was still possible to turn a blind eye to these events, they convinced themselves that nothing would happen to them. For, after all, they said to each other, we Jews have been living in Poland for generations, for hundreds of years even. We have served in the army; we have created all kinds of wonderful institutions to promote music, theater, art; we can take a large part of the credit for the economic prosperity of the state (much to the resentment of the non-Jewish Poles themselves, it has to be said). We live a full Jewish life here, and at the same time we are an integral part of the national and cultural life of Poland. There is nothing to worry about, there will be no changes here, nothing and nobody will interfere with our lives. No, Poland is not Germany. Let the German dog bark far away from us, he will not come here.

This however was not Reizele's way of thinking. Her instincts and natural intelligence warned her that the address was on the wall for the Jews here, too. Her premonitions gave her no rest and she began to search in earnest for a way to leave her town, her home. She was loath to remain there. Whether her life would be different somewhere else did not concern her. The first thing she had to do was get away. But to where? That was the question. Where could a young woman alone, the daughter of a Rabbi, go? Her only solution was to find a man who would take her away with him. Only a husband could extricate her from the net in which she was trapped. All Reizele could do was pray with all her heart that her wish would be fulfilled.

*Occasionally, ambitions and fantasies can be fulfilled, if you know to seize the slightest or the incredible opportunities that fall your way, and hold them in both hands, realizing*

*that the golden opportunity may never come again, and recognizing the moment of decision, to be in the right place, at the right time and to have the emotional strength and good sense needed to take advantage of the opportunity.*

To Reizele's great good fortune, something of this kind fell straight into her lap. One bright, hot day, she was doing the regular weekly food shopping at the market, walking from one stall to the other, buying a kilo here, half a kilo and two kilos there, when she sensed a man standing next to her. Tall and brown-skinned, with a thick mustache over fleshy lips, sparkling brown eyes and wild, curly hair, this man was dressed in the uniform of the Soviet Army.

Do you need help? he asked softly. Reizele raised her head so that she could see who had spoken, and a blush spread over her face. She had never seen him before in her life, but the animal magnetism he exuded made her whole body tremble. No, thank you, she replied. He continued to stand next to her, murmuring that from the moment he had first seen her he could not take his eyes off her. He was serving in the Soviet Army and was here on leave, visiting a family of a Polish landowner. From the second he caught sight of her, he said, he could not get her out of his mind. Reizele said nothing; she just listened to his words, feeling weak, as if all the blood had drained out of her body. When she finished the rest of her purchases, however, she allowed him to help her carry her basket.

Let's go somewhere we can talk, he whispered to her from under his thick mustache. No, no, I have to hurry home, she protested, willing her legs to take her away as fast as possible from the temptation which threatened to overpower her.

Reizele continued shopping as usual almost every day at the market, but found herself looking out for this Russian soldier, sending him a sweet innocuous smile whenever she saw him. Cautiously and gently he pursued her, standing close to her whenever he could. Reizele tried to hint to him, with a reproving glance, that she was a Jew, that she was not appropriate for him. Had he not heard of the German racial laws forbidding any connection with a Jew? But no, he reacted, the hell with them, in any case, what did he have to do with those vile German laws? He is Kazakhi and he does not care. On the contrary, her Jewishness excited him, her modest dress aroused him more than the most revealing cleavage. Reizele was both moved and flattered by his words, which convinced her that he really wanted her.

This attractive young man caused Reizele to experience emotions she had never felt before. The budding feelings of turmoil she had tried so hard to repress began to surface and she finally recognized them as they were. She could not turn a blind eye to what caused her to feel such strong desire: And to add insult to injury, this was for a man who was not a Jew!

What would her father say if he knew? Cry? Put her under detention? Kick her out of the door? This assumable fatherly reaction only strengthened her craving for that man – and she responded to his wooing.

Oy, oy, Reizele, what are you doing, she asked herself as she hurried to meet him, whoever he was. Arkadi, his name, Russian or Kazakhi, who cares, alighted with desire and fear, in the hideaway he had suggested to her, one of the stalls in a barn which the friendly landowner had put at his disposal.

Reizele, swept up in the adventure that occurred in her way, succumbed willingly to his passionate embraces, listening to his words of love as he nestled against her: Come away with me, you're mine, I want you. Let me take off your clothes, let me kiss your lips, ah, you're so sweet. And Reizele, lying in his arms, on the blanket he had brought to cover the scratchy straw, gave herself to him and let him kiss her over and over, again and again, to her immense delight, and alarm. She was eaten up with passion, stained by shame at what she had done. With these jumbled emotions, Reizele made her way home, dazed and withdrawn, hugging her scandalous secret to herself. Her parents discerned a change in her, but did not understand which possessing spirit had entered into her body. The evident strain she was under, her comings and goings, her estrangement from them and withdrawal into herself, gave them no rest.

What has happened to you, are you ill? they would ask. And she would respond, nothing is the matter, everything is fine, don't worry, just leave me alone.

In truth, however, her guilty feelings about her repeated transgressions could not stay bottled up for much longer within her; they would soon burst out. It was becoming impossible for her to lead this double life, being an innocent girl, attached as she was to her family, and at the same time, infatuated with a gentile man whose touch made her body throb on the straw, in the secrecy of their hiding place, and with whom, she felt, she wanted to stay forever.

No, she could no longer continue with this double life and keep her terrible secret to herself. So Reizele decided to accept his suggestion to run away with him, even though it made her feel that a sharp thorn had been pulled out of her flesh with one painful tug.

Behind the plan which Arkadi laid before her, was the idea that they would begin a new life together in another place, in the nearby town of Belzec, where he had relatives, Katya and Piotr Polski. They were Polish farmers, about his own age, in their twenties – and childless. These relatives owned their small farm, where they could live as long as they liked.

Relatives of yours? But you are from Kazakhstan and they are Polish, so how are you related, asked Reizele, dumbfounded. Not that his family background was of any particular concern to her, but from the little information which Arkadi saw fit to tell her, she more or less understood this bit of his family tree: His father was Russian-Pravoslavic, whose family had been forced to emigrate to Kazakhstan at the end of the nineteenth century, as part of the Czar's edict to settle Russian and Ukrainian farmers on Kazakh land. In spite of fierce resistance by the Kazakh people to the foreign invaders, and after much bloodshed and wars instigated by the Russians on the Kazakhs, the Russians succeeded in 1936 in forming a Soviet Republic in Kazakhstan. Half of its citizens were Kazakhs, the remainder – Russian and Ukrainian.

But what about your mother? asked Reizele curiously. In response, Arkadi shrugged his shoulders, mumbled something about a Kazakh woman from one of the Turko-Mongolian tribes which had invaded Kazakhstan in the sixteenth century, with whom his father had fallen in love and they got married. That was how Arkadi had come to be born there. What was her religion? Arkadi had no idea; they had never talked about it at home. Anyway, he himself did not believe in anything, in any religion.

Arkadi had known about the family connection with Piotr Polski from childhood, when his father told him about his cousin who, instead of going to Kazakhstan on the forced emigration convoy, managed to escape with his family to Poland, where Piotr was born. When he reached the age of looking for a wife, he married Katya, a Polish Catholic from Belzec.

Only when Arkadi was conscripted into the Soviet Army, three years before war broke out, did he meet Piotr and Katya. His terms of service allowed him relative freedom of movement. He found out where his Polski relatives were, and made contact with them. This soon turned into a close friendship, which, once Arkadi had told them that he had lost his heart to a Jewish girl, led Piotr and Katya to invite Arkadi and his lover to come to live with them.

Reizele was so warmed and secure by Arkadi's protective feelings towards her, that she agreed to his suggestion, while justifying to herself that even before she met Arkadi, it had been her ambitious wish to leave Zamosc. Reizele believed that the hand of fate had directed her toward this turning point, and she wasted no time on doubts and misgivings. Yes, she decided without more ado, she would run away from home with this man, even if he is a Christian, a Moslem, or whatever he is, all the same for her.

At dawn, on a cold and a misty morning, the first of September 1939, Reizele packed her few clothes and belongings and crept out of the house furtively. She had left a note for her parents and family, which she knew would shock them to the core. It said: I've left home; I'm going away from here. Do not worry, I'll be all right. She left the note on the kitchen table and went to meet her lover, who was waiting for her by the barn, wearing civilian clothes, standing next to an old truck. Reizele hid her face, in case the few people around at that early hour would recognize her and discover the fateful – shocking step – from their point of view – she was taking at those very moments. The truck revved up quietly, and set off slowly on its way south to Belzec, on the Lublin-Lvov road, where they would be living with Arkadi's relatives, Katya and Piotr Polski.

All of a sudden, fate had taken a sharp turn and turned normal life upside down. The everyday life that chugged along slowly, as it had done for many years, when even the daily hardship is so familiar, since it contributes to the sense of security and stability both in the personal lives and in the lives of the close-knit community, with one overwhelming stroke, sweeps you away by a devastating tidal wave, deep into the darkness of the unknown echo, powerless to resist.

Reizele and Arkadi started out from Zamosc in the highest of high spirits, on that first of September, 1939. The thought of their new life together in Belzec made them happy and excited. However these feelings were dispelled as soon as they arrived at their destination, where they were told the terrible news that the Germans invaded Poland. They felt as if they had been hit with a sledgehammer.

That first evening at the Polski house, Reizele made the acquaintance with Piotr and Katya. Naturally, the happiness of the meeting was overshadowed with anxiety caused by the news that had greeted them on their arrival. But even this disquiet could not weaken the intensity of their passion, and as soon as they were alone, they fell into each other's arms on the wide bed in their room.

Early the next morning, Arkadi put on his rucksack and went off to join his unit, which was assembling not far from Belzec, on the borders of Poland and the Soviet-Union. The Soviets still appeared to be convinced that nothing bad could happen to them, thanks to the guarantee of their security undersigned in that so recent pact with the Germans.

✦ ✦ ✦

With a lightning strike of ferocious severity, and in less than a month, the German troops invaded Poland and conquered it. All the Polish lines of defense collapsed; their equipment was out of date and no match for the German armaments. They were totally unprepared for the aggression they now faced. It was as if a bantamweight fighter had been placed in the ring with a heavyweight champion. The outcome was decided long before the start. One hundred thousand highly-trained, well-equipped German soldiers, with tanks and artillery, were backed up by the intimidating Luftwaffe. Infantry soldiers blew up houses and sowed havoc among the inhabitants who fled in all directions, while pilots carried out aerial bombardments without pause in their single-minded quest to crush, to conquer, to dominate.

In their advance towards the East, German planes bombed the town of Zamosc, and five hundred people were killed, including Jews who had fled from the west of Poland in the hope of finding shelter there from the invading Germans. But to no avail. They fell out of the frying pan straight into the fire. Death held out its arms to them precisely in the place where they had sought refuge.

After the bombardment, the Nazi soldiers entered Zamosc and on the 14th of September, 1939, took control of the town, but only for two weeks, and their presence was hardly felt. Before the townspeople could hardly turn around, the Germans had left, and the Russians replaced them, in accordance with the Molotov-Ribbentrop Pact. The Soviet Army began to take control of the city, but soldiers from the Red Army were to be found in Zamosc for only a mere week, while border adjustments were being carried out between the Russians and the Germans. Afterwards they departed, and Zamosc found itself in a vacuum. Without a doubt, the departure of the Russians from the town saved the lives of very many Jews – perhaps as many as five thousand – who took the opportunity to flee in their wake to the Soviet Union. Hence their lives were saved, because immediately afterwards, atrocities began to be perpetrated on the Jews who remained in Zamosc.

Once again Zamosc filled with German soldiers. This time they immediately began to issue orders and decrees with the purpose of constraining the lives of the Jews: Denial of their human rights; ban on economic activity; prohibition on moving their place of residence; the concentration of all bank deposits belonging to Jews into one bank, and the freezing of these assets; and the height of degradation and dread – to wear the yellow star, a badge of shame. Any Jew caught without this shameful patch on his sleeve would be shot, like a rabid dog.

In these first stages of the war, wearing the yellow patch did not save the Jews from abuse and humiliation. One day, Reizele's father, Rabbi Reznik, went to visit a sick Jewish man to give him a blessing and pray for his recovery from illness. The Rabbi cautiously made his way through the old quarter of Zamosc, the stunningly beautiful town which Emperor Jan Zamoyski had established in the sixteenth century. His vision and initiative had spawned a town of architectural grace and unity, for he had employed an Italian architect to design not only his palace but also all the municipal buildings in a majestic and highly-decorated style. The magnificent basilica was equally elegant, as were the many buildings belonging to the wealthy Armenian businessmen living in the town.

Rabbi Reznik crossed the town square; houses painted in all the colors of the rainbow were built close together on each side of the square as was common in all European cities in that period. He passed by the splendid municipality building, with its clock tower, and the magnificent cathedral, in the Gothic-Romantic style of architecture, the flag of the Polish eagle fluttering at its spire. Rabbi Reznik came out of the shadow formed by the massive cathedral, intending to walk home along one of the alleys leading to his house from the town square. Wearing the yellow star on his sleeve, he was suddenly stopped in his tracks by three Nazi soldiers who emerged from an alley across from where he stood. They started to curse and taunt him, calling him dirty Jew-boy; those books you are holding, what are they? Your Torah? Your sidur? So you have been to visit a sick man, have you? With a derisive look on their faces, and a rough jab of their elbows, Rabbi Reznik's hat and yarmulke went flying off his head. While laughing wildly at his distress, one of the thugs pulled out of his bag a pair of scissors; his comrades restrained Rabbi Reznik's shoulders and hands, and to the accompaniment of their shouts of glee, he began to lop off the Rabbi's beard and side locks.

Low as the dust, frozen to the spot, powerless to move a muscle, feeling as if all the blood had left his body, there laid the Rabbi while Nazi thugs held him down and abused him; while weeping tearlessly for the loss of the outward proclamation of his pride in his Jewish faith, his people's tradition, his own identity and personality. It was as if they had not only cut off his beard and side locks, but as if they had cut off his limbs from his body.

Kicked and beaten, his beard and side locks raggedly cut, and with the Nazis' vulgar insults still ringing in his ears, Rabbi Reznik was released by the three thugs. He staggered home, wisps of straggly hair sticking to his cheeks as poignant reminders of his once full beard. When he limped into his house, he sat on a low footstool for a full hour, not moving, stunned beyond words, his family standing around him, shocked and distressed by his appearance. Suddenly he started to cry out, shattering the silence: God Almighty, what have You done to us? What have WE done, how have we sinned? The Rabbi waved his arms in entreaty in the direction of the heavens, while his family stood bewildered, with eyes full of tears, their faces contorted by fear and shock.

Depression of the spirit, wage psychological terror on the Jewish inhabitants, denigrate and humiliate them, trample on their self-respect and crush their morale.

These methods of intimidation were carried out by the harsh Nazi regime on the Jews as if they were warming-up exercises to prepare them for the final goal of carrying out their physical destruction: The ban on engaging in the professions or in business, the yellow patch, verbal abuse, the burning of holy books, the public shaving off of beards and side locks, the kicks and the blows – all these were done as if to transmit to the Jews the message that this was the very worst things that would befall them. And indeed, what could be worse than the humiliations and loss of autonomy, the antagonism towards your social and intellectual positions, the confiscation of your property, and above all – the negation of your religion and beliefs, of what made you who and what you are? But in spite of all these insulting, degrading and cruel acts, they were still able to feel, at this stage, that their sensibilities had not yet been stilled by the Nazis. They still felt that if they lifted up their arms to Heaven and cried out for the Lord's protection, they would receive it, and He would not authorize these tyrants to continue to persecute His chosen people.

Afterward, when the physical torments would come – starvation, forced labor, mass killings – the human spirit would lose its will and ability to question, to wonder where was their God – their all-powerful, merciful, compassionate God. The spirit of the people would be blown away in the winds of a terrible storm, leaving their poor body condemned to torture and ultimately extinction.

Reizele had let the vagaries of history dictate the changes which transformed her life. At the same time, she still did not know that had she not taken advantage, as it were, of this extraordinary chain of events, her life would have been cut short within a very brief time. She slowly began to understand the immense stroke of good fortune she had in being able to leave Zamosc, her birthplace, on the very day that war broke out: she felt exactly like someone whose life was saved at the very last minute from a fatal accident.

From newspaper reports and rumors which flew in the air from mouth to ear, Reizele was aware of the orders and restrictions imposed on the Jews of Zamosc. Later on, she heard of Jews being abducted in the streets and sent to work in forced labor battalions; of the closure of all the Jewish schools and cultural activities, and of the Jews having to pay high taxes and ransoms, protection money and bribes so as to preclude themselves from being sent to forced labor and other torments. But these payments only postponed the harsh plans of the tyrants, and in the end did not help elude them. The Nazis first took all the valuables and property belonging to the Jews, and after that, took their lives. From all of this, Reizele was saved. She possessed a residency permit as a Christian citizen which Katya had arranged for her, and was also helped by the fact that no restrictions were imposed in Belzec, for the simple fact that no Jews lived there.

In December of the same year, the Gestapo set up a

Judenrat in Zamosc, consisting of twelve public officials, who were ordered to recruit six hundred forced laborers each day. These laborers were sent to the work camp which had been established in the city and surrounding villages. There were even some hundreds who were sent to Belzec to build the concentration camp which it had been decided would be set up there.

At the beginning of April 1941, the Nazis set up a ghetto in Zamosc, and the Polish mayor ordered all the Jews of the town to move there by the first of May. The Poles agreed to wait a month for the Jews to abandon their houses and their physical, economic, cultural and spiritual strongholds in which they had lived their lives in Zamosc for hundreds of years. Using whips and firing wildly in all directions, the SS ejected the Jews from their houses, until no inhabitant remained. The Zamosc ghetto was an open one, in the neglected neighborhood of Komarov. Although it was not surrounded by a wall, it was only possible to leave at certain hours of the day, while the non-Jewish Poles could come and go as they pleased. There was a postal service functioning in the ghetto, and a hospital was set up in order to contain an outbreak of typhus there. A committee to help refugees was established, and a communal kitchen, too, which for a token price, distributed hot meals. All in all, the conditions were not intolerable.

Reizele could not begin to imagine the terrible suffering which her family was undergoing. They had been forced to leave their house and go live in a rundown apartment in the ghetto. Nor had she any idea that immediately after the Jews had left their houses in the old quarter, the Polish townspeople rushed to strip them bare of all their furnishings. But that was not enough for the Poles: they then forced their way into the magnificent synagogue, where they plundered it in a frenzied covetous orgy. They fell ravenously upon every item of value, all the holy and valuable objects – Menoras, silver Torah crowns and pointers, rich embroidered covers for the Ark of the Law and the Torah Scrolls themselves. They ripped up rare books with elation, everything which they could put their hands on, they savaged like mad dogs. Within a few hours, nothing remained of the synagogue except for bare walls.

More than a year would pass before Reizele would learn of the bitter fate which befell her family – when she watched them in secret, when they were mercilessly and cruelly deported to their death.

✦ ✦ ✦

For an entire year Reizele cradled herself in the security of the Polski household in Belzec. She helped them in the house and on the farm, and Arkadi came to visit them all from time to time. At one and the same time she was both bowed down by a heavy burden of guilt, and infinitely grateful for the good fortune that had brought her there, and thus saved her from the suffering which was the lot of the Jews in every Polish town, including her own birthplace, Zamosc.

In December 1940, Reizele discovered that she was in her third month of pregnancy, a situation which made her feel both ambivalent feelings of happiness and anxiety. Many questions preyed on her mind: How and where would she, an unmarried mother, bring up her son, his father a non-Jew, his mother a Jew among gentiles? What would be recorded on his birth certificate? Would the birth of a baby not reveal her origins? There was no one Reizele could confide in about her fears. Arkadi was rarely there, he was away in the army most of the time, especially now, when the war was being waged vigorously in Western Europe, and country after country fell under the spiked boots of the Nazi Fuhrer.

Poland was only the first bite of the bird of prey which was devoured by her, but who knew which would be the last country torn apart by its sharp talons? Rivers of blood were spilled, and all the treasures of the former lives of the vanquished, and too often they themselves, were buried under the ruins. However, Russia, so the Russian leaders believed, would be spared this horror, based on the non-aggression treaty signed between them and Germany. They were under the illusion that the Germans would not harm them, even they knew that a fiercely-fought war was taking place not too far from their borders.

When Reizele informed Arkadi that he was due to become a father, the expression on his face gave her no clue as to whether he was happy or troubled by the news, or maybe he was simply unhappy about the timing, which could hardly have been worse.

Do not worry, he told her over and over again, I'm sure that before our son is born everything will have quietened down. Even if the war in Western Europe is not over, we are far away from it, and anyway the Germans will not dare to come here – we have signed an agreement with them.

Arkadi went on to explain to Reizele that if Stalin was not concerned, why should they be? Let those Nazis make as much havoc as they want in Western Europe. Here we are well protected in our own corner. Anyway, Stalin has already annexed the three Baltic States to Russia, which collapsed like a house of cards, and he can now put military bases there.

Finland too, who had fought bitterly against the Soviets, had lost the battles and was forced to give up and give us large areas from its country. So, when you think of that, how could it ever enter the Germans' minds to try to conquer a colossal country such as ours, when we have already annexed several countries in the north, to our huge country?

Reizele was reassured. All she was now concerned about, was for her pregnancy to proceed peacefully, and for her to be able to bring her son up in peace and quiet, the peace that would come after the war ended, very soon indeed.

Katya Polski, a nice woman with a pleasant face and short curly bright hair, took Reizele under her wing as a family member who had returned to her home after a long absence. She was very moved and excited by the idea that Arkadi would soon be the father of a baby, boy or girl. She herself was childless and medical tests had proved that she was barren and could never have any children. That is why she was so delighted to know that at least she would be able to cuddle the baby of Reizele and Arkadi in her arms.

Katya was a practical woman, and knew that what Reizele needed was a safe shelter in her home. She knew that Reizele's status could not be left vague indefinitely, so she invested all her efforts into acquiring official papers, so that Reizele would have the legal documentation to stay in Belzec.

Katya knew that the draconian racial laws passed by the Nazis forbade those of the Aryan race to have a relationship with Jews, Gypsies or members of any other race they considered inferior. She also knew, that according to those same laws, Arkadi's Kazakh origins – and even her own – would not pass muster for them to be considered of pure Aryan stock, since the Slav peoples, from the point of view of the Nazis, were fit only to be servants of their Aryan masters, if and when the Nazis took control of their countries.

The racial laws, full of the ugly seeds of destruction, will not stop me, Katya vowed. The most important thing now is to turn Reizele into a legal resident of the town. Quietly and efficiently, Katya secretively began to exploit her good connections with a high-ranking official in the government so that he could use his influence with the Population Registry. Her plan was to have Reizele registered as a Christian and as a resident of the town.

Look, she said unblushingly as she lied to her well-connected contact, my cousin has come to live with me, and she has lost her identity papers. Do me a favor and give her new ones. She is living in my house and needs the right papers. There is no need for you to worry your head about all the details. Katya played on her considerable charm to wheedle this portly, balding, influential man away from his suspicions as to Reizele's origins, while she tucked into his hand an envelope stuffed with banknotes.

No, no, this is just a little present for you, no connection, she said, smiling at him while he carefully placed the envelope full of zlotys into an inside pocket of his jacket. Just register these details and sign new papers for her; this is her name and her address, and here is her picture. All you need to do now is to arrange for an identity number.

Thus, with charm and efficiency, Katya convinced the official to give her the new papers for Reizele or, as she was now registered, in the name Raymonda Polski. Within the space of a morning, Reizele had become a Polish Catholic, a cousin of the Polskis, who had come to their town and made her home with them.

In order to earn money to pay for her daily keep, Reizele began to work in a garment-making factory. She was no different from the other workers, a Christian girl with an authorized resident's permit. Her head was bent over the heavy sewing machine from dawn to dusk, just like the heads of all the other tens of workers. It was demanding work, but she had to earn her bread, and the meager salary Arkadi received was not sufficient to cover her expenses. She also had to plan ahead and put money away for when the baby arrived.

With the whirring of the machines buzzing in her ears, she reflected on the metamorphosis she had undergone: She had changed her name, and her religion and soon she would give birth to a child that aroused so many questions in her mind.

What kind of hybrid would she produce? What would be his identity, his religion, his nationality? Russian or Polish? Would he be half-Jewish, a quarter Christian, a quarter Moslem? Reizele's thoughts ran further away to her unfortunate family whom she had left behind in Zamosc. What would they say about their grandchild she was about to give birth to? She was sure they had sat *shiva* for her, seven days of traditional mourning, as if she were dead. To go off with a gentile man? What disgrace, what a sinful shame she had brought on the family!

All connections had been broken off with them, and all she knew about what had happened to them were the terrible rumors that made her stomach turn over, but now she needed to gather all her physical and emotional strength together to overcome the lack of confidence she felt regarding the role of mother, which she would soon be called upon to fulfill.

In spite of her ever-increasing girth, nobody suspected that Reizele was pregnant. She did all she could to hide it, wearing loose clothes that left ample room for her growing belly, so that her co-workers and the management would not suspect her condition. During the last month of her pregnancy, when it became impossible to conceal the tell-tale bulge, Reizele informed the management that she would stop working. Her instincts told her that it was better for nobody to know about the impending birth, and she waited patiently at home, hidden from view.

Arkadi had promised her that he would come to be with her on the day that the birth was expected. He would come and take her to the hospital, he promised. However, when labor pains began, he had not arrived, most probably because army duties made it impossible for him to get away. It was Piotr who drove her to the hospital. It was on the morning of the 22nd of June, 1941.

They had not yet arrived at the small, rather dilapidated hospital, when they heard the roar of airplanes in the skies. A hail of bombs fell nearby. In a state of panic, Piotr, beset with worry about Katya, whom he had left alone in the house, helped Reizele into the hospital, where a kindly nurse took charge of her, and immediately returned home to his wife.

Reizele, by that time, was in an advanced state of labor, so she was hurried straight into the delivery room. There was no time for anyone to ask for personal details, or to fill in official forms. They helped Reizele up to the narrow bed, and she lay down, her whole body racked with the excruciating pain of labor. At that moment, Reizele heard an announcement over the loudspeakers that war had broken out in the East and that the Germans were advancing towards the Soviet Union!

They must be mad, thought Reizele, while praying that the baby would be born as quickly as possible. And yes, thank the Lord, while she was still straining and pushing, the baby's head emerged within an hour of her being helped up onto the delivery bed. Simultaneously, a deafening noise shook the rickety walls of the old hospital. A wing of the hospital had collapsed from the intensity of the bombardment the Luftwaffe was inflicting on the town; the walls of the delivery room shook all the while her body shuddered with the last efforts needed to bring her baby out of her body.

On the selfsame day, when Yuzhi emerged to the world and was placed in his mother's arms, Operation Barbarossa began.

✦ ✦ ✦

It is still debatable whether Hitler subconsciously knew when he embarked on Operation Barbarossa that it was doomed to fail from the start, and would ultimately lead to his army's collapse.

Barbarossa was the nickname given – because of the red beard he wore – from the twelfth-century Holy Roman Emperor Frederick. Of all the military and other operations Frederick Barbarossa waged, he is best known for initiating the Third Crusade, together with Philip II, king of France, and Richard the Lionheart, king of England, in order to free holy Jerusalem from Ottoman rule.

Barbarossa was not privileged to arrive at his destination because he drowned in the sea. A sudden storm capsized his boat and many of his troops had been lost with him. Barbarossa was therefore unable to achieve his objective, although those Crusaders who remained, continued on their way, conquered Acre, and gained a decisive victory at the battle of Arsuf against the armies of Salahadin. However, in Jerusalem, the Crusaders were overpowered by the Ottoman army, leaving Richard the Lionheart as their sole commander who finally preferred not to fight to the death, but to come to an agreement whereby Jerusalem would remain in the hands of the Ottomans, while the Crusaders would strengthen their presence in the coastal region between Jaffa and Acre. And so King Richard sailed away and returned to England.

The personal failure of Barbarossa, due to his death during the Third Crusade, came to haunt Hitler again and again during the operation called by the nickname of that red-bearded emperor. So why call the invasion of the Soviet Union by the name of someone who had failed to achieve his goal? It may be because Hitler had been influenced by a legend he had heard in his childhood about Emperor Frederick Barbarossa: On a high mountain in Bavaria, the Emperor slept among his knights, sitting around a stone table, while ravens flew all around him, and he dreamed that when the birds ceased flying, he would wake from his sleep and return Germany to its former greatness. This was in fact Hitler's own dream, not only while he slept, but also while awake: The dream of a great Germany, which impelled him to embark on his fanatical attempt to conquer the Soviet Union. He certainly did not lose any sleep over the pact of non-aggression, signed only two years ago by his own Foreign Minister and which was due to be in effect for ten years. A powerful Germany, he thought, could only be built by the conquest and annexation of all the vast territories of the great Soviet Union – he would not let loose the grip on his dream.

With his characteristic megalomania and arrogance, Hitler was convinced that the campaign against the Soviet Union would last only few weeks. He mentally ticked off the many factors contributing to his optimistic prediction: Two million of his troops were already in place on the Russian border in readiness for the invasion; and huge numbers of bombers and artillery were available.

Hitler also thought that after Germany's invasion of Russia, a revolution would break out there, the Soviet regime would fall, and his ally, the Japanese, would invade the Soviet Union from Siberia. Hitler did not learn from the bitter experience of his predecessor, Napoleon, whose attempt to conquer Russia did not succeed. He did not take into sufficient consideration either the vast dimensions of the country, or the invincible might of General Winter, which had stopped Napoleon literally in his tracks.

The beginning of the campaign was, for the Germans, an unqualified success. The Russians were completely unprepared, and Stalin himself was caught with his pants down: He had refused to believe the warnings of his allies about the Germans' plans to attack his country; his military equipment was antiquated; he had virtually no officers, having had most of them murdered in the 1930s during one of his periodic outbursts of paranoia.

Thus, in June 1941, the German Army advanced within the Soviet Union at great speed. Using the techniques of lightning strikes, the Soviet Army was bombed from all directions, and the Russian command was in a state of utter panic and lost control of its army.

This, then, was the state of the world when Yuzhi made his appearance into it. German planes strafed Belzec with bombs without a moment's pause, causing a whole wing of the hospital to collapse and the walls of the delivery room to shake, while Reizele's body was trembling with the effort of releasing her baby from her womb.

A few hours after she had given birth, an order was given

to evacuate the hospital of all patients and personnel. Many physicians and nurses had already escaped in the terrible panic of the bombardments, and it was not possible to continue to care for patients in those dangerous conditions. No one knew, or cared to know, what dangers lay in wait for them outside, and every patient who could stand on his own feet was sent home, each man to his fate, whatever that would be. But Reizele did not want to go and took advantage of a few hours to rest and make her arrangements for leaving the hospital. As long as her baby was asleep in his crib, she stood and gazed through the window to wait for Arkadi's arrival.

He must come, she said to herself, our baby has just been born, the Germans have attacked us, and all at once we are at war. She reflected that Arkadi had not stood by his word: He had promised her that the Germans would not dare approach the borders of the Soviet Union and here they are invading, bombing and killing us! Reizele would wait for him until he came. She was not going to move an inch, she insisted, and the staff let her wait there, in spite of the danger.

The noise of the airplanes slicing through the sky did not shift her from her place. Biting her lips out of sheer tension and nervous feeling of all the conflicting emotions she was experiencing, a sudden wide smile spread over her face. Here he was! Here at last! Sweaty and filthy, his black hair covered with dust, his uniform hanging loosely on him, his glance was full of concern and fear.

Arkadi approached her. He belted orders out of his mouth, without even giving her a kiss.

Come, we have to get out of here, an army vehicle is waiting for us. It is parked quite far away, we have to go straightaway, a bomb could fall on us at any moment.

There was no time. Reizele hurried to the crib, took the baby out of it and held him in her arms. She wrapped him in a blue blanket and held him against her chest. The baby seemed as not accustomed yet to his life in this new world, and showed no signs of hunger.

Reizele trailed after the man who had come to take her away, trying her best in her weakened state to hurry, run, escape from there, together with all the hundreds of others desperate to get out of danger and reach their homes or the nearest train station. Every moment was crucial. Arkadi marched slightly in front of them, to lead the way to the vehicle which would take them away from that hell.

While they hurried, a bomb landed among the crowd. A squadron of screeching German planes emerged from beyond the clouds and rained down on them bomb after bomb. One of the bombs succeeded in scoring an almost direct hit. Flames, smoke, incredible heat. Hundreds of people stumbled, fell, collapsed as they were killed or injured in the onslaught.

From the blasts of the bombs and crush of the crowd of panic-stricken people, Reizele fell to the ground. All around her was confusion and shouting, screams, moans, smells of burning.

When the wave of bombs stopped, she raised her head cautiously, and sat up slowly, examining herself, limb by limb, to see if she suffered any damage, but no, what a miracle, she had no injuries. A few seconds of blocked mind had passed, when suddenly she was aware that her baby had disappeared, thrust out of her arms by the bombs.

Seized by panic, Reizele jumped up as though she had been bitten by a snake, and began to quickly search for her baby. She jumped over the injured people on the ground among the dead, shoving and being shoved by the hordes of terrified people, crying and shouting, Where's my baby? Yuzhi, my little Yuzhi, where are you?

Around and around she searched, until she came across a familiar blue blanket in which her baby had been wrapped. Like a parcel, it lay on the ground, motionless, without uttering a sound. Reizele stooped and slowly lifted him, breathing deeply and praying that he had not been injured. She gently felt his body, bent to feel his breath on her cheek, and uttered a sigh of relief. He was alive, he was healthy and intact. He was not even crying. Reizele turned her eyes to the heavens and silently gave heartfelt thanks to God. She recovered her wits immediately, propelled with renewed vigor to get away from that valley of death.

But where could she run to? And where in heaven's name is Arkadi? Why isn't he here to help us get out of this hell?

Terrified by bad feelings, she began searching for him between the wounded and the dead bodies. She was pushed and shoved by the mass of the escaping people.

She will not leave here without him, she must find out what has happened to him.

Ignoring the moaning and calls for help from the injured, she suddenly came upon him. He lay there at her feet without moving, his arms and legs outstretched, his uniform stained with blood and a trickle of red dribbling from the corner of his mouth. Reizele stood there, rooted to the spot, stunned beyond belief. Was it possible the Fates had decreed that on one and the same day she would receive the gift of a son and the life of her son's father would be cruelly snuffed out? What a tragic coincidence! But wait, she said to herself, perhaps he is not dead, just unconscious. Reizele bent over him to see if he was breathing, but at that second her baby, cradled in her arms, began to cry. Because her movements were then restricted, she gently touched her husband's body with the tip of her shoe but there was no response. She stayed in that position for several more minutes, staring at the man lying motionless before her, but no signs of life came from him. She was left in no doubt that there was no breath in his body, and that he had slipped away from life.

✦ ✦ ✦

Reizele did not shed a tear. In her heart of hearts she wanted him dead. Perhaps it was preferable. This situation seemed to her a complication she might be better without. She felt as if she was a puppet on a string, pulled this way and that by unseen forces behind the stage of life: A young woman from a strictly Orthodox Jewish family gives birth to a son of a non-Jewish man of Russian or Kazakh origin, of unspecified religion, perhaps Pravoslav, whatever that was, Christian Orthodox, Moslem, even an idol-worshipper, who could be sure? What kind of a future would she have with him, with this fearful war breaking out on her doorstep? Indeed, perhaps it would be better to go back to her parents' house? They could not be so hardhearted as to turn her away with a baby in her arms. But how would she get to Zamosc? All the roads were swarming with Nazis hunting down Jews, and her parents' large house would probably already have been turned over to a Polish family and her family forced to enter the ghetto. What a ridiculous idea, to even think of returning to Zamosc with a day-old baby! The one person she needed at that moment was Arkadi himself, who would shield and protect her from those seeking to harm her, and help her and her baby get to her parents' house. But Arkadi was lying at her feet, dead. Now there was no time to be lost, for at any moment another wave of bombers could strike.

Reizele began to look around her: There was a jumble of dead bodies and injured people on the ground, with a mass of petrified survivors picking their way through them. She asked herself what on earth she was going to do now, and it took no time at all for her to realize that the only thing for her to do was somehow to reach Katya and Piotr – without any help from anyone!

She waited until the stream of people thinned out a little, which enabled her to walk without being pushed along by them. Still tired and weak from giving birth only hours ago, she clutched her infant tight to her chest and walked blindly on. As if she were a puppet being moved by forces unseen, her body did not feel like hers, her legs seemed to move without being directed. All she could think of was the imperative to reach her target: the Polskis' house.

Airplanes returned to the skies, bombs were dropping all around, but she managed to keep going. As long as I can stand on my feet, I will keep going, she repeated to herself like a mantra. As long as I have breath in my body, I will get home. She trudged on and on until, at dusk, she reached her destination. A second after Katya took her baby from her arms, Reizele collapsed. When she awoke, she immediately asked to nurse her baby. Katya had already diapered and clothed him, and in that short time, she had already taken the little one to her heart. Katya brought the baby to Reizele and put him to nurse. He is hungry, she said. Hesitantly and awkwardly, Reizele grasped her breast and put it near the mouth of her baby, lying across her body. Before she had worked out how exactly to proceed, in which position to hold him, the infant himself found her nipple and put it between his lips, and began to suckle, almost violently, not letting up the nipple for a moment!

To his great good fortune, his mother's breasts were overflowing with milk and from that day on, Yuzhi sucked and pinched and bit his mother's breasts for many months; he sucked avidly and swallowed and drank his mother's sweet milk until he was sated – for the rest of his life. The white liquid dripped down his throat, the smell went up his nostrils, milk took over his brain and filled all his being, until once he was eventually weaned, he could not anymore stand the sight or smell of that white liquid, and could not bear to drink any milk, either from the cow or from the goat. No drop of milk touched his tongue for the rest of his life, and even the thought of milk made his stomach turn.

After she had laid the infant to sleep in a makeshift crib, Reizele told Katya and Piotr everything that had happened to her since Piotr had left her at the hospital, that same morning, that horrible day in which she had not only given birth to her son, but had also been deprived of her man, her protector, her beloved. Words rushed out of her mouth as she described the terrifying experience of her escape under bombing, the maimed, the scattering dead bodies in the field.

Arkadi is dead. I saw him bloodied and motionless, lying on the ground, she told them unhesitatingly.

When Reizele began to absorb the implications of the situation on her status, she suddenly felt she was a stranger there. The thread which had connected her to Katya and Piotr Polski was Arkadi, and now the thread was broken.

What will I do? What will become of me and my baby? she sobbed. I do not want to be a burden to you. It was only because of Arkadi that you let me stay here with you, and now he is dead, and what am I to you? If the Germans find out that you are sheltering a Jew in your house, it will be terrible for you. They will shoot you on sight, as they do to everyone who hides Jews in their house, she went on. So please help me get back to Zamosc. I will go back to my family there, they'll take me back even if they are still furious with me for what I did to them. Circumstances change things, especially when it is your close family. Please help me return home to my family, even if they are in a stinking ghetto, she pleaded.

Katya and Piotr looked at each other while listening patiently to Reizele. Without saying a word, each knew what the other was thinking and had come to the same conclusion.

No, certainly not, said Katya with conviction. There is no chance that you'll find your family still living in their house. The Germans expelled all the Jews from their houses and sent them to the ghetto two months ago. They declared that by the first of May, no Jews would be left in the old quarter of Zamosc. Presumably your family was also turned out of their house. So where would you go? To the ghetto? With your baby? Thank the Lord that at the very last moment you were saved from the catastrophe which has fallen on your town.

You will stay with us, my dear, you and your baby will be safe here. We will hide you. There is just one thing: the forged papers I arranged for you will not guarantee your safety if they catch you, so perhaps it will be better if you don't go out of the house at all; and don't think of returning to work. Stay here, take care of your baby, and the work you do in the house and on the farm will cover your keep. In any case, as you know, we are unfortunately childless, so for us your son is like a gift from God, for as long as you are under our roof.

Katya's warm and calming response reassured Reizele, and all the tension and fears evaporated from her mind. They will take care of her, they will hide her identity, how wonderful is this good Polish family, one of the rare few who agreed to endanger their own lives for the sake of a Jewish woman and her infant son.

Reizele shut herself up within the four walls of the house, not venturing outside. For the sake of her son she was willing to suffer the restrictions of staying in hiding which were, in fact, not intolerable. The Polskis provided her with all she needed. They turned the basement of their house into a children's room, even decorating it so it would be more pleasant, and looked after her son devotedly, while he was hidden downstairs, in the basement.

As the days turned into weeks, and the weeks into months, being limited in her movements to the house eventually began to weigh Reizele down. She felt like a prisoner in chains and fetters. Freedom winked at Reizele from outside her prison cell, and she could not bear the enforced isolation any longer. She felt she had to throw off the chains which prevented her from moving freely.

When her son had finally been weaned – after more than a year – and had begun to eat solid food, Reizele decided that the time had come for her to go out into the bright light of day, and feel the warmth of the sun on her back. After all, no one in that small town knew she was a Jew, and on the very day her son was born, war had broken out in the East and a bomb had set the hospital ablaze, which meant that all hospital records would also have gone up in flames, including the initial sketchy registration of her name and other details, which had probably not even been completed due to her hasty arrival and immediate transfer to the delivery room. In any event, there was no documentation relating to the newborn baby because of the panicked evacuation of the hospital in the aftermath of the bombing. No papers, no birth certificate had accompanied Yuzhi's departure from the hospital. It was as if Yuzhi was considered not to have arrived in this world. So, why did she need to hide herself away? So she beseeched her benefactors to release her from her hiding place, take her out with them and present her to the townspeople as one of their Polish relatives. There is no problem with that, her papers confirmed her as a Christian, and even her name had been changed to Raymonda. They would never suspect her of having Jewish origins. She was sure that no harm would come to any of them if she ventured out in the open.

Katya agreed and her husband nodded his head in consent. All right, come with us to the church on Sunday, hold a prayer book, kneel when everyone else kneels and move your lips as if you are praying. Nobody will suspect you, and even the Germans never interrupt prayer services, especially now when they are busy searching and catching Jews hidden in the town.

✦✦✦

No ghetto had been established for the Jews in Belzec, for the simple reason that no Jews lived there. However, the Nazis very quickly, with their well-known ferocious efficiency, set up a death camp there to implement Operation Reinhard, the code name for murdering the two million Jews in the General Government region of Poland. The death camp was a kilometer south of the Lublin-Lvov railway station.

The original anti-tank trenches dug there turned into mass graves. This was not a concentration camp where some inmates were kept alive for slave labor. The Belzec camp was designed as the final solution for the problem of those Jews who still had the audacity to hang on to their lives: They were dispatched to a swift death immediately on arrival. The clothes of the victims had been stripped from their bodies; in the last indignity of public nakedness, they were taken to have their hair roughly shorn and immediately after, they marched to the showers whose taps released the fatal gas.

The exceptions were, as in the other death camps, the tens of strong males who were selected to carry out the most grisly jobs of heaving the dead bodies of the victims from the gas cells into a mass grave, and later wheeling them to the crematorium to be burned.

No Jew remained alive from the Belzec death camp. To be more precise, there were three survivors from that terrible killing center, which was one of the first the Germans put into operation. For that reason, Belzec was not as well known as the other death camps: No eyewitnesses could come forward to expose the horrors of that place of mass killings.

Reizele took the risk upon herself. She so much yearned to walk freely in the streets that her longing suppressed her doubts and hesitation about worshipping a God not her own.

It was on Sunday, the first of September 1942, when Reizele went with Katya and Piotr to the church which stood in the square in the center of the town. Katya had asked her neighbor, a dour and unsympathetic woman by the name of Mrs. Ohlenburg, to do her a favor: Would she be good enough to keep an eye on the boisterous toddler, who was then over a year old, while his mother went with them to church? This childless widow, usually ill-tempered and gruff, agreed to look after Yuzhi, so Reizele, Katya, and Piotr set off for church, where they merged with the congregation, kneeling, swaying, chanting as appropriate.

The thought came to Reizele while she was bent on her knees, imitating the movements of the worshippers around about her, falsifying her religion. She had not only changed her name, and her identity, she was now pretending to belong to a religion she did not believe in. She barely recognized herself, barely knew who she was any longer – she had lost her whole identity!

Reizele was seized with pangs of guilt about coming to church, but now it was too late. There was no going back. The sounds of the majestic organ accompanying the sweet soprano voices of the choirboys were both sweet music to her ears, but also filled her heart with immense longing for the Chassidic melodies her father sung in his synagogue: she could hear in her mind the congregation, who would join in with gusto, their prayers sincere, from the bottom of their hearts. She stood there in that church like a robot, kneeling down, praying, and chanting Mass with the rest of the congregation, no one suspecting for a moment that her piety was not as genuine as theirs. At the end of this, her first Mass, she even forced herself to line up with the other congregants to receive the Holy Communion wafer in her mouth. When she allowed the wafer to touch her tongue, only her tremendous strong will to remain alive enabled her not to spit it out.

When the prayer service ended and everyone filed out of the church, all of the sudden, the tranquility of the town square was disturbed by the screeching of the tires of trucks and horns being sounded.

One by one, the trucks juddered to a halt in the wide square, and SS soldiers jumped out, armed with clubs, pistols, and rifles. Ignoring the worshippers coming out of the church, they released the tarpaulin covers which closed each of the trucks, and with coarse shouts, and kicking and prodding with their guns, they commanded the human cargo loaded in the trucks to get down and wait in the square for orders.

With drawn pistols and rifles, scores of Nazi soldiers kept guard over some four hundred people, women and old men, children of all ages, who crowded together, terror-stricken, in the center of the square, not one of them daring to try to escape.

Reizele stared at the trembling Jews standing in the square, scared out of their wits, powerless. They were broken spirits, their bodies as thin as sticks after many months of suffering and indescribable torments in the ghetto and in forced labor. Her shivers went up her spine when suddenly some of their faces looked familiar to her. At that same moment, she heard someone nearby mutter they are the Jews from Zamosc! Reizele, her fears confirmed, hid herself behind Katya in case someone standing there would see her, and God forbid, point a finger towards her. Concentrating on their faces she began to recognize, one by one, her former neighbors and acquaintances, her teacher, the milkman, the vegetable seller, the mailman, and many others.

In utter horror, she found her eyes focused on the faces of her family, realizing that they too were part of that wretched convoy, and there, she suddenly came upon her mother and her three younger siblings, who stood huddled together frozen with terror.

As she was still scouring the faces for people she knew, her heart lost a beat when her eyes cached her father's image. He was standing there alone, separated from his wife and children. Yes, her father, the man who had given her life, stood waiting with the hordes of others for the end of the search by the Gestapo for any Jews who had managed to escape from the villages around, to find their way to hide in the town. And here they were, like a pathetic little herd of sheep smoked out of their hiding places, while the Nazi soldiers pushed and shoved, kicked and whipped them, terrified them with the butts of their rifles in their backs, bending down to shelter their poor bodies from these assaults. All of them gathered in the town square, the old, the young, women and children, all on their way to certain death, of which not one of them was aware.

Reizele continued to focus her gaze on her father. She could see him standing there, barely able to eke out his strength. Round-shouldered, shorn of his beard, dressed in tattered clothes, a torn cap on his head.

Where was his yarmulke? Or his *streimel*? Oh my God, what tortures this man has undergone, he must have had to do the hardest of hard labor, to look like that.

At the same time, she realized that at all costs he must not see her staring at him, for one look from him in her direction could reveal her identity and implicate her. But in spite of her anxiety, she did nothing to avoid meeting his gaze. Her father's eyes seemed to be searching her out among the people who were still standing at the entrance to the church. His glance identified the face of his daughter, which he could see behind the large hat of some woman. Their eyes met for the briefest time, in mutual acknowledgement, although not a muscle moved on their faces, neither of the father nor of the daughter. Their eyes betrayed no sparkle, for danger lurked in such an exchange. All they could permit themselves was a stolen glance, a glance of hopelessness, a glance of parting forever – an anguished farewell.

This brief glimpse of Reizele pierced her father's heart like a sharp sword, realizing his daughter had sunk so low as to abandon her religion. Here she stands with all those gentiles at the entrance to the church, an apostate. But perhaps it was better that way, the miserable father thought. The saving of a life overrides not only the Sabbath but also keeping one's religion. She is a forced convert, he rationalized. No doubt she'll come back to Judaism. The consolation of knowing that her life had been saved was a hundred times greater than the pain of her apostasy.

Reizele continued to gaze at the people standing confined

and crowded together. Her eyes searched for her brothers and sister, other than the ones she had already seen in the square. And where were her aunts and uncles, her grandmothers and grandfathers, had they been murdered? Or perhaps they had been able to escape? Or maybe had died in hunger and sickness? Who knows?

The mass of pitiable human beings began to move forward, goaded and threatened by rifle butts forced against their bodies and the sound of shots in the air. Reizele saw, through a veil of tears, her father and mother and her younger brothers and sisters holding on to each other, their eyes full of fear and misery. They stumbled on, towards an unknown destination, to the death camp, to be put to death by poisonous gas. Their murderers, with their Judas smiles, would entice them to go into the huge cell, to be washed and soaped and disinfected. You will come out of here clean and fresh. Hurry, take all your clothes off, and go into that room. You will need to have a shower, wash your hair, and get rid of any lice. And, like meek lambs wanting to believe the cruel fox, they all obeyed.

What choice did they have? They took off their clothes, followed all the instructions they had been given, and went further and further towards the point of no return when those shower taps were turned on, not to emit cleansing water, but to rob them of their lives. No one who entered those showers emerged alive.

Afterwards, when the gruesome plot of mass murder became known, Reizele could imagine what her family went through. Her mother, a modest soul all her life, the respected wife of the respected Rabbi of the town, forced to remove all her clothes and walk in her nakedness along the lengthy path bordered on both sides by an electrified fence to the killing place. In the space of twenty minutes, her mother and all her beloved family were reduced to a heap of bodies. Naked bodies, which the more muscular Jewish males removed from the gas chambers in a huge pile and brought them in wheelbarrows to the anti-tank trenches, which became a mass grave for those put to death in Belzec. This image would stay with Reizele all her life.

Later, towards the end of the war, when the Nazis wanted to cover up the evidence of their horrific crimes, and to remove all signs of the death camp, they dug up the bodies from the trenches and brought them to the crematoria, where they were burned until all that was left of them was a grey dust of ash. Into the emptied graves were thrown fragments of bones and the ashes of burned corpses.

Reizele bit her lips and continued to lead a double life: Her papers attesting that she was a Christian protected her from *actions* and transports, from the ghetto and from the death camps; these forged documents which changed her identity and her religion, erased her personality, nullified her upbringing – but not her faith.

It is possible to convert to another religion, but not to another faith. Her faith had not disappeared; she only had to lock it away deep within her heart.

Two different, opposing worlds. This was the reality of her life, and these two worlds caused Yuzhi to live in a state of confusion from the minute he was born. He was not brought up to have any faith, in fact he received only the essentials for survival: food, drink, a place to sleep, not enough love, and a deliberate disregard of any kind of education regarding his religion, his nationality, or family traditions. To an outside observer, Yuzhi absorbed the symbols of Christianity in the house he lived: Crosses decorated the walls, and watching the members of the household cross themselves ceremoniously before eating, before going to sleep, and on various other occasions.

Reizele's main concern was to survive the everyday ordeal which made her most fearful, that the secret of her origins was not safe from the Polskis' neighbors. Because she did not want to give them any opportunity to gain any information about her from her son, she kept him closeted in the house and would not allow him to put his nose out of the door. So he lived, like a cornered mouse who begins to squeak and tries to scratch his way out of his dark hole, often breaking into sobs, mostly unhappy and frustrated.

Another two years went by and Reizele continued to stay in Belzec, with Katya and Piotr, until one day, the bitter hand of fate shuffled all the cards and led her to an enforced and lengthy separation from her son. But by the same token, fate was generous enough to bring out the best of the bad, and initiated Reizele's meeting with Ruvke, a momentous meeting that would lead them from the horrors of a Death March to the *chuppah*, their wedding canopy, to a happy marriage.

# 3
# Among The Jaws

Ruvke had a happy childhood. His parents, Nachum and Gittel Kirgelik had a large and spacious house in the center of Warsaw, where he grew up with his two brothers and a sister. His father dealt in timber and had a concession to cut down trees in the forests surrounding Warsaw, to be used in his large furniture-making business in the industrial quarter of the city where he employed many workers, both Jews and Polish *goyim*, manufacturing high-quality furniture for the wealthy people of the city.

In line with the centuries-old attitude of *goyim* in Europe towards Jews living in their countries, that of Nachum Kirgelik's workers was marked by a similar ambivalence. One the one hand, they valued and admired the Jews, but on the other hand they envied them, and were hostile towards them to the point of overt hatred. Their respect for the Jews' creative skills could change direction in the blink of an eye to animosity, and from verbal abuse to the limits of physical violence.

Jealousy and hatred against the Jews were always present, if not on the surface then in the recesses of the soul, frequently bursting out in an excess of resentment and an accusing finger setting towards them in general, and in the country of the current accuser in particular, declaring that the Jews kept a stranglehold on the country's economy, and that they robbed away the livelihoods of the country's true citizens, the Christians.

So, in a nutshell, according to this bigotry, the Jews ruled the economy of the country and thus deprived the rest of the citizens of their rightful livelihoods, the fruits of power and capital. In most nations of Europe, a large majority of the citizens held the deeply-felt conviction, going back generations, that the Jews controlled the economy of their country. The demagogues had brainwashed them that millions upon millions of poor, deprived citizens were being held for ransom by that people who constituted a very small percentage of the population, who prevented them from developing or prospering! No matter that poverty ruled wherever Jews were scattered about in small villages and scarcely knew where their next meal was coming from; no matter that even in the larger cities they lived huddled together in crowded alleys far from the majestic squares inhabited by the well-established of the city. In fact, most Jews were bowed down by the heavy burden of earning a living in menial work or the hard physical labor of working the land. The brainwashed people's eyes were blind and refused to see the proofs of statistical evidence to be found in every village and city. Their eyes registered only the well-to-do, like Nachum Kirgelik, who, by working all hours of the day, and by the sweat of his own labor, had prospered honestly. But to the *goyim* of his town he represented the "international conspiracy" of Jews – including the poor and the downtrodden majority – whose ambition was to control their economy and rob them out of their livelihoods.

Those fuelled by hate needed only a match to light the fire. The fire was lit, the flames grew higher and higher and sparks shot off in all directions in the 1920s and 1930s. At that time of economic depression, there was no work to be found, food was scarce, and people were desperate for somewhere to live: but there was a scapegoat for all this suffering, in the form of the Jews. The Jews had taken away their jobs, their houses, their money, their livelihoods. No more than this was necessary to provide fertile ground for a fanatical regime, which promised a car for every worker, on the condition that those who did not belong, were considered an enemy of the state, and would be gotten rid of.

In the beginning, they spoke of emigration, of expelling the Jews from Europe and from Germany in particular. At the start of the war in 1939, Hitler made an impassioned, cynical and sarcastic speech in which he called on the nations of the world to accept Jewish immigrants from Germany. Take them, take them! he exhorted. If you feel so compassionate towards them, and if you are so impressed by their wisdom and abilities – open the gates of your states and let them in! Needless to say, no one raised up the gauntlet of Hitler's challenge, and no state opened its arms to admit the Jews en masse. Apart from the few Jews who had had the foresight to pack their suitcases in good time and the luck to find a country to accept them, the vast majority of Jews stayed where they were. They did not see the handwriting on the wall until it was too late to do anything about it, for they had convinced themselves that their rights were carved in stone with a sharp knife, never to be changed. They refused to believe the signs which could be seen by anyone with eyes and ears, which gathered weight and momentum like a snowball coming nearer and nearer to them; ultimately plunging into an abyss by a force which would cause their swift destruction.

✦✦✦

For very many years, Nachum Kirgelik had been a man held in high regard. He was on good terms with the Polish nobility, he sent his children to Polish schools, and he was altogether of a liberal outlook. His Judaism was confined to his home; he kept to the traditions but did not stringently observe all the laws of the Torah.

He was a man of high position in the synagogue, and his opinions were listened to, not because he was a big scholar in Torah, but because he was a generous benefactor to the synagogue. After all, he who pays the piper calls the tune. By virtue of this, he was called Rabbi, Rabbi Nachum. At home a Jew; amongst his Polish acquaintances a Pole, like them. Poland had been the home of his family for hundreds of years and he would do all his duty by her. In the 1920s, he was even called up to serve in the Polish Army, and did his army service faithfully and well, like every other Polish soldier in the country.

Ruvke was Nachum's youngest son, tall and handsome, with blue eyes and blond curly hair. Nachum decided to send him to the Academy of Music, where he learned to play the violin. His middle son, Anshel, studied engineering at the most prestigious college of technology, and his eldest son, Yudele, learned all the ins and outs of the wood trade from his father and helped him manage their flourishing business.

His only daughter, Naomi, born after all his sons, went to the girls' school connected to the synagogue in Warsaw. She was more educated in the Jewish religion and its practices than her brothers. She and her mother would go each Sabbath to the small neighborhood synagogue near their house, an old wooden building, surrounded by mature, gigantic trees which cast a tall shadow on it as if protecting it from misfortune. Naomi and her mother would sit in the ladies' section high up in the gallery, and Naomi felt that if she just stretched her arms up a little, she could touch the roof. They peered down to the main hall of the synagogue, at the men wrapped in their prayer shawls, rocking backwards and forwards in the intensity of prayer, reading from their prayer books words of praise to the Almighty.

The women tucked away far from the activity of the synagogue hall, were envious of the men being able to show their devoutness in this way; while they muttered the same praise with their lips. They could only peek through the curtains high above at the Torah scroll when it was taken out of the Ark, although their fathers and brothers and husbands could lovingly touch its cover and even lift it up reverently and with the utmost care to show it to the whole congregation. It was as if the wings of the heavenly Protector were extended to shield only the men's section of the synagogue.

As for the women, what could they do, ignored up there

in the gallery, but carry on a quiet conversation, one to each other, or nodding their heads and smile at acquaintances; but still they all were resigned to the fact that at least they were present in an atmosphere of holiness, even though only few of them actively participated the prayers, heartily.

On a black and dreary Sabbath, the first of September, 1939, Naomi and her mother, Gittel, were sitting on the front bench of the ladies' gallery of their synagogue while the men of the family, Rabbi Nachum and his three sons, Yudele, Anshel, and Ruvke, took part in the prayer service below. It was a tranquil day in early autumn, the scent of falling leaves in the air. Suddenly, in the middle of the prayer service, the men still enveloped in their prayer shawls, each holding his *siddur*, there was heard the thunderous roar of airplanes overhead. The noise was ear-splitting. Bombs dropped all around, sowing destruction and devastation.

Terror-struck, the worshippers clutched on to each other, holding their heads and stuffing their fingers in their ears to deaden the blast. They may not have realized it, but their whole world had metaphorically crashed down upon them.

The damage to their synagogue had not been caused by a direct hit to the roof, but a bomb had landed in the small courtyard surrounding it. In the middle of the courtyard was a tall tree with enormous branches spreading outwards and upwards from the thick trunk. It was this tree which took the impact of the bomb; the crackles and hisses of the massive trunk breaking into splinters filled the air, and the stately tree collapsed with all its weight onto the pitched roof of the synagogue, and flattened those under it. Most of the women who were sitting nearest to the part of the roof which collapsed were killed or injured. The majority of the men downstairs were trapped between the walls, which the intensity of the bombing caused to catch fire.

Some of those who were able, climbed up to the windows and fled in all directions, taking their lives in their hands.

The elderly and more infirm tried to get themselves out of the path of the menacing flames, which were licking at the crimson curtain in front of the holy Ark. Some of the men were injured, others fled through the doors and rushed up the stairs to the ladies' gallery to help the women trapped underneath the roof, which had collapsed and buried them under its heavy weight.

Reb Nachum and his three sons leaped up the stairs to the ladies' gallery to help the trapped women. Fearful of what might have happened to Gittel and Naomi, they began clearing the debris from the bodies of the dead and injured. To their consternation they discovered the mangled body of Naomi, lying among the destruction. Overcome with sorrow and distress at the sight, and crying out in anguish, they saw Gittel out of the corner of their eyes, sitting on the edge of a broken bench, her head tilted back. It was clear that the shock had rendered her speechless.

Remarkably, apart from some surface scratches, Gittel had not been injured.

Later, in the house, the Kirgelik family wept bitterly and mourned the beautiful Naomi whose life had been cut short so tragically. After Gittel had recovered a little from the intense initial agony, she could not be consoled, and felt a heavy burden of guilt that she had not been able to save her daughter. She would willingly have taken Naomi's place. Gittel felt as if one of her limbs had been cut off, and even the terrible events which were to come could not erase the memory of her beloved daughter who had perished in front of her eyes.

✦✦✦

The Germans conquered the entire territory of Poland in a lightning strike of ferocious intensity, and harsh edicts began immediately to beat down on the Jews' heads like hailstones. One day, German soldiers raided the Kirgeliks' wood factory.

Citing the recently decreed policy of confiscation of property belonging to Jews, they declared that their furniture-making factory would be commandeered in order to help with the war effort of the Third Reich.

The Nazis' first step was the seizure of the Kirgeliks' business. Their second step was to forbid them to trade in timber from the trees cut down from state forests; the third step was the cancellation of the official concession allowing them to cut down the trees. At this stage, the Germans still allowed Nachum and his son Yudele to continue to work in the factory, but as ordinary workers. Not only was their income considerably reduced, but also their status and their self-respect. Worst of all was being compelled to transfer the work of a lifetime, the business which was their pride and joy, into the hands of the Nazis. It was a body blow for them, that the tyrannical regime which had taken control of their country could, overnight, confiscate their property. They received no legal warning, no explanation.

Only frozen words were shouted into their ears: You are Jews, this is the law, it's all legal according to the Nuremberg Laws passed a few years ago.

Their Jewish faith, which had been source of pride to them, now became a cause of their degradation. So, they said to themselves, let the bastards take our business, we are not afraid of hard work. We will wait it out until better days come, may they come quickly in our time, Amen.

The Nuremberg Race Laws, formulated in 1935, were unsurpassed in their malice and severity, discriminating as they did between blood and blood. Little by little, the Jews discovered that their rights had been obliterated and that their lives became more and more constricted. What they had formerly taken for granted was now prohibited: they were forbidden to work in a business of their own; refused entry to places of culture and entertainment; libraries were closed to them; books written by Jews were publicly burned; Jews were barred from attending schools or institutions of higher education.

All these restrictions, and many more, fell like a ton of bricks on the heads of the Jews, among whom was Ruvke, the youngest son of Nachum and Gittel, who was nineteen when the war broke out.

One day, Ruvke went as usual to the Academy of Music where, with other students he was taking part in violin practice. The lesson was interrupted by the entry of two German soldiers accompanied by the principal of the academy. The soldiers pointed at a number of students, as if they were common criminals being taken into custody. This one, and this, and this, and that one. Ruvke was one of the four students taken to the office of the principal. In a voice empty of emotion he informed them that, as Jews, they would no longer be able to study in the academy. Whether he was concerned for his expelled Jewish students was difficult to tell. Certainly what was paramount in his mind was the continued existence of his academy.

Ruvke grasped his violin in his hands as he stood listening to the principal, who sat comfortably in the well-upholstered chair behind his large writing desk, telling him to take his belongings, his violin, his notebooks, his music case, and leave the academy. Immediately! That was all. No apology. No regret. No farewells to the friends he made there. From one minute to the next, take your things, Kirgelik, and get out of here. Now!

This was his punishment for being a Jew, being kicked out from the academy. Punishment, for the meantime only. In every institution of education throughout Poland, there were similar scenes of expulsion. One after another their gates were barred to Jewish students, teachers, and lecturers, and everyone who had studied or taught there, was dismissed in disgrace. Anshel, Nachum and Gittel's middle son, was similarly thrown out of the college where he had studied engineering.

In spite of these harsh edicts, the Jewish community of Warsaw did not give up, and with startling rapidity opened its own educational institutions. The teachers, who had been deprived of teaching in their former schools and colleges, found employment in the new Jewish institutions. In this situation, Ruvke thought himself fortunate indeed to be able to study violin with one of the most famous music teachers in Warsaw: He took advantage of his opportunity and his playing and technical proficiency improved by leaps and bounds – much faster, in fact, than what he had achieved in the academy where he had studied and from which he had been expelled.

Ruvke was careful to practice his violin each day and continued to study with his revered teacher. When he played, the glorious sounds of music he produced with his violin were like lightning rays running marvelously on the dark walls of the bad days which they, and the entire Jewish community of Warsaw, experienced.

A year passed by, a year of cruel restrictions, economic, religious and cultural. The Jews in Poland were slowly strangled by them, while the war continued to spread in Europe like wildfire, and one country after another fell captive to the Nazi regime, which captured the Jews under their crushing boots.

✦✦✦

After his triumphant occupation of most of the countries of Europe, Hitler became obsessed by his ambition to increase the territory under his rule by the conquest of the Soviet Union. He did not let the Molotov-Ribbentrop Pact of non-aggression stand in his way. Hitler prepared to embark on the glorious Operation Barbarossa which, he believed, would last not more than a few weeks. In June 1941, a massive concentration of German troops stood at the Russian borders for the length of two thousand kilometers; German soldiers were augmented by Slovak, Romanian, Hungarian, Italian troops, and even the Finns, who still had their own account to settle with the Russians, accompanied them.

An army of two million soldiers was ready to invade Russia. During the first twenty days of the invasion, the Germans' advance was impressive. The suddenness of the invasion had left Stalin completely at a loss. His army was inadequate to defend the vast Soviet Union, and was bombed in all directions. More than two thousand Russian airplanes were disabled on the ground, and the Russian command was panic-stricken and lost control of the army. In mid-July, the Germans came within thirty kilometers of the approaches to Moscow. Another German division reached Leningrad, in the north, and besieged the city without respite for three years!

However, in spite of the Germans' swift initial advance, they began to slow down.

Difficulties soon multiplied like mushrooms after the rain: The German troops had neither taken into account the vastness of the Soviet territories, nor had they profited from the bitter experience of Napoleon. They too found themselves far from home, entrenched in deep mud holes in the freezing temperatures of the Russian winter; reinforcements of essential supplies did not reach them because of the length of the supply lines. But Hitler's goal was not abandoned, and the German troops pressed on, leaving death and destruction in their wake.

After the first shock of the invasion, Stalin began to recover, and put into operation a new missile system which was used in the defense of Moscow. The Red Army suffered massive losses – two and a half million soldiers were killed by the end of 1941 – but its morale was not broken. Stalin even adopted a scorched earth policy, and the deeper inside Russia the Germans penetrated, the more vulnerable they were to attacks from the Russian front. On the Leningrad front, too, the Germans suffered an unexpected setback: they came up against strong resistance by the citizens of Leningrad, who were willing to defend their homeland and their city to the last man, to the last drop of blood, spitting in the face of the savage attacks.

Stalin was careful to appeal and encourage his countrymen, the Russian people, to come to the defense of their homeland, Mother Russia, rather than to talk about the defense of communism. The ideology of communism was pushed under the carpet when fighting for the life and existence of the nation. Only when Stalin wished to rid himself of his opponents in the Soviet Union – both before the war and after it – did he state that they were enemies of communism, a reason to demolish them, and so he persisted in this ideology until the day he died.

The Nazis' ambition to make more territory available to the German nation was in direct contrast to their decision to reduce to the bare minimum the areas available to Jews in the countries they conquered. As a consequence, the idea took shape in the distorted mind of Reinhard Heydrich to establish ghettos for the Jews, to isolate them, to deport them from the Aryan race, the master race.

This was the bitter fruit of the racial doctrine which embraced the belief that the Jews were an inferior race with whom it was forbidden for Aryan citizens to be in contact. Just as if they were sick from infectious diseases, the Jews had to be locked into quarantine, to be imprisoned in hermetically-sealed ghettos.

It is ironic that it was Heydrich who formulated the plan to enclose the Jews in the ghetto and be one of the architects of the Final Solution of the Jewish problem, for all his life Heydrich suspected, as a man, that Jewish blood ran in his veins.

Had it not been for the war, Heydrich might well have

been a famous violinist. However, he was conscripted into the Navy, where he had a short romance with the daughter of the shipyard director. Nothing came out of it, because finally he decided to marry another woman and the father, who was furious at Heydrich's rejection of her daughter, had him dismissed from the Navy. This act had disastrous consequences, since Heydrich took advantage of the rise to power of the Nazis, to find himself a place within the vast Nazi Party apparatus. After a short interview, Himmler suggested to him that he should present his plans for setting up an intelligence gathering service as an arm of the SS. Heydrich did it within the space of twenty minutes and his plans were accepted, and within a short time he had propelled himself into being appointed head of the Gestapo. With the conquest of Poland, it was Heydrich who devised the scheme of evicting all the Jews from their homes in the centers of cities and putting them into a fenced off area, a ghetto, surrounded by a wall, where freedom of movement would be denied them.

The area chosen was the Jewish Quarter in Warsaw. The Polish Christians who lived there were removed to other housing, and in their place were crammed the Jews who had lived in the Christian neighborhoods of the city. Whoever possessed money, silver, or other valuables could get by in this new situation better than those without means. Most Jews however came into this latter category, especially those who had been ejected from their houses in the small villages around Warsaw. They were so poor that they entered the ghetto with just the clothes on their backs and were forced to live huddled together in public buildings such as schools and study halls which had been closed down, and other storerooms. Their situation was desperate.

The Jews were not only compelled to go to live in the ghetto, they were also forced to shut themselves inside the walls so that nobody would be able to sneak outside, for the wall was three meters high topped with shards of glass. The high, glass-topped wall sealed the Jews off almost completely from the outside world, after they were compelled, by an irony order, to build their prison with their own hands.

Amazing, but many Jews who were compelled to enter the ghetto were actually pleased at first to live in a place where they would have only Jewish neighbors, and there was a burgeoning of religious and social activity. These feelings vanished quickly when the conditions of living in the ghetto became intolerable.

In order to transmit efficiently all the Nazi decrees to the mass of Jews, the system of the Judenrat, the Jewish council, was instituted. For every twenty thousand Jews, a Judenrat of twelve people was set up to act as the point of contact between the Nazis and the Jews – the most unenviable role imaginable. Members of the Judenrat would have to meet face to face with the Nazis to be given the latest cruel and inhumane decrees which would have to be obeyed to the letter. They would then have to return to their brother Jews and see that these orders were carried out. It was the Judenrat who decided what to give to whom, and how much; the Judenrat who from time to time could obtain certificates for people to go out of the ghetto; the Judenrat who might be able to reduce the severity of an order; to alleviate the living conditions of the Jews imprisoned within the ghetto. On the other hand, it was the Judenrat who was forced to draw up the lists of the Jews for the Nazis who would be sent to the death camps, a heartrending task.

During the first stages of the war, many members of the Judenrat tried to the best of their ability to ease the lives of the Jews, both by obtaining a better supply of food and by setting up religious and social facilities in the ghetto.

However, with increasingly bad living conditions, the outbreak of diseases, the terrible and ever-present hunger, and people dropping dead in the streets, the role of the Judenrat became too difficult for them to bear. Some members of the Jewish council resigned, and there were some who even chose to put an end to their lives so as not to have to carry out the Nazis' wicked orders on their fellow Jews and – worst of all – to be in the position of selecting those who would be sent to their deaths. A thankless role, an impossible position.

# 4
# The Escape

The decree of expulsion to the ghetto landed on the Jews like a hawk swooping down on its prey. They had no warning or hint that this was about to happen. The first they knew was when Nazi soldiers raided the houses with Jewish inhabitants according to meticulously prepared lists and the soldiers carried out these heartless *actions,* house after house, knocking loudly on each door. The callousness of the *actions* was proportionate to the level of efficiency and zeal with which they were performed.

The soldiers did not waste time waiting for the door to be opened by the householder. The peremptory knock was only to herald the door being kicked in by the heavy boots of three or four SS storm troopers, guns cocked in their hands and barking orders in all directions: This house has been requisitioned; everyone will be ready to leave within two hours. You will take with you only the essentials; one suitcase for each person.

Each room was thoroughly searched, one after the other; the soldiers opened closets, looked under beds to see if anyone was hiding there, climbed up to the attics and down to the storerooms. In the villages around the city, they poked haystacks with pitchforks in case any Jew had hidden himself beneath the straw.

Only very few could escape: the storm troopers' intimidating dedication to their task made escape almost impossible. Small children and grandparents, women and men were pulled away from their houses with very efficient calculated steps. Their Polish neighbors did not need to know what happened to the Jewish families in their street. The Nazis took care to carry out the evictions in the middle of the night, while the Polish *goyim* were asleep, so they literally had their eyes closed to what was going on. Later on, they could claim, we were sleeping, we saw nothing, we heard nothing.

The Kirgelik family was not spared eviction from their house. Two SS storm troopers arrived before dawn one morning at their house and broke the door down in their customary manner. They burst into the spacious house, guns loaded and cocked, and ordered the family to dress and prepare to leave within two hours. An officer wearing the SS insignia of a lieutenant on his epaulettes followed the soldiers, his pistol in the belt of his trousers, his arms behind his back, leaving to his subordinates the job of driving out the family from the house.

Nachum, Gittel, and their three sons – Yudele, Anshel and Ruvke – were in a state of shock as, wordlessly, they packed their things. What, not to go off to work in the factory? Not to study or work? Obviously not, with the guns of the soldiers trained on them. No plea from them would avert the evil decree. They had no choice but to submit to it.

At the moment when all their possessions had been packed and they stood ready to go out of their house for the last time, Gittel broke down. It was not only because she had to part from the rooms which she had brought up her children for so many years, but also having to part from her beautiful furniture, which her husband, a skilled craftsman, had designed and made with his own hands; her prized paintings, her highly polished silver, her sparkling crystal vases, her bone china so carefully washed and stored in the breakfront after every festive meal. How was it possible that all of these would be taken from them in a flash by the heartless orders of these SS storm troopers, holding a gun to their heads? Where were they being sent? Where would they live?

The soldiers reassured them that there is no need to worry, they are just moving to another place, where they will have only Jewish neighbors. In the ghetto they will be able to live as much of a Jewish life as they like. So they should not worry. Ah, what a generous proposal.

Gittel had dressed herself in her very best clothes, pretending to look brave and calm. She wore a lace blouse under her stylish fur coat, put on her head a hat of velvet with a showy peacock feather, as if she was going to an exclusive party. Nachum, her husband, threw her a look of amazement. He had hardly remembered what a good-looking woman his wife was until now, when, faced with the fear and dread of the unknown, she stood next to him dressed in all her finery. *Davka*, in the midst of the *action*, Gittel showed herself in her very best light, and Nachum, distressed as he was, admired now her dark eyes and rouged cheeks. His heart was moved beyond words by her beauty and courage.

The storm troopers stood over them with watchful eyes and the goad of whips in their hands ready to lash out at them if they lingered. Gittel, however, managed to hide within the single suitcase which she was allowed to take with her, most of her jewelry and some of her elegant clothes. She could not imagine that within a short time these would look like rags.

At the same time a dramatic scene had occurred. When her husband and their sons each packed clothes and other things into one suitcase as had been ordered and they all were on the point of stepping outside the house, one of the storm troopers held up his hand to stop them. He called out to Ruvke and asked, what have you got in your hand? We said you can take only one suitcase with you, so why are you taking two? Drop one of them now! Ruvke, both embarrassed and frightened, recovered himself immediately, and replied, This is not a suitcase. It has my violin in it. I cannot leave without my violin, and the suitcase has my clothes in it. The storm trooper had already raised his hand to snatch the violin by force from Ruvke, who continued to hold on to it. But just before the violin was snatched away, Ruvke nimbly sidestepped him and placed himself in front of the officer, who had been standing a little way off, listening to the altercation.

With pleading eyes, Ruvke beseeched the officer to let him take his violin with him. Only when Ruvke dared to meet the officer's eyes he saw the look on his face, which showed he was sympathetic to Ruvke's plight. They both were each strikingly tall; the officer was older than Ruvke by only a few years, a handsome man, his eyes a light brown like the eyes of a ginger-colored cat, his nose straight as an arrow, his lips shapely and chiseled. The thought flashed through Ruvke's mind that, in other circumstances, they could well have been friends. But his main concern at that moment was to ensure that his violin stayed with him for, without it, life for him was not worth living. It was as vital to him as air. Building up his courage, he implored the officer, Please let me take my violin, too. I simply cannot live without it; I need to play it all the time.

The young Jew's determination, combined with his exceptional good looks and bearing, affected the officer's stony, or supposedly stony heart, and he asked Ruvke a little skeptically: How many years have you been playing the violin? How do I know that you are not a raw beginner? Ruvke met the officer's gaze, and said tentatively, You can judge for yourself. I'll play something for you and you'll decide how good I am.

Getting the challenge and putting all the rules to one side, the officer agreed: Play!

Nachum and Gittel, Yudele and Anshel stood open-mouthed at the sight of Ruvke taking out his violin from its case, tucking it under his chin and began to play a Bach Suite. From the very first notes, the officer realized that the young violinist was extraordinarily talented. Ruvke continued playing for a few minutes, until the officer told him to stop. All right, he said, you can take your violin with you. The officer indicated to the two storm troopers, who had been standing all this time quite taken aback by the exchange between their officer and Ruvke, that he was permitting Ruvke to take his violin, and that they should now continue with the *action*.

In the few seconds that remained before the Kirgelik family finally went out of their house, the officer's eyes met those of Ruvke, who mumbled his gratitude to him. I will not forget what you did for me; I'll remember that there was one good thing on this terrible day. Ruvke even glimpsed a ghost of a smile on the officer's lips before they were all hustled towards the convoy of trucks waiting there in the street, already full of their neighbors, from the very young to the very old. The trucks set off with the Jews for the ghetto, which would soon turn out to be their prison.

Within a very short time, Nachum Kirgelik was one of those Jews chosen to form the Judenrat, which would act as the point of contact between the Nazis and the Jews for the purpose of organizing the mundane details of daily life in the ghetto.

Rabbi Nachum's first job was to supervise the building of the wall which surrounded the ghetto. It was hard labor, like the slaves in Egypt building the pyramids. Hundreds of thousands of people built this wall, which distanced them from civilization, totally isolated them from the outside world, to stew in their own juice of starvation, disease, and death.

In November 1940, the work of building the ghetto wall was completed by those who would be hemmed in by it and never again allowed to breathe the free air of the outside world.

Thanks to Nachum Kirgelik's position on the Judenrat, his family was allocated relatively roomy living quarters in an apartment that had previously been occupied by Polish *goyim* and had been vacated so that the ghetto could be set up for the Jews. One hundred and ten thousand Poles were evacuated from the area of the ghetto, and they were immediately directed to live in the houses now emptied of their Jewish owners. After all, what was simpler than to go to live in the

Jews' homes, homes which had been forcibly evacuated within a mere two hours from start to finish?

Gittel and her family went into the rooms they had been allocated in the ghetto and found it hard to assimilate the magnitude of the decline in their standard of living. The rooms were those of impoverished Polish *goyim*, of the masses who lived at that time of economic hardship, constantly short of food. The accommodation lacked the most basic amenities, everything was damp and moldy, but there was one comfort: At least, said Gittel, we will be living only among Jews, the *goyim* will not be green with envy and thinking up new ways to harass us all the time. We'll be able to get on with our lives in peace, more or less. So perhaps we will be better off here.

Only a few days passed before Gittel saw how her short-sightedness and naïve thinking had prompted her misplaced optimism. The ghetto quickly became full to capacity. To the 138,000 original Jewish inhabitants of the Jewish quarter there, were added each day thousands of Jews who were brought in from other neighborhoods of the city. During 1940 and 1941, masses of Jews from villages roundabout were also brought to be crammed into the ghetto, which was already bursting at its seams, to its maximum.

The Jews, who had lived there before the war, were better off than those who had been thrust into it by the tens and hundreds of thousands, for they had been able to hide some valuables which they were sometimes able to trade for food. However, those who had come later, possessed nothing of value, lived in former schools in the most cramped conditions, with appalling sanitary arrangements, without water, heating, or cooking facilities, and with no source of income. In such conditions, disease and starvation were bound to thrive.

Forty soup kitchens existed in the ghetto to feed the mass of people, and although Kirgelik tried to obtain as much food as possible for them, it was only a drop in the bucket.

Both children and adults subsisted on potato peelings, which became the main source of nutrition and those without means, would lick and suck the leaves which blew down from the trees, or cook them to try to allay their pangs of hunger.

As time went on, diseases took hold easily and spread like wildfire in the crowded and unsanitary conditions. Whenever Kirgelik would walk along the street, children would clutch at his trousers in mute appeal, but he would have to tell them that he had no more food to give them, not a crumb, there was none left.

Conditions worsened each day. He would try to persuade the Germans to give him more food to distribute among the thousands of sick and starving who could barely stand on their feet, but food became more strictly rationed, and later, food supplies were cut off altogether.

Kirgelik would see the bloated faces of the children sitting on the snow-covered ground, their eyes staring without seeing, the wind and cold tore through their ragged clothes and burned their flesh – they were just skin and bones, without the strength even to call out for help. Like wounded animals, only a yelping sound emerged from between their lips, blue with cold – sights which Kirgelik could not banish from his mind day and night.

✦ ✦ ✦

Nachum Kirgelik's three sons were involved in a variety of activities in the ghetto. Yudele and Anshel were active in several different youth movements such as Hashomer Hatzair, Bnei Akiva, Beitar, and Gordonia, which operated in educational frameworks, held meetings and secretly published their own newspapers. Ruvke was not interested in joining any of the youth movements, and instead decided to concentrate on studying, and any spare time he spent on practicing the violin.

Several months passed in this way, accompanied by constant suffering and fear of what might come to pass. Eventually, Yudele and Anshel felt they could no longer bear the awful conditions, the poverty, and the terrible sights which confronted them each day, of dead bodies in the streets being carted away in wheelbarrows. Their one thought was how they could get themselves out of that hell-hole.

The idea first came to Yudele when the family was sitting down to the meager meal on Friday night in the light of the flickering Sabbath candles, which Gittel still lit and blessed in the customary way. Yudele vigorously wiped his mouth with the back of his hand and looked around the table. He then said, decisively: It is impossible to go on like this. I don't want to stay in this nightmare of a place. I feel that no one will get out of here alive. I want to go, leave, escape from here. Father, get me a permit to go out of the ghetto, even if you have to forge or steal it! Use your connections with those criminals! Find some way of getting me away from here. We are all starving; people are dying in the streets. The Nazis are already putting pressure on you to prepare lists of people for deportation. They are murdering them! Father, they are killing them! I have to get away; I have to escape from here! Yudele's voice had risen so that he finished almost shouting his words out.

A heavy silence fell on them all. Gittel covered her face with her hands and sobbed softly, as if she agreed with her son's decision and was even now parting from him.

A few minutes later, Anshel began to speak. He sounded as if he had been struggling to find his voice, so quiet and restrained was it, but he was determined that his family would know what he, too, intended to do. I have to get away from here too, he said. There is no point in staying, just waiting for who knows what to happen. The only certain thing is that we will all die if we do not move. So, I also need help to get out of here.

While his elder brothers spoke of their frustration at remaining in the ghetto and their plans to escape, Ruvke looked at them open-mouthed. He was astonished at their audacity, but at the same time he knew that it would be better for them to leave the ghetto. He also knew that he could not allow himself to think of escaping. He would never abandon his parents, nor could he think of leaving his violin, for to escape would mean leaving everything behind and leaving with just the clothes on his back. He could not possibly leave his precious violin behind.

Nachum Kirgelik needed a long time to recover his composure after the shock his two elder sons had caused him. After a prolonged silence, which seemed to deplete the room of air, he said in an unwavering voice that he agreed with their decision. You're right. At least save yourselves, go out to be free men, in spite of all the dangers. I'm confident that you will cope with all the obstacles you will come across. Better to make a run for it even with all the dangers, than wait here like a caged hen waiting for the knife of the slaughterer to slash its throat. I have had my head in the sand like an ostrich trying not to see the implications of those lists of people the Nazis are demanding from the Judenrat to be sent on the transports.

Transports, they call them! Nachum raised his voice, full of frustration and anger: In other words, transportation to their deaths. It is a terrible position to be in, to have to sentence your fellow Jews to death. The Germans do not pick those who are going to be sent to be killed; we Jews on the Judenrat have to do it ourselves. I cannot do it; I avoid it, run away from it. But there are plenty of others who are prepared to carry out these Selections. Letting out a sigh of despair, Nachum continued: And who knows when our turn will come. Yes, I agree. Take the bull by the horns, perhaps you two at least will be saved.

A day or two after that Friday evening, Nachum first put his mind to forge a permit for Yudele to go out of the ghetto.

He went as usual to the Nazi headquarters next to the gate of the ghetto to receive his orders. He used his acquaintance with those Nazi officers responsible for the comings and goings of the ghetto to take advantage of the temporary absence of the commandant from his office. He aroused no one's suspicions as he stepped into the office, and went straight to the table on which were set out permits for officials to use when they went out of the ghetto in the course of their work. Like a conjurer who hides something up his sleeve without anyone seeing his deft movements, he quickly pocketed one of the permits bearing the picture of a bespectacled young man, and calmly walked out of the room. Nachum left Nazi headquarters for his home, looking for all the world like a conscientious clerk fulfilling his duties to the best of his ability.

Yudele did not want to waste any time. Before dawn the next morning he left his home at the appointed hour for those with permits to go out of the gate. He was wearing a large hat, and wore glasses just like the man whose picture was on the permit he held tightly in his hand. No one raised an eyebrow at him as he walked calmly through the gate. The Nazi guard glanced at him, casually checked the permit he held, and waved him through.

The guards could never hear the pounding hearts of those fleeing people they waved through the gate, and were not aware how these smuggling the gate were absorbed in themselves, their bent bodies trembling under their clothes and their heads shaking down to the level of the asphalt under their feet.

Yudele made an immense effort to regain his composure, and set out on his way. He had to draw himself away from there, disappear, go out of the city, warily zigzagging between the houses and alleyways so that he would not be caught.

Now came Anshel's turn to escape. Nachum knew very well every brick in the ghetto wall, every crack and every gap. He made a sketch for Anshel of the precise point where he would be able to squeeze under the wall to the other side of the ghetto. The best time for him to make his escape would be at twilight, when the guards on duty in the watch tower changed.

Anshel wore a lightweight coat in order to make it easier for him to crawl under the opening of the wall. He kissed his father and mother, smiled wanly to Ruvke and hugged him warmly with all his strength. Then he went out of the house without a backward glance. He looked at his watch, and made his way to the wall. It was time for the changeover of the guards. When he reached the gap in the wall, he looked around, and when he was sure that nobody was watching him, he bent down and began to crawl through, hampered a little by the prickly thorns which scratched his legs, but determined not to let that stop him until he finally squeezed himself through to the other side of the wall – the wall which had imprisoned him, his family, and all the hundreds of thousands of Jews trapped within its bounds, sentenced to death without trial.

Anshel shook off the clods of earth from his clothes. He strode off quickly to get away from the ghetto area, merging with the people who were making their way to their particular destination.

❖ ❖ ❖

Emptiness filled Nachum Kirgelik's heart after the departure of his two eldest sons, who had taken their fate into their own hands. He tried to fill this emotional gap in a practical manner, by helping some of the thousands upon thousands of the most destitute people.

One day, when he was at the home of a young couple with several small children, the youngest, a four-month-old baby whose mother did not have enough milk to satisfy him and for whom Nachum had managed to obtain a daily ration of cow's milk, a woman of about thirty came into the room like a whirlwind. She introduced herself as Irena Sandler, a Polish

Catholic social worker, who was a volunteer in the Zegota resistance organization whose aim was to help Jews not only by providing food but by smuggling children out of the ghetto. As a Christian, she knew even before it became apparent to the occupants of the ghetto, that the Nazis' intention was to clear the ghetto of every Jew so she had come to persuade the parents to entrust the baby and their older children to her, so that she could get them out of the ghetto before the Nazis got their hands on them and murdered them.

Nachum Kirgelik was inspired by this chance meeting with Irena, and in the course of the next few months helped her with that extraordinary task of smuggling children out of the gates of the ghetto. His main task was to convince the parents to part from their children. When it was first suggested to them, most of them were adamantly opposed the idea; however, after Nachum convinced them that this was the only chance of saving their children's lives, they tearfully agreed to let Irena take them. The children too did not agree to leave their parents and their homes without a struggle. They could only be persuaded to part from their parents on the basis of a lie: Irena and her helpers told them that those who the children thought were their parents, had in fact adopted them, and that when they left the ghetto she would help them find their real parents.

The escape from the ghetto was effected by several means. The bigger children were hidden on the tram which passed through the ghetto each day. Early in the morning, Irena would hide the children underneath the seats of the passengers, helped by the tram driver who was bribed for his help in secreting the children there.

Smuggling the babies out was a more difficult matter: Irena had the use of a truck on whose sides were written in large letters the name and address of an expert plumber. On this basis she had received permission from the Nazi administration, a free pass, to go in and out of the ghetto at will. The babies were wrapped up like a parcel and put into the false bottoms of the various tool boxes in the truck. Toddlers were put into thick jute sacks as if they were bundles of work clothes. To stifle the sounds of the babies' cries as they went through the gate out of the ghetto, Irena and her driver sat a dog next to them which barked loudly at anything and everything, particularly when the driver would beat him vigorously whenever a baby began to cry. The dog's deafening barks would ensure that the cries could not be heard by the guards, and the gate of the ghetto would open for them the way to freedom, to life.

This was the method used by this extraordinary woman who, without regard to the certain danger to her own life, dared – and succeeded – to spirit 2,500 children out of the Warsaw Ghetto. She placed the children with compassionate Christian families who took them in, sometimes with, sometimes without, payment, who also endangered their lives and the lives of their whole families, to save Jewish children.

Irena Sandler kept a meticulous record of the name of parents and each child she helped escape, with the aim of reuniting the children with their parents after the war. These lists she hid in glass jars, which she buried in her garden.

Irena continued with her mission until she was caught. One morning, the suspicions of the guard at the gate were aroused when he heard the sound of children crying from the plumber's truck even over the dog's frantic barking. The guard poked around the tools and opened the tool box and a jute sack in which children were hidden. At that moment, Irena was taken to the headquarters of the Gestapo and was tortured. Her arms and legs were broken and she was beaten mercilessly. But Irena steadfastly refused to reveal the names of the children she was smuggling out of the ghetto that morning, and managed to hide from them the fact that she had been helping children to escape on an almost daily basis. She did not divulge even under hideous torture any information to the Nazis, until they gave in and sentenced her to death.

To her great luck, her colleagues in the Zegota underground, who were in close contact with the Polish Government-in-Exile in London, paid money to the Nazis for her release, and her death sentence was commuted.

When peace was declared, Irena's first task was to identify the parents of the children she had saved, according to the lists contained in the glass jars she had hidden from sight deep in the earth in her garden, and bring about their reunion. But to her great sorrow, the vast majority of these parents had been put to death in the gas chambers. Children, whose parents were not identified, stayed with the families who had protected them during the war, or were adopted by other families.

Did these children ever discover the truth about their origins? Did any of them ever returned to Judaism? Who knows? In all probability, most of them simply adopted their families' religion. Their lives had been saved but not their faith. Not their real identity as Jews.

✦✦✦

Postscript: In 2008, more than 60 years after the end of the Second World War, Irena Sandler was nominated as a candidate to receive the Nobel Peace Prize for outstanding bravery and humanity – regardless of the great danger to her own life – saving Jewish children from the clutches of the Nazis. Unfortunately, Irena was not awarded the Nobel Peace Prize, and one year later, at the age of 98, she died in her native Poland. Her heroic efforts during the war had been acknowledged by the State of Israel many years earlier, and she was awarded the title of one of the Righteous Among the Nations as well as being given honorary citizenship of the State of Israel.

# 5
# The Uprising

Ruvke remained with his parents, trying with all his strength to ignore difficulties and to rise above the terrible sufferings to which he and everyone in the ghetto was exposed. But not for long.

The Nazis had begun to empty the Warsaw Ghetto of its occupants. With the deportation of Jews from the ghetto, the growing sense of extinction seized him with the thought and feeling that there is nothing to lose anymore and that he must do something.

Whole families were removed from their quarters to a so-called unknown destination, to a place they all knew that no one would return from it. This spurred Ruvke and others like him to act. To go meekly like sheep to the slaughter? No. Not anymore!

It took only six days in late July 1942 to empty the ghetto of seventy-five percent of its inhabitants and transport them to Treblinka in an operation of ruthless efficiency. Those who remained were consumed with fear, a fear which provoked members of the youth movements active in the ghetto, under the leadership of Mordechai Anielewicz, to ready themselves to rise up against the murderers. The unaccustomed feeling of pride and the possibility of revenge enthused all of them and brought the disparate movements of the underground together, while the seeds of revolt took root in their hearts.

No one was under the illusion that the uprising would save the Jewish people or lead to the defeat of the Germans. It was just an expression of human dignity and heroism against all the odds. If they had to die, they considered, it preferable to sacrifice themselves in battle against the enemy, rather than waiting passively for their end to come, by being murdered cruelly. A leaflet which circulated in the ghetto, called on its occupants dramatically: Resist! Be ready to resist! Do not go like sheep to slaughter! No more Jews will climb of their own free will onto the death train. We will no longer stand by helplessly!

The younger members of the underground were fired with the idea of taking revenge and with the hope that they could save whatever could be saved; at the very least, they would save their own honor and the honor of all those who were ground down mentally and then physically, under Nazi domination. So, they began to collect arms and ammunition to fight the murderers when the time was ripe. They decided that they would strike the next time the Nazis began to send more Jews from the ghetto to the death camps. In the meantime, they obtained arms and hid them away, and improvised explosive devices. They waited with growing impatience to use them.

Most of the members of the Judenrat were against the rebellion. Nachum Kirgelik was one of the minority who encouraged the underground, and was proud of their willingness to sacrifice their lives for the sake of saving the human dignity of those who remained, and as a way to honor the dead. His support for the underground's call to revolt was a slap in the face to the newer members of the Judenrat, who carried out their duties on the Nazis' behalf to the letter. They looked on him as if he was a stubborn eccentric, but with the capacity to do them a lot of harm. Kirgelik was a thorn in their flesh. Who knows where standing on his principles and expressing his opinions, might lead them all? If one of the Judenrat stepped out of line, they knew that the Nazis could punish them all. So when his moral support for the underground was expressed much more vehemently and openly to his fellow Judenrat members, his pronouncements leaked to the outside world and reached unsympathetic ears.

During one of the stormy meetings of the Judenrat, the subject came up of taking a stand against the underground's planned uprising against the Nazis, Kirgelik stood up to speak. He surprised even himself with the passion of his words, as he inveighed against his fellow-members. He called them traitors, without any scruples, hand in glove with the murderers, stabbing their brother Jews in the back. Resist, Nachum said with fervor, support the revolt, do not just lie down under it! Rise up against those animals, those Nazis, before they slaughter all of us!

Retribution was not slow to come. Kirgelik's exhortation to the Judenrat to support the revolt was reported to the Nazis in the most derogatory and exaggerated way, as if he himself had instigated the uprising as a member of the underground.

Two or three days after the meeting, while he was walking along the street on his way to take food to some starving families, a jeep belonging to the Nazi police slammed its brakes beside him. Two uniformed soldiers, with the SS insignia on their armbands, jumped out, yelling: Stop, you dirty Jewboy. Get in the jeep! Before he had uttered a word, they had dragged him to the back seat and drove off at high speed. When the jeep stopped, they brought him inside to an isolated section of the headquarters, where Rabbi Nachum could see for himself some of the instruments of torture he heard were used against potential rebels.

Without much preamble, the Nazi investigator shot questions at him with the speed of a machine gun: Who are the people leading the uprising? How are you involved in planning it? Who else is involved? Kirgelik could not answer any of the questions.

When he replied that he only expressed his opinion but was not actively involved in any way, he immediately received a blow. If you only expressed your opinion, you would get a bullet through your heart, but for being one of the planners of the revolt you will suffer a lot if you do not tell us what we want to know. You are someone we worked with and trusted, and behind our backs you have been up to all kinds of tricks against us.

Kirgelik continued to deny any involvement in planning an uprising, but the more he swore his innocence, the harder the blows he sustained: They beat his head with clubs, put out cigarettes on his body, but he could not give them any information, because in fact he had none to give, but he could not convince his torturers of that.

Kirgelik felt that every time they hit or punched his body, or bent back one of his limbs until he felt it would break, he might not only lose consciousness but also his identity, his integrity and autonomy as a member of the human race. He was in danger of losing his belief not only in his physical existence, but in the whole world. What he had thought was unassailable – the totality of his self – they were destroying. He viewed the blows raining down on him as a kind of criminal trespass on his body, like a rape. But whereas in other circumstances it might be possible to use all one's strength to resist, and even to fight back, in any torture chamber – in this case, that of the Nazis – resistance was impossible. The blows he received worked on him almost like an anesthetic, and made him almost apathetic to them and to the tortures his body was subjected to. It was as if Kirgelik had become resigned to the situation. In any event, he thought, in a semi-conscious haze, they would soon give up when they saw that not a word could be forced out of him.

But the sadists who inhabited the world of the SS were not the type to give up. Himmler, the highest ranking officer of the SS, would not forgive them if they did not epitomize the spirit of the Third Reich, which was the torture and murder of the many people who were delivered into their hands. The SS investigators who tortured Kirgelik knew that in order to be considered loyal lieutenants to the Fuhrer and his ideology, they had to be capable of knowing not only to use the weapons of torture but also not to be moved one iota by the suffering that they inflicted on their victims.

Seeing Kirgelik's torments only spurred them on to further and further efforts to break him. Until, suddenly, they gave up: One of the torturers grabbed Kirgelik's neck with both hands and dragged him to the opening of a deep pit next to the door of the torture chamber, ordered him to bend down, and shot him in the back of the neck.

Nachum Kirgelik's body was still warm when it was thrown on to one of the wheelbarrows which constantly trundled through the streets of the ghetto collecting corpses of people who died from sickness and starvation. His body joined the other scores of corpses as if they were just bundles of garbage; they were wheeled out of the ghetto gates and buried in a mass grave. In the eyes of the Nazis, they were indeed just that: garbage, trash, to be disposed of in a dump buried deep in the earth which would cover any traces of their remains.

Ruvke and his mother, Gittel, were devastated to hear the terrible news from their neighbors, who had witnessed the abduction of Nachum and his being taken to Nazi headquarters. Some of them had seen his badly beaten body being thrown onto the wheelbarrow.

During the many months since the Yudele and Anshel's escape from the ghetto, Nachum, Gittel and Ruvke would try their utmost to help the most wretched of their neighbors. Gittel would from time to time go with her husband to distribute food, and tirelessly nurse sick children as best she could with the very limited means available in the ghetto.

The immense shock that Gittel received when she heard that her husband, the head of their family, had been murdered, caused her to withdraw into herself completely. She lived within her own closed, nightmarish world, isolating herself, speaking to no one.

However, Ruvke's reactions to the murder of his father were in startling contrast to those of his mother. He was seized with a burning desire to avenge his father's death, to revolt against those responsible for it. The morning after his father's murder, Ruvke got up early, put his violin in its black case, closed the case, and put it under his bed. This is no time for playing the violin, Ruvke said to himself. It is time to fight.

Ruvke went out of his house and strode confidently to Mordechai Anielewicz's people. Give me an assignment, he said to the organizers of the uprising. I'll carry out any mission you tell me to do. Ruvke immediately joined, enthusiastically, those who had been working with the utmost secrecy for the past two years making ammunition and hiding it in the ghetto.

The fervor with which the young rebels worked to plan the uprising constantly refreshed itself despite the fact that they knew in their hearts that they were no match for the overwhelming power of the Nazis. The chances of being sent to their deaths were very high. But every single person in the Warsaw Ghetto was sentenced to death, they reasoned, whether a slow death by starvation or disease there in the ghetto, or as merely another number chalked up on the slate of the millions of their fellow Jews gassed or shot. Their thinking was that it was better to die fighting the enemy, or at least spitting in his face, rather than standing in front of him powerless and trembling, hands raised in submission.

The Warsaw Ghetto did not deserve to fall without resistance, without a fight. Too many Jews had died there. From 1940, the ghetto held more than 400,000 people. By the beginning of 1943, only 60,000 people were left. Over 300,000 Jews were forced out of the ghetto in ruthless *actions*, making their way to the *Umshlagplatz*, which was the main conduit between the Warsaw Ghetto and the Polish quarter of the city; there they were mustered and left standing for hours without food or water before being hurled onto the trains which would take them to the killing centers. The SS headquarters was opposite the *Umshlagplatz*; sealed railroad cars awaited thousands of Jews there each day to transport them to their final destination, Treblinka.

In January 1943, the Nazis decided to empty the ghetto completely of any remaining occupants and send them to the death camps. They were too impatient to wait for their end to come at the hand of hunger and disease. Better to hurry them along to a quicker death by gas.

However, the operation of clearing the Warsaw Ghetto did not proceed as smoothly as its Nazi planners had expected, for it ran into unexpected difficulties: the ZOB, the Jewish Fighters' Organization, under the command of Mordechai Anielewicz, had resolved to resist the Nazis to the end.

In April 1943, the rebels suddenly opened fire on the Nazis from the windows of buildings, from bunkers deep underground, and even from the sewers, shootings from all directions that blasted the Nazis from the ghetto, shamefully, their tails between their legs.

The unforeseen uprising led the Nazis to call in German Army troopers to overcome the uprising and complete the evacuation of the ghetto. On the eve of Passover 1943, the Germans launched a military offensive on the Warsaw Ghetto. They estimated that within three days the rebels would be brought to their knees. However, they severely underestimated the rebels' determination to fight to the last, and it took not the three days of the Germans' original, demeaning calculation, but four weeks to overcome them! Against a fully equipped army of thousands of highly trained troops stood 700 inexperienced young men and women bearing a meager arsenal of home-made weapons. But what they lacked in arms, they made up for in zeal, daring, and heroism. They knew they were fighting not for the control of territory or the acquisition of riches, but for the survival of the Jewish spirit against all odds.

Ruvke and his brothers-in-arms transformed the sewers, the basements, and any and every hole a man could hide in, into military positions, and fought against the enemy without a thought for their own safety. The remaining Jews in the ghetto barricaded themselves into bunkers and aided the fighters until their dying breaths.

The uprising was finally subdued. On May 6, 1943, the bunker at 18 Mila Street was overpowered. Tear gas was thrown into the bunker to force the occupants out, and it was clear to the rebels that they had two choices: either to climb out of the bunker with their hands up, as they had been ordered, and fall into the clutches of the waiting, triumphant, Nazis, or to commit mass suicide. Mordechai Anielewicz, his wife, and other resistance fighters took their example from the zealots of Masada against the besieging Romans; they chose the second alternative. Anielewicz, the heroic young leader, shot himself in the head, and so did many of his comrade fighters.

Ruvke did not lose his cool. As soon as he heard of the fall of the bunker on Mila 18 and of Anielewicz's death, he determined to escape from his hideout. With the deafening blast of bombs falling all around, and thick smoke choking his lungs, he slithered out of the basement he had been fighting from, and ran to find somewhere to hide as far as possible from the preying eyes of the Germans and the danger of bombs. He crisscrossed the narrow alleys between the burning buildings until he arrived, gasping for breath, at his home, where he found his mother, Gittel, gripped by anxiety and fear as to the fate of her son. When she saw Ruvke, she fell on his neck sobbing uncontrollably, in a paroxysm of gratitude to the Almighty for returning her only son to her.

Mother, there is no time to lose, we have to move out of here as fast as we can. The Germans are going from house to house with flamethrowers to smoke out any Jews left in their houses, and taking them straight to the *Umshlagplatz*. Unless we want to stay here and go up in flames, we had better get out now. We will just pack two small suitcases with a few things, and my violin, of course, and we will be on our way.

His mother did as Ruvke urged, and they made a run for it, Ruvke grasping his mother's arm to help her as they made their way between the clouds of smoke rising from the burning buildings of the ghetto. They joined the thousands of Jews being marshaled by the Nazis in the direction of the *Umshlagplatz*, a short distance from the ghetto. There they were made to wait until the train came, which would transport them to their next hell on earth.

The train drew up to the *Umshlagplatz*. All the tens of thousands of Jews, who had remained in the Warsaw Ghetto until the last, were herded onto the train like cattle; worse than cattle, if that can be imagined, jam-packed with barely enough room to breathe.

But there is an element of good fortune in all things, and the good fortune of those on that particular train was that it was not destined for Treblinka. Every other train leaving from the *Umshlagplatz* had arrived at Treblinka, where the human cargo was sent straight to the gas chambers with the Nazis' expert efficiency and cruelty.

This train went to the Majdanek concentration camp, close to Lublin, where selections were carried out, who would live, and who would die. Thus those whose fate decreed who would remain alive happened to be in the right place at the right time – in that specific context – so that they were sent to the Majdanek concentration camp.

# 6
# With The Partisans

To the forest. No signpost directed those who sought its shelter, but many young people made their way there to find refuge under the cover of its wide-branched, thick-trunked trees. The forest, to run into, some from the fear of being deported to the ghetto, and some who had escaped from the ghetto for fear of the next coming stage in that horrible place, that condemned them to a violent death in one form or another, without trial, without appeal.

Yudele, not stopped by the guard as he walked through the ghetto gate, hurried quickly in the direction of the forest to freedom. Freedom not in its absolute concept: He knew that someone who had managed to break away from the confines of the ghetto or labor camp was still in danger, like an animal escaping away from its hunters, but that could still be considered freedom, compared to what he had experienced before.

Yudele walked for hours on end in dense bushes and trees; he had no idea who or what lay in front of him. He only knew with grim certainty who and what pursued him. The greater the distance he walked, the more he was conscious that the trees had thinned out and did not provide sufficient cover for him. He felt exposed, and hoped that he would find a place to hide in one of the villages round about. Perhaps some villagers who remembered him and his family from their past dealings with the Kirgeliks would not send him away, but would offer him food and shelter.

Yudele found a deep hollow in the trunk of an ancient tree which concealed him from prying eyes and waited for nightfall. From his hiding place he heard the barking of dogs and the shouts of the storm troopers in full chase after Jews hiding out in the forest. He curled himself up in the hollow of the tree, and prayed that the dogs' nostrils would not pick up his scent. Fortunately, the wind was blowing in the opposite direction, so he was not detected. The barking grew fainter, until it ceased altogether.

When darkness fell, Yudele came out from his cramped hideaway, stretched himself and began to walk onwards. His burning ambition was to join up with a group of partisan fighters, although he knew that this would not be easily achieved. He might have to be patient for several weeks before his somewhat unrealistic dream might be realized and he came across one of the groups of partisans carrying out guerilla warfare and sabotage under cover of the dense, vast forests.

He began to be beset by pangs of hunger and his mouth was as dry as the Sahara desert, so his most pressing need at that moment was to get some food to eat. Guided by the lights which shone behind curtained windows, he was able to find in the dark a track which led to a village. As he walked along the village street, he heard the voices of families talking contentedly around the table, eating their evening meal after their day's work. Yudele walked hesitantly up to the heavy wood door of one of the houses, and knocked on it softly. When no one came to answer the door, he knocked again, a little louder. He knew the owner of this farm. A short time before his father's timber and furniture-making business had been forcibly confiscated by order of the Nazis, the farmer had come to their factory and asked them to make him a large divan.

Now the farmer stood at the door, his eyes full of fear, asking Yudele what he wanted, as if he did not know what the son of the wood merchant wanted. Without waiting for Yudele to put into words what he needed, the farmer, who suddenly looked frightened to death, walked over to the dinner table, took a few slices of bread from the cut loaf and gave them to the young Jew. He pointed to the large barn where his horses and pigs were kept, and without any word he let him understand that he could stay there for a few nights, and Yudele understood him to gesticulate, wordlessly, and thanked him with a wave as he walked towards the barn to sleep on the straw.

Lying in the dark, Yudele remembered the warm bed of his childhood, with its clean sheets and soft comforter; even his bed in the ghetto, which he had lain on, was without too much discomfort. Now, however, he had to get accustomed to sleeping on scratchy straw, with the smell of the sty and the stables in his nostrils, or even in much worse conditions.

Still, beggars cannot be choosers. He already realized that if the choice is to suffer or to die, it is better to suffer, and to hope that better times will come, eventually.

*Suffering, like happiness, is unpredictable, unstable, uncertain. The only certainty about it is that it is constantly changing, like water, never still, rather like being on a seesaw; up-down, up-down, constant perpetual mobile. Up to the happiness, down to the suffering.*

*In contrast, death is unchanging, perpetual; it cannot be revoked, for it has no end. It is the end. At a time of suffering, it is the memory of the happiness people have at some time experienced, which provokes their present actions and determination to fight and struggle and look forward, in order to gain a better, a happier, future.*

At dawn the next morning, the farmer's wife came to the barn, a white scarf wrapped around her head in the style of Vermeer's models, frown on her face, spitting words abruptly, towards Yudele: You cannot stay here. The Germans kill every Pole who hides Jews in his house or on his farm. Besides the Nazis are roaming around in the forests sniffing out Jews who have escaped, Polish gangs who are also chasing after your blood. Believe me, they are even worse than the Nazis. If they find you here, they will either hand you over to the Germans or kill you on the spot. And they will not have any mercy on us, either, the bastards. We do not want to put our lives in danger, or our children's. Here, take this food, and when it is dark, go far away from here.

The farmer's wife threw him two corn cobs and half a loaf of bread, and disappeared behind the heavy wooden door.

*Being hunted, as if you were an escaped criminal. Albeit the crime you were guilty of was of having been born to a people, a religion, a faith, which you yourself had not chosen, but from the very moment of your birth, they were an integral part of your being, their traits were inculcated into your personality, lodging deep inside you; you identified with them completely, you were who you were because of them. Your Judaism became your defining feature, your tree of life, and you clung on to it with all your might. However, as a Jew, your life was a strange paradox. On the one hand, you took an immense pride in your origins and were convinced that your nation, your faith and your religion – comprising your whole world-view – had their roots and principles way back in the infancy of history. Your religion taught the highest ideals and ethics to the whole of humanity, including the religions which came long afterwards, that adopted these as their own creation, and denied their origin.*

*On the other hand, you have been made to crawl for centuries along the lanes of history, constantly beaten down by nations and other religions whose highest ambition was to destroy you or only to hate you. And so you live, all your life, on the pendulum of emotions, swinging from one extreme to the other, in better times in a state of impotent anger at the racial or social discrimination meted out to you because of your origin; in worse times being hounded to death by those intolerable regimes.*

*For thousands of years you have endured pogroms and decrees, persecution, segregation, blood libels and torture, expulsion, killing and destruction; but even in the darkest days you continued to hold on to life by the skin of your teeth, never giving up your Jewish faith which was an inseparable part of your being.*

All that day, Yudele hid himself between bales of straw. After dark, he put what remained of the bread in his coat pocket, and started out on his way. This became the pattern of his life of wandering, by day he would, with great effort, dig a hole deep in the earth and hide himself there, by night he would emerge from it, like a nocturnal animal in search of food, and knock on the door of a farmhouse to ask for bread. Some of the farmers opened the door with a face like thunder and would drive him off their land with curses, as if he was an evil spirit they needed to distance from themselves. Others, however, were more compassionate and would give him food and even allow him to bed down for the night in a barn.

The cold was beginning to seep through Yudele's clothes, chilling both his body and his state of mind; he feared how he would fare when snow began to fall, quite soon. He had to find himself somewhere for shelter and be able to sleep, not exposed to the elements. Wandering from place to place, hiding in tree trunks or dugouts covered by branches was tiring him out, and he was plagued by ever-present hunger and thirst. However, he thought it was too risky to stay in one place for more than a day, so he continued walking on and on, until one night he came to a solitary house on the edge of a small village. There was a heavy silence in the air, not even the bark of a dog disturbed it. A weak light glimmered through the heavy curtain at the window, and Yudele instinctively felt that he might be lucky enough to be able to stay there for some time. He was not wrong.

Yudele knocked quietly on the heavy door, and a woman of about forty opened it. She was very thin, with disheveled hair, and a face which, although weary, was still pleasing. She stared in surprise at the stranger who had knocked at her door, yet at the same time she looked as if she had been expecting him to come to her. Yudele stood there, his lips trembling with the effort of finding the right words. Snowflakes began to fall on his head and shoulders. I have run away. I'm looking for work; I'll do anything for you, Yudele mumbled, as if he were speaking to himself. A flicker of understanding passed over the woman's face as she stared at him, and murmured back to him, It's dangerous. You are a Jew, aren't you? But you can come inside, and we'll see.

Hesitantly, Yudele went into the house. The furnishings were in old style, and a fire burned in the fireplace and gave off heat which both warmed and soothed him. The woman closed the heavy curtains on each window in the house, murmuring that even though the house is on the edge of the village and there were hardly any passersby, it is better to be careful. Ah, what a relief.

Yudele learned that the woman, Alina, was a childless widow, and lived alone. Yes, she was in need of help. She would hide him, and give the gossipers no cause to spread rumors, for Polish gangs were constantly searching for Jews who had escaped from ghettos or work camps, and would leave no stone unturned to find them. I will hide you well, she repeated. My husband died recently and I am desperate for somebody to help me work my small farm.

Alina went to the trouble of making Yudele a hot meal, the first warm food he had tasted for many weeks. Snow continued to fall, and Yudele silently thanked the Almighty for bringing him to stay the night here, on this snowy night, may His blessing be perpetuated so that he might be able to stay here in safety for as long as possible.

Whatever Yudele received, he was grateful for, even if it was a simple wooden bed covered with a straw mattress in a dark basement, where he was concealed from any unexpected visitors. To Yudele this was a great salvation, and for some weeks he cleaned Alina's house, and fed the animals, among which were some pigs, two goats, and hens whose eggs he collected. Every few days, Alina would go to the open-air market in the center of the village to buy food for the two of them.

Alina was a woman who, so Yudele understood, not only lived on her own, but chose to distance herself from other people and was not in the habit of inviting them into her home. The sudden increase in the quantities of food Alina bought at the market raised some eyebrows among the curious villagers. Strange, a woman living alone, has she got any visitors? It is very odd, now of all times, with a war on, and shortages of everything, that Alina, who usually shuts herself away from everybody, has such a large appetite that she has to buy twice what she usually buys. Hmm ...

The prying eyes were like thorns in her flesh. The whispers behind her back she ignored, making herself out to be immersed in the business of choosing her products.

However, she was conscious of people examining her movements and of the meaningful glances the villagers exchanged with each other.

Another week passed, and Alina had the feeling that they were gossiping about her more openly and more disparagingly than before, even though nobody approached her to ask her anything directly. Apparently one of her nearer neighbors had seen that a man was living in her house and working on her farm. Theoretically, there was no reason in the world why he could not be one of her relatives who had come to help her out. But if this was the case, why was it all such a secret? Why did he not show his face to anybody? Alina grew more and more anxious, and afraid. She knew that in the blink of an eye innocent murmurs had the habit of turning into suspicions which could, in their turn, lead to denunciations and accusations.

She had no choice. Yudele would have to go that same night, for she could no longer put her own life in danger. I am very sorry, Alina said to him, but it seems that they are on your trail. You will have to move on, for your sake and for mine, too. You know what they do to someone who hides Jews: they slaughter him mercilessly.

For a moment, Yudele was frozen to the spot, imagining what lay in wait for him outside his safe haven, but he managed to murmur, You are right. I cannot let you take the risk of hiding me any longer. Without another word, he packed his rucksack with some food and warm clothing that Alina gave him, which had belonged to her dead husband. After his few belongings were packed, he was ready to go on his way.

Yudele was just about to open the door, when he turned to face Alina, standing behind him. He caught an expression on her face which he had never seen before. Her eyes were full of longing, as if they were pleading, Take me into your arms! After the long weeks they had spent under the same roof had been lived as employee-employer, mistress-servant, benefactor-beneficiary, each of them knew that not far below the surface lay the more primeval status of man and woman, their attraction suppressed, their passion unfulfilled. Neither Yudele nor Alina dared to express their feelings for each other by even the smallest gesture. But now, at the moment of their parting, all the previous, self-imposed barriers fell; like iron filings attracted to a magnet, their bodies flew towards each other in a passionate embrace and even their clothes could not dull the sparks of desire which passed from one to the other in the longing to stay forever entwined in each other's arms. All the pent up emotions of days and weeks were released in the embrace which, even in its midst, they knew would have to end in a matter of minutes. They did not even kiss, for they knew that they could not allow themselves to become overwhelmed by passion at that time and in that place. This was a farewell embrace, which conveyed the prayer and the hope that they would return to each other at some future time, whenever that would be, or if ever it would be.

Unwillingly, Yudele freed himself from Alina's arms, conscious of the danger which threatened. He picked up his rucksack and, without looking back, stepped into the darkness, making his way for the forest, to the partisans.

A little time after he had left the village, and invisible in the dense darkness all around, he heard the sound of barking. He realized that the barking was coming from dogs belonging to a Polish gang. After that, came the sound of rifle butts knocking against the door of Alina's house. Harsh voices, shouts, barking, but it turned out to be all right. Alina was safe, she had nothing or nobody to hide.

There is no one here in the house besides me. You can see for yourselves. Look wherever you want.

Alina was calm, innocent in the face of the obvious frustration and disappointment of the pursuers, who had been cheated of their quarry. The pursuers, eaten up with frustration and regret, returned from Alina's house with empty hands.

What luck, her instincts had been sound. He survived this near miss, and so did she.

Yudele stayed under cover of darkness, making his way as fast as he could between the trees and overhanging bushes in an attempt to get away from his murderous pursuers. He was sick to his stomach when he thought of what they would have done to Alina had they seen him coming out of her house. Whatever excuse or reason he might have thought up would not have satisfied them. They would have shot and killed her, destroyed all her possessions, and set fire to her house. That was what they did to people who were caught sheltering Jews. The cries and shouts of the wife, the pleas of the husband, the sobs of the children all fell on deaf ears. These gangs did not have the word merciful in their vocabulary. With them it was always loaded guns at the ready; the sound of ricochets of bullets would be heard in the village, and one after another a whole family would meet its death for having sheltered a Jew on the run. Sometimes, gangs would turn their guns on all the inhabitants, and then burn down the whole village.

Yudele's instinct for survival led him to steal a chicken roaming around in a yard, or a few potatoes from a barn. He was again forced to hide himself in holes in the ground which he had dug with his own hands, and conceal his hiding place with branches and bark which he had wrenched from the trees with the last remnants of his strength.

So at night he would sleep in these holes, and at daybreak he would have to knock on the doors of farmhouses in search of a little food. He was playing a kind of Russian roulette. He did not know these farmers, so it was always a question of whether they would help him or turn him in. It was impossible to predict what the outcome of a knock on the door would be. Hunger was his constant companion, and sapped his strength. It prevailed over everything else, and he would take any chance to relieve it.

Yudele set his sights on somehow reaching the partisans where they were hidden deep in the forest. He knew they were not content to hide themselves in tree trunks, waiting passively for whatever the next day would bring. They wanted to fight, to overthrow the Nazi troops, or at the very least to cause as much damage as possible to their military. Yudele swore to himself that he was going to be a true partisan, to fight the enemy to his last drop of blood.

The bitter cold entered into his bones, despite the warm coat Alina had given him, but it did not freeze his spirit. He walked on cautiously, trembling both with the cold, and with fear of the two disparate enemies he knew were hunting escaped Jews like himself: the Germans on the one hand, and gangs on the other. Yudele persisted on his way, deep, deep into the forest until at last he arrived at his objective.

Put your hands up. Who's there? Out of nowhere Yudele heard a voice, and saw in the darkness a man with a rifle whose barrel was pointed at him. He stood in front of him, and Yudele breathed more freely, for his instincts told him that the gun directed at him was not that of an enemy but of a man whose overriding concern was self-preservation.

You do not need to be afraid of me, I am a Jew. I have run away. I have been searching for you, mumbled Yudele in Yiddish to the man shrouded in darkness. Yudele's words convinced the watchman to lower his rifle towards the ground.

Come with me, the watchman said in a low voice. I am not sure our group has room for anyone else, it is too dangerous. But we will see. Yudele followed him silently, torn between hope and despair.

They came upon a group of men sitting in the dark, getting ready for the night, each man with a bundle of his belongings at his feet. Someone offered him a slice of fresh bread and a corncob, which he drew out of the red embers of the bonfire which flickered in the darkness like the stones on the breastplate of the High Priest.

How did they live, this group of partisan fighters? Did they also go timidly from farmhouse to farmhouse begging for a piece of bread? Certainly not. They had put an end to depending on the vagaries of the farmers for their existence, with doors slammed in their faces most of the time. These men were full of self-confidence, armed as they were with weapons which they had managed to obtain, thanks to their resourcefulness and initiative. They were determined to make their contribution to the war effort, and kept themselves going by eating anything that came to hand from the villages round about: they became adept at stealing chickens from the hen run, vegetables from the farms, and digging up potatoes the farmers had stored deep in the earth.

Yudele felt that at long last he had arrived at his goal. He was no longer on his own. However, his hardships were not yet over. On the contrary, they may have even increased. To put it mildly, he had not been welcomed with open arms by the partisans, and before he was accepted by them, he had to tell the members of the group the catalog of disasters he had endured, his decline from a house fit for a well-to-do family of good standing, to the tribulations of daily life in the Warsaw Ghetto. He told them how his sister had been killed by a bomb in Warsaw, and how he himself had escaped from the ghetto and had lived from hand to mouth in the forest until, with great good fortune, he came across them. He spoke of his heartache knowing that his mother and father and youngest brother were languishing in the ghetto, and of his brother Anshel, who had also decided to make his escape, although he had no idea at all what had befallen him. Yudele spoke of his father in the present tense, unaware of the enormity of the tragedy which had fallen on his family with the murder of his father.

His words made a great impression on the group of partisan fighters. As he spoke, the expression on their grim faces changed from wariness to welcome and they accepted Yudele into their ranks. No one had to drill into him the passion, the hatred, the sense of injustice which burned in his blood. He would be fighting for the sake of justice, and for the sake of life itself.

*Where justice cries to come out of the dark place it has been banished to, it is natural that injustice and evils cry out to be restored. The question is, which comes first, the feeling of injustice which becomes so oppressive that it demands justice to come out into the light; or the feeling that justice is ever-present in humanity but has been beaten down by the forces of darkness? It takes great strength, both moral and physical, on the part of the forces of light, to burst out with sufficient determination and courage, fighting back with all guns blazing, to release justice from its repression.*

Yudele stayed with the partisan fighters, and became a fearless rebel, imbued like the rest of his group with a fighting spirit which attacked the Germans whenever and wherever they could. They may have had only limited arms and ammunition, but they used these to sabotage the essential infrastructure the Nazis depended upon: They set up ambushes, bombed bridges to disrupt trains, disconnected communication cables, cut telephone and telegraph wires, destroyed power stations and damaged factories making war components for the Nazis.

All these activities were carried out all the while they were fighting for their own survival. Taking revenge on their enemy was the best and most effective way to survive. To continue to live.

The partisans increased in number by the day. Whole families joined them, women and children too. Some were survivors of *actions* while others had escaped from ghettos, had lost their way in the forests and had hidden themselves there for months on end. However they came to be there, they were glad to put themselves under the protective wings of the partisans, who had achieved enough independence in their locale that they did not need to curry favor with the farmers so that they might receive a piece of stale bread, grudgingly given. These new families knew how to take, but there was danger in their proliferation. The members of each family dug themselves a bunker, and holed themselves up in it, waiting for salvation to come: each day they survived seemed a miracle. Until the blow struck.

The Germans grew tired of being ambushed by the partisans.

They knew that the forest was full of Jews on the run, and were determined to hunt them down and kill them to the last man, especially now that it was clear that the partisans were joining up with the Russians. In retaliation, they attacked them cruelly.

The Nazis found Yudele's group of partisans completely unprepared. Although most of them had secreted themselves into the bunkers they had dug, this method of concealment was well known to the Nazis; so, with the help of dogs to sniff them out, and rifle butts to probe the thickets of trees and bushes, they would bomb the holes and hollows together with all their occupants.

On the morning of the attack, Yudele had come out of the hole in the earth, where he had secreted himself for the night with some other people, to stretch his cramped muscles and go in search of some food for his rumbling, empty stomach. He thought he might see a birds' nest with some fledglings that he would snatch, even though he sympathized with the mother bird, who would come back with a tasty worm or two for her brood and find the nest emptied of its inhabitants. Yudele's eyes were scanning the tree tops for nests when he heard the barking of dogs and the heavy stomping of the soldiers, which came nearer and nearer to where he was standing. Suddenly, the sounds of bombs blasted his ears.

The Germans are bombing the bunkers with everyone still inside! Yudele's brain flashed the warning to himself. They are coming nearer. What should I do, where should I hide? At the very last moment, Yudele discovered the only place he had a chance to hide, and like an animal under threat of being killed, he climbed the tree next to him, and with the speed of a squirrel raced higher and higher up the tree, clinging to the branches, until he found a branch strong enough to bear his weight on which he could lie without being seen.

Terrified, Yudele watched the Nazis approaching. Scores of soldiers, their savage dogs baring their teeth and growling as they came to the cover of each bunker which hid men, women, and children huddled together, trembling with fear. Sitting up on the thick branch, Yudele heard the loud order that was given, and immediately after, the thunderous sound of bombs exploding in the bunkers, filled the air, including the bunker in which he himself had spent the night. The remains of the bunkers were scattered over the area as far as Yudele's eyes could see from his perch at the top of the tree. Fires broke out on the ground, and shouts and cries of the trapped people in the bombed bunkers shocked him to the depth of his soul and his mind. What a horror!

For several hours, Yudele stayed flattened against the branch, while bombs were thrown into bunkers, killing or injuring their occupants. At last the voices of the SS soldiers and the barking of the dogs ceased, and they went on their way. Their mission had been completed.

Yudele survived this cruel attack. It was fortunate for him that the Germans wore peaked caps and did not raise their heads toward the sky. It would have been enough for just one of them to have looked upwards for him to have been caught. But it was his good luck that the eyes of the murderers were focused on those who had concealed themselves in the ground and not on anyone sitting high up on a tree.

Yudele came down from the tree, and when he saw that there was no one around, he began to run towards the bushes and trees, to search for survivors. When they all came across the bunkers, there were only smoldering ashes, and all that remained for them to do was to cry for their dead, and cover the bombed-out bunkers, which had turned into a mass grave.

After what he had experienced, Yudele was not able to stay any longer in this valley of death. On a momentary impulse, he was seized with the desire to run away from there as fast as his legs would carry him. There was no logic in his decision, he would be leaving behind his comrades and friends, but he ran in terror, as if pursued by the fiery tongue of a dragon. He ran and ran, escaping from himself, from his being, even from his body. A kind of lunacy had taken hold of him and would not let go. Something had cracked in Yudele's mind from the horrific scenes he had witnessed looking down from his hiding place high up in the tree, and he ran on as if possessed for a long time until his strength gave out, and he collapsed on the ground, abandoning himself to his fate, dazed and exhausted.

When he awoke several hours after sleeping as though unconscious, Yudele felt that his strength had returned to him. It was dusk, and he was beset by hunger. He got up, shook his clothes, which in some places were torn, and began to walk. He had no particular goal. He struggled with thorns and overhanging branches of the dense thickets he walked through, avoiding the hungry wolves roaming freely, as was entirely natural for their species. Yudele could not but envy them, that in spite of the fact that although they were hungry – as he himself was – at least they did not have to hide as he did from pursuers baying for his blood.

For several days, Yudele walked on, concealing himself when necessary, nourished here and there by the fruits of wild plants. Suddenly, in a flash of recognition, it came to him that he was actually retracing his steps. Amazed, Yudele found himself walking in the direction of the village he had come from. Weeks had passed since he had left Alina's house and now, suddenly, almost subconsciously, he found himself nearing the village whose far-off lights had beckoned him towards it.

Darkness had already fallen, and Yudele felt more confident. He hastened his steps.

And why not? He would return to Alina. The thought that he would see her in only a short time excited him. Would she be excited to see him? Would she be afraid to open the door of her house and her heart to him? Would she want him to be close to her, to be in her house with her?

Yudele banished any doubts from his heart. Positive emotions which someone has are generally shared by the object of these emotions, even if they have not been expressed in words. Yudele was sure that Alina had been as aroused as he by their passionate farewell embrace, when their souls had been joined together in love until the end of days, even though the danger hovering over their heads had forced them to part after only a few minutes. If Alina had not wanted him, she would not have clung to him in that way. It is not that feelings of love by one party are always reciprocated by the other, but it is not hard to distinguish between someone's longing or rejection towards you. Despite being desperately tired and hungry, Yudele felt in his bones, in the very fibers of his being, that Alina wanted him.

When Alina heard the knock at her door, she knew that it was not the harsh rap of hatred, hostility, or aggression. She sensed appeal, entreaty in the knock; it heralded the exhilarating return of the man she had longed for day and night without cease since the moment she had had to remove herself from his arms. And behold, he had come back.

Alina leapt to open the door, and even before she had managed to lock it securely again from the inside, she found herself swept up in Yudele's arms who, in that split second, became her lover. The two of them stood not moving, locked together, scarcely able to breathe, until they became a little calmer.

They closed the shutters and pulled the curtains, and sat close together at the dining table. Alina brought food and drink to Yudele, and even before he was satiated he began to tell her everything that had happened to him from the moment he left her house. Alina stroked him, washed him, and put him into her bed to warm both his heart and his body with her closeness. She was elated by his return, and promised him that this time she would conceal him so well that nobody would suspect that she had him hidden in her house. One day this terrible war will be over, Alina said. According to the news, it might even end soon.

# 7
# In The Anders Army

Anshel Kirgelik walked with hurried steps on the sidewalk next to the wall of the ghetto after he emerged from the narrow opening in the wall which his father had shown him. He bent his face downwards so as not to draw attention to himself to the few passersby. What concerned him in particular was that he should not fall foul of the Nazi soldiers, with eyes like hawks looking at everyone who passed them, and carrying out spot checks of people's identity cards: Heaven help him if he was caught with his papers, or without them. For someone without an identity, it was better that he should not be identifiable at all.

Anshel knew from the beginning where he should head for: To the east. He would make for the territories held by the Soviets. But his first step was to get out of Warsaw. From a distance he saw the uniforms of the SS, who had set themselves up as guardians of the racial purity of the city: His pursuers.

In as natural a manner as possible, he retraced his steps in the direction of the nearest tram station. He knew Warsaw like the back of his hand, and was well aware of the destination of the trams on that line. They went far out of the center of the city, bound for the eastern neighborhoods of the capital. He hastened to get on to the tram, which soon left the station and continued on its way. He did not arouse the suspicious of the German police, and in fact they took no notice of him at all. The days when Jews would be walking in the streets wearing the yellow star was long gone. Warsaw was now cleansed of Jews. They had all been flushed away like murky water down the drains of the Jewish ghetto.

Anshel was pushed into the midst of the throng on the

tram, and managed to make his way to stand by the exit door, ready to jump off at the first sign that anyone identified him or suspected him of being a Jew. But no, it was everyone for himself.

*Anyone who travels by tram or subway behaves as if he is totally alone, submerged within his own ego. People on a tram or a train exhibit the classic behavior of narcissists and egocentrics, gathered up inside themselves like sufferers from autism or all kinds of phobias, neurotically fearful of meeting the eyes of their fellow passengers who, they feel, are only lying in wait to intrigue their privacy. The more crowded a carriage, the greater the distance a passenger puts between himself and the rest of its occupants, as if he says, leave me alone.*

Anshel seemed to be the only person in that crowded carriage who with apparent nonchalance was looking sideways out of the corner of his eyes even while his heart was hammering away with anxiety and restlessness. When the tram arrived at the last station, he jumped down from the carriage and made his way quickly to the outskirts of the villages, to the paths, the woods, until he reached the open fields. There was no time to be lost, he must not linger, he told himself.

By a stroke of good luck, a farmer driving his wagon stopped beside him and offered to drive him in the direction of the village Anshel told him he was going to. Anshel knew it was in his interests to get out of German-held territory in Poland as quickly as he could. To the east, to the east, his ambition was to get to the east.

Darkness was beginning to fall after he got down from the wagon and started to walk on in the ditches passing isolated villages. Suddenly he heard the rumble of a truck, at first quite distant, then coming closer until its headlights blinding him with their glare. Anshel was unnerved, for he was not yet used to the sense of freedom in which he found himself. The thought that he was no longer imprisoned within walls that closed in on him from all sides still astounded him. At least he had the freedom to escape. That truck was almost level with him now: Was it pursuing him? Would it run him down, injure him? Should he get out of its path? All these thoughts came simultaneously into his head. He breathed a sigh of relief as the vehicle stopped beside him and the driver wound his window down slowly, and asked him if he would like to hitch a ride with him part of the way towards his destination. Anshel did not hesitate for a second and replied that he would be delighted to go with the farmer wherever he was driving. This suited Anshel's needs, for he needed to get to the east as fast as possible, and here he was being offered the means to do so. Driving for hours at night with the farmer would put a vast distance between him and the Warsaw Ghetto from which he had run away.

The unsuspecting farmer asked no questions of him, and was even good enough to offer Anshel some bread and vegetables he had with him. When he reached a bend in the road and changed direction, Anshel asked him to stop so that he could get out of the truck, and thanked him profusely for taking him so far along his way.

Anshel continued to walk on, day after day, eating anything remotely edible he found, sleeping in trenches and ditches, going deeper and deeper into the forests.

One evening, after nightfall, the sound of the Nazis' dogs hunting people down impelled him to run away from them for dear life, before they sensed his presence.

*Run, Anshel, run for your life; make a bolt for it. Run, Anshel, run! Running to escape, running with no aim in mind, running towards a particular purpose, running to no place, running until you have run out of breath, running to save your life, just run, Anshel, run on, run on, and on ...*

Suddenly he caught his leg on something large, soft to the touch, which barred his way; he could not tell exactly what it was, but he fell flat on his face onto it. What, for heaven sake, was it? Was it a stumbling block or a milestone?

Anshel stayed in that position for some minutes, darkness all around, until he got his breath back. He raised himself up with difficulty from where he had been lying, and for the second time, his breath was cut off, when he realized the nature of the obstacle blocking his path and across which he had been lying: It was a man's body.

Human corpses lying in a field or forest or in open spaces were not an uncommon sight during that period. Anshel had even gotten used to the phenomenon during his many months in the ghetto albeit he stared with horrified eyes at the bodies of women, children and old people who had died of starvation or disease and whose corpses were unceremoniously strewn in the streets of the ghetto before being flung onto a wheelbarrow and buried in a mass grave outside the gates. In spite of that, because he was so near to the body, and had even touched it, he felt sick to his stomach. Good grief, he felt so agitated that for a brief moment he even thought that he was guilty of desecration of the dead, or that he had gotten caught by an obstacle set up to trap the blind, or unseeing. The very next moment, however, he realized that the corpse was in fact fully dressed!

Anshel recovered himself quickly and the wheels of his brain began to turn feverishly.

In a flash he realized that a golden opportunity had come his way which he would not allow to slip through his fingers. As if searching for precious booty, Anshel began to rummage in the pockets of the dead man's clothes, knowing exactly what he was seeking. He wanted the dead man's identity card, the identity of this anonymous man, he wished to adopt for himself. His hands trembled as he groped through the pockets of the heavy coat until he found what he was looking for.

He held the booty in his hands with an air of triumph mixed with relief: here it was, the identity card, whatever name was registered on it, he would adopt. From that moment, he received a new identity, he would no longer be a nameless individual. Now he possessed a name, Polish or Russian, it did not matter a jot to him.

And now Anshel was combing the pockets of the dead man's clothes for something else, which he had the luck to find, some zlotys and a considerable number of roubles. It looked as if the dead man had also escaped to the east, but his luck had run out, who knows what had happened to him. In the prevailing darkness, who could know if a bullet had pierced his lung or entered his skull, or if he had had the misfortune to eat a poisonous plant, or if deadly bacteria had put an end to his life. But really, how the man died made no difference to him. Anshel straightened himself up, tucked the identity certificate and the money in the pocket of his own coat, and set out to continue on his way.

The identity certificate burned in his pocket like a hot coal: The certificate knew better than he did himself what were his name and his identify, beginning from that very moment. What a bizarre situation, Anshel thought. Here I am walking on with my new, unknown identity tucked into my pocket while my true identity no longer exists.

He now felt more self-confident. He only had to wait for the sky to light up at dawn to be able to see the certificate and learn the details of his new identity. In a little while it would be daybreak: the dawn of a new day, the dawn of a new life.

In the pale first light of dawn, Anshel sat himself down under a bush and, with trembling hands, drew the certificate out of his pocket. At that same moment an unwelcome thought came into his head: What if the identity certificate was that of a Jew? What would he do if the dead man was a Jew like himself, running away from his pursuers? What could he do with such a certificate? Like a gambler standing in front of the swiftly turning roulette wheel waiting – and praying – to see if the ball would come to rest on his number, so Anshel opened the certificate, overcome with emotion, and ran his eyes over the details recorded there: Polish. Christian. Older than himself by two years. Married, with a six-year-old son. Milush Grybacz.

Anshel's delight on reading the details on the identity certificate knew no bounds. He felt as if he had won all the chips strewn on one of the gambling tables.

Anshel continued on his way, walking during the day and sleeping at night in barns and stables, or in the undergrowth of woods, trying to evade the attacks which the Germans, accompanied by their ferocious dogs, carried out in the forests. He felt like a tightrope walker trying to avoid falling into the jaws of the lions far below him in the circus ring.

After a few days, Anshel arrived to the outskirts of a town on the Russian border. He did not hesitate to walk through the main street of villages he passed and buy himself food at the market there. Nobody stopped him or questioned him, and anyway, the certificate he had in his pocket gave him the weight of the highest authority in the eyes of those who would otherwise tear him to pieces.

In spite of the identity certificate of a pure-bred Polish citizen in his pocket, Anshel preferred not to have to go through checkpoints and inspections. To be on the safe side, therefore, Anshel-Milush skirted around the main approaches to the town and entered the town by way of the darkened side streets, where here and there the ruins of houses and bomb craters in the road still bore evidence of the damage German airplanes had inflicted on the Soviet Union during their invasion to that country.

Anshel headed towards the center of the town. His gut feeling told him that this place was within Soviet control. At last he had arrived at his destination. He still did not know what to expect, but at least he was rid of the threat of the German pursuers. Of the Soviet gulags and Siberian work camps where hundreds of thousands of Poles were sent to do forced labor – among them scores of thousands of Jews – he had vaguely heard. But at least their suffering was shared by all Polish citizens, not only Jews. Apart from that, he himself was now a pure-bred Pole.

Milush Grybacz. He rolled his new name around his tongue, enjoying it to the full. He was no longer Anshel Kirgelik.

*Get out Anshel, get out behind your cortex, force yourself to drop to the bottom of your conscious mind, and sit there until the day comes for your return. Until I call you back. Sit there quietly, Anshel, and do not show yourself to me again. Do not move from your place and let me steer my way out of the storm, until your hour will come again.*

The town came to life even before sunrise. To Anshel's astonishment, tremendous numbers of people began to fill the streets, the gardens, and courtyards. All sorts of men, women and children from young to old streamed into the streets, and Anshel mingled with them, astonished at this unusual sight. He did not know what was happening, or where all the people had come from, or where they were headed. Weeping and distressed, they were dressed in rags, he heard both Polish and Russian. Everyone seemed giddy with the freedom that had suddenly landed on them from nowhere. Depressed? In rags? And also free? What was happening? Where were they walking?

Anshel wandered through the streets of the town as if in a dream. Hunger pangs were making themselves felt, and he had not yet had anything to eat when he felt the urge to urinate. He turned into one of the courtyards almost obscured by overgrown bushes and beds of withered flowers surrounding a large empty building, the wind whining through its broken windows. While zipping up his trousers he heard the sound of sobbing behind him. Entreaty. Muffled cries. Anshel, surprised, turned his head, and was shocked to see a boy of about five or six years old standing under a large tree; the boy stared at him, and extended his hand as if asking him for something: perhaps for money, perhaps for a slice of bread.

Their eyes met, and they stared in surprise at each other for some time without moving. The boy did not lower his tearful eyes. With his beautiful almond-shaped eyes, he resembled the crying boy in the remarkable painting by the Dutch painter Franz Hals, and continued to stare at him. The boy's hand shook as he held it out to him.

Give me something, help me, his sad, tear-filled eyes pleaded. Without a word, Anshel came close to him, hesitantly he took the boy's hand in his own, and the boy clutched at it. They both walked slowly and cautiously towards a bench hidden away in the small garden. After several minutes of sitting there in silence, a silence pregnant with curiosity, Anshel tried to find out from the boy who he was and what he was doing there. But his repeated efforts to understand from the boy how he had gotten there and where he had come from failed. The boy was confused, shocked, and dumbstruck, and it was clear from the way he stammered his words that he had experienced severe trauma.

My f-f-f-f-f-ather is d-d-dead, and my m-m-m-mother is d-d-d-dead. Those were the only words the boy could utter. Anshel could simply not get another word out of him. The boy did not even know his own name, or did not remember it. Anshel began to despair of the situation into which he had unwittingly fallen, and sat there silent and thoughtful until suddenly, like a brilliant streak of lightning, an idea flashed across his brain. A sense of exhilaration spread over him, and he was enveloped by a sense of mission. You don't want to tell me your name? You do not remember it? Well, I will tell you what your name is! Anshel exclaimed to the boy. I will tell you right away what your name is! For as long as he could remember, Anshel had had no reason to smile, but now, swept up in a kind of elation, he grinned from ear to ear as he drew out of his pocket the identity certificate he had acquired, which had provided him with a new identity. He opened it and read out the name of the child registered there, the name of Milush Grybacz's son. Your name ... just a second, it is hard for me to read, yes, your name is Lova. Lova Grybacz.

That is it, Lova, that is your name now. So, Lova, what do you think of your new name?

For the first time since they met, a smile of happiness spread over the child's face.

L-l-l-ova, he stammered delightedly, his eyes sparkling, and began to pound his chest with pride while he shouted, I'm-m-m c-c-c-alled L-l-l-ova! I'm-m c-c-alled L-lova!! I'm called Lova!!!

The two of them got up from the bench contentedly, as though they were two close friends who had met up after not seeing each other for a long time. Hand in hand, they walked in the direction of the market to buy something to eat.

✦✦✦

It was a historic moment, a kind of redemption. Immediately after the German Army invaded the Soviet Union, in June 1941, Stalin decided to free all the hundreds of thousands of Poles remaining in the Siberian gulags where they had been sent from Eastern Poland to work in forced labor camps. Some months after June 1941, the Soviets also released from prison one of the most outstanding commanders of the Polish Army – General Wladyslaw Anders.

It was General Anders' good luck that the Germans revoked the Ribbentrop-Molotov Pact and invaded the Soviet Union, for if they had kept to the pact, he would have languished in a Soviet jail for many years, at least until the end of the war, and perhaps until the end of his life. And now, astoundingly,

Stalin decided that he would also conscript the Poles living in Soviet territory so that they could fight alongside him against the German invaders. Hence, General Anders was released and, by virtue of his rank, was called upon to establish a Polish Army on Russian soil, to be at its head, and to fight wherever he was commanded. The setting up of Anders Army was carried out contrary to the wishes of the Polish Government-in-Exile at that time, but Stalin held the whip hand, and the deed was done.

Anders was born in 1892 in a small village close to Warsaw, studied at a technical college in Riga and served during the First World War as a captain in the army of Czar Nicholas II. After the war, when Poland gained its independence, he joined the Polish Army, and fought as a Regimental Officer in the battle between the Red Army and the Polish Army in 1919. In the 1930s, Anders' rank was raised to that of General. At the outbreak of the Second World War, on September 1, 1939, Anders was commander of a cavalry brigade. Quite naturally the cavalry stood no chance against the overpowering barrages of artillery shells which the Germans unleashed, so Anders was forced to withdraw with his brigade to Eastern Poland, where the Russians had invaded; and thus he fell into Soviet captivity. Trapped on both sides, the Germans in the west had pushed him into the arms of the Russians in the east, who captured him and jailed him in the notorious Lubyanka prison in Moscow, where he was interrogated and tortured by the NKVD.

Now his luck changed. General Anders on his release from the Soviet prison, and after the German Army began to suffer defeats on the Russian front, was nominated to the greatest task of his life. He was charged with forming the Second Polish Corps, which soon became known as the Anders Army.

*Anders is recruiting soldiers for his army,* Anshel heard people saying excitedly in the market, after he and Lova had eaten and drunk their fill. Anders is also taking the soldiers' families, yes, women and children too, a real motley collection of people. Imagine, an army of soldiers with their children going along with them. That Anders is a real savior; everyone wants to join the Anders Army!

Anshel could not believe his ears. However, almost immediately the tremendous opportunity that had come his way seeped into his consciousness. He realized the benefits the army could supply him with: Regular food, shelter, a stable framework, and also the possibility of taking Lova along with him – Lova, his small hand tucked into his own, whom he loved more every moment. Anshel was swept into the hordes of people and, with Lova, walked along with them. The men enlisted in the army, and Anshel enlisted too. No one probed the details of his background, no one asked him where he had been released or escaped from. Anshel turned into a soldier in Anders Army – a soldier whose name was Milush Grybacz.

When General Anders appraised the new recruits under his command, he found a crowd of starving men clothed in rags. Out of the 1,500,000 Poles expelled to the Soviet Union from Eastern Poland with the Russian invasion in 1939, only a few hundred thousand of them had survived.

Anders built up his forces like someone rebuilding the ruins of his life, and transformed them from a motley crew into a well organized, disciplined, army.

The Anders Army was an incredible phenomenon: uniformed soldiers accompanied by every kind of non-combatant refugees – women, children, old people – who were given the same army rations as the soldiers.

Anshel and Lova were almost inseparable during that time. The boy was registered in Milush-Anshel's identity papers as his son, and so he was regarded. He slept at his side in the barracks, huts and tents; wherever his father laid his head, so did Lova.

It was clear to everyone that their presence in the Soviet

Union was only temporary, because Anders required a properly set up training camp where he could prepare his forces for battle. Negotiations between Stalin, Churchill and the Polish forces enabled the Anders Army to enter Persia, which at that time was within the sphere of British influence.

Thus it was that throughout the night a great multitude of people set out on their way. Of the 100,000 of them, only 20,000 or so were soldiers, the remainder being the soldiers' families and other citizens who accompanied them. Their number also included some thousands of Jews who had enlisted, taking the opportunity to escape from the Soviet Union, together with their families. In spite of the fact that they were not enamored of the Polish soldiers, whose derogatory comments had quite an overtone of anti-Semitism about them, the Jewish recruits much preferred to get themselves out of the hell of the gulags and put up with taunts of the Poles. Much later, in retrospect, they understood how wise their decision had been.

When the Allies informed the Anders Army that their mission would be to fight on the Italian Front, Anders had to urgently begin to train them in earnest for that assignment. The soldiers spent some months in Persia, carrying out arduous training exercises, while the civilians lived alongside them.

During the same period, word that hundreds of orphaned Jewish children were gathered with the Anders Army reached officials of the Jewish Agency in Palestine and they quickly took steps to save them. Emissaries of the Jewish Agency established a large orphanage camp outside Tehran, gathered the children there and started to prepare them for their immigration to Palestine – Eretz Yisrael. It became clear that most of the children were not orphans, but they were alone in the world. The parents of many of them were in Russia – starving and freezing in the dire conditions of forced labor camps – but chose to part from their children in the hope of saving their lives and getting them out of the inferno of the war.

Anshel was faced with a difficult decision. He knew that this would be a wonderful opportunity for Lova to reach Palestine as a Jewish boy without family; even though he would have to part with Lova, of whom he had grown so attached, it meant that the boy would not have to go along with him as the son of a Polish goy serving in the Anders Army. He was sure that Lova was a Jew: when they went to urinate, he saw that he had been circumcised. In addition, from the sketchy information that he had managed to extract from Lova, it was obvious that he had grown up in a Jewish family. Anshel came to the conclusion that for Lova's benefit, he should join with the children the Jewish Agency was gathering together to bring to Palestine.

With endless patience, Anshel spent hours explaining to Lova that for the sake of a brighter future he would have to go to the camp being set up for the children being prepared for their journey. He told Lova again and again that he would have a warm home, and that it would be better for him to be with other Jewish children rather than stay with him in the harsh conditions which awaited them. Anshel promised Lova that one day he would also come to Palestine and visit him there.

It was difficult for Lova to grasp the plan Anshel had put before him, and even more difficult for him to agree to it. The fear of parting from the man who had taken on the role of his father was unbearable to him.

When the Jewish Agency emissaries came to the Anders camp to take the children whose parents were dead, or missing, or imprisoned, Anshel handed over Lova to their care. He explained that he had found him wandering alone in a town on the Russian border after both parents had died, and had taken him under his wing in order to save his life. But now that you are offering to take Jewish orphans to Palestine, it will be better for Lova to be there, so, I'm entrusting him to you. Take good care of him.

Lova wept and cried and resisted, clinging on to Anshel, refusing to be parted from him. Tears pricked Anshel's eyes, too, but he told Lova again and again not to be afraid, and that he would be looked after better with the other children than he himself would be able to do for Lova now, when they were about to learn how to fight, and there would be no time for anything else. He explained that children would not be allowed to go along with the soldiers the way they could until now, because they would soon be fighting, perhaps far away. Lova did not stop crying, although when he began to realize that he had no choice in the matter, he agreed unhappily to part from Anshel, but allowing a little hope to lift his spirits.

The historic and epic journey of the Jewish children from Tehran to Palestine was fraught with difficulties. Only after frustrating and protracted negotiations, with obstacles continually put in their way, did the Iraq regime agree to allow the children to pass through their territory, from Kirkuk in Iraq, to Port Said in Egypt, where they boarded the train which brought them to Atlit.

A joyful and enthusiastic welcome awaited the children on their arrival in Palestine. From the moment of their arrival, the 716 children were known as the Tehran Children, and this label stuck to them throughout their lives, even in old age.

The Tehran Children were divided up into different educational tracks, according to what was the most suitable to each one – some to the religious track, others to the National Religious schools, and the majority to secular schools. Still others went to kibbutzim. None other than Henrietta Szold herself, who was then head of the Youth Aliyah department of the Jewish Agency, interviewed each of the Tehran Children to determine which framework was the most suitable for the child, according to his family background and religious practices, and to make sure that each child was satisfied with her decision.

Lova was so traumatized by the death of his parents and by

his anguished parting from Anshel, who had been his savior, that he seemed to be suffering from a kind of amnesia, as well as a mild brain dysfunction: He was unable to answer them when they asked him about his family's lifestyle. All he was able to answer was, My f-f-f-ather is d-d-d-ead, my m-m-mother is d-d-d-dead, p-p-p-apa M-milush, papa M-milush, I want p-p-papa M-milush.

Everyone who took care of the Tehran Children opened their hearts to them and did whatever they could to help them; however, they could not do the one thing that Lova wanted above all else. How on earth could they bring Papa Milush to little Lova, when it was clear that Milush was not in fact Lova's father and that he was serving in the Anders Army? Lova was classified as a child who did not come from a religious home, and was sent to a kibbutz in the Galilee, where he was adopted by a middle-aged couple with one teen-aged daughter.

✦✦✦

When the order was given for the Anders Army to leave Persia in order to start the first stage of their journey to Italy via Palestine, Turkey and Iraq refused to allow the soldiers and the refugees who were with them to pass through their territories. This left the Anders Army, together with the thousands of men, women and children in their wake, no alternative but to go by boat from Karatchy to Port Said in Egypt. From there they went by train to Palestine, where they arrived in February 1943. As soon as they arrived in Palestine, General Anders' forces were deployed with units of British soldiers in the Jezreel Valley to resume intensive combat training to prepare them to fight on the Italian Front.

Milush-Anshel was overcome with emotion when he arrived in Palestine and his feet touched the ground of his historic homeland, Eretz Yisrael. When he had crawled out from the wall of the ghetto, it did not occur to him – could not possibly have occurred to him – that within a comparatively short time he would arrive in the Holy Land. It also did not cross his mind that he would arrive there with a false identity, not as a Jew returning to the land of his forefathers, but as a soldier serving in a foreign army whose attitude to its Jewish soldiers was antagonistic, with more than a hint of overt anti-Semitism. Anshel was almost beset by feelings of guilt towards his Jewish comrades in arms, who suffered from hostility on the part of the Polish soldiers, even though his Jewish roots were as deep as theirs.

Anshel began to ponder what was keeping him in this army, and why he should be willing to be sent to fight in Italy. After all he was among his own people now, and he yearned to stay and join the many Jewish soldiers who, one after another, deserted from the Anders Army to settle among their own people, and very quickly became illegal immigrants to Palestine.

However, not every Jewish soldier deserted from the Anders Army. Anshel witnessed how one of the Jewish soldiers – Menahem Begin his name – rejected the urging of the Etzel underground to stay in Palestine and accept the role of commander of the underground movement. Menachem Begin refused to desert from the Anders Army. It was not in his character to do such a thing, nor did it correspond to his perception of the nature of military service. So Begin continued to serve in the Anders Army until he was officially demobilized, when he was immediately appointed commander of the Etzel – the National Liberation Organization.

After much heart-searching, Anshel decided that he, too, would not become a deserter. Something in his personality would not allow him to do an act like this. After all, they had saved him from the jaws of the Germans and the Russians, and had brought him to where he was now, providing him with all his needs. How could he do such a thing to the Anders Army at this crucial point, just when every man was needed to carry out the mission assigned to it in Italy? No, he would most certainly not desert them!

Anshel was now in two minds, that when the time was ripe he would return to Palestine. But not now. Not when the fever of war was throbbing through his veins. Anshel resolved that he would go with the Army under its Polish commander to fight on the Italian Front.

Anshel argued with himself for a long time whether to go to visit his beloved Lova before leaving Palestine for the Front. He longed to see him but was afraid of disturbing the boy's peace of mind; Lova had found a new family to look after him and attend to his well-being and education. If he visited Lova just to say goodbye to him, it would cause him much unnecessary suffering, to add to the traumas he had already experienced. No, he would not go to see Lova again for a parting visit, but only when he could establish a close and permanent connection with him. He would go to fight and if he survived, Anshel told himself, he would return to Palestine as an immigrant and reestablish his former name and identity, and throw off that of Milush Grybacz, who had provided him with his name. Until the appropriate time came, he would just have to lock away the memory of Lova in his heart, and cherish it.

At the end of the war, the soldiers of the Anders Army dispersed, each going his own way. Anders himself, of Polish birth, went to live in Britain, after the communist government in Poland deprived him of Polish citizenship and of his military rank. However, Anders had always been unwilling to return to Soviet-dominated Poland, where he would have been jailed and possibly executed. Furthermore, he even did not want to return to Poland to be buried there, but left instructions in his will to be buried among his fallen soldiers at the war cemetery in Monte Cassino in Italy.

But Poland did not forget him. After the collapse of

Communist Poland in 1989, General Wladyslaw Anders became a national hero. His citizenship and military rank were posthumously reinstated to him and many streets and schools named after him, including the main Anders Boulevard in Warsaw.

# 8
# Majdanek

Filthy concrete platform, screech of brakes, wailing siren, and like a stew pot that bubbles, seethes, and boils until it overflows all around the pot, the forty-five carriages of the train disgorged their human contents, to the accompaniment of the cracking whips of the Ukrainian police and SS soldiers, detailed to carry out their mission – to eject every single individual in this tormented and afflicted human cargo off the train until the very last one.

The train had taken several days to make its way tortuously from the *Umshlagplatz* in Warsaw, each carriage crammed to capacity, with no air to get relief from the sickening stench, until it arrived at its destination – the platform of the central train station in Lublin. The guards were ordered to ensure that not one person managed to hide himself away in a carriage, and they carried out their orders with their usual brutal competence until all that remained in the carriages were the bodies of hundreds of people who had died during this unimaginably hideous journey. Directed by the SS, the Ukrainian police scooped up the bodies and took them away in wheel barrows to be flung straight into the pit of a mass grave.

Ruvke Kirgelik and his mother Gittel were on this transport, among all the mass of terrified and wretched Jews arriving from the *Umshlagplatz* in Warsaw.

As soon as they came out of the carriage and blinked in the unfamiliar light, they, and all that terrified mass of people, were ordered to put the meager belongings they still clutched, onto the rapidly rising piles of bundles on the platform and to start walking on the Black Road to the final destination – to the Majdanek camp.

Ruvke had no difficulty leaving the few clothes he had

hurriedly thrown into a bag just before he ran from the burning ghetto, but he refused to part from his violin. He would not forsake his violin, so he held it tightly in one hand, and embraced his mother's shoulders with his other hand as a prop for her. She, too, had added her small bundle to the ever-growing heap of abandoned possessions, and was left with the shabby clothes she had been wearing when she ran out from the blazing ghetto.

The obliteration of the Warsaw Ghetto and the extermination of all its inhabitants were for them events which even the most vivid imagination could not have conceived would take place in real life; however, they managed to summon up all the reserves of strength they were not even aware they possessed, determined to bear their suffering and by this way defeat the cruel enemy.

Whips and shouts acted as goads to move this mass of human beings in the direction of the camp designated as their destination; they somehow dragged themselves along, but for many others this was to be a march to their deaths. Whoever was too slow to keep up with the throng, whoever felt dizzy or weak, and fell down, in particular the old, the sick, children, was shot in the head and removed away. Gittel leaned on Ruvke, who held her arm and would not let her succumb to the pain and exhaustion which threatened to overcome her.

Keep going, keep going, we can do it. It is worth the effort to live, he encouraged his mother, as he saw the murdered bodies falling all around them. They walked and walked, in the paths of the Black Way until they arrived at the gates of the Majdanek concentration camp.

The original purpose of that camp, built in 1941, was to serve as a camp for Soviet soldiers who fell into German captivity. In February 1942, when the monstrous extermination machine got under way, Majdanek became a concentration camp.

Ruvke and Gittel arrived there in April 1943, exhausted physically, mentally and emotionally. The euphoria they had experienced during the heroic uprising of the Warsaw Ghetto fighters, amongst whom Ruvke was an active participant, vanished in light of the dire situation they found themselves in. They were still unaware that the horrendous train journey in the cramped and stifling carriage, and their stumbling walk towards the Majdanek concentration camp were only the first steps on the way which would lead to their complete disintegration: the loss of dignity, loss of the human spirit, loss of humanity, and, after all these had been doused like one candle after another, the annihilation of their bodies in the final, Satanic, triumph of depravity.

The wretched convoy of people who had survived the journey and the trek to the camp, goaded onwards by the cracks of whips and the firing of revolvers, entered through the gate of the Majdanek camp to a vast square.

The process of selection began immediately. The Gestapo, the Wehrmacht and the SS lost no time in carrying out their directives, each in its own way, and with its specific aims, but all with fiendish efficiency.

The news from the Russian front did not augur well for the Germans. They were being routed by the Red Army, which had recovered from the initial shock of the German attack, and were being decimated. It was unbelievable to them. After all their victorious conquests in the West, to be routed in such a humiliating way in the East? This, then, spurred them on to an orgy of vengeful and swift destruction of the weak, the unarmed, the devastated, the innocents whom they declared enemies, such as Jews, Gipsies, and dwarfs.

Two high-ranking officers, with the emblem of the swastika on their armbands, stood in the center of the square and carried out the selection. One officer, whose rank was higher than that of his colleague, a doctor by profession, was short and stocky; while the other, was taller and younger. He had a congenial, even childish face, which looked as if he had assumed an expression of severity, but in vain, he looked nice and pleasant.

Soothing melodies of an orchestra, comprised of prisoners in their striped uniforms, provided a background to the routine atrocities carried out in the camp, as if to calm the fears of those about to be led to the slaughter, but who still did not know what awaited them there.

*Music and murder, what a distorted combination of a concept which challenges all the accepted laws of nature and of man. Music, which can make a human being soar to the highest heavens, used to serve the corrupt ends of those who have discarded every vestige of humanity, putting music to such cynical and nauseating use, to mask their most heinous crimes.*

Selection: The doctor, an SS officer, would closely scrutinize for a few seconds each person who stepped up to him out of the line. According to his impressions, and after asking a question or two as to each one's profession or work background, he would decide with the speed of lightning in which direction to flick his thumb: A young man with a strong body would be asked what he had worked at, and the officer's thumb would point to the right – to life. The old, the weak, children, the disabled, the sick – the officer would not need to waste his time asking even one question, his thumb would unhesitatingly point to the left – to death.

The column of people was long. Gittel felt that in another moment she would collapse. Only with extreme tenacity and the support of the strong arm of her son was she able to stay erect. But then, an event occurred in those moments that made her forget her pains. Out of the blue, they were conscious of a couple in their thirties, standing in front of them in the line. The man was tall and sturdy, the woman thin, pale, and of fragile build, who held in her arms a baby of about five months old. The couple looked as if they were eager to arrive as quick as possible to the head of the line, and the journey was taking them too long. So, in order to get there more quickly, they simply overtook the people waiting in line and moved forward rapidly, as if in their impatience they wanted the tiring procedure to be over. That was how they had come to be standing in front of Gittel and Ruvke.

In that second, quite involuntarily, they found themselves gazing at a charming child, his wide smile lit up his whole face. They were delighted to see him playfully squeezing his mother's cheeks and nose with his little fists, revealing his two tiny milk teeth each time he gurgled with joy, and Gittel was amazed at the tranquility and the sense of confidence the baby radiated. His large blue eyes glowed with hope, purity, a feeling that nothing could harm that new life in all its innocence; a bright light shone out of them as if to call to all who saw him, to follow him, see what a wonderful world we live in!

The line continued inexorably on its way, and even though the couple with the child had gotten ahead speedily by overtaking people in front of them, there was still a way to go until they reached the very front. The couple had thought it would be more comfortable for their child, that soon they would be able to cuddle him and take care of him sitting down, instead of standing up, crouched over. The baby's eyes were still calm and unworried, and all the time he kept peeping over his mother's shoulder, until the couple reached the head of the line, and stood facing the officers carrying out the selection. Suddenly, Ruvke and Gittel, whose gaze had never left the couple, realized that they had been separated. Parents were being parted from their children, husbands from their wives. What on earth was going on here?

Because the man was sturdy and well built, the doctor carrying out the selection immediately pointed with his thumb to the right. The Third Reich would not reject a potential member of the workforce such as he. As for the fragile-looking woman, she was close to collapse from physical and emotional exhaustion, standing for hours holding her child and the few essentials she had managed to keep with her. The officer had no hesitation in sending her to the left, together with her child. Babies who were once long ago cast into the river Nile, were in this terrible era automatically sent to their deaths in the gas chambers.

So the forcible separation of the little family took place, and immediately after it began a drama, with all the elements of a Greek tragedy.

The woman began to be jostled towards the left side but, when she saw that her husband was not behind her, began to shout to him: Leibele, I cannot manage on my own, come and help me. I can't manage, I am exhausted. I need you, don't leave me, come back to me, Leibele, Leibele! Her husband, distraught as he saw his wife and child being manhandled further and further away from him, could no longer after hearing his wife's frantic pleas, stay in the place assigned to him. He in his turn began to call out to her, Sheindele, I will not leave you, Sheindele. I am coming; I am coming – and Leibele stretched his arms out towards her. However, as soon as he began to walk over to her, the hands of those standing near to him held him strongly, while saying to him firmly: Do not move from here, do not go in that direction, everyone there is going to die. They are on their way to their deaths. You they are keeping alive. Take your life in both hands. You have to stay here!

But Leibele did not understand what they were saying. His brain could not grasp the implication of this perverted process, his ears did not wish to hear, and he threw off the arms which were preventing him from going to help his wife, and with his arms outstretched, began to walk towards her. Leibele did not even heed the order of the German soldier snapping at him to go back to his place: Go back, you idiot!

Idiot? Leibele questioned. Who is an idiot? An idiot is someone who is not ready to help his wife and son! So Leibele continued towards his wife. Everyone despaired of him and saw in him a man who, of his own free will, rejected life and walked, as if in a daze, to his death. Leibele reached his wife and child, and walked with them, their arms around each other, the family undivided.

When Leibele swiftly realized that where they were walking would lead to the point of no return – it was already too late. There was no way back for him, and the only help he could offer to his dearest ones was no more than to die together with them.

Ruvke and Gittel watched in shock as the tragic scene played out before their eyes, in spite of their not taking in its full significance. But they had no time to reflect on it because they knew that within a very short time indeed it would be their turn to stand in front of those who would decide their fate.

Ruvke was still clutching the violin in his hand as he and Gittel came nearer to the more boorish of the two officers, whose thumb indicated right or left like an automaton, albeit a deliberate and calculating one. As they continued to walk closer to the officer, Ruvke began to understand the significance of the selection, and when they arrived at the head of the line, he grasped the nature of the farewells he saw taking place between family members. With trepidation, they stood before the decider of their destiny.

Would they live, or would they die? Assigned to work, or to the incinerator?

Ruvke tightened his hand on his mother's shoulder in an attempt to still the trembling rippling through her bones, brought on by the fear that in no time at all they would come to a parting of the ways, wherever they might lead.

Then, unexpectedly, Ruvke's eyes fell on a familiar

face. A face he had seen long ago, which had made a strong impression on him – the face of a man who had done him a great kindness. Next to the higher-ranking officer with the unpredictable thumb which decided a person's fate, stood the handsome young officer, whose rank now was more senior than at Ruvke's first meeting with him. That officer had come to their house in Warsaw when *actions* were being carried out to force the Jews there into the ghetto, and had surprisingly let Ruvke take his violin with him in addition to the one suitcase officially permitted to each person to take. That was almost two years ago, and he had been in the ghetto for all of that time until the train journey. However, in spite of the long period that had elapsed, the features of the officer's face were etched into his mind.

Ruvke wondered if the officer would remember him. And now, here he was, face to face with him: what a strange combination of circumstances had brought about this second meeting. The officer had probably been transferred to Majdanek after the completion of the *actions* in Warsaw, and had been rewarded by the granting of a higher rank, and he was serving here as an aide to this hulk of a man who functioned as the Satanic Judge.

When the officer's eyes met those of Ruvke, there was a spark of sympathy in them. Ruvke, who had not taken his eyes off the officer's face for a second, immediately felt that the officer recognized him. Remembered him. Not a muscle twitched in their faces; only their eyes penetrated the carapace of pretense and communicated what could not be expressed in words. At the same moment, one of the soldiers guarding the bewildered line of people, pulled Gittel out of the grasp of her son and pushed her to face the autocratic officer. A brief glance at Gittel, quivering with terror and weakness, was enough for him to raise his thumb – and she was directed to the left.

A German soldier pushed her towards the group whose

next steps would supposedly take them to have their hair cut, to shower, and to be deloused.

Ruvke, anguished at being separated from his mother, had a sense of impending death at the sight of the weak, wretched people whose doom was already foretold. It was now his turn to stand facing the officer, his fate literally in the hand of the omnipotent officer. What have you got in your hand? Why didn't you leave that case with all the baggage? the thickset officer snarled while Ruvke was beginning to mumble his reply. It is my violin... I play the violin...

To his great astonishment, he saw the young officer turn to his colleague and whisper something into his ear, what changed the look on his face to one of consent. The Satanic doctor turned to Ruvke, whose eyes, trained on the young officer, expressed his gratitude, and said, You will have to be examined by the Committee that will judge if your playing is up to the standard we expect. Then we will decide whether you can join the camp orchestra. Without looking at Ruvke again, he raised his hand, and pointed his thumb to the right. Ruvke, however, still hesitated. The dreadful foreboding of what was going to happen to his mother, sent to stand on the left, welled up in him and when he stood face to face with the young officer, whose eyes had stayed fixed on his, he said in a low voice, My mother is a healthy woman, she can work. That was all, but even before Ruvke turned to join the men assigned to forced labor, he was reassured to see the young officer nod his head to him almost imperceptibly, as if to say, don't worry.

Meanwhile Gittel had joined the group of people sent off with a flick of the thumb to the left side; these mainly comprised woman, children, infants and old people who, after standing there for some time, were then directed to sit down on the snow-covered ground. They waited quietly, patiently, for whatever would happen next. It never entered their minds that what would happen next would be blatantly antagonistic towards them. Until their turn came and, group by group, they began to feel more and more apprehensive as they obediently carried out each part of the unnerving process.

Anyone who has eyeglasses – take them off, and put them on the pile; throw your walking sticks and crutches on a separate pile; on that pile there, false teeth; remove your shoes, tie them together, and throw them on the shoe pile. But before you do that, go over to the desk and leave with the people in charge all your valuables, jewelry, money, diamonds, gold, everything you have we will look after for you; no, no, we do not give receipts, there is no need. We will know what belongs to whom and return it to the right person when the time comes, you can depend on us.

The line next to the desk where they were required to leave their valuables grew longer. People were being forced to give up all their savings, everything they had worked so hard to save from their weekly earnings, zloty by zloty, until they had a tidy sum of money put away to marry off a daughter, buy a piece of jewelry, or for a rainy day. And here they were being ordered to hand everything over without a receipt? Or, to be more exact, knowing that they would never again, as long as they lived, see their valuables, which had become worthless.

Their eyes were full of tears as they handed over everything of value that they had managed to hold on to thus far: antique jewelry whose sentimental value they found so hard to part from: a ring handed down from generation to generation, from grandmother to granddaughter, a brooch a mother had given a daughter on her marriage. Some found it impossible to do this and chose to secrete a gold ring, a diamond, in their mouths, assuming an expression of innocence while turning their heads to the side, and swallowing the object. That was the best hiding place, from the mouth within a short time to the stomach, and from there to its natural exit, when it would be recovered far from inquisitive, greedy eyes. Yes, it will be a real good step to outwit these bastards.

I will not give up my gold and diamond to them. I will swallow them, so that I will not be swallowed up.

However, the Nazi soldiers had gotten used to this attempt to trick them, and their eagle eyes easily picked out those who had swallowed their treasures, to be marked with an X on their backs, at a later stage.

The first stage of the great fraud began with the women and girls coming into the barracks where they were told their hair was to be cut. In the center of the room were rough benches, and a row of men wielding scissors stood behind these benches to cut the hair which they would then contemptuously let fall onto the floor. The women were pushed, group by group, to sit down on the benches; the haircutters were Jews, whose luck it was to have worked in their former lives as barbers and thus were judged fit to live, at least for now, in order to carry out the task of cutting the hair from the heads of the women before they went for a hot shower. With chilling disdain, the barbers grasped in their hands hair of every type: braids meticulously plaited, which they chopped off with one slash of their scissors right down to the roots; manes of curls, those would take them only two or three attempts to slice off, destroying their prettiness; smooth hair, wavy hair, black hair, white hair, fair hair, and red, all the severed hair mounted up in heaps on the floor. It would be hastily gathered up in sacks, for in wartime, nothing was wasted, and hair could be utilized in naval submarines, or to fill mattresses, or for an abundance of other purposes.

The next order was to take off their clothes. Under the threat of whips ready to lash out and the barrels of revolvers pointed at them, stood women, and men, and children, children who had been torn from their mothers' arms, and all of them removed their clothes, coat, and dress, trousers, and underwear, women and men stood across from one another, he in his nakedness, she in hers, embarrassed and ashamed, quivering with fear and from the cold, such humiliation, to expose publicly the most private, intimate parts of their bodies; religious women who had all their lives been imbued with the value of modesty in deed and in dress, always with long sleeves and so concerned about the proper length of their dresses, to stand so, disgraced and dishonored.

*All the differences which exist between individuals when they are clothed, dissolve in a second as soon as they are naked. Without clothes people become a mass group melted together: Rich and poor; leaders of men and plebeian; great scholars and unschooled who do not even know their alphabet; God-fearing women and empty-headed young girls; wise men and fools, the educated and the ignoramus: every possible variety of individual that were brought to that place – because of the only thing they had in common – their being Jews.*

Like an unsuspecting flock of sheep surrounded by a pack of wild animals waiting to tear them from limb to limb, they stood encircled by brutal beasts brandishing whips, ready to lash out at anyone who dared to open his mouth; and not one person in that passive flock knew where their terrible destiny would lead them.

The Nazis, whose probing eyes had sought and detected those who had swallowed their precious jewelry or gold coins, now passed between the rows of the naked bodies and marked their backs with a large "X".

You have not deceived us, and anyway, very soon, what you think you have hidden away will not be of any use to you. We will get it out of you, like a treasure hunt. The "X" will show us where it is to be found.

The column of naked people, their hair roughly shorn, the beards of the men reduced to uneven stubble, began to make its way to the showers. The SS captain in charge of the procedure said to them soothingly: Nothing is going to happen to you. Don't be afraid. Just take a deep breath when you go into the showers. You need to be clean and healthy. A deep breath will strengthen your lungs. It will clear out of all the polluted air you have been breathing.

Someone asked the officer what would happen to them once they had showered, and he answered reassuringly: The men will have to work, building bridges and roads, and the women will do housework, in the kitchen, cleaning, those kind of things.

A glimmer of hope lodged in their hearts, enough to bring them, unresisting, to the death chamber. Young women, their infants still nestled onto their chests, old women, the frail, the sick, and the old, children, all walked on.

Gittel heard what the officer had said, and did not believe a word of it. Every detail of that humiliating route to the showers, the cold that froze her ears, exposed after so many years of being covered by her thick hair always tied back on her neck, the way her hair was callously cut off in one fell swoop from her head, above all the shocking public nakedness, could not be erased by the officer's smooth tongue. And now the stench of burning bodies began to reach their nostrils and their suspicions were aroused, just as the open door to the chamber came into view.

One of the women near Gittel decided to climb onto a small step to see if she could see what awaited them. Her incredulous eyes caught a glimpse of the unimaginable sight of heaps of bodies on the other side of the large hall with the showers, being piled onto wheelbarrows and brought towards the furnace, the crematorium, from which endless plumes of smoke filled the sky. This woman understood before anyone else what was going to happen to them all, that the soothing words of the evil SS guards were only intended to confuse their perception and ensure their cooperation in their own deaths. She began to shout out, Murderers! Devils! Our children's blood will be on your heads! But the SS officer did not hesitate for a second before whipping her across the face five times, and she screamed in pain. However, her scream was lost in the sudden command issued from the loudspeaker: Halt! Stop!

The officers guarding the mass of Jews stood and halted the column in its path. A soldier ran towards them, holding in his hand an order from a senior commander: Take Gittel Kirgelik back to the square, she is not go to the showers now. Take her to the haircutting barracks, give her a prisoner's uniform to put on, and send her back for a further selection. The initial selection was faulty. By order.

Gittel was shocked, and felt that her fate had taken a turn for the worse. Why was she being singled out and prevented from cleansing her body in a warm shower? Why were they returning her where she had already been, even before the shower they had promised everyone? She tried to protest this discrimination in a wavering, feeble voice.

But an order is an order, and, wonder of wonders, nobody was pushing and shoving her. Two soldiers accompanied her to the dressing room, and she returned, in the uniform of a prisoner, to stand in front of the same brawny officer whose thumb settled the fate of masses. Without a word, his thumb pointed to the right, and Gittel was sent to the women's barracks to join those whose right to life had also been decided by the same mercurial thumb.

On Gittel's departure, the column of people standing at the entrance to the shower chamber began immediately to continue on its way. The woman whose face was still streaming with blood after being whipped was alternately whimpering and cursing, until she was shoved by the pressure of those coming after her into the shower chamber. More and more naked bodies, more than could possibly fit into the space available, were compressed and pushed, body to body, suffocatingly close one to the other, and the heavy iron door was closed and barred behind them, clanging shut with an ominous clatter.

All of them, squeezed and crammed into the inadequate space they were forced into, waited for the healing water to revive their weary bodies. But instead of water, they were stunned to sense a stream of gas coming out of the shower taps: its scientific name, hydrogen cyanide, or Zyklon-B. The moans turned into cries of horror, people clambered and clawed at each other, one body on top of another, in a futile scramble to get out of the reach of the gas, starving them of air, as they even tried to climb up the smooth walls. In vain.

At that time, in April 1943, seven gas chambers were operating in the Majdanek concentration camp. There was only one crematorium, which had only one incinerator. But by September in the same year, a large crematorium with five incinerators was built, which accelerated five-fold the process of extermination.

Directly behind each stall of the showers into which the gas was piped, was a small cubicle where a member of the SS stood, whose responsibility it was to conduct the proceedings, a man who must have lost every trace of humanity, if indeed he had ever possessed it, for he had to be able to observe with blood-curdling concentration the effectiveness of the gas which he himself had released into the showers in causing the agonizing deaths of the victims, and confirm that not one person was left alive. He would then give the signal to open the iron doors on the other side of the gas chamber, and the Zundercomandos would then get to work on the disposal of the bodies.

Zundercomandos. What a pompous name for young, brawny Jewish men, strong and muscular, who in normal times, could well have been outstanding athletes, but who in these hellish times, fate had decreed would carry out the most foul work of all – to drag the bodies from the floor of the gas chambers, pile them up on wheelbarrows and bring them to the site of the crematorium to be incinerated.

Zundercomandos. They worked in two shifts, from five

o'clock in the morning until seven in the evening, and from seven o'clock in the evening until five the next morning. Smoke never ceased to pour out of the incinerator, even for a minute. They placed body after body into the furnace of the incinerator, shoved human bodies into the oven, bodies which only an hour before had been living and breathing men, women, children, filled with faith and hope, who had gone to the showers willingly to wash and cleanse themselves, as they thought, naked as the day they were born. Showers that did not delouse and wash their bodies, but put them to death by means of the poisonous gas they emitted.

Not every corpse was immediately put into the incinerator. The Nazis would not give up so quickly the treasures which, here and there, someone had managed to secrete in his body by swallowing a diamond, a gold ring or coin, in the hopes that he could cheat the insatiable German appetite of their hard-earned valuables. No, in order to identify those who had thought to do this, a large "X" had been marked on their backs, and now the time had come to retrieve what had been swallowed only a short time before.

For this purpose, a table stood at the entrance to the crematorium, used for the dismembering of bodies. A Nazi veterinarian wielding a sharp dissecting knife would slice into the intestines as if into the bowels of an animal and soon enough the treasure would find its way into the hand of the Nazi butcher. At the same time, he would take advantage of the custom to pull out the gold teeth from the mouth of the victim. Oh, how innocent they were, those unfortunates who had swallowed their diamonds. What hope there was in their hearts that after a short time they would set eyes on their diamonds again without a soul seeing and hide them somewhere safe until the day of freedom came.

Less than a handful of ashes remained of each victim, remainders of ash that became a sacred mountain, holy mountain, a memorial monument for all eternity.

✦ ✦ ✦

When Ruvke was sent to the men's barracks after putting on the striped uniform of a prisoner, he was still unaware that his mother had been removed from the convoy of Death and returned to Life.

There was total separation between the men's and the women's barracks. The two hundred twenty-seven barracks covered a huge area, laid out in such a way that there were vast distances between them. On the perimeter of the barracks were electrified fences topped by barbed wire, and eighteen watchtowers, in each a soldier manning a machine gun, ready to fire at any prisoners who dared to revolt or try to escape.

On Ruvke's arrival at the barracks assigned to him, he could not focus on the incidents – both astounding and terrible – which had occurred to him, because his whole being was overwhelmed by emotion. He was amazed by the intense sensation provoked by his meeting the eyes of the German officer; a warm flush radiated from his chest up into his throat, without his discerning exactly the nature of the connection between them. He could not grasp how it was possible for him to evoke such empathy in a member of an organization whose raison d'etre was to murder him.

*Amidst the debris of human life trampled and crushed to bits in the terrible inferno, some flicker of humanity may be left to shine through, like a bright star in a dark sky shrouded by threatening clouds.*

Ruvke looked at the rows of wooden bunks and speculated which would be the best place for him to sleep. The barracks were huge, each holding 800 men, with different facilities for sleeping. In one barracks the prisoners slept on straw mattresses on the floor, with one woolen blanket to cover them. In another, there were bunks with one man to each bunk, in three tiers; and in yet another barracks the wide bunks held seven or eight prisoners crammed together on one tier, also in three tiers. What a nightmare. Who could get any sleep wedged in like sardines in a can?

In Ruvke's barracks, there was one man to each bunk. He arrived just as the body of a man who had died from starvation or sickness, or both, was being taken out. With his death, he vacated a bunk on the bottom; such luck for Ruvke, who swiftly removed the blanket of the dead man and arranged his bedding so it would be as comfortable as possible for him – if it is even possible, or appropriate, to use the word comfort, in connection with such sleeping arrangements. He spread his blanket on the bunk and pushed his violin case under the bunk he would be sharing with two other men, all of them exhausted from the hard forced labor, from the first light of dawn until nightfall.

A mixture of languages could be heard incessantly, prisoners were brought to Majdanek from several countries in Europe – Holland, Belgium, Czechoslovakia. They were all plagued by chronic hunger and near death from the exhaustive compulsory labor which obsessed them day and night, losing any semblance of belonging to the human race to which they had belonged before they were thrown into that pit. They scarcely looked like human beings anymore. The human spirit in that place vanished as if it had never been, in the everyday struggle for a few more crumbs of bread, for another gulp of the thick soup stuck to the bottom of the pot. Every man for himself, trying to eke out one more day in the land of the living. Only the strong survived. All the others succumbed each day to exhaustion and starvation and if the Angel of Death, by some chance, passes over a weak man, the next selection will finish him off.

Each day transports arrived with relatively stronger men, so room had to be made for them, and so on, the sequence repeating itself endlessly, as the stronger ones quickly lost their vigor; the newcomers replaced them while these miserables, the plain folk, the obedient, who fulfilled all the orders; the disciplined workers who would never ask for anything more; these vulnerables who found themselves oppressed and depressed in that place whose smoke they saw, day in day out, rising from its chimney, within few months would lose their physical strength after they had lost their spirit. Little by little, they faded away, until doomed to annihilation.

Ruvke was determined not to yield to such a situation. Within a short time he understood that the battle to stay alive would not be won by being submissive. You had to excel in something, show leadership. In that place you had to know how to maneuver. That was the only way he could survive. And he had to survive.

Towards evening on the day after his arrival, when he had just received the ration of thin soup and a slice of stale bread doled out to the prisoners, two SS soldiers came into the barracks. They exchanged a few words with the kapo in charge, and called him to come with them and bring his violin so that it could be decided whether he was good enough to play in the camp orchestra. Ruvke was overcome with emotion, and followed them, his violin in his hand, as they made their way to the large barracks used for concerts. Some officers were sitting there, among whom was the officer who had behaved so compassionately towards him and whose name Ruvke still did not know.

Alongside the wall stood a number of prisoners, who were also due to audition for the orchestra. The tension in the air was almost palpable, for anyone who was only pretending he could play well, was sure to come to a bad end. One by one, the prisoners stood with their instrument at the ready, and played for the officers relaxing after a hard day's work. These officers, with their SS insignia, worked very hard indeed, effecting the extermination of a large quota of human beings each day. It was not a cushy job – what do you think – all those details to take care of. But they also loved to listen to music and music was essential in the camp to calm people down and get rid of their fears.

The job in hand was to fill the depleted ranks of the orchestra, so that it would be worthy of its name, and with that in mind they had to audition everyone who said he could play an instrument. So, let's start.

The first to play was a trumpeter. What a harsh sound he produced from his trumpet, the officers' ears rang with the cacophony, no, no, that trumpeter has not a chance of being accepted into the orchestra, thought Ruvke, and at once had the satisfaction of having his opinion backed up, as the officer in charge shook his head to reject the incompetent candidate and, with the speed of lightning, two soldiers hurled themselves at the trumpeter, grabbed him by the neck, kicked him, and flung him outside. While he was still wondering what would happen to him, he received a bullet to the back of the head and fell dead. For such a fraud, according to the Nazi laws, the only punishment is getting a bullet in your head.

Almost all the remaining candidates to be tested shuddered with fear at what they now realized would be their fate, too, should they fail. Ruvke, however, was confident in his proficiency, and waited calmly for his turn to show the officers what he was capable of. He would play his very best for them, pull out all the stops. He would give the performance of his life because it would be for his life. It would buy him the right to live, him they would not kick out, he had no doubt about that.

Another prisoner's playing failed to come up to standard and he too was dispatched to the next world with a kick and a bullet. After him came a man who asserted that he could play the contrabass, and one was brought to him from the back of the hall. Wonder of wonders, he astounded his hearers with his playing, embracing the ungainly instrument in a bear-hug and coaxing out of it wave upon wave of the deepest, most resonant sounds. Holding the thick bow in one hand, the fingers of his other hand progressed adroitly from one string to the next, producing the sonorous, low tones of the contrabass. The man and the instrument became one entity.

The contrabass player was admitted into the orchestra, and thus secured his life. Later, Ruvke heard that he performed in a famous philharmonic orchestra in his city.

When it was Ruvke's turn to stand up in front of the examiners, he adjusted his violin to sit comfortably under his chin, tuned the strings prior to playing, and when he was given the signal to start, began to draw out of his violin the opening notes of the Paganini concerto, the most difficult of all in the violin repertoire. His bow leapt and flew in his hand like a whirling dervish, the glorious music electrified the atmosphere, and a smile of sheer enjoyment began to spread over the faces of the listeners, who all sat, spellbound, until the chief examiner stopped him, having been convinced of his talent and excellent technique.

Now play something lighter for us, our orchestra does not play a full concert of serious music. It is usually music with more rhythm to it, something you can tap your feet to.

Ruvke sprang to the challenge, playing on his violin melodies guaranteed to please the ears of the listeners – marches, fugues, dances. Without a single exception, the examiners nodded their heads in agreement when asked if Ruvke should be allowed to join the orchestra.

Beginning the next morning, as soon as the morning roll call was over, Ruvke was ordered to play with the orchestra as instructed. Whenever the transports arrived, the orchestra provided musical accompaniment for the selections that were preformed in the square at the entrance of the camp. There was another particularly perverse use of their music – to perform each day when all those who had committed some kind of transgression were sentenced to death by shooting or hanging – a distorted execution ceremony.

Yes, indeed, every single day, Jews who had committed a particularly heinous and unforgivable crime during their imprisonment in the camp, such as stealing a piece of dry bread, or a sweater from the storehouse, or a potato from the kitchen, or were late by one whole minute for work, all these hardened criminals were, so the Nazis had decided, brought to this killing area in the camp. They were lined up there, and either shot or hanged. The gallows were a permanent fixture on the outskirts of the camp, and they also had to vary the method of killing. Thus, so as to minimize the sound of the bullet as it shot out of the gun, it was obvious that there should be an orchestra to play rousing tunes at the moment the sentence of death was performed, and silence those ordinary atrocities in the daily schedule of the camp.

It was also the orchestra's task to play pleasant music, in order to lull their senses and stifle any potential opposition, while the prisoners were stripped of their clothes, and to accompany them as they walked, naked, to the delousing showers. That was all. The orchestra was not needed to provide musical accompaniment on the way to the crematorium, the ears of the prisoners could no longer hear.

However, the musicians were required in the evenings to entertain the SS officers and the staff of Nazi workers, for they all loved music, and art. They were very cultured people, no doubt. In front of these listeners, the orchestra could play the immortal works of the great composers.

Culture, presumably, not only lifts up one's spirit. Culture can also create monstrosity.

For a number of days Ruvke had no idea what had happened to his mother. When he realized where the flick of the left thumb would lead the masses of shaved, naked men, women, children; when he understood the significance of the selection carried out before his eyes as he, and the other members of the orchestra stood to the side, playing tuneful melodies; and when he could see where all the wretched throng were being brought, among them his own mother – he was overwhelmed by pain, anger and grief for his mother, who had perished.

Until he found out what had happened. One evening after nightfall, Ruvke had just finished licking the last drop from the bowl of soup which was the prisoners' evening meal, when two soldiers came into his barracks, and after they explained to the kapo what they had come for, they told Ruvke to wrap his blanket over his thin prisoner's garb to protect him from the freezing cold outside, and walked with him towards the narrow iron gate which separated the prisoners' barracks inside the fence from the living quarters of the staff officers outside the fence. The soldiers knocked on the door of the furthest lodge in the row of staff quarters, and it was opened before him, leaving Ruvke altogether bemused.

A welcoming hand invited him to enter, and he found himself face to face with his benefactor, the officer who had, for some reason he could not fathom, allowed him to take his violin with him on the day of the *action*, when he and his family were removed from their house to the Warsaw Ghetto; and again, very recently, at the time the selection was carried out, because of this same officer's intervention, he was allowed to take his violin with him to the barracks and was even chosen to play in the camp orchestra. His whole body trembled with fear and emotion.

My name is Gregor Wolfgang, the officer said simply, and moved towards the small drinks bar in the corner of the room. He picked up a bottle and began to pour a drink into a couple of glasses. Instead of his starched uniform, Gregor was wearing a long white shirt. His face was flushed, and his eyes sparkled. This must be quite a surprise to you, he said, turning to Ruvke. Let's have something to drink. Whiskey? Cognac?

A liqueur? Here's a liqueur. You are not used to drinking? What a shame. Prost!

Ruvke began to realize that the officer was already drunk to the point of babbling. There was a half-empty bottle on the table, and the officer's hand shook slightly when he poured himself a second glass. Later on, Ruvke understood that the monologue and confession he had heard that evening from the Nazi officer would not have taken place had he not been under the influence of alcohol. The alcohol had enabled him to unwind enough for him to forget the formal behavior usually required of him, and allowed him to bare without reserve all his emotions to Ruvke, the Jewish prisoner.

Gregor seemed to have made a fateful decision to unload a considerable burden which had been weighing on his conscience, a burden pressing down on him so heavily that he felt he could not keep it to himself any longer. It was fortunate that Ruvke knew German; this had made it possible for him to approach Gregor in his home in Warsaw about keeping his violin, and now helped him to understand the torrent of words which flowed out of the officer's mouth as he began his confession.

You know that I saved your mother, right? Gregor sat himself down in an armchair and motioned to Ruvke to sit across from him. Ruvke shook his head, speechless with astonishment.

I have no idea what happened to my mother. Wasn't she sent with all the…? his voice trembled. Gregor cut his words short and explained to him, while raising his glass, that after he had told the medical officer at the selection that Ruvke played the violin well, and he was sent to the barracks, he saw Ruvke's distress and unspoken entreaty as his mother was directed to walk towards the gas chambers. He told Ruvke that he had whispered to the medical officer in charge of the selection to have that woman returned. He had no need to give any explanation, just get that woman, what is her name – check her name – back here, and immediately the messenger ran off with the order in his hand to stop the process, and a minute before she was pushed into the gas chamber with all the other wretches, your mother was saved, and sent to the women's barracks to join those who were chosen as fit to work.

Ruvke's eyes opened wider and wider in admiration as Gregor recounted how his mother had been saved from death. I cannot thank you enough for what you did, he said in gratitude and amazement. But why did you do it, how could you convince them to do what you wanted? And aren't you afraid that one of the officers or guards will gossip about you because you brought me here this evening?

Gregor took another gulp of his drink and replied simply: No, I'm not afraid. By the way, this evening there is a party for all the staff commanders and they are all having a good time, enjoying themselves, getting drunk, stuffing themselves in the camp commandant's house, quite far, in the forest. I didn't want to go, and pretended that I didn't feel well, stomach ache or something like that. They wished me a speedy recovery, and off they went to enjoy themselves. Apart from that, I can ask for practically anything I want from the commandant, because I am the son of a very high-ranking officer in the Wehrmacht headquarters in Berlin. The CO who decides who will live and who will die cannot refuse me a request. I requested that he order to bring back your mother and he agreed. It was in his interest too. Why should not he suck up to the son of the person who may be responsible for recommending him a higher rank?

But you asked why I did it. Well, I will tell you. You know what happens to most of those who are brought here. Sooner or later, they will end up in the gas chambers. Yes, it is dreadful, but let me tell you that it is a comparatively merciful way to go. This method of putting people to death, by gassing them, the way we do here, is a lot more humane than the way we killed people at the beginning of the war. We have progressed, become more efficient – what can I say. I know it seems cynical to you but it is the truth. I can see with my own eyes how we have become more efficient – there is more humanity in our methods. I can see by the look on your face that it is enough to make you burst, the concept of efficiency in murdering human beings and the word humanity in the same breath, but I can tell you that gassing is definitely preferable than being shot in the back, bleeding to death, and falling into a hole onto the layer of people shot just before you, their bodies still warm and bloody.

Don't think of me as an out-an-out idealist who spared the life of the mother of a Jewish youth. Look at my hands, they are stained with enough blood, even if my heart is disgusted by what we are doing here. So why did I do it? Why did I rescue your mother? To be honest, it is hard for me to answer that question, even to myself. Perhaps it was to atone for my sins. To clear my conscience a bit. And why you, of all people? Maybe because I was impressed by the way you look, your whole appearance, but mainly because ... you are a violinist. When I was a child I also learned to play the violin, although I did not stick with it. After I'd been having lessons for a few years, I could see that I'd never be a great violinist, so I stopped playing. It was simply too hard for me. Therefore I admire your persistence, and your ability to play at such a high level. Incidentally, didn't they expel you from the Academy of Music where you were studying? I can see from your face that they did, of course they did, as a Jew, but in spite of that you play amazingly well. It is not only that you are talented, it is also your determination, and that is what gave me confidence in you. You should know that you are the first, the only, person amongst all my friends and acquaintances that I have told about what happened to me at the beginning of the war, and what I'm going through now. There is something about you that speaks to me, that allows me to open my heart.

For the sake of my sanity, I feel I must unburden myself

about the dilemma I find myself in. Me, Gregor, the son of an SS officer, one of the high-ups in the German Reich, I am an officer myself, and I am fed up with everything we, the Germans, are doing to the Jews, and not only to Jews, but to the whole human race. In murdering millions of human beings, our own humanity is bleeding to death.

But do not for a moment think that I did not lose my own humanity, Gregor continued, as his confession opened the door to the dark places of his mind. I also got carried away by the Nazi propaganda and saw in National Socialism the solution to everything. Even before war broke out, I enlisted in the army, did my training and became a commissioned officer. I preferred to serve in command headquarters work – that is, until war broke out against the Soviet Union and Operation Barbarossa got under way, and I was ordered to join one of the advance units which invaded the Ukraine. That operation changed my whole life, all my opinions, attitudes – feelings were turned upside down. I will explain to you in a minute why I am still here, serving in a concentration camp. I admit to you that I have participated in one of the cruelest extermination operations in history, and compared with that, the war on the Eastern front – even with air bombardments and artillery barrages – is as pure as the driven snow. For what's more vile than to shoot innocent people in the back, who then fall into a pit, which becomes their grave?

We were ordered to kill, to shoot Jewish civilians because they were declared our enemies. I felt I wanted to rebel against that but I was a small cog in that huge machine, and I could do nothing against it. The effects of political history change people's personal lives, as you should know.

Anyway, the situation got worse and worse until the resolution was officially adopted to physically annihilate all the Jews. Of course this sickened me, but just like millions of other Germans, I am in no position to protest or influence anyone to my way of thinking. Nobody asked me what I want.

I am only a cog in a machine. What was drummed into us is that we have to be completely callous, pitiless. There is a job to be done, and we have to do it, without our personal feelings entering into it.

Before we invaded Russia, our commander explained to us that our objective was to identify and eliminate everyone behind the lines that we suspected of being a threat to our forces, that is to say, every Bolshevik, every Jew, every Gypsy. They defined Bolsheviks, Jews, and Gypsies all of them, as our enemies, so we advanced towards the cities of the Ukraine. The Red Army had fled from them in panic after our planes bombed them to smithereens. Before they abandoned the cities further east, the Red Army put explosives into lot of buildings so that they would smash us to bits when we got there. When we came into small towns and villages, we finished off to the very last man, we did not leave a single one left, everyone who seemed an enemy, the Bolsheviks and the Jews, until we got to Kiev.

We were drunk with victory. Our commanders boasted that within a week or two Kharkov would fall, and Odessa would collapse at our feet a few days later, and by the time we got to Moscow, we would have taken about half a million prisoners. All the Reds were in panic, and we were sure that within a month we would be in the capital. I remember that even with all the euphoria in the air, I asked the commander, what if we do not manage to take Moscow? Winter is coming. Are we ready for it?

Even at the start of the invasion in the East, my instincts told me that the plan to wipe out all the Jews would not do us any good at all; it would not help us diplomatically, nor economically. What was it for? It was just a terrible waste, a pure waste of manpower, as I told my commander. If we go ahead with this, there will be no way back. No withdrawal. We will be tied to the outcome of the war and if our whole way of thinking is wrong, then we are finished. You can imagine that what I said was dismissed out of hand, waved away like an irritating fly: This is what the Fuhrer has decided, this is what the Fuhrer wants – your problem is that you think too much!

When we got to Kiev, the whole city was burning and in ruins, after the Soviet NKVD people had put explosives in public buildings and private homes and set fire to them before they fled. They left tens of thousands of people without a roof over their heads. So it was decided to get the Jews out of their houses and eliminate them. The commander of the operation, named Blobel, came up with the idea that when the Jews were forced to leave their houses, to their deaths, they would have to hand over the keys of their house with its address written down on a paper tied to the key, so that the house could be handed over to homeless Ukrainians.

The place chosen for this massacre was to the west of the city, next to the Jewish cemetery, near a deep ravine, which was ideal for this job. It was called Babi Yar. There was also a station there for freight trains, which Blobel said would make it easier to convince the Jews that they were being taken there for resettlement in other areas of the Ukraine. Blobel did not want to leave us in two minds about the need to kill all the Jews of the city. The Jews who will be taken out to be killed are worthless, anti-social parasites. Germany cannot bear even the thought of their existence, he said again. So they prepared maps of the area, chose squads to carry out the mission, worked out the best way to get there, arms and food for the soldiers. They thought of everything, even cleared a place for people to put their valuables, 150 meters away from the place where they were about to be shot, the valley of death.

Ruvke's startled eyes never left the face of the man sitting opposite him during this saga of awfulness. He felt as if the man opposite him did not hear his own words, as if he were in a trance, or had been hypnotized, rather than speaking from his memory. Gregor continued his story as if still in a trance,

Ruvke had not uttered a word.

On Sunday, our people stuck up orders all over the city, calling on the Jews to report the next morning opposite the Jewish cemetery because they were going to be resettled in other areas of the Ukraine. They were told to bring with them baggage weighing 50 kilograms, and the keys to their houses. So, the next day, September 29, 1941, the morning of the Day of Atonement, Yom Kippur, the most holy day, when the Jews atone for their sins, the Jews began to stream into the streets. I decided to stay in my office and not be a part of any of this, especially after hearing Blobel laughing cynically and saying with glee that these Jews are certainly going to do repentance for their sins today, ha, ha. I took myself out of earshot of his mocking, and said to my commander that I had to prepare an important report so I would not be present at the spot. However, my attempt to get out of going did not work, because a bit later a more senior officer than me came into my office and called me to come with him, saying that the order had been given from the high-ups that all officers had to be present there. I had no choice, so I went to sit in the jeep with my driver.

It was freezing cold. We drove past ruined buildings, the embers of the fires still smoking, and then through the main streets, I saw groups of Jews walking westwards from all parts of the city, in long lines, family by family, calm, not in a panic, carrying their things in bundles on their backs, or in knapsacks, some of them in wagons pulled by skinny horses. People from all the side-streets joined the mass of people, which was by now becoming like a swollen river when all its streams empty themselves into it: Women and children, and old men with yarmulkes and long sidelocks, must have been rabbis. They were singing and chanting religious melodies every step of the way.

There were hardly any young men. They had probably joined the Red Army or fled before we got there. All this crowd of people seemed calm and composed, because what they had been told was that they were going to the ghetto, they were going to Palestine, they were going to work in Germany, and so on and so on, as many options as the brain could take in. Other rumors were also flying around, such as that they were going to be killed, but those rumors were quickly dismissed and we relied on their total disbelief that such a terrible thing could happen, so they encouraged each other to hope for the best.

*Hope that is born from the fear of what tomorrow might bring. The damned hope!*

When I arrived at the place where they were all gathering, opposite the Jewish cemetery, barbed wire fences made the area into a sort of corridor, and Wehrmacht police and Ukrainian guards lined both sides of the wire fences.

From there, it was no longer possible for them to go back. Not a single Jew could retrace his steps. A bit further on they put some tables, and everyone who passed by them was commanded to place his house keys on them, and all his 50 kilos of his valuables. On the very last table, they were ordered to strip and put their clothes and shoes on the table. At this stage, they began to suspect something, but they did not say a word. Anyone who dared to ask a question got a blow from the butt of a rifle the police held ready. The people were all naked now, their bodies shivered and shook from the cold. Then the troops who were to do this job came and separated the men and the youths from the women and the little children, who were loaded onto trucks which would take them down to the ravine while the men had to go down on foot. To tell you the truth, I hoped I would not have to be at that place, but Commander Blobel appeared and raked me over the coals; he said they had been waiting for me for hours there, and that I should be there because the Brigadefuehrer said every officer has to be present.

An order is an order, so I sat in my car and drove behind the trucks carrying the women and children to the ravine. When we arrived, the men were already there. The women and children were taken off the trucks, and the Ukrainian police put all them together. They did not know it, but these were to be their last moments alive.

From the ravine we could now clearly hear the sound of guns firing non-stop, each shot put an end to someone's life. The women began to panic, but were helpless – there was nothing they could do.

And then the Ukrainian police divided up the women and children into small groups and brought each row to the edge of the pit. The firing squads kept shooting at them without pause, shooting women, children, and old people in the back, who then all fell into the pit atop the bodies of those murdered moments earlier.

At the end of each round of firing yet another row of people was lined up to stand at the edge of the pit, their faces turned to the pit, and immediately they got a bullet in the neck. Three firing squads took part and the whole gruesome operation was done very quickly.

On the slopes of the ravine the numbers of bodies grew and grew, so the Ukrainians then dragged the rest of the condemned people over to the stacks of the dead white bodies, and forced them to lie down on top of them or at their sides so as to use every possible centimeter of space in the ravine. The firing squads came towards the people lying on the bodies and shot each one of them to death.

The problem that arose then was that not everyone was immediately killed. Many were just wounded and they shouted in pain, so in the short time between the executions, our officers had been ordered to go and look at the bodies. If someone had not been killed outright, but was badly wounded, they would take their revolver and finish him off, put an end to his suffering. I stood at the top of the hill with a group of officers, and it was clear that this butchery taking place literally in front of their eyes made them feel frantic, like me, but we could not say a word. To cheer us up, we got lot of delicious food, but I had completely lost my appetite and only took some bread and an onion. When we finished eating, my commander said that I should get my revolver ready for my turn to go down to the ravine to give the poor wretches an easier death. That is the officers' job here, he said.

I was horrified, weighed down by a sense of revulsion as I walked along to the ravine. I got there, to the bottom, where the Jews who had been pushed to the edge of the gorge were shrieking in terror when they saw the terrible, terrible scene. They struggled and refused, and the Ukrainian guards thrashed them with steel-tipped whips to force them to go down to the pit and lie on the bodies. The children also struggled and tried to escape, but were caught and made to lie down and the firing squads wasted no time, shooting them straightaway. Many of the people were only wounded but it did not faze them, they just went on to fire at the next lot of victims. The wounded shouted and writhed in pain and I was frozen to the spot in horror and could not lift my hand. Then one of the officers took me by the shoulders and shook me and pointed his gun at the bodies contorted in agony and said, for God's sake man, put an end to their agony!

A merciful death they called it. What a shocking paradox, to put murder, slaughter, together with the concept of mercy. But there is no denying it, if you are going to die anyway, better to die straightaway than to linger on among the corpses and die in slow agony from your injuries. So that I could get to some of the wounded, I was stumbling around. I almost fell. I had to tread on oozing bodies. I was up to my ankles in blood and flesh, it was horrendous. I was filled with disgust but I knew I had to do whatever had to be done to save the injured from even more suffering, so I began to shoot at everyone who moved. I convinced myself that I was being humane to these people so that they would not suffer more. I went on like this, stepping on the bodies and shooting those twitching or shuddering, until out of the blue I came across a youth of about seventeen or eighteen lying at my feet. I had almost stepped on him, thinking it was a corpse, but he suddenly lifted a finger to me and raised his eyebrows so I would not shoot him. I'm alive, his eyes declared, let me live, do not shoot me. I felt that he was telling me that I should spare him, he wasn't wounded at all. He must have thrown himself into the pit a second before the burst of gunfire reached him, and pretended to be dead. I did not hesitate for a second. I dropped my hand holding the revolver and nodded to him, that, yes, I would give him his life. He could run away; wait till dark, the firing squads would leave, and then he could make his escape. The youth blinked his eyes once to show his gratitude, then closed his eyes and made out that he was dead, and I went on, shooting the injured lying there moaning, every one screaming in pain, until I was literally sick to my stomach and, like a madman, I started to jump over the corpses and ran out of the ravine. Like someone possessed, I ran until I had to stop and vomit everything up, all the feelings of revulsion and disgust I'd swallowed. I was there for a long time. I could not stop vomiting everything, and with my last ounce of strength, I managed to drag myself to the officers' post, put down my revolver and said, I cannot go on anymore, and collapsed.

They gave me some hot tea to drink, that made me feel a bit better, and my officer calmed me down and said he could understand me, no problem, you do not have to do anymore of this, adding that it was always possible to find people who are happy to take over the job of killing. Don't worry, you carried out your assignment bravely.

Some other officers said that they could not carry on either, and all of us knew that although nobody would punish us for this, we also knew that because we could not stay in the field until the end of the killing, we would pay for it by not getting a promotion. I knew that when my father got to know that I had collapsed, he would be disappointed in me, and I was right. When I told him on the phone what had happened, he said that he was ashamed of me, and began to preach at me for not being able to meet the challenge. Naturally I did not tell a soul that I made it possible for a Jew to escape from that slaughterhouse and save his life. If it had become known, they would not only have been ashamed of me, but for something like that, I would have been court-marshaled and paid a heavy price.

It was my good luck that I fell ill the same day and was ordered to rest. I don't know if I had gotten some sort of infection or whether I was in shock from everything I'd seen, but it was an acceptable reason not to be there at the killing site any longer, since they went on and on shooting without a stop for another three days, from first thing in the morning until last thing at night, the firing squads shooting to kill and the officers shooting to relieve the agony of the ones the squads had left half-dead, until all the Jews in Kiev had been destroyed and no trace, no remnant, no survivor was left of them.

Ruvke was shocked beyond words, nauseated by what he had heard. He sat stupefied, without moving, across from Gregor, who continued to speak to him as if hypnotized.

For a few days I lay in the sick bay, and after that they sent me to a convalescent home near Lake Como in Italy, and when I was well again, I was transferred to the unit which among other things carried out *actions* in Warsaw, removing the Jews from their houses, and I was appointed the officer who went with the troops. That is where I met you for the first time and let you take your violin with you to the ghetto.

Gregor suddenly put his head in his hands and began to murmur, I don't know how I could do it, how I agreed to do it, but in fact I did not agree to do it! I was dragged into it! Gregor raised his head. No, I'm not making any excuses, and I do not justify it. But that was my fate. To avoid such a situation, I should not have been born at all. And having been born, I could equally have been in the same situation as the murdered Jews whose bodies I stepped on. But I was born in the place and to the family I was born to, and that brought me to the dreadful state I am in, that I also did not believe that there was any need to do something like that. My gut instincts told me that it would lead nowhere. It was as if we were lemmings in a mad dash to jump over a cliff, and that from the point of view of history this terrible adventure would not last long, and no country would remember us for the better because of it. To annihilate people, whole peoples, because of their origins? It makes me sick. Conquering countries is one thing. But slaughtering innocent people, murdering a whole people as an ideology? It is unacceptable.

Ruvke was beginning to feel uncomfortable, listening to these shabby excuses, and gathered up his courage to ask: So what are you doing here. Here they are murdering masses of people! All right, the method is more advanced, people die faster, suffer less, but they're still losing their lives! And you're helping these murders to take place!

Gregor waved his hand to silence him and said apologetically, To tell you the truth, when I got here, I did not realize what they were doing, although once I did realize what was happening, I decided to get myself away from this place. So in a few days' time, I will be leaving the camp. I applied for a transfer ages ago. I want to be sent to fight on the Russian front. I know our situation there is very bad. We were defeated at Stalingrad and the German Army is withdrawing from Russia but we still have not given in. The campaign has not yet been decided. It will take a long time, and I want to join the combat units fighting the Russians. I feel I should put my own life on the line, and whatever happens to me, happens, I do not care if I get killed in battle.

Maybe that is the punishment I'm giving myself for not being true to my real self. I am off to the front to face the guns of the enemy, I have no problem with that. I will always be able to comfort myself by saying that at least I saved one Jew from that terrible massacre at Babi Yar. I am sure that he managed to get himself out of the mass of corpses he was lying in, stand on his feet and escape from there once it was dark. That is one person I managed to save, and now I've also saved your mother.

Gregor unexpectedly stopped talking, and his face looked drained with exhaustion. He got up heavily from his chair, and told Ruvke to get up too, picked up the blanket Ruvke had come in and quickly wrapped it around him saying, with a weary smile, now you can go. Go back to your barracks and don't say a word to anyone about meeting me here, or what I told you. Ruvke pulled his blanket around him more closely, preparing to go out into the cold. He was still shocked by what had occurred that evening, and unable to take in what he had heard. He stood for another moment facing his benefactor, who, despite what he had revealed to him, Ruvke still regarded as a knight in shining armor compared to the rest of the pigs wallowing in the muck of the pigsty.

He said quietly: In spite of everything you told me, I will remember you for the good in you. I owe my mother's life to you, and also my own. You are a ray of light in the darkness ... I will remember you, Gregor Wolfgang. Maybe one day I will be able to repay you for this.

A glimmer of a smile reached Gregor's lips, a pitying smile which understood that the statement was spoken out of naivete and that it was inconceivable that the intention behind it could ever become a reality.

No, to Gregor Wolfgang, the German officer, it was the most far-fetched thing he could possibly imagine that one day in the not-too-distant future, Ruvke, the Jewish prisoner from the concentration camp, would indeed repay him for the good deeds he had done to him.

✦✦✦

Twenty years went by until the horrifying massacres carried out by the Nazis at Babi Yar became known to the world. In 1961, the poem written by the Russian poet Yevgeny Yevtushenko about Babi Yar was published and was translated to English by Ben Okopnick, a lament rising from the blindness of the heart, which shocked the world.

*No monument stands over Babi Yar. A steep cliff only, like the rudest headstone. I am afraid. Today, I am as old as the entire Jewish race itself.*

Only fifteen years after the lament set hearts on fire, a monument was erected in the ravine where the massacres had been carried out. The immense monument was intended to memorialize the victims, but no place was found on it for any mention of Jews, who were the overwhelming majority of the victims. It took many years, before Jews were permitted to erect in the present-day park of pine trees their own monument, made of brown marble on which a menorah was engraved with an inscription in Hebrew, in memory of the scores of thousands of Jews murdered in that accursed site.

No evidence remains of the slaughters at Babi Yar. In 1943, the Nazis took care to obliterate completely all traces of the massacres which they had carried out, and they succeeded in what they set out to do. Nothing is left. Only memory, only guilt. And there is a legend saying that each time when there is a very rainy winter and the ravine of Babi Yar becomes flooded until the water rises up the banks, the skeletons and skulls of the murdered float to the surface and come to knock on the doors of the residents of the city of Kiev, in particular on the doors of those who received the keys to the houses of the Jews who were brought with the most depraved cunning to the ravine and did not return. The skulls and skeletons knocking on the doors come to remind them of their part in this vile crime.

✦ ✦ ✦

With excitement and emotions in turmoil, Ruvke came out of Gregor's quarters and almost ran the whole way to his barracks. The two soldiers who had waited to accompany him back paced one on either side of him in case he tried to run away, and the guard at the gate which separated the prisoners' barracks from the staff quarters nodded him to go through without saying a word.

Ruvke reached his bunk breathless, his heart pounding and his eyes cast down, when he waited for the roll call, which was taking place just as he arrived, to be over. When it ended, he curled himself up on his bunk, as if he wanted to be swallowed up in it and sink into a deep sleep. But he slept only fitfully. The details of the bloodbath at Babi Yar, which Gregor had described to him, passed before his eyes again and again and became embedded in his memory; but at the other end of the gamut of emotions, he was elated by the intense joy of his mother's miraculous rescue from certain death. Conflicting emotions raced around in his mind: Was Gregor some kind of sub-human murderer, or was he a human being able to rise to a higher level of humanity and save someone, even at the risk to his own life and trapped though he was in circumstances forced upon him?

Gregor's case was exceptional and differed from that of the other murderers who did their hideous work in the valley of death. Ruvke, as self-appointed counsel for Gregor's defense, in his own mind, convinced himself. He managed to slip away from the butchery at Babi Yar without taking an active part in it, and without deserting from the army; what he saw with his own eyes literally made him ill. He even showed mercy to a youth who had not been wounded in the massacre and gave him the chance to escape and save his life. He did not pretend to be what he wasn't. Many of the others who continued to murder line after line of innocent, unarmed people did so out of sadistic enjoyment, or closed their minds and eyes to what they were doing, disciplined to a fault and carrying out any task they were ordered to do with blind obedience, even if that meant that they were knowingly overriding their own views and also their own conscience.

This tangle of emotions and thoughts kept Ruvke awake for long time, until he finally gave way to exhaustion, and fell asleep.

From the very next morning, the routine of the camp became an unrelieved nightmare, with roll calls morning and evening, and a precise tally of all those going out as slave laborers outside the camp. On their return from each day's backbreaking work, the sweet melodies of the orchestra greeted the laborers in a mockery of welcome. The men were hardly able to put one foot in front of another after hour upon hour of shoveling rocky soil, or paving roads, or burdened by bearing sacks of such weight on their backs that they buckled under them. It was with heartless irony that they were exhorted to march in fives in time to melodious tunes as they came into the camp, each holding in his callused hands or attached to his belt his tin bowl. This hard labor, much of it even superfluous, turned the men into mere skin and bone. They looked like walking scarecrows, limping along like ducks, their feet a mass of bloody, infected sores caused by ill-fitting shoes.

Men like these had reached the nadir of humanity, the very lowest rung of the ladder. They could sink no further. Everything, including the most basic things, had been taken from them. They were left mere shadows of themselves; wretched, powerless, their self-respect in shreds, their lives as independent beings a remote memory. They scarcely looked like men any longer, were hardly recognizable as members of the human race. How much easier, then, to put such creatures to death, for it was not necessary to consider them fellow human beings anymore.

Ruvke had a stroke of luck. Within a short time he was transferred to the barracks the Nazis had placed at the disposal of members of the orchestra where they could rehearse together and go from there together to play wherever they were ordered to. The conditions were better, the food was more ample – they were treated more tolerably.

Ruvke's violin had saved him from the worst possible destination, the one the left thumb of the officer in charge of the selection would point to, and also from the preferred alternative, forced labor. He adapted himself to the irony of the forced labor to which he had been allotted, that is, to entertain the victims on their journey to their deaths, and to amuse those who led the victims to their deaths. He just had to close his eyes and make an effort not to break down.

# 9
# The Delation

Her false identity, her change of name, the replacement of her true religion by another – according to her forged papers – all these lay a heavy burden on Reizele, as if huge hailstones were falling on her soul from a gray sky weighted with wrinkled clouds like pouched face of a hundred years old man. However, Reizele did not forget for one moment that her false identity and the pretense of her conversion had saved her life and that of her son, and even though performed through force of circumstance and only for outward considerations, her mind was in a state of turmoil. She comforted herself that on her false papers, there was no record that she had a son. Yuzhi had not been registered anywhere so, for all intents and purposes, he did not exist, and better that way. As long as the Nazis were hunting human prey day and night, it was safer that no one should know of his existence, and therefore no one would know that he was the son of Arkadi.

Deep in her heart she rejoiced about his death, although on the surface she managed to feign the mien of the grieving widow, and when Katya and Piotr discovered where Arkadi was buried – the three of them went to the grave with wreaths. Katya and Piotr murmured prayers and crossed themselves, as if to salute Arkadi's memory, but Reizele contented herself with a token bow towards the grave as she laid her wreath on it. She could not possibly have made the sign of the cross on her chest. Her whole upbringing, together with her Jewish education etched into the core of her soul and of her whole being, would not allow her to perform that simple, but so meaningful gesture.

Reizele's memories of Arkadi were fading little by little.

She had spent these two years of the war in Belzec, two demanding years, closed in as she was most of the time in the house, keeping her son out of sight in case an evil eye would fall on him, and bringing him up in hiding, a child who had never known the everyday, simple joys of life lived openly. He grew up in the confined darkness of his cellar, full of fears, and Reizele, who did the best she could to take care of him, had to draw on all her emotional reserves so as not to give way under the strain.

Two years of a cruel war spent in a place where the reek of burning bodies of her family reached her nostrils each and every day from the extermination site. Reizele could not get in her mind what the citizens of Belzec thought and felt as they calmly went about their daily lives when, only a stone's throw from them, the mechanism of extermination was at its zenith, cruelly putting an end to the lives of people of all kinds, of all ages, of all races. Did they not know? Did they not hear? Did they not get a whiff of that odor? Or perhaps they simply ignored what was going on. They preferred not to hear or see or feel or smell. Maybe they said that, anyhow, there was nothing they could do to help.

Either way, Reizele forced herself to do the same, with the feeling of someone who has something vile in his mouth which he is forced to swallow, otherwise it would swallow him up. The one glance that she had exchanged with her father, as he stood in the town square near the church before he was taken with his family to the final destination from which no one returned, never left her for a moment.

Reizele tried as much as she could, not to be in the company of others, voluntarily isolating herself almost completely from people so as not to have to answer their prying questions. As the weeks turned into months, and the months into years, all the pretenses she was forced to adopt, both regarding her own self and towards her surroundings, caused her to feel more and more saddled with frustration.

What especially concerned her were the suspicious eyes of Mrs. Ohlenburg, their next door neighbor, small in stature but with large dark eyes as prominent as a lizard's coming out of its rocky hole. Reizele sensed the neighbor's malevolence towards her even when wishing her good morning, for her eyes could not hide her jealousy and hostility. Reizele felt that her neighbor was aware of her true identity, and that she was just waiting it out until she had the evidence to prove her suspicions, and Reizele would fall into her hands like a ripe peach. For her part, Reizele underestimated the possible consequences of having a distrustful neighbor and did not realize the harm which that unpleasant old woman could do to her. She only regretted that they had to welcome her in the house, but unfortunately Katya liked her and needed her, so Reizele would have to put up with her presence – until she stumbled headlong into a trap which sealed her fate.

One day, when Katya and Reizele were sitting in the entrance of the house, Mrs. Ohlenburg came from her house on some pretext, she had run out of milk; just a cup of milk, please, she will take it by herself, no problem; while Yuzhi was playing with the cat in the basement, where he lived and slept and played; the mailman had arrived and delivered a letter to Katya from one of her relatives in Lublin. Both concerned and eager, Katya took the letter out of the envelope and read it. Her eyes sparkled with excitement as she said that it was from her cousin. They've had a happy event in the family, their son Andrzej's wife has given birth to a daughter. This is their first grandchild, and they are inviting us to celebrate with them, to come and visit them. Katya read from the letter excitedly, come and stay with us for a few days, they write. We are waiting for you. You are invited, we'll be delighted if you come.

Katya dropped the letter down on her lap, sadly. No, she will not be able to accept the invitation. Her husband, Piotr, had begun to suffer from a difficult kidney ailment, which meant that he had to take medication every single day and would not be able to travel anywhere, and obviously she would not leave him on his own. Ah well, what a shame. But even while she was still bewailing her lost opportunity, a glimmer of an idea came into her mind. Just a minute, Reizele, why don't you go instead of me? They are also Arkadi's relatives, and you know we think of you as his wife, and mother of his son, so go off for a few days. Travel about a bit, relax, you have nothing to worry about. Your papers are in order. You are registered as a born Christian and nobody will suspect for a second that you are a Jew. No, don't worry about Yuzhi. We will look after him very well, you can be sure of that.

Neither of them had the remotest idea that Mrs. Ohlenburg's heart pounded with joy when she heard this, standing out of eyesight in the kitchen. Neither of the two women saw her frozen to the spot like a statue, while her eyes twinkled with wicked intention. Katya's slip of the tongue, when she said that nobody would think that Reizele was a Jew, confirmed what she had suspected. Of course that woman is Jewish. I was right all along, Mrs. Ohlenburg gloated to herself.

Reizele did not need much time to consider this generous suggestion of Katya's, for the scent of adventure wafted from it, and she was more than ready for something to relieve the intense boredom of her everyday life. In spite of her anxieties regarding Yuzhi, who was always restless, she welcomed the opportunity which had come her way to travel to another city, to meet new people, to join in the celebrations. She would be away for only a few days, and then she would come back to Belzec. Yes, she told Katya, she would go. She knew that nothing would happen to her son, for Katya always took care of him devotedly and Mrs. Ohlenburg would help her. Yes, she would go – it would be a breath of fresh air for her, revive her; she deserved it. Reizele was quite swept away by the anticipation of the journey to Lublin.

On the day she was expected to go, she packed her clothes

into a large bag ready to set off on her way. She had earlier debated with herself whether to take her jewelry and the money she had saved with her, but decided not to because in every journey there was the danger of being robbed. So she would leave her valuables where they were hidden in a box in a small dresser in the cellar next to Yuzhi's bed. The box was locked, and she kept the key hidden behind, so that even the owners of the house or anybody else could not open it.

Reizele was relaxed and cheerful before she set out on her journey. Katya gave her the exact address of her relatives in Lublin. Reizele kissed her son goodbye and parted from Katya with a warm hug.

But the evil eye which was fixed on her, determined her fate. No sooner had Reizele left the house on her way to the station to catch the train to Lublin, than Mrs. Ohlenburg scurried off to the headquarters of the Gestapo which was located on the edge of the town not far from the concentration camp.

What impelled her to go and inform on the Jewish woman who had found shelter with a good Christian family? No, of course she would not betray Katya and her husband for hiding this Jewish woman, certainly they could not have known the truth about her origins, they were strict Catholics. The Jewish woman hid her true identity from them. It must have been her boyfriend Arkadi who obtained the false papers for her in the name of Raymonda Polski, but he was killed by a bomb and there is no point in looking into all the details. What is important is that you must get a move on now, because that Jewish woman masquerading as a Christian is at this very moment on the train for Lublin, and you can get hold of her before the train gets there.

Reizele's eyes drank in the changing scenery from the windows of the train. She was enjoying to the fullest the wide green fields and the country cottages, but tried to avoid any conversation beyond the most trivial with her fellow passengers, replying to their questions with a pleasant smile, yes, a short journey, only three hours, the train is due to arrive soon.

And then it happened. The moment the train drew into Lublin Station, all the passengers stepping on to the platform were directed by SS troops to pass only through the train station building, and were not allowed to leave as they wished. Everyone was ordered to go into the station hall via one entrance and, afterwards, to go out to the street via the exit on the other side of the hall. Disgruntled and apprehensive, the passengers were crowded into the hall, SS soldiers standing by the exit, closely scrutinizing the papers of each passenger before they were allowed to go out. The line of people moved forward slowly, but Reizele was not concerned, after all, her papers were in good order, she was registered as a Christian, her name was Raymonda Polski, her photograph was there for all to see. She even gave the sullen policeman a fleeting smile, and for a split second he almost smiled back at her, but the moment he cast his eye over her papers and noted the name recorded there, the look on his face changed and became hostile. It was the look of a man who had found what he was expecting to find, and was shocked to discover it. The hint of a smile had frozen before it reached his lips. The Nazi soldier immediately handed over the papers to his superior officer, standing beside him, who ordered Reizele sternly to follow him.

Reizele was taken to the interrogation room of the railway station, shaking with fear.

What had happened? Why did they suspect her? After all, her papers were in order! Before she could make out what it was all about, a volley of questions was fired at her:

Where are you from? Where were you born? What were your parents' names? What is your real name? Who got these papers for you? When did you arrive in Belzec? These are false papers. What was your husband's name? It is lucky for him that he is dead. People are killed for forging papers for Jews. Now admit to me that you are a Jew and that your papers are forged.

When she tried to deny her origins, she received such a blow on her face that the pain pierced her ear. Reizele was stunned. It was the first time in her life that hatred had made someone hit her. An act of injustice. When she did not answer the questions which rained down on her, the blows came faster and became more violent.

When the investigating officer indicated to her the means of torture he intended to use on her if she did not tell them the truth, such as stubbing out lighted cigarettes on her body or tearing out her fingernails – and those were just the initial ones – she gave in. She decided that there was no point in keeping silent. She would never be able to stand up to torture. They would be able to extract the information from her in the end, so why suffer needlessly?

Like someone who accepted the inevitable and made his peace with the worst that was likely to happen to him, she said, all right, I'll tell you. Yes, I am a Jew. She told her investigators about her parents' home in Zamosc, about going off with a Russian soldier who took her to his relative's house in Belzec, but he was killed in the bombing. She told them everything, except for the fact that she had a son.

She did not volunteer the information, and they did not ask. Arkadi had brought her to his relatives without telling them that she was Jewish. No, Katya and Piotr knew nothing about her origins. It was Arkadi who had arranged the new identity papers for her, saying that she had lost her original ones. Reizele looked her investigators in the eye and spoke quietly and with confidence, as if she had come to terms with whatever they would do with her. She also took into account that she might be killed.

Her investigators listened to her story with faces like

stone, which became more severe as she proceeded with her confession. When she finished speaking, silence fell for perhaps a minute or so, broken only by the sound of her breathing, which seemed to her to tick like the pendulum of a clock in an empty pit.

Come with me, ordered the investigating officer in a voice as cold as ice. He stood up and went outside and pointed out with his finger ahead: Go over there, to that barracks at the end, where all the people getting off the train that had just arrived, and go with them to wherever they are being taken to.

He ordered two soldiers to escort Reizele, and they roughly hustled her off to the barracks which was teeming with the mass of people who had just emerged, dazed, from a long and tortuous journey on a train so crammed that they had hardly been able to breathe. Jews, Gypsies, and others from Czechoslovakia, Belgium, and Holland, who had been declared enemies of the Third Reich were in that transport. SS troops and Ukrainian police surrounded the frightened throng of people, keeping a stern eye on them in case someone tried to escape from the bitter fate which awaited him.

Like a sheet of paper set alight by a tongue of flame, the command spread rapidly among the crowds of people to go out through the exit door of the train station. Whole families and individuals, every man for himself, then began to drag themselves in the direction of the open fields, to the south of Lublin, towards the unwanted destination, the Majdanek concentration camp.

Reizele walked with the miserable and stumbling crowds, still shocked by the confrontation she had had in the station, lost in thoughts; people around her, the weak and the sick, were stumbling and falling and the SS soldiers were shooting them to death.

Reizele was aghast from the terrible sight of murdered

people that were pushed away to the sidewalk, but tried hard to ignore the scenes and continue to walk blindly like a sheep in the herd.

Suddenly she was aware of a strikingly beautiful young woman, not more than eighteen years old, walking not far from herself. She was wearing an expensive fur coat, which she kept pressed to her body with both hands, as if she was afraid that it had a will of its own and might fly off her. It looked as if the coat was dearer to her than its face value. It even occurred to Reizele that the bulging pockets might well be stuffed with very expensive valuables. Without noticing, she found herself walking alongside the young woman with the fur coat.

By the side of the road lurked some Poles from the area, watching the convoys of Jews being led to the camp, greedily awaiting their chance to make off with some of the booty the Jews had with them.

While she was walking, deep in thought, Reizele heard a low moaning sound. She turned her eyes in the direction of the sound, and saw two Polish women begin to drag the young woman at her side, trying to pull the fur coat off her by force. The young woman resisted with all her strength, trying to fight them off, but without success.

Reizele did not consider whether she should get involved, but instinctively went to the young woman's defense, and began to struggle with the two women who were trying to steal the fur coat. She pushed and hit them with her fists, but she was no match for the two covetous women, whose lust for the coat and the treasures they hoped to find hidden in it, overcame all resistance to part from it. All the while, the women jeered that in any event the Nazis would take it from her, but neither Reizele nor the young woman, nor anyone around them understood what they were talking about, for the coat belonged to her – it was her property, and the four women continued to tussle for possession of the coat, a mixture of pleas and curses could be heard from the four women, until the Polish women triumphed over the Jewish women who had fought them, and stripped the young woman of her coat. Laughing with delight, they hurried off with the booty in their hands.

The young woman whose coat had been stolen from her, began to sob and wail bitterly, her face as someone who was in deep mourning, bemoaning his fate. Between her sobs, she started to tell Reizele her sad story, how her husband had been killed before her eyes during an *action*, when he had refused on principle to leave his house with the SS soldiers, and cursed the soldiers roundly.

The bastards shot him simply to shut him up, and shoved me into the truck which brought us to the railway station. And now they have stolen my coat, that breaks my heart more than anything else in the world.

Reizele was at a loss to understand why the theft of her coat, expensive though it might have been, distressed her as much as it did. Only later did it become clear. Pleasantly and gently Reizele tried to soothe the young woman until she was a little calmer, and so they walked on together, while the woman – who had not told Reizele her name – wept constantly, the tears running down her face; she could not, or would not, open her mouth to say a word, as if she was shielding a secret locked into her heart, so Reizele left her alone.

Reizele was still stunned by what had happened to her at the railway station, and by being manhandled by the soldiers accompanying the crowds, as well as by the struggle with the Polish women over the theft of the fur coat.

The young woman dragged herself along in silence, she and Reizele by her side, walking together with the terrified and exhausted procession of men, women, and children of all ages and conditions. When they fell down, the Nazi police would shoot them and kick their bodies away of the way.

She summoned up every vestige of willpower to walk in as dignified a manner as possible in spite of the blows she had received earlier, as well as by the kicks and punches all over her body from the Polish women.

When the convoy reached the gates of Majdanek, it flashed through her mind to what a trap she had fallen into. What also concerned her was the thought of what Katya's relatives would say when she failed to arrive at their house in Lublin, and what Katya would think when they told her that Reizele had never reached them.

Reizele had no doubt that the rigorous patrols at the railway station had been set up in order to catch her. She was their target. She had no doubt that that witch, Mrs. Ohlenburg, had informed on her. That jealous and resentful fat, almost dwarf-like woman had gone to the Gestapo Headquarters in the city to speak with the commandant.

Listen carefully, there is a Jewish woman masquerading as a Christian. She has managed to get false papers, but she is a Jew, I'm sure of that. She looks such and such, the name written in her papers – Raymonda Polski – is not her real name. Now is your chance to get hold of her. She has just left to catch the train for Lublin. Make sure she never comes back to Katya's house. No, Katya certainly does not know she is Jewish. She deceived Katya. Leave Katya alone, just catch that Jewish woman. I don't want that Jewess pretending to be a Polish woman, as my neighbor.

Reizele shook off these loathsome thoughts and began to glance around her, shocked to realize that they were standing in a line for a selection to be carried out. The young woman now standing in front of her had dried her tears and was immersed in her own thoughts, as if she had suddenly woken with a start and grasped what was going on.

Yearningly, she gazed at the many women holding babies in their arms; however, when she saw the stout SS officer wave his thumb to the left or to the right and that all the women holding their babies were sent to the left, while the men and the young, healthy-looking women were sent to the right, she was struck with a flash of insight that heaven had sent her those Polish women to steal her coat from her. After thinking it over, she turned to Reizele, and her face radiant, whispered, to Reizele's astonishment: I want you to know that I'm delighted that the Polish women took my coat. Look where the women with babies are sent to. Thank you for trying to help me, but the finger of God sent them to me to take my coat off my back.

Reizele looked more intensely at the uniquely striking face of the young woman, her large, widely-spaced eyes revealing her inner beauty, a face and eyes which would never be erased from her memory. I do not understand why you are suddenly so happy that they stole your coat when you wept so bitterly then, she wondered, and in response the young woman came closer to her and whispered in Reizele's ear her mysterious secret: Because I had hidden my baby in the coat. I thought that would save her, although now I'm sure that she has been saved because my coat was taken from me. It is the finger of God, she repeated, overjoyed.

Without responding to the gasp of surprise which escaped from Reizele's lips, she pressed her fingers on her hand as a farewell gesture, and hurried to overtake people waiting in the line, hurrying to reach the front. Reizele followed her with her eyes and managed to see her stand in front of the all-powerful officer whose Satanic thumb directed the bearer of this skinny body, shaking with fear and cold, to the left.

Not only did Reizele not want to get to the front of the line quickly, she even slowed her pace to let many others overtake her, as if she wanted to delay for as long as she could receiving her sentence. She had no reason to push herself forward. It was not a soup kitchen where they doled out food to everyone in the line. The column of people slowly advanced and the single line became two; those who would live, and those sentenced to die. Beyond being shocked and pained when she saw where the young woman was ordered to, and her great surprise to discover that she was the mother of a baby girl, she suddenly heard an orchestra strike up. The music, which was at first gentle on the ears, grew louder and louder, until it became a veritable roar. The column advanced quickly now, and as well as the music, the loudspeaker relayed again and again an order that everyone must place their jewels and money on the table specified. Reizele blessed the instinct which told her not to take the jewelry with her, and the money that she had managed to stash away in the dresser in the cellar next to Yuzhi's bed. She put her bag on the pile of suitcases.

No, you will not need your clothes here. We will supply you with suitable clothing, the striped clothing of prisoners, once every two months a change of underwear.

The long line moved ahead and grew shorter, and the music made her feel almost dizzy, while she could see the selection being carried out – those sent for delousing and to the showers, and those sent to the barracks for forced labor. Although her heart was pierced by sorrow by the tragic fate of that beautiful young woman callously sent to the left, Reizele straightened her bowed body and lifted up her head confidently, so as to look her best – healthy and strong.

Reizele moved forward as the line progressed, and when she came closer to the officers carrying out the selection procedure, she turned her face towards the group of the musicians dressed in the striped uniform of prisoners, to see, not only to hear.

It was not a large orchestra, some violinists, a contrabass, a few woodwind players, each one engrossed in his own sheet of music, sending off with their playing those wretched people designated to be sent to the barracks of slave laborers, or those even more unfortunate sent on their last journey.

The stench of burning bodies which had begun to reach Reizele's nostrils left her with no doubt. It was the same stench she had smelled in Belzec. Reizele continued looking at the orchestra band and found herself watching, as if hypnotized, one of the violinists whose bow danced up and down the strings of his violin, as if he were holding a magic wand, while his shortened golden curls fluttered gently in time to the music. His eyes were closed most of the time, as if he was totally absorbed in the music or maybe, she reflected, he closed his eyes to save himself from looking at the faces of those about to be murdered in a very short time.

Her eyes darted from person to person and suddenly they found the young mother amongst all the women, children, and old people ordered to walk on the fenced-off track leading to that fiendish preparation for their deaths: having their hair cut, being forced to undress, the delousing. The young woman sought out Reizele, and managed to send her one last eloquent look before being hustled into the pitiful horde of people being propelled to their deaths.

Through the mists of consciousness, the young woman slowly understood where she was being led. When she was ordered to undress, and she stood with all the terrified women whose babies were held protectively close to their chests, she realized how lucky she was. How much she had to be grateful to those two Polish women who had torn her coat from her, for not only would they discover her jewelry in her coat pockets, but also her baby daughter, who she had thought in her innocence to save by hiding her in a secret pocket of her coat. Ah, how naïve and stupid she had been. But now, as she sensed that this was her last hour, she was comforted by the thought that at least her daughter would remain alive.

✦✦✦

The two Polish women returned with good cheer to the

home of one of the women, a small apartment on the outskirts of Lublin, the heavy fur coat in their hands. They lost no time in rummaging through the pockets of the expensive coat, and to their great delight found gold and silver jewelry and other valuables. However, even though they thought they had completely emptied all the pockets, it seemed that the coat was heavier than it should have been. They searched the coat again and again, until, incredulous, they brought out from a concealed pocket a large package.

Their hands shook with the anticipation that they would find a cache of treasure. Opening the package, they were astonished to find, wrapped in the finest clothes, an infant of no more than a month old, alive and breathing.

Once they had recovered from their surprise, the woman in whose house the baby was discovered, instantly decided to adopt her and bring her up as her own daughter. To the women's delight, the baby began to cry and they began to care for her by giving her sips of milk to drink. They noticed that around her neck was a gold necklace with a pendant, on which something was engraved in letters they could not read. With trembling hands, the woman who would be the baby's adopted mother removed the necklace from the baby's neck and put it out of sight in her jewelry case, which she kept hidden in a drawer of the dresser in her bedroom.

The remainder of the jewelry they found in the coat the women divided up between themselves equally, but the woman who decided to adopt the baby gave her friend a considerable part of her own share as compensation to keep her from telling a soul about the Jewish baby they had found and about the baby being cared for as her natural daughter, as she would register the baby in the Population Registry.

And so it was, the Jewish baby was brought up in the house of the Polish woman, a strictly observant Catholic; she grew up to be a clever girl, with a strikingly beautiful face, and her big, widely-spaced eyes produced a startling effect on anyone who saw them. When she completed high school, she went to university to study medicine, and at the end of her general medical studies specialized in pediatrics and worked as a physician in that specialty in a hospital in the city.

Some years afterwards, the mother who had brought her up, died. Not long after her mother's death, the daughter, who had mourned her mother like every daughter mourns a mother, was surprised to receive a telephone call from a woman who presented herself as someone who had in the past been a friend of her mother's.

The friend seemed very moved when she asked to meet her. When the two met, the friend told her immediately that the mother she considered to be her mother was not in fact her birth mother and that she was actually the daughter of a Jewish woman who had been murdered in the concentration camp Majdanek. She told the daughter that she had been found, an infant, in the coat which two Polish women – her adopted mother and herself – had forced her mother to give up on the way to the concentration camp where she had, without the shadow of a doubt, perished. The daughter was stunned to hear this extraordinary story from this mother's friend, and asked her for proof that it was indeed true.

Confidently the friend said to her, look in the drawer of the dresser in the bedroom where your mother kept her jewelry box and you'll find a gold necklace with a pendant. Engraved on it is a name in letters we do not know how to read, but if you come across the necklace and find out what is written on it, you can be sure that you were born to a Jewish mother. When you come to think of it, you were lucky that your real mother could not take you with her in the coat to the camp, otherwise you would have died with her.

Quite dumbfounded, the daughter went home, and zealously searched exactly as she had been instructed within the drawer of the dresser for the box, hunting through the heap of jewelry and adornments piled into it, until she found a gold necklace with a pendant on which were engraved letters in a language she did not understand, presumably Hebrew.

In the meantime, she continued with her everyday life and with her work as a doctor until the day she went on holiday and traveled to relatives of her mother in Czechoslovakia. Purely by chance, she came across two men walking along the street dressed in black, who she assumed were rabbis. Impulsively, she approached them, showed them the gold necklace she wore round her neck, and asked them the meaning of the inscription, telling them everything she knew about her origins. The rabbis looked at the inscription on the pendant and straightaway said to her that that was the name of her mother, a Jew, inscribed in Hebrew lettering: There was no doubt that she herself was Jewish. The rabbis added that if she wanted to be certain of that, it would be best if she wrote to the Lubavitcher Rebbe in New York, telling him her whole story, and he would decide for himself, knowing all the facts. The daughter did as they advised, wrote to the Rebbe, and the Rebbe replied, saying that he was certain that she was Jewish, and because of this, it would be best if she left Poland and went to live in Israel, where she could take care of the health of Jewish children.

The daughter accepted the instructions of the Rebbe as a sacred mission, and did exactly as he had told her. Within a short time, she resigned from the hospital where she had worked, put Poland behind her, and came, with the status of a new immigrant, to live in the capital city of Israel, Jerusalem. It took her only a few months to learn Hebrew in an *Ulpan* (an intensive language study program) and when she was fluent in the language, she was accepted to work in a hospital in the center of the city as a physician in the pediatrics department. Her good fortune improved even more when she was lucky enough to meet quite soon a wonderful man whom she married. Her daily life was one of pleasant routine, she put her professional training to good use – until one day fate took a course which changed her life, as if a miracle happened to her.

◆ ◆ ◆

At last Reizele stood face to face with the man who would decide if she would live or die. Upright, tall, he stared directly at her, examining her with his gaze. What did you work at, he asked, and Reizele replied, I worked in a sewing factory. He gave her another fleeting look, taking in her youth and strong build, and his despotic thumb directed her to the right. Just before she was sent to the women's barracks, she stole a glance at the violinist in the orchestra, and this time she was surprised to see him following her with his eyes.

Ruvke felt the magnetism in the air when Reizele focused her gaze upon him, as if hypnotized by him and simply had to follow his every movement; this in turn made him open his eyes to look intently at the beautiful eyes which had captured his heart. While she was standing face to face with the officer whose thumb decided the fate of thousands, Ruvke waited tensely to see where the dreaded thumb would send her. When she was directed to the right, he felt a sense of relief.

The impressive appearance of the woman clad in fancy clothing, her high-heeled shoes torn and scuffed from the long walk she had endured, pierced his heart as an arrow shot straight from a bow. A minute before Reizele was taken from there, their eyes met and the intense look which passed between them became etched into their minds as if it had been engraved onto basalt by a rod of iron. It was a look of understanding towards the other, of intimacy achieved in a moment equivalent to what might be achieved after years-long acquaintance.

Whoever does not grasp the significance of a certain look, will not understand it even after a long explanation.

That glance of burning intensity between Reizele and

Ruvke entered the totality of their beings, and remained seared into their hearts long after Reizele was hustled away to make room for those who came after her in the column.

Reizele was pushed and shoved inside a barracks overflowing with women who were fortunate, or unfortunate, enough to be sent to that barracks where they would live, at least for the time being, barracks of those assigned to forced labor, each one of them trying to catch her place in the corner of her snuffed soul.

While the harsh Jewish kapo, whose sadism had secured her life, was dealing out blows left and right as she conveyed commands and threats with the speed of a machine gun, Reizele looked around for a place to rest her head. Somewhere towards the back of the barracks she found a place on a vacant bunk, spread the one blanket each woman received on the layer of straw which served as a mattress, and without even looking around, fell onto the bunk to try to soothe her pain and calm herself after the trauma of all the tragic events she had gone through during that one long, drawn out day.

What will happen to Yuzhi now, when his mother had suddenly vanished from his life? What would Katya think when she realize that Reizele had disappeared, after she failed to arrive at her family's house in Lublin? How had she come to fall into the trap which that bitch of a jealous neighbor of Katya's had set for her?

Delation on people paid off handsomely for the informers. They received not only a pat on the back, but also monetary compensation or other benefits and – we will remember you warmly for your efforts in helping to exterminate that inferior race, that vermin in our midst.

Bursting with pride, and with no sense of remorse – on the contrary, her conscience was now clear – for, like all her fellow-informers, she withheld nothing which could affect the interests of the German Reich in any way.

Mrs. Ohlenburg set off home with a spring in her step and the deep satisfaction of the vengeful and vindictive after informing on Reizele at Gestapo headquarters. When, after some days had gone by, she saw that Reizele had not returned home, and heard from Katya that Reizele had never reached her relatives in Lublin, she knew that her mission had been successful. Her joy knew no bounds. What a blessing, we have gotten rid of that Jew, she said to herself. Yes, she would be happy to help Katya look after Yuzhi, her son.

# 10
# On The Death March

Under the reign of terror of the Kapo in charge of the barracks, Reizele began her life of forced labor. A slave rather than a laborer. She was assigned to work in one of the barracks where hundreds of women had to sort out and fold and pack the innumerable heaps of clothes of all those sent to their deaths with an autocratic flick of the thumb to the left. Fur coats, wool coats and expensive, elegant clothes, separating them from the cheap, worn clothes, and pack them up to be sent off to massive warehouses in German-controlled territory, destined to enrich the German treasury.

Empty out the suitcases of the victims – fold, sort, pack – here we do not make clothes, here we pack them for dispatch. We have a heavy quota to fill, so anyone who is lazy, or a latecomer, or cannot keep up with the pace, will sooner or later be making their way to the incinerator.

One morning at dawn, at the daily roll call, fifty women, among whom was Reizele, were ordered to carry out a rather bizarre task. They were ordered to bring baby carriages from the camp, to the railway station, three kilometers west of Majdanek, where they would be loaded onto a cargo train.

Baby carriages? These that had belonged to the poor babies and their poor mothers, who were sent to the gas chambers together and had died together?

Orphaned carriages, empty of their rightful occupants. Baby carriages without babies. What will be done with them? It is none of your business. The Nazis know what the carriages will be used for, so get a move on and get over to the barracks where those carriages are standing, uninhabited and forsaken. Put them in rows, five to each row and get going. Now!!!

The women began to walk forward, each woman pushing

a carriage in front of her, and the kapo walked behind them, bringing up the rear, whipping the backs of those dragging their feet, barren women, the same as women who have given birth, all trying out wheeling and pushing an empty baby carriage, starting to realize their own situation, yearning for their own babies, not knowing what has happened to them as their grown up children who have been cruelly grabbed out of their arms. But they had no choice. They had to carry the carriages ahead, which kept getting stuck in holes in the roads caused by the bombs. The thin head scarves over their ears hardly provide any protection from the freezing cold, but they are not allowed to slow down, even though each of them is shivering with cold and fatigue.

Falling and tumbling, the fifty women continued on the three kilometer trek until, out of breath, they at last reached the platform of the train and handed the carriages over to the man in charge of loading them onto the train.

Weak with hunger and thirst, with the daily food ration only a meager slice of bread and a bowl of watery soup, the women hauled themselves back to the camp. Reizele reached the barracks and stretched herself out on her bunk, all her limbs were aching and sore.

The image of the empty baby carriage kept returning to her mind and she remembered wistfully how Yuzhi had looked when he was a baby. She imagined him now pointing at her accusingly: Why have you abandoned me? Why have you disappeared? I need you, I'm longing for you! This little accusing finger drove Reizele to burst into tears, her body shook with sobs for a long time. Fatigue, cold, and longing for her son made her heart pound. It seemed to her that only yesterday she rocked her son to sleep in his cradle, and today she had to wheel the empty carriage of a baby who had been murdered, and that thought made her cry even more bitterly. She sobbed loudly, openly, as if she had at last shaken off all the restraints which had until now kept the tears from streaming out of her eyes. A kind of delayed reaction had shed light on the terrible situation she was in, just bad luck. Why did she take it into her head to go off, leaving her son, and her safe haven with Katya? What a miserable decision she had made!

Reizele's body was still shuddering with the force of her sobs when she became aware of a gentle hand stroking her forehead, the hand of someone who sought to comfort her and soothe her pain. I can see how hard it is for you. I feel for you, said the woman who was bending over her. Here is something to give you a bit of strength, a small piece of bread I put aside from last night's rations. Come, eat. Reizele looked at her through eyes red with weeping, and wordlessly expressed her gratitude to the woman for the compassion she had shown towards her.

The woman was older than Reizele by a good many years, and whose bunk was very close to hers. It is useless to cry, you will spoil your pretty eyes. You need to save your strength just to stay alive each day. The woman's face was pale and drawn but still good-looking, and all the while she spoke, she continued to stroke Reizele's forehead. Reizele looked at her with admiration, and wondered how this older woman, who looked so frail, had such inner strength and wisdom and had managed to find just the right words to comfort her. She wiped her eyes with the back of her hand, and said: You're right. I must not give in to weakness. My name is Reizele, what is yours? The woman answered, Gittel, Gittel Kirgelik is my name. Very soon they discovered that they both worked in the same huge barracks folding and packing the clothes of those murdered, and also of the prisoners who were still being kept alive.

From that evening, they were always together, friends whom fate had thrown in one another's path, although they had no hint of the surprise fate had in store for them.

## Loves In The Shadows

For her part, Reizele disclosed to Gittel only a fraction of her life story and concealed most of it. However, Gittel told Reizele with complete openness all about herself, how she and her son, also a prisoner in the camp, had been brought to Majdanek from the blazing Warsaw Ghetto, after the Nazis had murdered her husband and after the Warsaw Ghetto uprising which her son had taken part in. Gittel also told her how she had been on the verge of being dragged with all the others into the gas chamber but had been brought out, literally at the very last moment, and sent to this barracks. She admitted that at the beginning she felt a little frustrated, thinking that she had been prevented from having a warm shower. Now, of course, she knew that when those showers were turned on, it was not water but a deadly gas which came out from them, and she knew that she had been saved from certain death. To this very day, she still has no idea at all how this had come about.

What an absolutely fantastic story, Reizele answered. But curiosity was aroused by what had happened to Gittel's son, and she plucked up her courage to ask Gittel casually, by the way, what does your son do in the camp, what forced labor has he been assigned to?

With a sigh of relief, Gittel replied, thank God, he's a gifted musician. He plays the violin, so he was accepted to play in the orchestra. I've already managed to see him from a distance a few times. He always gives me a smile and carries on playing. Oddly enough, he behaves as if he's not a bit surprised to see me still alive, even though he saw me being sent in the direction of the showers. It is strange, very strange how he wasn't surprised when he saw me on my way to work from the barracks. As far as he knew, I was supposed to go to the gas chambers! But that doesn't bother me. I'm just as relieved as I can be that he wasn't sent like almost everybody else here to hard labor and doesn't have to haul heavy loads on his back every day. Playing in the orchestra is a good job, even if the musicians have to accompany people walking to their deaths, and play to drown out the sound of the rat-a-tat of firing squads gunning down in a killing ceremony.

Reizele's heart fluttered with excitement when she heard that Gittel's son played the violin in the orchestra and, making an effort to keep her voice as controlled as possible, suggested to Gittel that perhaps one day on their way to work, or if they had a brief break, or if any kind of opportunity arose, they should try, accidentally, as it were, to come upon the musicians. You must be longing to see your son, aren't you?

Reizele just wanted to be quite sure that the handsome violinist who had captured her gaze on the day she had arrived at the camp was indeed the son of her new friend Gittel.

The opportunity came up to see the orchestra when a lot of women, including Reizele and Gittel, were ordered to leave the clothing barracks and go to work in the vast kitchen where food was prepared for the Nazi staff officers. Among the onerous jobs they had to do, was to carry large saucepans from the kitchen to the dining rooms in the officers' barracks.

They had to walk quite a distance, their shoulders aching from the heavy weight of the saucepans they held, but on the way back they were free of this burden and they were more able to enjoy the open spaces they walked in, compared with being confined all day to the barracks, hunched over a table as they folded and packed clothes. There was another, important, advantage to working in the kitchen: They did not feel constant pangs of hunger, for it was always possible to find a bite of food to put in their mouths in addition to the paltry bowl of soup they got as a daily portion.

Yes, to be out in the air certainly eased the burden of carrying the heavy cooking pots, and now it seemed as if they would be able to take a peek at the musicians from close up, when the sounds of the orchestra were vying with the thunderous gun shots of the firing squad as they carried out that daily executions.

In the short intervals between each piece of music, or when they all went back to their barracks after their long day's work, the musicians were forced to write out the musical notes of each piece of music for themselves. The Nazi deputy commandants of the camp did not provide them with any sheet music, so the musicians wrote them out on paper they were given, and conducted the rehearsals according to them.

One rare sunny day, Reizele and Gittel were on their way back from taking the saucepans from the kitchen to the officers' dining rooms. When they had to pass by the large square used for executions, they approached the area where some prisoners had already been assembled to watch the gruesome ceremony, which was practically part of the everyday routine in the camp. The orchestra was there, waiting to strike up the instant they received the signal, which would be synchronized with the start of the executions.

Ruvke was among the band of the musicians, placing his violin under his chin, and holding the bow in his hand, ready for the order to play, when out of the blue he glimpsed his mother walking in his direction, gazing at him with a look of deep love. But who is that walking beside her. It looks as if they know each other, walking together and coming near. It cannot be, it's the woman from not long ago – the one who stole his heart when she looked at him! Ruvke fixed his eyes on hers, gave her the hint of a smile. They looked at each other as if an invisible power had bound them together. While he was still rapt in the midst of this enchanted moment, the orchestra struck up a rousing march – violins, trumpets, and drums. Ruvke began to move his bow up and down the strings, playing with all his heart and soul as if he were playing only for her, not paying any attention to the tens of prisoners who gathered from all directions to watch the gruesome scene.

At that time, the tens of the wretched victims, those

criminals who stole some bread or a shirt or a potato, that were lined up in a long row, were ordered to crouch their faces towards the ground, and with a thundering roll on the drum, the order came to shoot, and two soldier-assassins, one at either end of the row, each with a gun in his hand, began to walk down the row with measured steps, making of this horrific incident almost a ceremony, as one abject victim after another, in turn, met his death by a bullet in the back of the head. The soldier-assassins knew how to do their job with precision and efficiency, leaving only one bleeding hole in each skull where the fatal bullet had entered.

Within only a few minutes it was all over. The tortured lives of those sentenced to death came to their violent end, the hopes and ambitions of those remaining alive were crushed under the weight of the fear of a similar end in that same place and by the same means.

This surreal ritual of routine murder being carried out against the background of drum-rolls and trumpet blasts and the squeak of bows stroking the violin strings, left Reizele standing rooted to the spot, mesmerized by the nightmarish scene, but also fascinated by the violinist whose eyes she still sought.

Gittel had to tug at Reizele's arm in order to pull her away from that spot, to disentangle her from the overwhelming jumble of emotions which engulfed her – the shock and the revulsion of being a witness to the killings, and at the very same part time the feelings of love which had begun to blossom in her heart. Is that your son? Reizele asked Gittel. Yes, that's my son. What's his name? – Ruvke, but that's enough of your questions, let's get back to the kitchen before they say we are late, and you have seen what they do to latecomers.

From that time on, Reizele took advantage of every moment she was not at her work, to try to be where the orchestra was playing, in order to see Ruvke, whose looks and bearing had so enchanted her. Ruvke, she whispered his name to herself, who had inspired her love for him and felt in his answering gaze which pierced her heart that he cared for her in return.

✦✦✦

The exciting rumor began to be heard that the German Army was retreating from the Soviet Union, the Russians were overwhelming the German Army and making their defeat all the more decisive by their scorched earth policy. Not that that eased the prisoners' hunger, but at least the hope that freedom would soon be seen on the horizon warmed their hearts to some extent. The Nazi guards in the camp were irritable and anxious, and their eyes flashed with even more evil intent than usual. They were obsessed by two particular missions which they were determined to carry out before it was too late: To increase as much as possible the daily tally of killings, and to obliterate every trace of the evidence of their gruesome deeds, which were a matter of day-to-day routine to them.

The furnaces were working at a crazy pace during this period, burning one thousand bodies each day, but even this was not enough for the murderers.

The Nazi staff at Majdanek suspected that the prisoners were planning a revolt in the camp, as had happened in other places like the Warsaw Ghetto uprising and the rebellion in the Sobibor death camp.

Some attempts of prisoners to break out and escape of the camp, drove the Nazis to wipe out the prisoners in Majdanek by additional, and very cruel means.

That is how they planned the massacre which was euphemistically known as Operation Harvest Festival.

At the end of October 1943, 300 of the healthiest and strongest prisoners were ordered to dig three massive ditches alongside the crematorium, from where a foul stench filled the air, night and day.

When the digging of the huge ditches was completed, and

their dark mouths were opened to swallow as many bodies as possible, on November 3, 1943, trucks were driven into the camp with loudspeakers blaring out deafeningly loud music which could be heard in every corner of the camp. On the same morning, as they stood during the usual roll call, SS guards began to walk between the lines of the prisoners and pull out groups of 100 of them, women and children, old people and men, the most frail, those who were little more than skin and bones, pushing them towards the deep ditches, forcing them to undress and to lie down in the ditches. Before the wretched people understood what was going on, firing squads standing at the edge of the ditches shot them to death and groups of another hundred of people were pushed and pulled to the open ditches and were forced to undress and lie down one next to the other, one on top of the other, while machine guns and sub-machine guns sprayed bullets into them, devastating them body and soul.

The strident marches and dance music burst out from the loudspeakers so as to shut out the sound of the shooting guns, and the prisoners who were still managing to hold on to their lives, did not grasp what other sounds the music was hiding. Ruvke, however, knew that the music was not being performed purely to gladden the hearts of the listeners. As a part of an orchestra he knew that its task was to silence the noise of bullets being discharged, one by one, into the row of prisoners fated to be murdered in the public square; or to calm the fears and suspicions of those on their way to the gas chambers. But knowing this did not help him when he could not lend a hand to any of them.

The slaughter in that horrified day, continued from dawn to dark, non-stop, that bloody day of the Harvest Festival when what was harvested was 18,400 victims whose lives were cut short, until the music heard throughout the camp seemed to echo the crackle of the constant gunfire.

Brawny Jews, whose strong build had led to their being

chosen to carry out the next stage of these sickening proceedings, were brought to the killing site in order to cover the ditches with lime, ditches which had become mass graves, whose blood still cries out from the depths to the unfeeling world.

Executions were also carried out in the fields outside the camp where ditches had been dug for the murdered prisoners to fall into, who met their deaths by shooting. The thunderous booms of Russian artillery and the blasts of the bombs they were dropping near the multitude of German soldiers left no doubt in the minds of the commandant of Majdanek that the end was approaching, and that they had no time to complete the quotas of murders they had been ordered to perform nor to destroy all the incriminating evidence of their deeds. How many bundles of paper was it possible to burn? They were in such a hurry that the smoke from the bonfires of paper mixed with the smoke coming from the crematoria, until they had to extinguish the flames from both sources. Time was running out for them, they had to get themselves far away from there.

Before they abandoned the camp, the Nazis managed to destroy the crematorium but not the gas chambers nor most of the barracks which held the prisoners. There was no time left. The wheel of fortune had turned, and instead of being the hunters, they were being hunted, and the only option they had was to flee.

The main task they set themselves just before they fled was to empty the camp of as many of the surviving prisoners as they could, in case they fell into the hands of the Russians who, at the end of the war, would use these eyewitnesses to point the finger of guilt at them.

Thus began one of the cruelest episodes of the war, the removal from the camp of all the prisoners still alive and force them mercilessly to march out of the camp, into the fields, onto the roads, through villages in the direction of the railway stations where trains would take them to westwards, far from the extermination camps in Poland, to the territory where the Nazis still ruled with an iron fist, to be exterminated there.

About one thousand people were taken out of Majdanek on the forced march. Most of them were dressed in threadbare clothes, their shoes full of holes, some were even barefoot. Anyone who could, put a coat or blanket around himself. The guards used whips and the barrels of rifles as goads, and this convoy of ragged wretches was forced to stumble through the freezing cold, the snow settling onto the shoulders of the men, women and children. All their strength was required just to put one foot in front of the other. Even at the outset, the weak, the old, and the sick began to slip and fall, and each one who collapsed received a shot to his head and was roughly flung out of the way. The white snow turned red from the victims' blood, and the Germans who marched at the rear, threw the bodies into the ditches at the side of the roads which had been dug beforehand, at the edges of the villages along the path of the death march.

Before the women in Reizele's barracks were pushed out to leave the camp, she had somehow managed to find a warm coat to wear and urged Gittel to put on her shoes and the coat, and wrapped a blanket around her shoulders. She clutched her arm and pulled her out of the barracks before the kapo came and dragged her out by her hair. But Gittel was not willing to leave the camp before she saw her son. I want to walk with Ruvke. I will not go without him. The men and women are not separated now. Look, everyone is walking together. I have to find him, and Reizele agreed with her with all her heart. She was longing to meet again the man who had so moved her. The two women began to hunt for him, looking in the direction of the men's barracks, and the musicians' barracks, their eyes searching among the hordes of prisoners.

Ruvke will not leave without me. He is bound to be looking for me, murmured Gittel as if to herself, and suddenly, in the midst of all the turmoil and confusion, she saw Ruvke's blond forelock cut short, and saw him looking anxiously for his mother, who he hoped he would find, together with her young friend with whom he had fallen in love at first sight.

Look! Here he is, called Gittel, and rushed over to him while Reizele walked by her side. Their faces sparkled with happiness as they fell one upon other. They hugged and embraced each other, Gittel clinging to her son as if she would never let him go. But Ruvke was concerned also about somebody else. While he was still holding his mother close, he saw Reizele over her shoulder, standing at her side, aroused by her closeness to him. Ruvke turned his face towards her, and his hand reached out for hers, which responded eagerly, their two hands linked in the heat of shared emotion, clutching each other longingly, in wonder, unwilling to separate one from the other.

And then, their throats choked with emotion and unable to utter a word, Gittel, Ruvke and Reizele turned towards the gate of the camp to join the mass of prisoners setting out on this death-defying journey.

From the very first minutes, even before they had gone out of the confines of the camp, Gittel felt that she basically did not want to go on the march. It was not only that she knew that she was too weak to survive the walk in the snow and the cold, to an unknown destination. There was another aspect to it, which she could not as yet define, which perturbed and upraised her resistance. Was it because of having to walk? To march? No, it was the fact that they were forced to escape. And why, and to where they were fleeing? From the Russians, the Russians who were the enemy of the Nazis, but who were presumed to come to save the prisoners of Majdanek? This flight had nothing to do with her, it was the defeated Germans who had to run away, and she did not have to lend her hand to it, for it was against her interests! To these hesitations were added the smoldering desire she had become conscious of, when the two young people who were standing next her, quite strangers to each other, had clasped and joined their hands together. That moment had shocked her, and she was not able to dismiss it from her mind: With a spark of intuition, she suddenly understood why Reizele had been so keen to see her son, something she had managed so successfully to hide from her, until that instant when their hands had clasped in unspoken passion.

And so, in light of the feeling of mutiny against her enemies which rose up within her, but also because of the unspoken covenant her son had entered into with her young friend, she came to a decision: I shall stay here. There is no point in going out of here.

Death will come whenever and wherever it comes, here or there, what is the difference? And life, what about life? You may find the breath of life even here, in this corner of this God-forsaken place. Who knows? Gittel looked around her, they were surrounded by savage guards and kapos, armed with whips and guns, goading and whipping and threatening and hitting anyone within arm's reach. The thought of the advancing Russian Army had shocked them to such an extent, that had even increased their sadistic outbursts, so they behaved like a herd of wild animals running rampant over their captives.

Gittel decided that she would not let herself be tormented in this way. She would stay here, whatever the consequences would be.

Little by little, she slowed her pace and began to retreat from the crowd, maneuvering her way carefully in case her son and the young woman with him would notice her absence, and for fear that the Nazis would come after her and force her onto the terrible march. Suddenly it occurred to her that, strange as it seemed, the extermination camp was a place which held out a greater chance of survival. I'm going to stay here, she said to herself, after all there are others who are not able to go, and in all the chaos and rushing about, they will not notice that I'm not there. So, step by step, she tentatively, cautiously, made her way back, as a person trying to walk among the drops of rain, to avoid getting wet. She trudged along as slowly as she could, moving almost imperceptibly, towards her barracks. When she reached it and went inside, she saw that there were indeed still some women there, lying on their bunks, too feeble even to try to sit up. Gittel slowly walked the length of the barracks, looking at the bunks ranged in tiers in the large hall, that most of them were empty. She did not even know why she was looking so intently at the bunks, until the thought came to her that in order to find something, it was necessary to search for it. Her eyes darted here and there until they fell on the thing that she had subconsciously been searching for. Here it was, a piece of bread which probably had dropped from someone's hand in the panic of being forced out from the barracks. Some wretched woman had no doubt secreted it away like a precious jewel to be used in time of need.

*Who can understand the mind of a person who, even in time of extreme poverty or hunger, still hides some food behind, in case a time of poverty or hunger should strike him!*

*Like in old age, one keeps saving money and other valuables, buried them deep in his safe or bank accounts and denies himself enjoyment and pleasure, so that he will still have something left for the future, for his ... old age.*

*There are no boundaries to the fears of human beings of the doomed days to come...*

Gittel took the slice of bread which, at that time and in that place, was valued more highly than gold, and continued to walk slowly down the huge hall, this time knowing what she was seeking, examining closely the rows of bunks. Her efforts were not in vain. She found on another bunk a quarter of a loaf that must have been stolen from the kitchen, she said to herself.

Gittel walked back to her own bunk and sat herself down on its edge. With lifeless eyes, she began to chew the bread, although it stuck in her throat. She has to hold on just a little longer. She must eat something to stay alive. She was plagued with thirst and thought of the heaps of snow which had piled up outside the barracks that would help her quench her thirst. She realized that now there was nobody responsible for providing food, even if they had only doled out a thin slice of bread and some can of soup. Suddenly the kapo seemed to her a benevolent angel who had deserted her. The kapo had at least obtained food for them.

Gittel lay on her back, sighing both with relief and distress, but in her excitable state, she could not close her eyes. Her temples were throbbing with fear and emotion and she was filled with an overwhelmingly strong feeling of rebellion. She was rebelling not only against her own imprisonment and torments, but also against the horrific circumstances she had been caught in, together with all her fellow Jews.

She was infused with long-hidden mental strength which entered her consciousness as if it had sprung up from the depths. To consider my people, the Jews, who gave the world the Bible, the Ten Commandments, developed sciences, established major philosophies, brought prosperity to the countries they lived in, and cultivated a just and fair society wherever they lived – they are such an inferior race and because of that they are doomed to death? And all the Jews who were prominent in the arts and culture of so many countries – including Germany – the writers, artists, musicians, world-class scientists and inventors, were all these inferior? And why were the ordinary Jews to be disdained and vilified, those who struggled to make a meager living, bringing up their families to be loyal citizens of the state they lived in, and their forebears had lived in, while at the same time remaining faithful to their religion – what was wrong with them? Was it only because they clung to their Jewish religion?

Despite her fatigue and exhaustion, feelings of injustice and revulsion gnawed away at Gittel with an intensity which she was unable to shake off. As much as she tried not to think of the existence of the God who allowed His people to be crushed and annihilated, she found herself returning again and again to the question, Where was our God, to whom we pray every day of our lives, to whom we pay tribute and praise? She got no answer to all her questions, but she knew that she would never abandon her faith in the God of the Jews, despite of all the disasters that had fallen on their heads. Full of faith in her God and religion and the Jewish people, Gittel finally fell into a deep sleep.

The Russian Army was advancing, and the blasts of the explosions were increasing in intensity. The Russians were pushing forward aggressively, and the Germans were being defeated! The thunder of bombs echoed in the vast camp of Majdanek. Some of the watchtowers were destroyed, the guards having abandoned them and all the officers and staff who had served with blind obedience in the camp, were in panic.

Hastily the Nazis had wanted to empty the camp of its occupants and drive them out from the areas of Poland to the west which were still under their control. That terrible march claimed the deaths of around half of those who took part in it, who fell and died, or were shot. Only those who were not as frail arrived at the railway station, where they were loaded on to crowded trains, as if they were cattle, to be taken to an extermination camp – to be murdered.

Only the most wretched prisoners, the sick and the weak, those with no strength even to stand on their legs, had remained in the camp, where death, lurking all around, would carry them off by cold, starvation, thirst, and disease.

✦✦✦

Persevere. Keep walking. Overcome the horrors. The hand holding hers caused a seed of hope to be planted in her heart, a sensation that this hand would not be taken away from hers and that she would not remove her hand from his.

The first to notice that Gittel was not walking with them was Reizele. Where is mother … I mean, where is Gittel? Alarmed at not seeing her with them, but unable to search for her, the two of them continued walking. There was simply no possibility of turning around, retracing their steps, asking about Gittel. We can only hope that she will come through all right, replied Ruvke. I know my mother, and I think she is bound to have gone back to the barracks, and not have come on the march at all; smart of her, she could not have lasted out here. What we have to do now is not to weaken, to carry on somehow, look what is happening all around us.

The convoy of people in front of them ran, stumbling, falling, shots rang out as they received a bullet to the head as they fell, their blood turning the snow red, and those still able to walk trudging through the deep snow saturated with the blood of the dead.

Ruvke and Reizele were surrounded by the corpses of the victims, their own feet stumbled, hunger gnawed at them, their throats were dry as the Sahara desert, their eyes watered from the cold, but it was forbidden to fall behind for even a minute, if they wanted to stay alive.

I cannot go on for much longer. I can hardly breathe, whispered Reizele, but the look of loving tenderness in Ruvke's eyes encouraged her to keep up her pace, and carry on walking hour after hour. In a very short time, everyone still alive would arrive at the railway station, where the cattle cars of the train would transport them to that dreaded destination, the extermination camp, where the cruelest fate of all awaited them. Treblinka? Auschwitz? Buchenwald?

Ruvke was determined to find some way to escape from this forced march before nightfall or before they reach the dreadful train station. He would escape – he must escape. Whatever will be, will be. He had already spotted an isolated granary in the secluded yard of an abandoned farmhouse not far off from the disastrous march they were involuntarily taking part in. So, amid the jumble of people and guards who brandished their whips and fired their guns indiscriminately at the miserable convoy, he took advantage of the twilight when the guards temporarily relaxed their vigilance, to signal to Reizele to follow him. Taking great care that the Nazi guards, or those they were walking with, would not become aware that they were trying to escape, they slipped away nimbly, crawling like lizards.

Ruvke led the way, and Reizele followed closely behind him until they had only a short distance to cover, and they would be inside the granary. The door opened at a light touch, and they went inside. Panting after all their efforts, they fell in a heap onto a sea of smooth hay and straw.

Without saying a word, but drunk with a sense of freedom, at least for the time being, they covered themselves with straw, stretched their cramped limbs and rested to regain their strength and allow themselves to breathe deeply and slow the rapid pounding of their hearts. The heat of the animals which could be felt in the granary warmed the cold air which froze their bodies, and they lay on the straw for a long time, until they felt calmer.

And then, slowly, they tentatively began to explore with gentle fingers each other's body, they edged closer to each other, lay entwined together, and held each other close with rising passion, as if they were swearing to stay linked as one forever.

Without a word, for words were unnecessary in the face of their mounting emotions, they fell asleep in each other's arms, inseparable in their oblivion.

Love had come upon them unwittingly. Love had them in its clasp without either knowing a thing about the other's past, and would not be diminished by anything in that past.

After sleeping deeply for a whole day, they awoke in a panic to the roar of engines all around them. The darkness of the granary was penetrated by just a few shafts of light so they were unable to see more than a hand in front of their face, but they heard the noise of aircraft, and the heavy boots of infantry troops coming nearer and nearer. The first fearful thought that occurred to them was that, in spite of being so cautious, they had been noticed by the Nazi guards as they ran from the march, and they had been caught in their hiding place.

Everything is lost, we're finished, they thought, still rubbing their eyes after their long deep sleep, not yet completely awake. Like a man resigned to a harsh sentence meted out to him, they stood up and raised their hands in submission to the muzzle of a gun cocked at them. But the tall soldier standing opposite them did not threaten them, or shout at them, or shoot. He suddenly dropped the barrel of his gun, and rested it in the straw. To their astonishment, he smiled at them, and said: Don't be afraid, I'm Russian. The war here in the east is over. We have won!

Seeing the dismal condition they were in, the soldier said, wait a minute, I'll be back quickly. He went out, leaving them standing there without having moving an inch, still amazed and bewildered. He came back a few minutes later, holding a loaf of warm bread, which he had taken from a stock of loaves in his army truck, in one hand while his other hand held a large mess can full of drinking water. Take them, I suppose you have not eaten or drunk for ages. You have been saved. The Nazis have gone. They have run away, the bastards. Eat and drink something, and go back to sleep. You can sleep peacefully now. Without another word, the Russian soldier turned on his heels, opened the squeaking door to the granary, went out, and closed it behind him.

Ruvke and Reizele were so astonished at this turn of events that they did not even have the strength to eat the fresh bread they had been given. We have won? Nobody is hunting us any more? They looked at each other, and grinning from ear to ear and shrugging their shoulders in disbelief, sat themselves down on a bundle of straw and began to take slow gulps of the cold water, passing the can one to the other after each had downed two gulps of water, until they had emptied the can. When their thirst had been quenched, Ruvke broke the loaf of bread into two, and gave one half to Reizele. They began to bite into the bread ravenously and chewed it with increasing appetite, right down to the very last crumb.

Their deep sleep had revived them, and the food and drink they had received, gave them renewed vigor and they felt their strength return to them.

Reizele and Ruvke sat side by side, trying to control their strong emotions and the magnetic attraction each of them felt for the other: Only yesterday they had been close to annihilation, now they sparkled with the elation of their new-found freedom.

Ruvke was the first to stand, and held out his hand to the woman who only a short time ago had come into his life and captivated him, and about whose past he still knew nothing. He even had no idea how she had come to be sent to the extermination camp. At the same time, he felt that he had found his soul mate. He stretched out his hand to her to help her up from the mound of straw she had been sitting on, and when they stood facing each other, their hands gripped as if they wanted to combine all the strength in their bodies and make them one. Their lips touched, light as the fluttering wings of a butterfly. Then, all their senses on fire, the heat of desire emanated from their bodies, their tongues in the other's mouth as if they wanted to swallow the other and be swallowed up, their breaths intermingled, as their bodies fused and, murmuring soft words of longing and joy.

As passion overcame them, they fell onto a thick carpet of straw and, embracing uninhibitedly, quickly removed their clothes and the one began to penetrate the other's body with enormous hunger of desire, with the ecstasy of an explorer discovering a hitherto unknown continent with its mountains and valleys, rivers and caves. This was Ruvke's first experience of intimacy with a woman, and he was astonished not only by being absorbed into a woman's body, but also by the magic of the attraction itself, the indescribable rapture which spread into every fiber of his soul and sent waves of uncontrollable spasms throughout his body, and so they lay together for hours, exploring the secret places of their bodies, each time rising to a peak of delight and afterward taking pleasure in blissful serenity.

For a long time they lay in each other's arms, without speaking, until Reizele suddenly sat up and shook herself. She then lay back on her back and said in a business-like tone, completely at odds with the feelings of passion which had overwhelmed her only minutes before.

Now that the Germans have gone, we can go back to Majdanek to find your mother, and after that, we will have to go to pick up my son from Belzec.

✦ ✦ ✦

From the time his mother went out of Katya and Piotr's house and did not return, Yuzhi behaved like a child who was a stranger to himself, as if he had lost a limb. The child was in a confused mental and emotional state which expressed itself in extremes of behavior: One minute he would be as quiet as a mouse, introverted and taciturn, deep in thought; the next he would burst into tears, for no apparent reason, and had frequent nightmares, from which he would awake screaming; opening and shutting doors, searching for her upstairs and downstairs as if in a constant game of hide-and-seek, yelling where is my mother? Where is she, even though he knew that his mother had not hidden herself away temporarily in a closet or somewhere else in the house out of sight, but had simply disappeared from his life. Had she run away? Had she abandoned him forever? What could he know, this small child brought up in the dark, hidden from the outside world? None of Katya or Piotr's explanations convinced him to believe them. And what was there for him to be convinced of? That his mother had gone to visit relatives but had not arrived at their house, and that we do not know if she will ever come back to us?

Katya and Piotr believed that Reizele was dead. The rumors and, now, the certain knowledge of the mass murder of Jews in every country conquered by the Nazis, left no doubt in their minds that Reizele had been caught and sent to an extermination camp, or that she had been shot trying to escape, or that she had been tortured to death, or that she had become ill and died. Who knows what had become of her?

Even if they did not know exactly what had happened to Reizele, they were as sure as they could be that there was no chance that she would return. No Jew returned from the inferno. Several months had already passed since Reizele had left the house so cheerfully to visit their relatives in Lublin, but had never arrived at her destination. Day after day, night after night, Yuzhi never stopped asking sadly, Where is my mother? Where is my mother? Katya could never give him an answer which would satisfy him, or in fact any answer at all. She herself lost her rock-like stability in the uncertainty of the new situation she was faced with, sometimes laughing with unfounded optimism, at others weeping as she reflected on what their lives had become. Katya felt herself sliding into an abyss of gloom and realized that she had to overcome this, for all their sakes. She came to the decision that the best thing she could do was to teach Yuzhi to regard her as his mother. He is only a small child, just three years old. He is still very malleable, he'll forget. So, in all kinds of ways, she began to persuade him to look upon her as his mother. She bought him a necklace with a gold-plated cross and hung it round his neck. I'm your mother, Yuzhi, I'm your mother, Yuzhi, my sweet boy! She called him sweet, although the natural sweetness of children of his age was not present in his personality, and by degrees he became disagreeable and bitter. The disappearance of his natural parents and the strain and uncertainty which plagued Katya and Piotr all the time became absorbed in Yuzhi's consciousness. Consequently, he was a very insecure little boy, and expressed his unhappiness in frequent outbursts of rage, and unfriendly, even hostile behavior. His speech was fluent but indistinct, as if was speaking with his mouth full of food, so that all the content spilled out and filled the air with shattered words. But Katya wanted him as he was. She had never had a son, and had always longed for one. And now she had one. He was with her all the time, her own son, doing all the things that mothers do: She fed him, hugged him, kissed him, put him to bed, sang lullabies to him – go to sleep my baby, close your pretty eyes, angels up above you, watch you from the skies

Katya's determination to adopt Yuzhi as her son was completely encouraged by her husband, Piotr:

When the war is over, we will go to the Ministry of the Interior and register Yuzhi as our son. He has never been registered in the Population Registry, so there will be no problems about that. He will be ours! Our son! However, Katya, that good-hearted soul, could not rid herself of the feeling of guilt that skulked in her heart even as she rejoiced at being granted the gift of a son, for she knew that her good fortune had only been made possible by the death of Yuzhi's mother. But as time was going by, Katya's guilty feelings became repressed so deeply in her subconscious, that she failed to be aware of them any longer.

# 11
# Stirrings Of Freedom

Gittel slept long and deeply, a sleep which enabled her to escape the harsh realities of her life. She awoke to the sounds of the creaking of the wooden floorboards upon which heavy boots were treading, and loud voices of cheers and cries of happiness hovered around her ears. It took her a little time to come to herself and sit on the edge of her bunk, as she was still light-headed from hunger and her throat was hoarse and dry. At last she managed to open her eyes fully. She was astonished to see walking through the barracks soldiers in bulky, crumpled uniforms, not the starched and ironed uniforms of the Germans, their boots thick with dust. The soldiers were staring, aghast, at the shadow-like figures of the ashen-faced women standing mute in front of them and the women walking to and fro, like ghosts who had lost their way.

*Happy are those who have lost their way; happy are those who have been saved from the destructive way but still have not revealed their way to freedom, which was long forgotten and suddenly ready to burst out of the darkness of their life.*

Out of the mix of voices Gittel heard the deep bass voice of a Russian soldier who approached her and stood at the side of her bunk. He was a tall man, about 50, a few years older than herself, the brown stubble of his beard was streaked with silver.

You are all released and free, he said to her, and soon we will be bringing you something to eat.

We are released? To where? Gittel asked in surprise. At that moment she started to realize that the barracks, which had housed women sentenced to hard labor or condemned to death, and was her safe haven, had suddenly collapsed under her feet. Now, at her age, in her condition, she had to move away from there? To begin to wander along a road full of obstacles, of hardships? What would she do? Where would she go? She was completely alone! Her whole family scattered in all directions. Her husband, Nachum, had been murdered in the Warsaw Ghetto by the Gestapo; her son Yudele had run away; her son Anshel had run away; and now she had become separated from her son Ruvke, who was on the death march. Who knows what has happened to him? Oh, what a distorted irony of it, that of all her family, she might be the only one to survive and have to cope all by herself with whatever the future held. How on earth would she manage?

✦ ✦ ✦

Majdanek was the first concentration camp to be liberated by the Allied forces, and the Russian soldiers brought food and drink to the remaining survivors in the camp. Those broken, starved souls, the oppressed and the depressed, fell upon the food, and still some of them, so ironically, even blessed *she'hecheyanu,* thanks to God, for the food they received.

Only very slowly did it enter into Gittel's consciousness that she was free to leave the camp. Although the war was still not over, and the Germans continued to control western Europe, stirrings of freedom had come to Majdanek. But Gittel herself was not able to take advantage of this newfound freedom, for she had nowhere to go. She had no one to go to! She had no one to go with! And she had no strength to go anywhere!!

The Russian soldier who had broken the astonishing news to her of the liberation, would himself bring her mugs of hot soup, slices of fresh bread, and corn. Gittel would eat them in silence, her expressive eyes showing her gratitude for his kindness. It did not cross her mind, yet, that the Russian soldier was trying to become close to her. Compared with the other women remaining in the barracks, Gittel looked much better than they, and the pallor of her face and her slimness only accentuated her beauty.

One day, the soldier introduced himself to her. My name is Sergei Moldakov, what is yours? She took a long time to answer, hesitating whether to give any information of importance to a man who was virtually a stranger to her. In the end, she said, Gittel, and thus they began to strike up a friendship.

On the next few mornings, while Gittel was eating with relish the food Sergei had brought her, she found herself listening with great interest to his life story. At the beginning, Sergei was sitting on the bunk opposite to hers but after few days he came to sit next to her, touching lightly her hip, a kind of a gentle touch, which made them both shiver pleasantly.

He was conscripted to the Russian Army some years before the war, and it was his good fortune that he had never risen above a low rank, for Stalin had liquidated thousands of army officers in the 1930s, which had spelled ruin for the Red Army. He was not a communist, but had always been poor. He never had any ambition to become an officer, and that is how he was saved from being liquidated; his rank now was First Sergeant. Does he have a family? No, no more, but he had had one. Tragically, before war broke out, when he was serving in the Ural Mountains, a long way from his home, he lost his whole family. His parents, his wife, and his two daughters were all murdered in a pogrom the Russians carried out against the Jews. There was no shortage of pogroms against the Jews in Russia, Sergei said bitterly.

During the war, he was responsible for supplies in one of the units defending Stalingrad during the siege, and was then posted to an artillery unit pursuing the fleeing German troops. Yes, there too he was in charge of getting food and uniforms for the Russian soldiers who were trouncing the Germans at every turn. How did Napoleon put it? The army marches on its stomach.

We reached the outskirts of Eastern Poland, and every town, one after the other, was liberated, and you can take my word for it that I took care that the stomach of every soldier in my unit was full, while the German soldiers were starving because nobody worried about where their food was coming from. The German troops were bogged down in the mud and the snow. They did not have proper winter uniforms so they froze in the cold. They were just overwhelmed by us. Now that we have liberated Majdanek, I have to stay on here for quite some time to collect and process the mass of records and documents the Germans did not have time to destroy when they ran away, and sort out the evidence, witnesses and so on; put together all the equipment from the factories in the camp. There are a hundred and one things I have to do, including organizing food and equipment for the command staff, soldiers and, of course, for the prisoners who are still here, and – very important – I have to make sure that everything is recorded accurately.

Sergei's face was wrinkled, but pleasant and open, full of strong expression, and this, together with his deep voice, his forelock of silver, generous mouth, and warm, brown eyes combined to give the impression that he had a good heart, was a decent man, the salt of the earth, and Gittel felt completely at ease with him. A wonderful sense of belonging to him suddenly came over her. Sitting next to him, the loneliness and fear she usually felt dissolved and she was enveloped in the warmth of his nearness.

Where do you intend going when you leave here, he asked Gittel.

She shrugged her shoulders despondently, and said in a low voice, I have no place to go. I have no strength to leave. I have nobody to go with.

Sergei looked at her with his warm, brown eyes, and said in his deep voice, which gave her a pleasant thrill: If you have nowhere to go, stay here in the meantime. I am a Jew, too, you know, you've touched me deeply. I also have nowhere to go or anyone to return to, so stay and I will take care of you.

Gittel could hardly believe this stroke of good luck which had suddenly come her way; she nodded her head in agreement, and said, yes, I will stay. I will stay here, with you. If my son is still alive, I am sure he will come and look for me here. I trust you, Sergei. I will stay.

Sergei's eyes shone with emotion. This woman, with her pale beauty, had very much moved him. She did not lose her humanity, as many of the women there had. I will help you, he said to her. I will look after you, you need not worry, but first of all you must get your health back.

✦ ✦ ✦

As soon as Ruvke and Reizele had eaten and drunk their fill from the generous food rations the Russian soldiers had brought them, they set out to look for somewhere to live in one of the villages in the east of Poland, which had been liberated. They found themselves a ramshackle house abandoned by its owners, who were most probably Jews forced out of their house and sent in an *action* to an extermination camp.

Although the house was dilapidated and had obviously been ransacked, no Polish *goyim* had taken it for themselves to live in; and now here they were, taking the house for themselves. They washed up, and found some clothes to wear, picking them out from the piles of men's, women's, and children's clothes which were flung in heaps on the floor – anything to get out of the prisoners' uniforms which were such a tangible reminder of the horrors of the extermination camp. Then they sat themselves down on the floor, and began to tell each other all about their lives, revealing their innermost secrets.

To get my mother out of Majdanek and to go to Belzec to get your son from there? The striking news that Reizele had a son, surprised Ruvke, and he repeatedly urged Reizele to tell him how that had come about. Reizele, however, kept putting off telling Ruvke, but after a lot of hesitation finally gave in. But what in fact did she tell him, which version of her life did she tell Ruvke?

Reizele gave Ruvke a very curtailed account of everything that had happened to her, and spoke in a dry, businesslike way, without emotion.

Oh Reizele, what fairy tales are you making up for your lover, revealing just a little and hiding so much? What is this about some yeshiva bochur from Zamosc, Mottele – was that his name? – who took you right after your wedding, from your parents' house on the very same day that war broke out, to relatives of his family in Belzec, where you gave birth to your son and, on the very day that he was born, Operation Barbarossa began and your husband was killed by a bomb, and when the Germans conquered Eastern Poland you hid herself away in the house of neighbors – *goyim* – who kept you concealed in a dark cellar, until by some miscalculation on your part, you could not resist a proposal to go to Lublin with the forged papers you had, and you were caught by the Gestapo, falling victim to a gossipy neighbor, who informed on you for being a Jew and for that reason you were sent to Majdanek, and the rest is already known. Reizele sighed deeply, and added dryly: That's how everything happened, but I must go now to Belzec to get my son.

*It's difficult to get emotional when you are telling a fabricated story, because that would mean you are lying twice over. First, you have concocted the story and second, you have to express emotions you do not really feel.*

Ruvke must have suppressed any misgivings he had about Reizele's sad story, or perhaps his brain did not absorb the contradictions which protruded from behind the smokescreen of facts she related to him; the most outlandish of them could have come straight from the plot of an old movie, where it was hard to tell the difference between fact and fiction. Ruvke had no interest in going into all the details, and he was especially not interested in asking what kind of man her late, unfortunate, husband had been. He felt that Reizele was avoiding the issue and he went along with it. Indeed, Reizele was still not ready to tell him the truth about her relationship with Arkadi. It was not only in Yuzhi's consciousness that Arkadi did not exist: Reizele also hid his existence from Ruvke for many years.

What had most affected Ruvke was the existence of the son who waited for his mother in Belzec: That is really a wonderful idea, he replied cheerfully to Reizele's suggestion. We must not lose any time about going to Belzec and bringing your son to live with us. But on second thought, it would be better if we go in separately: I will sneak in to the Majdanek camp through a hole in the fence, to look for my mother, and you will go to Belzec to get your son. All we have to do is decide where we will meet up.

Yes, of course, we can do that, said Reizele. I know where I want us to meet. I want us to meet in Zamosc, where I was born. I want to go there and try to find out if there is anyone at all who survived from my family. Perhaps I will find someone who managed to hide himself away, or at least to find out what happened to all my family, my grandfathers and grandmothers, my aunts and uncles and their children. Even if all of them were taken to be murdered and I will not find anyone of them alive, I still want to go back to Zamosc, to knock at the door of the house I was born in.

To knock at the door of her family house, as a stranger, and even if the house was occupied by Poles, those trespassers who will consider her a trespasser. She would think of a way for her and her son and Ruvke and his mother to live there and wait for the havoc of war to blow over.

They allowed themselves a few days of rest, and spent their nights enjoying the pleasures of love. Before they parted, Reizele wrote down for Ruvke the exact address of her family's house in Zamosc and each one of them went his way.

It was a warm spring day when Ruvke, alternately on foot or in a car which stopped to offer him a ride part of the way, neared the extermination camp, all of whose entrances he knew so well. He did not attempt to enter by the main gate as he suspected that the Russian soldiers on guard there would not allow him to enter. He looked for, and found a hole in the fence, knowing that the electricity which had run between the spikes of the barbed wire had been deactivated. On that fence so many prisoners, choosing to gamble between freedom and death, had lost their gamble and, in trying to make a run for it, had been electrocuted. That deadly fence only benefited those desperate souls who could no longer bear the unbearable suffering. They threw themselves onto that fence, thus putting an end to their hopeless lives. Now the fence was harmless – there was no reason to be afraid of touching it.

Ruvke slithered under the spiked barbed wire and crossed into the area of the camp. The watchtowers stood empty, some of them had been destroyed by the bombs the Russians had discharged onto the camp. There were no German soldiers to be seen anywhere around. They had all fled, the bastards, like rats leaving a sinking ship, reflected Ruvke, as he began to make his way through the vast areas of the camp which seemed surreal, but at the same time, animated with life of a new kind.

Ruvke knew where he wanted to go, even before he went to look for his mother. He hurried to the barracks where he had lived with the musicians of the camp orchestra. It was deserted, which convinced Ruvke that they had all gone on the terrible death march, and had indeed met their deaths there in those inhuman conditions. Musical instruments had been flung at random – trumpets and drums and violins thrown in every direction, the broken bow of a violin tossed in a corner.

None of the musicians had any need for their instruments. They all were on the march, where there was not any attempt at pretense. The death march was not accompanied by the tuneful melodies of musicians, nor even by dirges. The crack of gunshots putting an end to the lives of the weak and the stumbling were the only sounds to reach the ears of the wretched marchers.

Ruvke's heart ached as he looked around. Here was the bunk of the trumpeter, and here the drummer had slept and here the saxophonist, but there was no need to go on, for he had a most important, urgent, task to do there in that barracks. With mounting excitement, and knowing exactly where he needed to search, Ruvke bent down to look under his bunk. His hand trembled as he drew out his violin case. Nobody had found it, neither the fleeing murderers nor the incoming conquerors. For the time being, a musical instrument was of no interest to anyone. Ruvke could hardly believe that his precious violin was once again in his possession. He grasped it tenderly with both hands, and held it close to his chest, closing his eyes and with a feeling of an ecstasy. It was as if a pet puppy had disappeared, and after a long time was suddenly discovered hiding under the bed and, when he jumped up to his owner, wagging his tail, his owner felt a rush of joy.

With his violin in his hand, Ruvke then set out in the direction of the women's barracks where his mother had spent her miserable time.

On his way, he looked into one of the abandoned barracks which still gave the impression that it still contained a semblance of life. Indeed, here and there, he saw people wandering about, still in a kind of daze – survivors of the horrors, the deprivation, the inhumanity – looking like ghosts; skeletons, somehow held together by a thin covering of skin tightly stretched over their bones, their eyes staring out of their skulls.

Even the Russian soldiers took no notice of him. Ruvke then understood that the gate of the camp was wide open and the few former inmates who were left in the camp, those human scarecrows he had seen, were trying to plod their way in the direction of a free life, towards freedom. Their lives were no longer embittered by a kapo. They were not plagued by hunger or exposed to the cold in thin clothing, There was no more backbreaking work, and no more selections to the gas chamber. Even if they did not have enough strength to get up and dance for joy to celebrate the end of the terrible suffering they had endured, their hearts felt the lightness of liberation, and they came and went through the open gate of the camp as they wished, and felt like a narcissus opening its petals in the first warmth of spring after being buried in the earth for the duration of a cold, hard winter.

Ruvke went into the women's barracks and walked around, but he saw only a few skinny women, their faces pale as a sheet, who could scarcely drag themselves even a few meters. His mother was not there. Desperate, he walked in the direction of a barracks some distance away which had formerly served as SS headquarters. It turned out that the Soviet Army which had liberated the camp was using it as their headquarters, and Russian soldiers were seen coming in and going out, each one intent on his own work. Nobody prevented Ruvke from going into the huge office, and he walked up to the officer sitting behind a large desk. Without any preamble, Ruvke said, I am looking for my mother. She stayed in the camp. She was not with the prisoners the Germans forced out of here to go on the march before they fled. Perhaps you know where she is, her name is Gittel Kirgelik. I am her son, please help me find her.

The officer shrugged his shoulders as if to say, I have no idea where she is, and pointed in the direction of the uniformed official, an older man, who was going through the documents on the far side of the room, saying, ask Sergei, he looks after whoever is still in the camp.

Ruvke could not have had the inkling of an idea that this Sergei would know his name when he told him his mother's name. I know a lot about you. I see you found your violin, said Sergei with a smile, and put down the papers he had been holding. Yes, your mother is here in the camp. Come, I will take you to her. And so, without another word, and marveling at the turn of events, Ruvke followed Sergei to one of the barracks of the camp staff, or, to be more precise, to the most distant barracks that served as the staff quarters, which was in by far the best condition, after the Germans had run off in haste. When they went inside, Ruvke found his mother dozing in an armchair.

He could hardly believe his eyes. At best he had expected to find his mother lying helpless, weak and ill, on her bunk in her old barracks, bereft of all hope, but here she was, looking as if she had recovered from her long ordeal and regained her health. Sergei had taken care to bring her nourishing food to repair the ravages of hunger and put flesh on her bones, and now, considering all she had been through, she looked relaxed and well, confident in herself and whatever the future would bring.

While his mother was still rubbing the sleep from her eyes, Ruvke had a moment to think, and looked around him. The room seemed strangely familiar to him. A flash of awareness rising with the speed of a rocket through the folds of his memory reminded him that he had, in fact, been in this room once before! He had stood exactly where he was standing now! This was the barracks where the compassionate Nazi officer, Gregor Wolfgang, had lived! This was Gregor's barracks! Good grief, I wonder what happened to him, thought Ruvke, with some emotion. If he really was sent to fight on the Russian front, as he wanted, it is doubtful if he is still alive. But it is also possible that he might have been taken prisoner by the Russians.

Ruvke was shaken out of his reflections by the voice of his mother, who on opening her eyes and seeing him standing there, was overcome by deep emotion, and said, Ruvke, oh, my Ruvke, is it really you here with me? Ruvke nodded to her, and bent to kiss her, delighted to see his mother in such relatively good condition. Sitting across from her, and holding her hand, he was seized with an urge to tell her about Gregor even before hearing what had happened to her since they had parted. Sergei also sat himself down next to them to hear the amazing story Ruvke began to tell them. He told them a great deal about Gregor but restrained himself from telling them about his participation in the Babi Yar massacre, as he did not want to awaken feelings of grief, mourning and hate in his mother.

Isn't it the most incredible thing, that just because I play the violin, he told them, Gregor felt he must get Mother out of that mass of people who were due to be gassed just minutes later! He saved her literally at the very last moment! Gittel, incredulous, said, haltingly, I never knew how that happened, why out of everyone I was taken out of there just before it would have been too late, and given my life back. It was a miracle. So now, at last, I know that it was thanks to my son, that somehow he made that Nazi feel compassion. I even do remember him when he came to our house in Warsaw to deport us to the ghetto and how he agreed to let you take the violin after he listen to your marvelous performance. Yes, it is unbelievable...

Sergei had not said a word, but sat in deep in thought. Now he said, that Nazi who saved your mother from being murdered – if I ever meet him in one of the prisoner-of-war camps the Russians have set up , I will repay his kindness and do everything I can to have him released from captivity.

It was not hard for Ruvke to understand that Sergei, who

had come into his mother's life as a guardian angel, would sooner or later be joining the family in Zamosc, which would thus be adding another member to its ranks.

After Ruvke and Gittel's reunion in the barracks, which Ruvke would always think of as Gregor's barracks, Ruvke spent a few days there with his mother. And then Sergei drove them in an army jeep to the house in Zamosc which had formerly belonged to the Reznik family.

✦✦✦

The small town of Belzec was liberated by the Russian Army in the summer of 1944. The death camp close to the town had already been emptied of the prisoners who had all either been put to death in the gas chambers or had been shot standing at the edge of a ditch and buried in the trenches made by tanks. The Nazi murderers had destroyed the camp in its entirety, and not one of the buildings, installations or furnaces remained standing, so that no trace was left of the existence of the camp. The last surviving Jewish forced laborers were sent to the Sobibor death camp to be murdered there, so that they could not serve as eyewitnesses to the heinous crimes carried out by the Nazis, while all the Nazi murderers themselves fled for their lives for fear of the Russian troops who were racing towards them.

One day a woman turned up at Katya and Piotr's house in Belzec. She was dressed in the ill-assorted clothes of a peasant, which hung loosely on her thin frame as if from a hanger. Her pale, lined face showed that hunger, thirst and fatigue had taken their toll of her and she stood at the entrance of the house, unable to utter a word or even to stretch her lips in a smile. Reizele had walked for much of the way there, with only an occasional ride in a truck or jeep or a farmer's cart, journeying for hours on end on dirt roads. Her strength sapped. She was on the point of collapse.

Katya had been busy in the kitchen when she heard a knock at the door. She went to see who it was, the knife she had been using to chop the meat still in her hand. She stood rooted to the spot, bewildered, trying to identify the woman whose face indeed seemed vaguely familiar to her. For some time Katya stared at the woman standing feebly in front of her, and slowly a glimmer of comprehension came to her brain. Raymonda? she asked her, softly. Are you Raymonda? The woman nodded her head in confirmation. At that moment, when Katya recognized her, she felt she would burst with fear, emotion, and exhaustion, like a cork popping out of a bottle of champagne. She could not stay on her feet any longer and dragged herself to the armchair in the entrance and collapsed on it in a dead faint.

After some time, she woke up and was still blinking in the light when she saw Yuzhi, bending over her. Mother, mother, he whispered, as if he was afraid that he might wake her from sleep. Mother, mother, the words rang in her ears like an insistent melody, and, smiling widely, she stretched out her arms to him and enclosed her little boy in them, hugging his body close to her chest with joy and relief.

I have come back to you, my darling, Feel me, pinch me. It is me, it is really me. She whispered in his ear, I've come back to take you away from here, with me.

Katya saw the emotional reunion between mother and son, and knew immediately the course events would take even before Reizele had spoken. Her instincts told her that Reizele had not come back simply to stay on with them in their house. Because Katya was the kindest and most good-hearted woman imaginable, she reconciled herself at once to the bitter new reality she had to face. All her illusions about adopting Yuzhi as her son were shattered. She knew in that moment that she would never have a son.

Katya went into the kitchen to get some food and drink ready for their lunch. Piotr arrived home to eat, and his joy knew no bounds when he set eyes on Reizele, who they had been sure there was no hope of seeing ever again.

They all sat down to eat together, and Reizele waited until Yuzhi had got up from the table and went to play. She told them as best she could everything that had happened to her from the moment she had arrived at the railway station in Lublin on her way to stay with their relatives in the town. Katya and Piotr listened with genuine sadness to what had happened, but they could hardly believe their ears when Reizele said: I am sure that if your neighbor Mrs. Ohlenburg had not informed on me and caused me to be sent to the hell of the Majdanek death camp, I and Yuzhi would have been living here with you for a long time. Who knows? Although I want you to know that I am as sure as I can be, that your neighbor, that friend of yours, caused me to suffer agonies which I will never forget. I think that the disappearing of a mother from her child, like what happened to me – completely, unexpectedly, and without any warning, for so many months, has probably harmed Yuzhi emotionally for ever. Because of that, because of her, I must take my son away from here. I cannot think of living next door to that poisonous informer for even one single day. As far as you two are concerned, I will never be able to thank you enough for everything you have done for me and Yuzhi. You saved our lives, and I'll never, ever forget you, dearest Katya and Piotr.

The couple was astonished to hear Reizele's accusation of their neighbor's part in her being sent to the Majdanek camp. Reizele got up from the table and went down to the cellar and packed her and her son's belongings. Katya followed her, her face still white from the shock she had received. She did not see Reizele draw out from the box she had hidden in the dresser next to Yuzhi's bed the jewelry and money she had secreted away before she had set out on the journey which had led her to that hell. These might now be of use to her in the next stage of her life. Reizele said nothing about the person she had fallen in love with, whom she had first seen in the death camp. She said merely that she had decided to go to Zamosc, where she had been born and had grown up and would ask there if she could be given a room to live in her parents' house, which no doubt was occupied now by a Polish family which had either taken it over themselves, or had received it – legally – at the hands of the authorities.

Holding her bundle of belongings in her hand, Reizele was ready to leave the house with her son, when Katya suddenly stood in front of her, barred her way and said with some determination: Just a minute, Reizele, I cannot let you leave before I am quite sure that what you told us about Mrs. Ohlenburg is true. I need to see how she reacts when she comes face to face with you, and hear what she says about your allegation that she informed on you to the Gestapo. Even if she denies it, I'll be able to judge if she really did that terrible thing or if you're mistaken. It is impossible to leave such a thing hanging in the air without knowing if it is true or not. I'm going to get her. Wait till I come back.

Katya rushed out, and knocked on the door of her neighbor and said to her come to me, I've got a surprise for you. A few minutes later, Katya returned, and they all stood in a tense silence waiting for Mrs. Ohlenburg to step inside the house. With a smile of anticipation on her face, wondering what surprise Katya had in store for her, for surprises from friends brightened up one's humdrum everyday life, Mrs. Ohlenburg could hardly contain her excitement to see what surprise her good neighbors the Polskis, had for her. However, her smile froze on her lips immediately when she saw the figure of a woman standing in the middle of the room, whose accusing eyes were fixed on her with revulsion. Mrs. Ohlenburg stared at the woman in disbelief, as if she had seen a ghost. She immediately began to choke and gasp, as if the air was too viscous to reach her lungs; her eyes bulged in their sockets, and she had to hold on to the back of the chair to steady herself while her other hand she placed over her heart as if it would burst out of her chest. Coughing and wheezing, Mrs. Ohlenburg again raised her eyes to look at Reizele, who all this time stood fixed in her place like a statue, mute, tight-lipped, while the accusatory expression on her face showed all the contempt and hostility she harbored against that dwarf-like woman, who began to mumble: Jesus Christ, you have returned! How? Thanks be to God that you have returned. I'm so sorry, you have no idea how I regretted what I did. I know it was a terrible thing to do, please forgive me, I did not sleep nights. Looking past Reizele to where Katya was standing, she began to mutter, I thought I was doing you a favor, Katyanka. I only wanted you to be able to have a child. It was only for you that I informed on her, although I really did not mean any bad to come from it. And look, thanks be to Mary, holy mother of God, you have come back safe and well. I see that nothing bad had happened to you! You just look a bit weary, but no harm has come to you.

Like a heavy stone dropping into the depths of the sea, the tearful Mrs. Ohlenburg sank down into a chair, blew her nose and dabbed at the crocodile tears which oozed from her eyes. It was all a pretense. As if casual words of apology could erase the terrible crime she had so eagerly committed. But for Reizele, Mrs. Ohlenburg's spontaneous confession was sufficient – a confession that without a doubt Mrs. Ohlenburg would regret for the rest of her life, after the consequences of making it bounced back in her face.

Reizele picked up her belongings, and took Yuzhi by the hand. On the threshold of the house, she stopped for a moment and turned to look at Mrs. Ohlenburg, who sat slumped in the armchair, subdued and defeated, and spit out just one word towards her: Scum!

Reizele started to walk out of the house and Katya ran to catch up to her. She hugged and kissed her, and stroked Yuzhi's head while whispering, At least she did not deny it.

At least we do not have to live with the feeling of did she or did she not, which would have gnawed away at us forever. We know the truth now, and I can promise you that that woman will never set foot in our house again. Here comes Piotr. He will drive you to the railway station. God be with you.

✦ ✦ ✦

It was dusk when Reizele arrived in Zamosc from Belzec. She came to the house where she had been born and spent all her childhood and youth, and knocked on the door. She wondered who would open the door in answer to her knock. Would they welcome her? Would they treat her kindly? Would they be polite to her? Or would they callously turn her away from her house?

They were polite. When they heard that she had once lived in the house, they opened the door to her without a word and signaled to her to come in. They were pleasant people, at least they seemed so on the surface; a middle-aged couple with three children running around. The children immediately began to play with Yuzhi, who was still overwhelmed by the sudden freedom which had come to him completely out of the blue. Yuzhi could not remember ever having spoken with other children! He had in effect grown up alone in the dark! Now he stood facing them, motionless, his face frozen until, little by little, a smile spread across his face. The children held out a toy dog to him, and it appealed him so much that he smiled at it. Yuzhi began to relax, to look around him, to respond to the children. The adults could not take their eyes off the children playing together. They continued to watch them for some time until they could not put off any longer the matter which Reizele had come about. It seemed to Reizele that they had no feelings of guilt or embarrassment towards her. To put it bluntly, it was obvious to her that there was no chance that her house would be returned to her. There would be no return. We are occupying this house quite legally.

Reizele quickly assured them that she had no intention of suing them for her portion of the house, even though her parents and her brothers and sisters had been forced to leave and go into the ghetto three years ago and were then sent to be murdered. No, she has no hard feelings towards them. All she wanted was to be allowed to live there for a short time. She had only recently managed to escape from a terrible death march after being thrown out of the concentration camp which the Nazis emptied of everybody still alive. I have to be here, she pleaded, to wait for my friend and his mother to come. Please let me live in part of the house. I promise not to disturb you, the war is still going on, so I just need to stay here for a short time, then I will go on my way.

This alien family, who had in effect inherited the house instead of Reizele herself, agreed that they would let her stay in the house for a time – until the war is over. They felt no compunction about their position, and were certainly not willing to forgo their rights to the house for Reizele, but they would not throw a little boy and a woman with pleading eyes into the street just before nightfall. The hostility they felt against her they repressed in the very back of their minds, closed off, as it were, behind an iron curtain.

You may stay in the servants' quarters, two-and-a-half rooms, they said to her. Reizele remembered that place where her family's servants had lived as a shabby little place, with its own separate entrance. However, in comparison with the barracks in Majdanek, it was the height of luxury to her. So she would live in the servants' quarters. It did not bother her. Her hosts put out some food and drinks for Reizele and Yuzhi, but did not seem especially interested to know anything about her. For her part, Reizele did not intend to say a word to them about what she had gone through.

Later, when Reizele lay in bed, she could give vent to the tensions which had weighed her down. She murmured to herself, thank God, she had survived and her son was now with her. She realized that she could not complain about her fate to anybody, neither to the Almighty. She did not feel the way Gittel did, who had an account to settle with God; she did not point an accusing finger at the heavens or feel paralyzing bitterness because of the injustice which had ruined her life. She determined to harden her heart, to grow a thicker skin, to do her best not to fall prey to memories, particularly those which threatened in the dead of night to disturb her hard-earned respite. She snuggled under the blanket and told herself to look on the bright side, to the future that she would be sharing with someone she loved and who loved her. At the same time, the painful realization came to her that she had no idea at all what exactly had happened to the Jews of Zamosc, and to her family in particular. Only snippets of news had reached her, apart from the fact of their annihilation, which she knew with bitter certainty to be true. She knew no more than that.

Before Reizele dropped off to sleep, she did not imagine for even a minute, that the information she sought about the fate of the Jews of Zamosc and especially about her own family, would strike her between the eyes and make her heart beat faster with the speed of an eagle and pile up like a heap of dung on the threshold of her awareness.

The next morning, Reizele asked her hosts if they could look after her son, Yuzhi, for two or three hours. Could he please play with their children's toys while they were in school? They agreed to this and, once Reizele could see that Yuzhi was quite happy with the whole new charmed world of toys to play with, she kissed him and went to have a look around the town. She was very curious to see what had changed, as if she was rediscovering her much longed-for roots. She walked slowly through the streets which had once been so familiar, and now seemed foreign to her. She was shocked to realize that all the houses that had once been lived in by

Jews were as if they had never belonged to Jews. The same was true of the shops and workplaces. Everything that had once had a Jewish stamp to it had disappeared: the familiar figures in their traditional mode of dress, the men with their beards and sidelocks, the women with their head coverings and modest clothes. All the Jewish communal institutions had disappeared, no sign of anything Jewish remained. Polish citizens had quickly taken their places after the Germans and the local townspeople had made Zamosc *Judenrein* – a town emptied of its Jews.

Reizele wandered around the streets tirelessly, and without realizing it, her legs were taking her towards Zamenhof Street, to see if the central synagogue of the town where her father served as the Rabbi all the years of her childhood and youth was as she remembered it. She expected to see the magnificent building with its sacred inscriptions over the entrance and the paintings on the walls depicting scenes from the Bible – Noah's Ark, Adam and Eve and the serpent, the illustrations of animals and surrealistic depictions of people. Reizele was extremely curious to see the synagogue, and even if she did not delude herself that she would find even one worshipper, she did indeed think she would find it in the same state as it had been before she left the town.

She was still at the corner of the street when she heard a lot of noise and commotion, and wondered where it was coming from. Reizele was shocked and disappointed to find when she neared the building, that it was no longer a synagogue, but an elementary school. It was obviously an intermission between lessons, and the children were playing and running around in the yard.

The Zamosc central synagogue had become a school. No sign remained that it had once been a most beautiful Jewish house of worship, the massive menorah was gone; there were no decorations, no Ark of the Lord. There were only bare walls in the classrooms where the pupils sat on their benches.

Reizele stood for several minutes leaning on the fence, hardly able to believe her eyes, stunned by the magnitude of the disaster, of the total eradication of every sign of Jewish worship.

It took her some time to become aware of somebody standing nearby, a gaunt man, unkempt, his hair matted, his face lined, although he was probably not more than forty. He gradually came nearer to her, with cautious steps, looking at her closely between each step, as if to be quite sure that his eyes were not deceiving him, until he mustered up the courage to ask her: Are you Reizele? Rabbi Yechiel Reznik's daughter? His voice trembled with emotion. Yes, I am, she answered, astonished to see this Jew standing in front of her. Are you from here? Were you able to hide out in Zamosc for all this time during the war? In spite of all the odds, did a Jew manage to survive here?

The man shook his head sadly. No, Reizele, there is nobody left here. There are no Jews here. A few thousand joined the Soviet Army when they cleared the town at the beginning of the war, and that is how they survived. But in the town itself, no Jew was left here, and none of them survived. I am the only one who went through every one of the seven levels of the *Gehinnom,* of Hell, and survived. I was imprisoned in Majdanek and left the camp only yesterday. I decided that the first thing I would do before trying to pick up the threads of my life would be to come back to Zamosc, to see what was left of the town I knew, and what I would just have to keep in my mind as a memory.

Reizele was so astonished to hear this, and cried: You came back from Majdanek? But I also come back from Majdanek! Didn't they force you to go on the death march? How did you manage to survive that march, and come back to Zamosc? How was it possible?

No, it wasn't like that, the man replied. If I would have gone on that march there would not have been any chance of returning here. Everybody who was forced on the march and did not die on the way to the railway station – either of exhaustion or by falling down and getting a bullet in his head – was sent to the death camps. Nobody came back from there.

You are wrong, replied Reizele, I came back! I was on that march, and I managed to escape with my friend, and both of us survived.

They were each keen to hear the other's story and Reizele, who only the day before had decided to overcome and conceal the bitter memories of the horrors she had experienced during the last years of the war, was now longing to know all the details of the terrible experiences her family had endured before they were sent to Belzec, and to hear what happened to all the others she had not seen when she had exchanged a last heartrending glance with her father that day in the town square – her brothers, her sisters, aunts, uncles, grandfather, what happened to them? Yes, he knew them all. You cannot imagine the sheer savagery, the suffering, the plunder, and more than anything, the thought that at any moment you could be killed for no reason.

The two of them walked slowly through the streets, and came to the square where the church stood. The statue of Jan Zamoyski, founder of the city, was still there – he was still astride his horse. They continued on their way into the vast square on all of whose four sides were ornate palaces and the City Hall, which towered over all the other buildings.

Let's sit down here on the bench, Reizele's companion suggested. But, looking around her, she bit her lip and shook her head, and said, no, let's go away from here, this place makes me shiver. It has came to symbolize for me everything that has been stolen from me and from every Jew in my town. Let's go and sit down there, in that garden behind the buildings, where nobody will see us.

The man, who had introduced himself to Reizele as

Zalman, followed her and they sat themselves down on a bench there. Zalman immediately began to tell Reizele all about himself.

I was a well-to-do-man, a wealthy man, even, in business. I had a large shop in the center of the town, selling clothes and shoes. I only knew your father as one of his congregants when I came to pray in his synagogue on the Sabbath and holidays. He was a dear man. I remember seeing you from time to time as a young girl, until you suddenly vanished, even before the war.

Reizele answered him apologetically. I left Zamosc the day war broke out in Poland, the first of September 1939, and went to live in Belzec. But please tell me what happened to you, and to the Jewish community in the town from that time.

Zalman was silent for quite some time, as if he had to put in order his chaotic thoughts and memories of the horrors the Jews of Zamosc had experienced, and unearth them one by one from the deepest recesses of his mind: You cannot imagine how lucky you were to have left Zamosc on that ominous day of all days, and to have gone to live in a town where there were no Jews. Only a week after you left, Zamosc was bombed and 500 people were killed. A week after that, the Germans occupied the town, and immediately issued orders that Jews were forbidden to drive a vehicle, and that they were not allowed to leave Zamosc! So we were all trapped. After only two weeks in the town, they suddenly upped and left and the Russians came and took over, just as the pact they had signed provided for.

But the Russians were here only for one week, and then they left. By that time a few thousand Jews from Zamosc joined them and left the town with them. That was a brave and wise move on their part, because they saved themselves from the terrible tragedy which happened to all the Jews who were left in the town.

What happened to the Jews who remained? Reizele asked him with growing anxiety.

At the beginning, Zalman answered her, they managed to find somewhere to hide. In the week between the Russians leaving and the Germans returning, there was a kind of vacuum. The Jews were afraid of the local Poles terrorizing them, beating them up, robbing and cursing every Jew they came across. When the Germans came back to the town, they put themselves up in government buildings, and immediately began to snatch Jews off the streets for forced labor. They turned us into their servants before we became their slaves. To start off with, we cleaned their rooms, their cars, and other menial, degrading work. We were too afraid to open our shops, and stayed in our houses, but the Germans issued an order that we had to open the shops, and if someone did not obey it, that would be an indication that he had left Zamosc with the Russians, so his shop would be impounded and broken into. That is exactly what they did. They broke into shops which stayed closed, and confiscated all the goods. I opened my shop, and hoped that would prove that I was still in the town and they would not touch the shop, but that was just a fraud, because one day the Gestapo broke into my shop and seized all the contents. In just one day, they robbed me of everything I had in the shop. That is what they did to all the Jewish merchants in the town. I was lucky that I had some money and valuables put aside, so I was not left without anything. I also had enough money so that I could bribe those greedy Nazis, when it was still possible to bribe them. In fact, all the time the Jews would bribe the Germans as long as their money held out, although money only delayed the Nazis for a short time from carrying out their evil intentions.

To help them seize businesses and property, and collect money and goods from the Jews, and then send them on forced labor, and later to their deaths, the Germans set up the Judenrat. Right from the day the Judenrat was set up, the Germans demanded that they recruit 250 Jews for forced labor. At the same time, they demanded blood money, that is, huge amounts of gold and all kinds of supplies, so they would let the Jews get an exemption from this decree or other. Even so, new decrees fell on our heads like rain each morning. Beginning in December 1939, every Jew aged 10 or over had to wear the yellow star. That badge of shame made it easier for the Germans to catch a Jew, who would then be sent off to hard labor or be beaten.

It did not take long before they took all the Jewish men to labor camps outside the town, where they were housed in barracks overrun with fleas and bedbugs. I was one of them, and your father, the Rabbi, was also taken to the labor camp. Those bastards were completely heartless. On the measly bit of food they gave us, we had to go out every morning for hours of back-breaking work. The work manager of the camp, an SS officer, a real sadist, would walk every morning among the forced laborers and fire his pistol wherever his fancy took him and everyone who had the bad luck to be within range, would be hit and fall down. Dead. But, bad as the situation was, at least we had some consolation knowing that our families, our wives and children, were still in the security of their homes. That thought comforted us, although they were so afraid that they did not go out of the house at all during the day. Only in the evening would the women go out to draw water from the well, and go to the baker to buy some bread to eat, to stave off their hunger. But things did not stay like that for long.

In March 1941, two days after *Purim* there was a new decree, to move all the Jews who lived in the lovely old quarter of Zamosc – to Komarov, that run-down neighborhood on the outskirts of what they called the new town, where the poorest Poles lived in tiny, dilapidated houses. So all the Jews still left in the old quarter of Zamosc were forced to leave their houses, their neighborhood, everything, and move to much worse conditions.

That was how the Zamosc ghetto was established. It was actually an open ghetto, but Jews were forbidden to go out of it. However, Poles could come into it, and there were even Poles living in it, who had been there before it was set up and did not want to leave.

Naturally, we were not allowed to sit with our feet up all day. The Germans were then preparing to invade the Soviet Union, and they needed all kinds of work to be done, building airfields, paving roads, laying railway tracks, preparing hay and straw to use in barracks – and who do you think had to do all that? Only the Jews, who had all been moved into the ghetto, and the road which crossed it on both sides was crowded each morning with Jews going to work, each one with his bit of food in his hand. Women were also recruited to work.

Reizele could hardly wait to ask if her parents had been there, had her mother worked? I don't remember your mother, Zalman told her, but there were women there who had not managed to hide. They were pulled out of their houses, using the lists the Judenrat provided for the Gestapo. However, I did see your father setting out day after day with all those who had to do forced labor for the German Army. In comparison with what happened afterwards, the situation was still tolerable, but it did not take long for it to change for the worse.

The Judenrat soon had to find for the Germans not only people for forced labor. The Nazis suddenly demanded that they hand over people who would be deported from the ghetto. The Judenrat themselves had to fulfill these quotas for the Germans. What was this deportation? Where to? The rumor which went round the ghetto was that they would be deported to the Ukraine, to areas which had been captured from the Russians. Just like that, pull the wool over their eyes so that they would not be afraid to gather in the market square.

The first deportation took place on April 11, 1942, when

German-mounted police surrounded the entire ghetto and nobody was allowed to go out from it. They went into the office of the Judenrat, and gave them their orders, and members of the Judenrat went out straightaway to the Jews' houses telling them to go to the market square and assemble there. By one-thirty that day, thousands of Jews had gathered. They'd gone of their own free will, naively believing that they were being sent to the East, to Russian-occupied areas. Most of those who had come to the square were women and children, all of them dressed in their best, but men also joined them, holding their documents attesting to the vital work they were carrying out for the Germans. These documents gave them confidence that nothing bad would happen to them, for they were essential workers, but the Germans snatched the documents from their hands and tore them to shreds. Three thousand people were due to be deported that day.

They were all made to stand in the square for hours on end, until late into the evening. The hours of standing had worn them out, it was torture for them. They suffered terribly, and when at last the signal came for them to move off, they had to make rows of fives, and began to walk forward, and without any warning, the Gestapo opened fire on the convoy, and all those walking in the last rows were shot and killed. The rest of the convoy continued to walk on until they reached the railway station where a train of thirty boxcars stood. They climbed into the boxcars, with all the bloodied bodies of those murdered, and the train set off on its way, the last journey for all those crammed on to it, to Belzec. To their death.

The next morning the Jews still left in the ghetto went off to work, exactly as if nothing had happened. We all thought that the deportation the day before would save us from another one like that. We thought that we had already filled our quota of those to be deported. We were very innocent to think along those lines, it was the innocence and gullibility of victims, apparently, which made it so much easier for the whole extermination machine to be successful. Anyway, only a month went by, and on May 17, 1942, orders were posted again on the doors of the houses which stated that occupants of the ghetto – this time only the old – were to meet up in the market square before sending them out from Zamosc. Many of the adult children of the old people did not want to let their parents leave without them. Every day Jews were murdered in the streets or where they worked. It had become a matter of routine in Zamosc, and this had made them understand that their old parents would not survive for long. So that they would be spared such a terrible fate, they found all kinds of places for their parents to hide in, the way I did for my parents. However, what did the Judenrat do? They went in search of the old people whose names appeared on the list that they themselves had prepared for the Gestapo, and took those they found to the market square, and those they did not find – they took their adult children instead and put them in jail. That is what happened to me.

I refused to let my mother and father be rounded up in the market square, so they put me in jail. When they finished rounding up the old people, the Gestapo pushed them onto the train which would take them to the death camp. However, after they were already on the train, but before it had gone out of the station, the Germans were told that the carriages were needed to transport senior SS officers, and that they would have to get all the old Jews off the train. So the Nazis pulled them out of the carriages and forced them at gunpoint to cross the railway lines, and run like crazy towards the cemetery close by, all the time close on their heels, lashing out wildly. When they reached the fence of the cemetery, they began to fire at them, one by one, until they had murdered all of them.

Reizele, aghast, began to tremble and murmur, as if speaking to herself, so that's presumably how my grandparents met their deaths, shot and murdered by the fence of the cemetery.

That is why I did not see them on the transport from Belzec with my parents and brothers.

Reizele then started to tell Zalman about that same terrible day when she had seen her father and mother and three of her brothers brought like a herd of animals to the market square in Belzec and made to go on foot towards the death camp on the outskirts of the town. Zalman nodded his head slowly to confirm Reizele's assumptions, and went on to tell her the circumstances of that same horrendous transport her family had been sent on to their deaths.

Two weeks after the old people were murdered at the cemetery, two weeks in which the remaining Jews in the ghetto went out each morning to do forced labor and still hoped that there would be no more *actions*, the Gestapo once again surrounded the ghetto to round up another quota of Jews to send for extermination. But the Jews had by now learned a bitter lesson from the previous times, and hid themselves as best they could from having to make up the numbers for this *action* – and only few hundred Jews were caught in the net this time. When I was on my way to work the next morning, I was told that in the small *action* the day before, Rabbi Reznik, his wife, and some of his children were caught. Because there were not such large numbers of Jews this time, they were driven in trucks to Belzec. From what you have told me, they were taken off the trucks in the square near the church, where you saw them, and the same day were marched to the death camp.

After that *action*, Zalman continued, there were not so many Jews left in the ghetto, so it was decided to reduce the size of the area they could live in. The Jews were ordered to go to live only in buildings to the right of the road which crossed the ghetto, which meant that they were separated from the non-Jewish Poles who were still living in the ghetto area. Even after this, the Jews continued to go out of the ghetto every morning to work as forced laborers for another three months, and there were no other *actions* during that time. However, anyone who dared to show his face in a street where one of the Gestapo happened to be, would be shot and murdered, just for the fun of it, as it were.

On October 18, 1942, at five o'clock in the morning, the Gestapo again surrounded the ghetto and ordered the Jews to assemble in the market square, where police guards with a machine gun were on a freight car. The muzzle of the machine gun was trained on the Jews gathered there. Because of what had happened before the last *action*, the Gestapo did not leave it to the Jews to come of their own free will to the square, but went from house to house ordering all the inhabitants to go out of their houses and get to the point of assembly. My family and I were among them. The first thing the Germans did was to poke into the pockets of every Jew and take out anything of any value they had tried to bury there; watches, money, jewelry. At that deportation *action*, in which my family and I were among those being deported, Gestapo men from Lublin arrived to inspect all those due to be sent on the transport, such a ceremony, they even photographed two children they pulled out of the crowd there. When all the high and mighty Nazis had gone, the transport began to go on foot to Izbecia, a small town next to Zamosc, and when we got there, we saw that many Jews from the villages round about, were also crammed in there, what made Izbecia almost a Jewish town. The Nazis piled us in there as if onto a heap. We were terrified to show our faces in the street, because of the danger of being shot by an especially cruel Gestapo commander, who rode his horse through the streets and fired on any Jew who crossed his path. Just for fun.

After only three days, some soldiers appeared in the town, dressed in black, by the side of a long train of 50 boxcars to be filled by Jews who would be deported to Belzec. The Jews, including me and my family, were forced to run towards the train with the soldiers viciously driving us on. They snatched the watches from our wrists, even removing the boots from anyone wearing them. They shoved as many as could stand into the boxcars. The train then set off for the extermination camp.

I and my family were very lucky, since the boxcars were overloaded and could not take everyone who had been forced to run to the train. My family and I, with many others, were sent back to our places. But not for long, because after two weeks, more soldiers in black came with another train of tens of boxcars to transport all the Jews who had been left behind. The evacuation lasted for three straight days, because the Jews had tried to find somewhere to hide, and to get them out of their hiding places, the soldiers in black went from house to house with Polish firemen equipped with axes and water cannons. The firemen tapped the walls and floors, and when they heard a hollow echo they immediately smashed the wall or the floor with an ax, and aimed a powerful stream of water into the area. It was very effective, for immediately Jews who had been hiding there emerged with their hands up, soaked to the skin and shaking with fear. The Polish firemen sneered contemptuously at them and beat them until they saw blood coming out of their bodies, and then emptied their pockets of anything of value they had still managed to hang onto.

Then the Jews were taken to a narrow building housing a cinema, where they were held for eight days and nights without food or water, and not even allowed out to use the toilet.

When the eight days were up, the Nazis started to bring out of the cinema building groups of 30-40 men, and led them to the Izbecia Jewish cemetery, where they were all shot and killed. My family and I managed to survive all these *actions* by finding a good hideout. But then we decided that there was no point in hiding any longer. With no food or water, with such terrible suffering, we found it too hard to go on, so we came out and turned ourselves over to the enemy.

Not long after, on November 11, 1942, thousands of Jews came out of wherever they had been hiding, either of their own free will, or were dragged out by force. We were forced to run outside of the town, the Nazis surrounding us, while they were actually doing a Selection: Young men and strong men they ordered to the left, and everybody else to the right. I was one of those sent to the left, to life, but the rest of my family, my father, my mother, my wife and my daughters, all of them, all these innocent victims, were led towards the Jewish cemetery to be killed. That is how my family was taken from me. I watched them walk further and further away from me, each one clutching in his hand a heap of machine gun bullets, the ammunition the murderers used to kill them when they reached the place where they would be slaughtered. The machine gun ready to fire bullet after bullet from its wide mouth, and when all the wretched people arrived there, and the machine gun was filled with the deadly bullets those victims had been carrying, the gun started to fire, indiscriminately, and put an end to the lives of the thousands of Jews led there, murdered every single one of them, who were shoved group by group to stand in front of the machine gun. That is how I lost all my family. After all the terrible suffering we had gone through, all the effort we had made to survive, which took their toll on our bodies and souls, were for vain. I am the only one left. I stayed alive because I was good work material, so I was sent with other strong youths in that Selection to do grueling work from morning till night.

They carried on with the transports to the death camp every day for the next few days. Every day the train would be filled up with Jews who had been concentrated in Izbecia from all the towns and villages around. The trains took the Jews to Belzec and Sobibor. No one escaped from that terrible death, not even members of the Judenrat. After they had done their dirty work for the Germans, the Germans had no intention in keeping them alive, and they were also deported to their deaths. My turn came for deportation, too, and I was brought on one of the last train transports to Majdanek. I don't need to tell you the terrible conditions I suffered in the camp; the cold, the hunger, the exhausting, back-breaking work. But, as you can see, I survived. I somehow hung on with my last bit of strength until the Russians arrived and liberated the camp. And here I am now, telling one of my landsleit, a girl from my own town, all my troubles.

Reizele and Zalman sat for a long time without speaking. What each had heard from the other had left them physically and emotionally drained, and they needed time to recoup their strength, to get their breath back before they could say another word.

Tears streamed down their faces; their throats were choked with sobs. When they were a little calmer, Reizele asked, What do you plan to do now? Where are you going? I am staying for a bit with the people who took over our family's house. Do you want me to ask them if they agree to let you stay in some other part of the house? I have no idea if they will agree for me to bring another Jew there, but I can ask.

Zalman cut Reizele short. No, no, you don't need to. I am not going to stay here. I came just for a last look at the place. It is not what it was, and never will be again. Without Jews, I do not feel as if I belong to the town any more. I am leaving today for Warsaw. Against all the odds, I managed to stash away enough gold coins to keep me going until this bloody war ends. And then I am planning to go to America. One of my uncles had the good sense and the good fortune to leave Poland just before the war broke out. I am going to look for him and make a new start. So that is it.

Zalman slapped his thighs with both hands to indicate that that was the end of the meeting. Time was short, and the conversation had taken longer than he thought it would. Zalman rose, congratulated Reizele on her incredible survival from the jaws of death, and wished her success for the future.

Without another word, he turned walked away.

Reizele never saw him after that, and never heard another word from him.

✦✦✦

It happens not infrequently that someone who is on tenterhooks to hear good news, biting his fingernails down to the quick with high hopes, is then bitterly disappointed and feels as if he has gotten a slap in the face when his hopes are dashed. Fortunately, it can go in the other direction, too. You think that the worst is going to happen, and suddenly you have a stroke of unexpected good luck which lifts your spirits as high as the sky.

What Reizele was worried about at that time was if Ruvke would come to her there, in Zamosc, and if he would bring his mother, Gittel, with him, or if she would hear that Gittel had died in Majdanek of starvation, cold, exhaustion, or disease. During those tense days, Reizele tried to make the servants' rooms as comfortable as she could for whoever would join her to live there. She went to the market several times to buy groceries for her and her son, and to put some away in the store cupboard in case Ruvke would arrive with his mother, oh, please God, make it happen.

And it did! They arrived. Reizele had not identified the humming noise under her window as coming from the engine of some vehicle. The noise suddenly stopped, and she immediately heard the rattle of the door knocker on the door to the main house, and the housewife's voice telling the inquirers to go around the back to the servants' quarters. To her! And here they were!

When Reizele saw Gittel coming towards her slowly but with steady, confident steps, she was beside herself with happiness. Like mother and daughter, they fell into each other's arms, and hugged and kissed, wiping away tears of joy. Reizele could not believe her eyes. How wonderful that you are here with us, and then broke off to embrace her beloved Ruvke. He turned a little and beckoned towards a man standing near the door, and introduced him to Reizele. This is Sergei. If he had not taken care of my mother, she probably would not be here today.

Very moved, Reizele brought out some of the food she had bought that day at the market, and listened enthralled to the story of how Gittel and Sergei had met. But almost immediately, Sergei got up from the table and explained that he had to get back to the camp. He was on duty, but promised to come back as soon as possible to visit them whenever he could, and with a shy smile he added that after he was discharged from the army, he would come to live with them.

Now it was Yuzhi's turn to make his acquaintance with the man, who from that day onwards, he would regard as his father, and with the woman who, from that same day, he would call Grandmother.

A new chapter had now opened in Yuzhi's life, with additional characters in his family story, as well as his mother, Reizele; his father Ruvke, and Grandmother Gittel. But who was the man who had fathered him? In his truth, it was Mottele, who had been killed on the very day of his birth.

Many years would pass until the curtain would be lifted on Yuzhi's origins, and when the truth was finally revealed, he would be utterly astonished and shocked.

Sergei came often to visit his new family, feeling very happy whenever he was with them. He had deliberately refrained from physical intimacy with Gittel, for he would not allow himself to approach her in that way yet, as she still had not fully recovered from the ravages of the war.

However, it was already clear to each of them that the connection they had forged was so strong that nothing could break it, and as they had the rest of their lives in front of them, there was no need to rush. At this stage, what Sergei most wanted to do was to provide good, nourishing food for Gittel and her household, and he would bring them the field rations the Russian soldiers received in Majdanek, which built them up, put flesh on their skeletal bodies, and strengthened their bones and muscles. They were all content in the two-and-a-half rooms they had been allotted, Reizele and Ruvke slept in one room, and Gittel and Yuzhi in the second. It was not very spacious, but the servants' quarters of the Reznik house seemed to them enough for the time being.

In the course of the next few days, Reizele told Ruvke and Gittel what she had heard from Zalman about the terrible events which had led to the annihilation of the Jewish communities in and around Zamosc, that preciously vibrant center of Jewish life. When they went out to walk a little around the town, their steps were as slow and hesitant as if they were mourners at a funeral. The townspeople she saw in the streets, busy with their everyday concerns, she wondered, were they not aware of a certain emptiness, a lack, in the absence of the Jews from their town? And if they did, was it a heavy kind of emptiness like a shortage of breath, or a light, fresh air that now they could breathe easier? Reizele tried as hard as she could, not to give way to the profound grief she felt about the loss, the catastrophe, the terrible and total destruction of the community she had known and respected, and treasured. No, it doesn't make any difference to her now, what the *goyim* of the town feel. Deep in her heart she knew they were breathing fresh air. But maybe, in the future, they would change their attitude and understand the great loss, the evil, the injustice from that crucial, aghast long period.

As for herself, in those moments, she felt she was a victim. Victim of the life she has to endure, to live and see, day after day, the degradation and devastation, physically and mentally, of the ugly, cynical, hypocrite world surrounding her.

One day Sergei arrived out of breath and in quite an

emotional state. He asked Ruvke to get in the jeep straightaway and go with him. Ruvke did not understand a thing about any of it, but had confidence in Sergei's judgment. There is no doubt that there is something important he has to do so urgently and a good reason for him to be in such a hurry. Sergei drove fast all the way, and explained excitedly to Ruvke that he had heard that a camp for German prisoners-of-war had been set up not far away, and that last night they had brought in hundreds of German soldiers taken captive by the Russians. I don't forget for a moment the German officer who saved Gittel from certain death, and I thought it was worth driving to see the commander of the camp and check if that Wolfgang is one of the prisoners there. If he is, we must try to do something to help him. Ruvke was overcome, and thanked Sergei from the bottom of his heart for making such an effort on his behalf.

Sergei and Ruvke arrived at the camp, and went straight to the camp commander's office. They were greeted by the commander himself, Druyanov, bearing the equivalent rank to colonel, a stern expression on his face, and by his deputy. Sergei saluted formally. The commander said, hardly looking at them, hurry up, say what you want, we have not got all day. Then he raised his head in a sparkling memory, looked at them more closely, and in a second the expression on his face changed and his pursed lips broke into a wide smile. Sergei was nonplussed, for it took him a little more time to realize that he and Druyanov knew each other very well.

Druyanov got up from behind his desk, and went over to where Sergei was standing, and they hugged each other like old friends. The difference in rank between them was no barrier to the comradeship each of them felt, and after they sat down at a table at the other side of the office, drinks and sandwiches were offered.

How are you? Druyanov asked Sergei. Where you are now? What a surprise to see you here. Sergei too expressed his surprise and pleasure at their meeting, and wanted to know from his friend the commander what had been happening to him since they had last seen each other. He asked him how long he had been there and was told that only two weeks ago Druyanov was appointed to be commander of the camp, and that just the night before they brought German prisoners who had been captured by the Russians straight from the front to the camp. The two of them turned to Ruvke, amazed at the reunion he had witnessed, and began to explain to him how they knew each other. Words came fast and furious as they showered him with the details of their long acquaintanceship serving in the army, and in particular during the defense of Stalingrad.

For a long time they both told Ruvke their experiences in the battle of Stalingrad. After a short pause, Sergei could not contain his curiosity about where else the commander had served and what had happened to him since they had gone their separate ways. Ruvke realized very quickly that Druyanov was a Jew, and that he seemed really pleased to have the opportunity to reminisce about the operations and battles he had taken part in along the way, and he talked on and on for a long time before he asked Sergei the reason he came to the camp.

I served as the commander of an infantry battalion when we invaded Hungary, Druyanov said enthusiastically. After besieging Budapest for months, we broke through and conquered the city. The Germans, who had controlled Hungary before we got there, had moved out beforehand, after they had finished killing all the Jews in the country, except in Budapest itself. That stinking job they left for Szalasi, the Hungarian Prime Minister, who they had appointed, knowing they could rely on him to annihilate the Jews of the capital. You cannot possibly imagine the scenes of horror we saw when we came into Budapest after the siege ended. The river Danube was red from the blood of the Jews who had been killed just a short time before and their bodies were thrown into the river. The Danube was full of thousands of bodies, and there were branches of trees, and parts of bridges which had been destroyed and were floating on the water. All the bridges connecting the two parts of the city – Buda and Pest – had been bombed, and our army was ordered to bomb and destroy parts of the city so that we could get control of the country out of the hands of that same tyrant Szalasi, who ruled with an iron fist. Yes, he and his thugs from the National Socialist Arrow Cross Party had Hungary completely in their power. No sooner had the Germans left the country when Arrow Cross gangs, like dogs straining at the leash, started to attack Jews in the streets of Budapest and murder them. At the same time, they dragged thousands of Jews from the ghettos to the edge of the Danube and lined them up on high ramps they had built up on the river banks to stop the tides. They ordered the Jews to face the river, and those Hungarian fascist thugs then shot them in the back so that they would fall into the water, which turned red with their blood, and their corpses floated in the river for days. Someone who was there, a Hungarian, told us that he saw with his own eyes that the Arrow Cross murderous beasts, to save on ammunition, tied the Jews one to another with ropes after they were standing in rows at the edge of the river, and only fired at every third or fourth man. The ones who had gotten a bullet in the back would fall into the water, dead, dragging the others who had not been shot with them, and these others would still be alive when they went under the cold, bloody water and drowned.

    The lilting tune of Johann Strauss' Blue Danube waltz did not ring in the ears of the Nazi murderers, nor in the ears of the Hungarian murders, nor in the ears of the Russian conquerors, and certainly did not uplift the hearts of the Jews of that beautiful city, Budapest, who were murdered with unimaginable cruelty on the banks of the charming river that flowed through the center of their city. The Danube was not blue during those terrible days, but turned red from all the blood spilled into it, and from the shame of the horrendous, unforgivable crimes committed on its banks.

Ruvke, shocked by what he had heard, could not hold back from asking, But what about the Nazis in Hungary? What did they do in all this, with the Jews who lived in the cities and villages outside Budapest, in the rest of the country?

Druyanov grimaced as he replied: When the Russian Army entered Budapest after it had been besieged for 100 days, there was not a single Jew left outside the capital. They had all been sent to the Auschwitz death camp. The Germans occupied Hungary, even though Hungary had collaborated with them and fought with them against the Red Army. However, at some stage, Germany began to suspect that the Hungarians were about to enter into negotiations with the Allies, and that gave them the excuse to invade and occupy Hungary. They immediately started to get rid of all the Jews still there, and worked literally around the clock, as they knew that the Red Army would reach Hungary very soon.

Under Eichmann's leadership, they gathered all the Jews together from all over the country into overcrowded, rat-infested ghettos, without food or water. The Jews were not in the ghettos for long, only for a few weeks, and then they were brought by train to Auschwitz. As soon as they got off the train – hundreds of thousands of them – they were sent to the Birkenau extermination camp, and immediately pushed into the gas chambers. The Jews of Hungary were in Birkenau for not even the space of one day. The crematoria worked non-stop, at full capacity to burn all the bodies from the gas chambers. It took only three months, from May to July 1944, to annihilate all the Jews in Hungary who lived outside Budapest. 450,000 people, most of them women, children, the old and the sick were put to death there.

It was not that the Nazis gave up on murdering the Jews of Budapest, but they were sure that Szalasi, the new head of government they had put there, would finish the job.

The Nazis had to appoint a new head of government then, because they did not look kindly on the previous Regent, Miklos Horthy, who ordered a stop to the extermination of the Jews so that he could pave the way to making a pact with the Allies. Because of this he was deposed and replaced by the Hungarian murderer Szalasi, who finished the Nazis' dirty work, sending Arrow Cross gangs of thugs to round up and murder Jews in Budapest with unbelievable barbarity, even choosing the River Danube to be the grave of thousands.

The commander of the camp glanced at his watch and said he was astounded that the time had passed so quickly; however, he immediately resumed his story, as if he had suddenly remembered to tell them of an incident that had taken place during the German occupation of Hungary and which he had heard from one of his superior officers, a staff officer, who received in great detail all the information on the course of the German occupation. It appears, said Druyanov, that there were some Jews who survived in Budapest. In 1943, one of the leaders of the Jews in Hungary, a man called Rudolf Israel Kastner, if I'm not mistaken, set up the Aid and Rescue Committee to help the Jews after he was told about the annihilation of Jews in Europe from eyewitnesses and connections he had outside Hungary. Once this became known to him, he immediately tried to convince the Jews in Hungary to leave, to escape while they could, but they did not want to listen to him. They did not believe him. So he decided that he himself would set up a rescue operation – the Aid and Rescue Committee – and initiated meetings with the Nazi leaders who were organizing the transports of Jews to Auschwitz. Kastner even met Adolf Eichmann himself, who was at the head of the administration carrying out the extermination of the Jews of Europe, and proposed giving him a handsome ransom in exchange for allowing the Jews to be transferred to a neutral country. Eichmann considered the proposal and said that he would agree to it if he received 10,000 trucks. Are you with me? The Nazis had lost an enormous amount of their ammunition and weapons and desperately needed trucks, so they were even prepared to forgo the murder of several thousand Jews in order to get those trucks.

Blood for trucks they called the deal, and as soon as they had Eichmann's agreement in principle, Kastner's deputy, Joel Brand, set out for Istanbul to put the proposal to the British, assuming that they would support it and provide the funding. Here they had the opportunity to save Jews who would otherwise all be murdered, was what he told them. But the British Minister for Eastern Mediterranean affairs in those days, Lord Moyne, was known to be very pro-Arab and would not even meet the Jewish messenger, Brand. In fact, instead of meeting with him face to face to hear about the proposal, he ordered him to be arrested, so the matter was never discussed at all. Lord Moyne had no interest in saving Jews, and there was saying that after he'd had Brand arrested, he said to his deputy: What, I should pay a ransom to save Jews? What would I do with a million Jews? If I've got it right, it was that same Lord Moyne who paid for his anti-Jewish policy with his life. Just a few months later, two young men – Eliyahu Bet-Zuri and Eliyahu Hakim – from one of the underground movements in Palestine assassinated him. Unfortunately for them, they were caught, sentenced to death, and hanged.

Druyanov paused for a little, and then went on to tell them the sequel to this episode after Lord Moyne's outright rejection of Brand's proposal. In the end, following long drawn-out negotiations between Kastner and Eichmann and after a large amount of money had been paid to the Nazis, most of which was collected from wealthy Jews in Budapest who had been promised a place on the rescue train, the train did in fact leave Budapest in July with 1,684 Jews on board, among them several members of Kastner's family, and children and young people. If my memory is correct, the train did not go straight to Switzerland, as the Nazis had promised, but stopped at the Bergen-Belsen concentration camp. Only after more negotiations there, when the leaders of the Jewish community had to hand over more money to the Nazis, were the Jews allowed to continue on to Switzerland from the camp, some in August, but most in December, and eventually they all arrived in Palestine-Eretz Yisrael.

Sergei glanced at his watch and said that he would love to hear about all the battles Druyanov took part in during the war, but unfortunately time was getting short, and they would soon have to be on their way. Only then did the commander remember that he had not yet asked them why they had come to the camp. So what brought you here? Sergei explained to him that they had come to look for one of the German prisoners-of-war, that is, if he was in fact in that camp. I would be grateful if you let me look for him and if he is here, I want to ask you to do everything you can to improve the conditions of his imprisonment and, if it is at all possible, to release him. Sergei told him briefly how that German officer had saved the life of Ruvke's mother, who he had gotten to know in Majdanek and with whom he intended spending the rest of his life.

Druyanov gave them a free hand to go looking among the hundreds of prisoners who had arrived in the camp for the German prisoner who had saved the life of a Jew, who had refused to continue to serve as an SS officer in the death camp, preferring to be sent to face danger and death on the Russian front, from which indeed few returned alive. First of all find him, then we will see what we can do for him, said Druyanov.

Sergei and Ruvke, accompanied by the deputy commander, were determined to do everything in their power to find Gregor, and went doggedly up and down rows of prisoners sitting on the bare ground where here and there heaps of snow were scattered along. The prisoners, their uniforms dirty and tattered, their eyes lifeless, appeared shamefaced and depressed. It was hard to imagine that these same miserable officers and ranks had only a short time ago proudly given each other the Nazi salute, Heil! while clicking the heels of their polished boots as they did the goose step.

Ruvke and Sergei continued to search up and down, up and down, for a long time, until Ruvke suddenly spotted Gregor, sitting on the ground, pale as a ghost, his head bowed in humiliation, his uniform stained with mud and dirt, his stripes dull and discolored on his shoulders. Yet, even with these radical changes in Gregor's bearing and appearance since the last time they had met, Ruvke had no doubt that it was he.

When Gregor noticed Ruvke looking for him, his eyes lit up with a spark of joy, of hope, of thanks, and Ruvke pointed to him and said to the deputy commander, this is the man. Tentatively, Gregor got up from the ground and stood facing Ruvke, moved and incredulous. They stared at each other, a bemused smile on each of their faces, neither able to find the words to express their amazement at meeting here, of all places. They stood without moving, overcome with emotion, until an overwhelming impulse led each to hold out his arms to the other and they hugged each other with great emotion, speechless. It was a hug of thankfulness, such a warm hug they could have been brothers meeting after a long period of separation.

Gregor was the first to find his voice after he had calmed down a little. Astonished, he asked, How did you find me? Ruvke answered him only: Do you remember that I said to you when we met in your barracks at Majdanek that I hoped that one day I would be able to repay you for the good turn you did for me? For saving my mother? I am sure you never thought it might happen. But here I am. I remember what you did then, and came to find you, and recommend to the authorities that they give you better conditions of imprisonment, and if possible even release you. Gregor was at a loss for words with excitement, and just managed to stammer, it is unbelievable, unbelievable.

Ruvke then introduced him to Sergei, who told Gregor to follow him. The commander of the prisoner-of-war camp was very doubtful that it was in his power to release a prisoner just then. What's more, Druyanov said, there is nowhere to release him to. Where would that German officer go? He cannot go back to his unit, because it was disbanded, they were defeated, and most of the soldiers were killed. Go back to his country, to Germany? The Allies have now invaded the continent of Europe and are bombing Berlin day and night. It is just one mass of ruins, who knows if his house is even standing! But I can promise you that I will do everything I can to make things easier for him and to release him as soon as it is allowed.

Ruvke and Gregor parted from another the best of friends. Gregor was so moved by seeing Ruvke again and being assured of his help that he had no words to thank him for all his efforts on his behalf. He just expressed his hope that one day they would meet again. Give me a pen and paper and I will write down for you my address in Berlin, Gregor said, and in a neat hand did as he said. Ruvke folded the piece of paper, put it in his pocket, and patted it affectionately as if he had received a precious gift.

Sergei and Ruvke returned to Zamosc in good spirits, feeling that they had discharged an extremely important moral obligation. While they were all sitting around the table at dinner, they told Gittel and Reizele about everything that had happened on that emotion-filled afternoon at the prisoner-of-war camp.

Before he went to bed, Ruvke took the piece of paper with Gregor's address in Berlin out of his pocket, and put it between the pages of his notebook, a safe place, ready for the day when he could make use of it.

# 12
# Rape In Italy

Anshel, in his assumed identity as Milush Grybacz, a Polish Christian, was very proud that he had continued to serve in the Anders Army and had not been tempted, like many others, to desert ranks and stay in Palestine as an illegal immigrant. Anshel knew the consequences of desertion, as did all the Jewish soldiers who chose to desert the Anders Army and stay in Palestine. They were aware that they would be giving up their personal freedom, and that they would be in constant fear and hunted down by their pursuers – the British soldiers – so they would have to hide themselves away in very uncomfortable conditions for a long time.

The Polish commander at the head of the Anders Army turned a blind eye to their desertion, partly because he was glad to get rid of the Jewish soldiers in the Anders Army, but also because he realized that it was quite natural for Jews to want to stay in Palestine, as they considered it their homeland. Thus the Poles were not the cause of their hiding themselves away.

It was the policy of the Mandatory Government regarding desertion from a foreign army as a severe crime, since these deserters were illegal immigrants whose presence in the country used up places in the quota of immigrants which the British were prepared to absorb. According to the British White Paper of 1939, there was no room for flexibility. From the British point of view, these deserters had to be deported. Where to? That was of no concern to them.

So, stern measures were therefore taken to find these deserters, and British soldiers would carry out spot searches in places they suspected the deserters to be hiding, probing anywhere and everywhere; great efforts were indeed invested in these vigorous searches. The loyal soldiers of the King did not leave a stone unturned in their quest to find these deserters at all cost. They hunted them down in villages and towns, in kibbutzim such as Ein HaKovesh and Hulda, where deserters had in fact found a place to hide and the kibbutz members hid them and sheltered them and defended them with all their might. The kibbutzniks would not give their friends away and would not let this biased, pro-Arab Mandatory Government, discover their whereabouts so that they could deport them.

When the British failed to find the deserters of the Anders Army, their response was simply to reduce the equivalent numbers of certificates allotted to aspiring new Jewish immigrants.

Anshel did not desert. Not so much because of his loyalty to the foreign army in which he was serving, but more for a sense of adventure that was opening up to him, of being present at a crucial moment in history and participating in a strategically critical battle at this stage of the World War, whose aim was to defeat a cruel enemy, that for him this ruthless enemy had not only conquered the country of his birth and exiled him from it forever, as well as threatening to destroy the whole world, but had exterminated his people, the Jewish people, in the most barbaric ways imaginable.

So certainly he did not want to miss the chance to contribute even in a small way to the defeat of this enemy. Therefore he continued to serve with the soldiers in the Anders Army, which made up part of the British Forces, and after a short time they were sent to play their part in the fierce battle which was taking place to capture Monte Cassino, in Italy.

Monte Cassino. For many months the Allied Forces had been trying to take the historic church and monastery situated high on a peak overlooking the small town of Cassino, on the coast between Rome and Naples. Monte Cassino had first been taken by the Nazis, when, following the defeat of Mussolini and his surrender to the Allies in 1944, the Germans broke through to the north of Italy.

Monte Cassino was a strategic vantage point of the highest importance, in regard both to artillery and air battles, and the mountain itself, with its monastery and the jagged terrain surrounding it, made it a grueling challenge to capture. The Allied Forces decided to invade Italy from Sicily, which they had taken after they had defeated the Germans in the North African campaign; however, because of the complexity involved in breaking through the almost impenetrable fortifications of the Germans and reach the mountain top, they were forced to withdraw again and again.

Only after the Anders Army arrived with the British Forces, under the courageous and inspired leadership of General Anders, the hilltop was conquered in March 1944, together with the church and the monastery, which were regarded as a legitimate target for capture, in spite of its immunity as a holy and historic site.

Monte Cassino was conquered, and the Anders Army waited to advance to Northern Italy with the aim of taking the city of Bologna and freeing it from its Nazi occupiers. However, Anshel now began to have doubts as to whether he really wanted to continue with his unit to the next objective. After the tough battle of Monte Cassino, which he had miraculously survived, uninjured, he was physically and emotionally drained of energy. Suddenly he found himself unable to keep pace with the soldiers in his unit. With his rucksack on his back, his gun tucked into his shoulder tab, he blocked out off his mind the moral question of whether it was or was not the right thing to do, and decided to stay.

Anyhow, with all the chaos and pandemonium around him, no one would notice his absence and no one would care: A huge number of soldiers had fallen or been injured in that battle and Anshel had buried the corpses and rescued the wounded, but now that the battle and its aftermath were over, he felt so traumatized and exhausted that he had no energy to take part in another battle.

There were 850 Jewish soldiers who fought with the Anders Army at Monte Cassino, and 126 officers. There were 22 Jewish soldiers killed in the battle, and 62 were injured. 126 of the Jewish fighters received awards of valor from General Anders himself, who declared at the end of the war that, from the time when the Jewish soldiers left the ranks of the army in the Eastern Mediterranean campaign, they fought so heroically on the battlefield and also excelled at whatever they did.

Anshel viewed himself as a Jewish soldier fighting with the Anders Army, despite the fact that on his official identity papers he was registered as a Christian. But now he realized he had to take some time to recover from the distressing physical and psychological exhaustion he felt overwhelmed by.

Anshel knew that the French Army stood at the ready to break through the German line of defense in the South Lazio region, capture the German military batteries, break through beyond the military batteries of the allies, and thus open the path to the center and north of Italy so as to enable the Allied Forces to conquer the whole of Italy. Slowly, the seeds of a decision began to sprout in Anshel's brain. He would stay in this region, where there were many villages and peasants working the fields, simple farming people. He would live quietly for a time here in the hills, surrounded by nature. And so Anshel turned his back on his unit and walked on his own for several hours along a footpath in the hills until he came to one of the villages, whose breathtaking views and the pastoral peace and quiet aroused in him a strong desire to stay there. He walked to and fro along the lanes, and passed by the church which stood in the middle of the square. Anshel carried on walking until he came to the edge of the village where there was a substantial house set in a large courtyard with several small cottages scattered around it. The house was set apart from the rest of the houses in the village, and this gave Anshel a sense of security; he felt that this was where he would like to settle for now. Wondering whether the landlords would turn him away, he knocked on the door and asked if he could sleep there. He thanked his lucky stars that he had managed to save some money, from his army pay, for just such a contingency, for now he could allow himself to rent a place to sleep and perhaps even enjoy a hot meal once a day.

The door was opened to him and the Cachumare family, that later on Anshel found out consisted of an older couple and their two daughters, one called Nadia, who was married with three children running around her. Her husband had been drafted into the army and so was not at home. The other, the younger daughter, Silvana, who looked about twenty-five, and was unmarried, with the fleshy lips and impressively large breasts of a country girl that from the first moment Anshel felt her eyes wandering all over his body, measuring him up with lusting eyes.

The Cachumare family were at first somewhat suspicious of Anshel. But, after they had heard his request for a place to sleep, and a hot meal, for payment of course, and after they had looked him up and down from every possible angle and come to the conclusion that he posed no danger to them, they willingly agreed to let him have one of the small cottages near their house. The cottage was in a rather neglected spot, but certainly made adequate temporary housing. There was a wide bed with a straw mattress, a sheet and blanket, a table and chair, and a bowl for washing with a full jug of water next to it. Apparently, the gun tucked into his shoulder tab had made a favorable impression on the family, giving them the confidence of being protected, and Anshel was relieved to be accepted by them. He stepped into the large house, which was evidence of the comparatively good situation the household was in, and saw several full sacks of basic foodstuffs standing in the corners of the room, which had been filled and stored well in advance for the time when there would be a shortage of everyday commodities. That time had already come and was felt in their day-to-day lives, for shortages were being felt more and more with each day that passed.

After Anshel had something to eat and drink, and had a wash, all he wanted to do was to stay there alone, and relax for ever in the calm of the countryside.

Anshel could already understand and speak basic Italian, and he listened willingly to the babbling members of the household as they chattered about the way the war was going and told him how worried they were about the alarming state their country was in, for the Americans were in control in the south and the Germans in the north. What did they know? They were simple, ignorant people, most of them totally uneducated, plain farmers, but Anshel enjoyed their company, and they related to him as if he were the prodigal son returned home.

The only help Anshel could offer them was to reassure them, in light of the threat of the Allied Forces' invasion onto their land, and to try to make them understand that this invasion would be an important step towards bringing the war to an end. Anshel realized that the capture of Monte Cassino was only one stage in making a breakthrough for the Allies to enter the Boot, for they would still have to destroy other military batteries and fortifications which the Germans had built in order to block the advance of the Allied Forces in Italy. It will take another battle in this area, and then we will be sure of victory, Anshel reassured them confidently. You do not need to panic too much when you hear airplanes or see bombs dropping. There is nothing we can do about it, after all, we are at war, you and I, but it will be over soon and everything will be back to what it was before. Neither Anshel nor these naïve villagers could have forecast in their wildest nightmares the atrocities which would take place in their own homes, within only a few days.

Not far away, in his role as Allied Commander in Italy, General Mark Clark proposed the idea that soldiers from the Moroccan Goumiers who had served under his command in the French Army, and were experienced in fighting in mountainous terrain, would be the ones chosen to penetrate the fortifications the Germans had built on the Gustav Line to stop the Allies from reaching central Italy and the north. According to the same plan, Moroccan soldiers would also capture the Fiato and Maio military batteries, break through the Mossoni batteries, and thus open up the way to the center of Italy and the north. It was a highly difficult mission to achieve, and in order to motivate the Moroccans soldiers and encourage them to give it everything they had, the Commander of the French Army guaranteed the Moroccan expeditionary force, inducements and benefits that they had not imagined even in their wildest dreams. This commander promised them that everything would be theirs for the taking. They could do what they wanted with everything in the area they captured – both human beings and property of all kinds. If you succeed, he told them, you will get everything you want. After you win, you can go anywhere in the area you have secured for us; you can have all the Italian women in the villages. You will have a free hand to do whatever you like with them; you can take their houses and everything you can fill your hands with; drink their fine wines – for three whole days! For seventy-two hours you will be lords and masters over everything that comes your way, and afterwards none of you will be punished or have to give an account of what you have done.

Those soldiers from the Moroccan Expeditionary Force – what did they feel to hear those promises, which were intended to spur them on to success? What could those strong-bodied, fierce fighters but quite feeble minded, think the Commander had in mind, if not to ensure that their hearts and bodies would build up massive amounts of adrenaline which they would release by fighting like lions, with every ounce of strength they had. Some would call that boldness and bravery, and within two days they broke through the Gustav Line, slaughtered all the German troops who had defended those fortifications, and broken through to secure the much-needed route so that the Allied Forces would be able to advance to the center and the north of Italy and free those areas from Nazi occupiers.

And then began the horror. The Moroccan soldiers of the Expeditionary Force brought victory, and now they demanded the reward promised by the French Army, that made good its promise to them, in full. As soon as the successful campaign was over, the Moroccan soldiers were driven in trucks belonging to the French Army to the villages in the area, which they had by their own efforts captured, and uninhibitedly took for themselves the rotten fruits of war which had been promised to them before they went into battle: Rape, plunder, slaughter.

The members of the Cachumare household, like all the villagers in their region, went to bed as soon as it was dark after a day of strenuous physical work. That evening, they made their usual preparations before going to sleep for the night, when they suddenly heard from not far away the sounds of cries; women shrieking, children wailing, men bellowing, and gunshots. Anshel was still sitting with the family after they had all eaten a simple but tasty supper, and he knew that these sounds boded ill.

The shouts seemed to be coming closer, and he went outside to try to see what was causing all the noise. He was astounded to see Moroccan soldiers jumping down from the trucks which had brought them straight from the battlefield to the villages. Dirty and sweaty, their eyes gleaming with a fiendish leer, their faces blackened, with guns in their hands, group by group they burst into the houses, and here they were, coming closer and closer to the Cachumare's house, which fortunately stood at the very edge of the village. Anshel had immediately grasped what was happening when he went outside, and ran as fast as he could to his cottage to take his gun to threaten the two Moroccan soldiers who were fast approaching the house. However, while Anshel was still searching for his gun in the dark cottage, he heard the women, Nadia, Silvana, and their mother, screaming. Rushing out of his cottage holding his gun, he saw Silvana running towards him in panic, fleeing one of the Moroccans who was hot on her heels, but who was, luckily for them, unarmed, for he had left his gun propped up against the door of the house in his haste to get his hands on a woman.

When Anshel saw what was happening, he did not hesitate, but shouted to the soldier to stop while pointing his gun at him. The soldier did in fact stop in his tracks, instantly realizing the danger he was in from the cocked gun. Made an about-turn, and began to retrace his steps. Anshel almost let him get away, but suddenly saw that the soldier intended to return to the Cachumare house in order to find another victim to rape. Anshel cocked his gun but, so as not to shoot a man in the back, called out to him in pidgin French, ola monsieur, and the soldier instinctively turned his head towards him, and the next second, Anshel pointed his gun at him and shot him in the head. The soldier slumped towards the ground, drenched in blood. Only then could Anshel turn his attention to Silvana, who was trembling with fear, and bring her into his cottage. He sat her down on the only chair and told her to wait for him until he got back.

Silvana stayed in the cottage, and Anshel ran off to the house to rescue the other women, the mother and the elder sister, Nadia, from the ravages of the other soldier.

The second he arrived at the house, he saw the Moroccan

about to lie himself down on Nadia, who he had forcibly laid on the floor, pushing her dress up over her thighs while snarling and grunting and baring his rotten teeth at her. Nadia was trying to kick him and get him off her, screaming Mama, Mama, but of course to no avail. The soldier pinned her to the floor so that she could not move her arms, her mother and father and her children were all standing horrified seeing all this and screaming, but were powerless to do anything to help her. While the struggle was going on, and the Moroccan soldier had almost succeeded in achieving his aim, Anshel thundered at him to stop, and pointed the barrel of his gun at the rapist. The soldier, who did not want to give up his prey, raised himself up from the body of the woman pinned under him, and tried to grab his gun, which was lying on the floor a short distance from him.

But Anshel was too quick for him, and kicked the gun out of reach of the rapist. When the soldier saw that he had no chance of gaining his end, and to spare himself from being shot at by the gun directed at him, he got to his feet and ran out of the house while zipping up his trousers and, in his haste, leaving his own gun behind him there.

He consoled himself with the hope that there were plenty of other fish in the sea, many more women there in the village he could easily rape, whose husbands were not at home to stop him. After all, they could do what they wanted in that region, the Moroccan Expeditionary Force had been promised that they could rape and plunder to their heart's desire.

Thanks to Anshel, the Cachumare family had been saved, but powerful shockwaves were felt in all the villages of the region. Like swarms of wasps, the Moroccan soldiers spread out over all the villages in the area, bursting into houses and forcing themselves on every woman between the ages of 12 and 80 who was unfortunate enough to be there. They would lay them down by force, rip and choke and beat and rape, and if their husbands or brothers or husbands came to rescue the women and girls from their stranglehold, they would shoot them and kill them, to get the men out of their way and let them do whatever they wished.

Between April and June 1944 on the Laccio Line in Italy, 2000 girls and women of all ages were raped; 800 men were murdered trying to defend their wives, daughters, and sisters. For three days and three nights, acts of rape and murder did not cease, and during this time scenes which could have come straight out of Dante's Inferno took place, where lust, gluttony, avarice, violence and treachery reigned. The Moroccan soldiers stole from the villages 80% of their produce, 90% of their animals, and naturally they ransacked the houses and went through wardrobes and drawers and hiding places for valuables, and robbed the inhabitants of their jewelry, clothes and money. And all of this was with the knowledge and collusion of their French commanders, who turned a blind eye to the chilling crimes carried out by the Moroccan soldiers.

After the rapists and murderers had left the villages, it turned out that almost all of the women who had been raped had been infected with gonorrhea and syphilis, and only a short time after that they infected their husbands. A tragic epilogue was that in the months to come, many of the women and girls gave birth to unwanted children, a large proportion of them deformed.

And then the outcry erupted, an outcry of the raped and the plundered, and immediately the French acknowledged their responsibility for these atrocities, and compensated the victims, the women and girls who had been raped – who were afterwards known as Moroccaniata – with between $12,000 and $17,000 each. In addition, the brutish soldiers were put on trial, and many of them were sentenced to death while their French commanders were not punished and got away with this appalling affair without a stain on their characters.

After that terrible incident, Anshel decided that he could not stay in that place any longer. The open wound that the Cachumare family in particular, and the village in general, had suffered was too deep, and Anshel could not see himself living there and sharing the burden of their constant pain. It was enough that he had been able to help them and rescue them, but he could not stay there impotently and predict the consequences of that terrible invasion of their village by the barbaric Moroccan soldiers. And if that were not enough, he had an urgent personal reason to get away from the place, something which happened on that horrendous, unforgettable evening, something connected with Silvana, who had been waiting for him in his cottage while catastrophic events were taking place only a stone's throw from her place of safety.

Anshel returned to his cottage tired out and taut with tension after he turned the two Moroccan rapists out of the family's house, one of whom he had killed and the second had bolted. Seemingly, the rumor spread like wildfire that an armed man was in the house, and that stopped other soldiers from trying to burst in there. Anyhow, Anshel was sure that Silvana was sitting on the chair, as he had told her to do, waiting for him to return so that she could go back home once all was quiet there. Anshel came in to his cottage, took off his sweater and undershirt, and by the light of his torch washed his face and arms with water from the bowl. He was just drying his face when he noticed that there was a naked woman lying, her legs parted, on his bed.

Thanks be to the Holy Mother that you've come back. I was worried about you, whispered Silvana longingly to him, and Anshel found himself faced with a situation that he had never been in. Silvana, what do you think you're doing? Get yourself dressed straightaway, and go back home; you cannot stay here, he stammered in shock. The sight of a naked woman was a new and strange experience for him, but Silvana's response was to hold out her hand to him invitingly and whisper, Come, sleep next to me. I'm afraid to go out of here. I feel safer with you. Come and lie down next to me.

Conflicting emotions began to struggle in Anshel's head and heart. His head ordered him to send the woman who had invaded his bed away, by force if necessary. However, his heart and all his senses yearned for the sight of the nakedness of a sensuous woman who desired his nearness and, as in a wrestling match where there can only be one winner, Anshel's heart won over his head. While at first he had felt a strong distaste to enter into a situation – and into a bed – that had suddenly been imposed upon him, his objections weakened, and he found the temptation impossible to resist. After removing only some of his clothes, he agreed to lie down next to her on the mattress, keeping his distance from her as much as he could. However, Silvana proved herself as a woman who had had plenty of experience with men – something which had not crossed Anshel's mind – and she edged closer to him, her body burning with passion, and slowly and sensuously she made his head spin by stroking and embracing and kissing him all over his body once she had removed the rest of his clothes. He only murmured to her, you must not do this. We should not get carried away, but his resolve had disappeared in the face of this overwhelming temptation.

Anshel had never before experienced physical contact with a woman, and at that moment he felt submerged beneath her huge chest as if drowning, her breasts quivering, so tempting, so stimulating, rubbing against him, but he would not succumb. He would not touch her, although his head did not listen to his body and Silvana's intimate caresses higher and higher along his thighs made his blood rush through his veins, and he felt his organ swelling and getting erect, although he did not intend this to happen. He simply did not understand how this happens, and then Silvana raised herself up and slowly pressed herself against him so that he entered her body. She began to move slowly, rhythmically, up and down, groaning and panting with desire, her movements growing faster and wilder until Anshel could no longer restrain himself and he felt a powerful, unstoppable stream gushing inside him until it spilled over into the limitless cavern of her body, such a tremendous physical sensation that an involuntary low scream released itself from his throat. He had never in his life experienced such a sensation, but at the same time, he felt as if he was raped by that woman.

For Anshel, this was an act without relating in any way to the woman. His body was on fire, but his heart was untouched. His hand had not stroked her, his arms had not embraced her, his lips had not kissed her. There had been not a scrap of affection in what had taken place between them.

His body soon returned to itself after its unfamiliar exertions, and Anshel felt that all he wanted to do now was to sink into a deep sleep. Without a word, like a woman who is offended when her lover does not respond to the love she bestows on him, or perhaps from an insight into what Anshel felt, Silvana got up from the bed, dressed herself quickly, and very quietly left the cottage.

The next morning Anshel awoke even before dawn, when the world was still in darkness, already clear and determined what his next step would be.

Before he had even rubbed the sleep from his eyes, the thought came to his mind that it was better to suffer from shell shock when fighting on the battlefield than to suffer the terrors of war here in the village where he had deluded himself to find the tranquility he craved. That is it, he would take himself off, and rejoin his unit. He would go in the steps of the Anders Army on foot, by car, or by train. The roads now were full of all kinds of vehicles in which soldiers of the Allied Forces had invaded central Italy in the thousands, and were now advancing northwards to wrap up their occupation of the whole of Italy. He would have no problem in hitching a ride; in the end he would find his unit. He had kept all his army papers. He would tell his officers that he had fallen sick, he had caught some sort of terrible infection, fever, the shakes, and could not keep up with the rest of them, and suddenly he found himself left behind on his own and lucky for him, some good-hearted villager found him almost fainting on the hillside, and brought him to his house and took care of him. There was no doubt in Anshel's mind that the army would understand the situation and accept the reason for his absence, and not consider it desertion.

The events of the terrible night – the incidents of rape and plunder that he knew were still going on in that village and, in fact, in many of the villages all around – made him want to get out of the village as fast as possible. But in addition to that, what he had gone through himself by being raped added to the urgency of his wanting to leave the area at once. He had been deflowered against his will, an act which produced in him a strange, unpleasant feeling, and he was forcing himself to overcome it, repress it. After all, it was not as if his hymen had been perforated, he reflected with a certain irony, so he would forget the disagreeable but at the same time intensely exciting experience and get on with his life. He would once again take part in the battles to liberate the Po Valley, and would fight until the nightmare of war came to its end.

Anshel quickly packed his belongings into his rucksack, tucked his gun into his shoulder tab and secretly went out of the cottage. He turned his head away as he passed the blackened body of the Moroccan soldier he had shot, as if passing the corpse of a dog or a cat, and hurried down the mountain slope in the direction of the road swarming with vehicles which led to the north.

## 13
## The Collapse

No victory celebrations follow a blood-soaked battle, since victories in battle and occasional conquests offer no guarantee of final victory in the war. Therefore, when the aggressor is the one who initiated the war, he suspects at a certain stage in the campaign, or even before he began his offensive, that in spite of all his partial victories, he might come to a bitter end and be defeated; so, as a measure of protection, he arranges his escape route in advance.

Such a feeling began to simmer in Hitler's heart even before his initial offensive in the war, and it came to the boil when he decided to invade Russia. It goaded him on to take steps which would ensure his continued existence, his protection and security, and be able to function both physically and operationally, if and when he would arrive at the stage where he would have to flee and hide.

Thus, in 1936, two to three years before he opened the war and invaded to Poland, the Nazi leader began to build a bunker at a depth of 7-10 meters underground, in the grounds of the magnificent Chancellery in the center of Berlin. The area of the bunker was 600 square meters, and it was cast in reinforced concrete, which no bomb would be able to penetrate; it was spacious and fitted with every technological advance of the age, and was designed to function as a safe hideaway for himself and his cronies, the ministers and underlings who were subject to his orders, with their wives and children.

The work of building the bunker continued during all the years of the war, especially between the years of Hitler's attack on the Soviet Union and his withdrawal from Russian territory. It was not that Hitler thought for a single moment of surrender. That was something he would not do in any circumstances, even if hundreds of thousands of his own soldiers and millions of his citizens were to fall in battle or be sacrificed to death on the altar of his hugely inflated ego.

For a man to ask forgiveness, for a leader to be able to admit defeat, requires him to possess a certain amount of honesty, integrity, and sanity, and to be able to see reality in its true colors.

These traits at that time were not to be found in the Nazi leader's personality, if in fact he ever possessed them. Without any intention of admitting defeat, Hitler went down into his bunker accompanied by a significant number of his ministers and their families. Each of them had rivers of blood on his hands; vicious cronies that had not only brought the Holocaust on the Jewish people, who had been slaughtered by them with vicious cruelty, but also rained down ruin and destruction over the whole of Europe and on the German nation itself. Germany not only paid the price for Hitler's madness in the millions of people killed, and in the millions of German Marks paid in compensation to countries invaded by them. In addition, he caused the German people also to go on their knees for many years in order to beg forgiveness from the world in general and from the Jewish people in particular.

For Hitler, hiding in his bunker was inevitable, given that the free world did not stand by in light of the reign of terror in Europe, which the Nazi dictator had imposed. England was licking her wounds from the thousands of bombs the German Luftwaffe had rained down on London and other major cities, resulting in death and destruction on a massive scale, but did not capitulate. The United States suddenly woke up and faced the enormity of the horror and the danger it posed only after the surprise attack on Pearl Harbor – the US Naval Base on the island of Hawaii – by the Japanese, Germany's ally, in which battleships and cruisers were sunk or damaged, and thousands of soldiers and civilians killed. It was a slap in the face for America, and, humiliated and angry, the United States determined to fight back. As for the French, they experienced at first-hand the terrors of the Nazi tyranny when their country was invaded by German troops. Accordingly, the British, the Americans and the French, all joined together to put their shoulders to the wheel, and coordinated for two whole years the planning of one of the most complex and glorious campaigns in world history, the campaign which went by the name of Operation Overlord, the great invasion by Allied Forces of the coast of Normandy in Occupied France, which took place in June 1944.

British, Americans, and Canadians – 175,000 troops of the Allied Forces – crossed the English Channel with army equipment which included 50,000 vehicles – motorcycles, bulldozers, tanks, armored cars – which were used, thanks to the help of members of the French Underground, who fought at their side to establish beachheads in the face of fierce resistance from the German Army which had at its disposal 11,000 planes and more than 5,000 boats and other sea-going vessels – until the Germans were overwhelmed.

It was not only a question of superior weaponry that decided which side would win and which suffer defeat. Luck also played a part in Operation Overlord. The Germans did not foresee that the offensive would take place on the beaches of Normandy. They had prepared to fight and defend the Calais coastline, which was closer to the coast of Britain. This brilliant feat of deception was conceived by Churchill and Eisenhower.

Another state of luck was when at the very time of zero hour of the offensive, Hitler was enjoying his slumbers, and had forbidden anyone to wake him up; and above all, the illustrious Commander in his army, General Rommel – who had conquered all the countries of North Africa and was only a hair's breadth away from invading Egypt and Palestine – had been invited that evening for a celebratory dinner far from the Front. In addition, the victories of the Americans and the British were due to the daring and inspiring leadership of Churchill and Eisenhower, including their brilliant deception of the German commanders, which enabled them to overcome the Nazi enemy; and – more than anything else – to the hundreds of thousands of young inexperienced soldiers who stormed the towering cliffs of the Normandy beaches. Wave after wave of soldiers carrying their personal weapons emerged from the holds of the boats and landed in front of the immense coastal cliffs; they did not despair in the face of the bloodbath which killed 2,500 soldiers on the first day of the landing, but succeeded in advancing and go across, to establish footholds and secure the beachheads before annihilating the enemy. These were soldiers who showed initiative, and acted on it, and made crucial decisions in the heat of battle, which led to the success of this most complex operation. It is both ironic and paradoxical that these soldiers grew up in the 1930s, which were bitter years of economic depression all over the United States of America; they were youngsters who had read the anti-war books of the period which had cynically described patriots as fools, and draft dodgers as heroes. But when the acid test came, and they were forced to come to the defense of their freedom, they fought bravely and heroically and proved that soldiers from democratic nations are not meek and mild but are able to defeat soldiers from totalitarian regimes steeped in fanaticism and blind obedience.

Like the wave of a tsunami crashing out of the sea onto the shore, taking all in its path, so did the Allied Forces invade the European countries which had been conquered by the Nazis. One after another they regained their independence, France and Holland, Czechoslovakia and Belgium and Denmark, until the Allies invaded Germany and struck her the sharpest and most threatening blow, particularly in Berlin, where the Fuhrer had taken refuge, like a rat deserting a sinking ship.

Since January 1945, Hitler had been holed up in his bunker deep underground, from where he conducted the war. At that stage it was essentially his personal war, and not a military war, against his assailants. Haunted by paranoia and manic-depressive, he swung between high hopes and deep despair; he would direct his forces at the Front – who had already been crushed and decimated– to go on the attack, a situation which only his sick imagination could conjure up as reality. Although he knew and felt that the end of his rule was very near, the urge to destroy still burned within his bones. He had said more than once that if he fell, he would cause the whole world to fall with him.

Even when he heard the powerful bombs resonating as they rained down on the capital city, killing thousands of citizens, damaging and destroying buildings, ruining his rule and the nation's pride, who were turned into dust and ashes amid the debris of that once magnificent city; even when he realized that the end had come, he did not want and did not agree to surrender, against the advice of his army commanders. Thus, with each day that he refused to concede defeat, German citizens were killed in their hundreds and thousands, and hundreds and thousands of public buildings or buildings of historic significance were destroyed to their very foundations. Hitler's authority over the senior officers and ministers who surrounded him and who behaved as if they were hypnotized by him, was still enormous, and no one dared to disobey him even though they realized that he was leading them all to the edge of the abyss.

However, when all was said and done, the Nazi leadership was on its way to collapse while a series of acts of treachery was being carried out, pointing the finger of blame one at another, all of which impelled many of them to commit suicide in despair. That was also the last resort for Hitler, when he eventually realized that the game was up.

In a short ceremony in the stifling underground bunker, he married the woman who had been his mistress for 15 years, Eva Brawn; each of them declared to the Registrar of the marriage that they were of pure Aryan descent. The very next day they closed themselves in their room, the new husband and wife, and put an end to their lives. Hitler shot himself once in the head, and his wife swallowed a cyanide pill. They had left instructions that their bodies were to be burned in a pit which had been dug in the garden above the bunker, leaving no recognizable remains, in case they fell into the hands of their enemies. Hitler preferred to put an end to his life by shooting and having his body burned rather than to take the chance of having his head put under the blade of the guillotine with the whole world exulting in his end. He detested the idea of being put on trial, facing the hostile world and to have his crimes flung in his face, knowing that he had no defense claims. It was thus as clear as daylight to him that at the end of the trial he would be sentenced to be hanged on a high gallows in the town square and his body sway back and forth, disgraced forever, like the body of his friend and comrade-in-arms Benito Mussolini who, after being executed, had his body strung up on a lamppost and displayed in the main square in the city of Milan. He, Hitler, would not demean himself. He would not admit defeat or express regret for his crimes, and he would allow nobody to preach to him about his wrongdoings. And thus he turned his back on the world and chose to die by his own hand as a lily-livered coward. He had brought on himself only a fraction of a fraction of what he had brought on countless others, by choosing to have done to himself what he had commanded be done to the millions of his murdered Jewish victims who had become heaps of holy ashes – to have his body burned.

All that remained of him was a small amount of tainted ashes, ashes which were scattered among the dust of the rubble and debris of the capital of his crumbling empire. Foul stench of tainted ashes that would burn forever in the throats of all human beings, and especially in those of the Jewish people.

Only after his death could senior officers of the Third Reich sign the unconditional surrender, which carved up their country and divided the cake of the crumbling, ruined regions between the Russians who controlled the east, and the Americans, who controlled the west. As for Berlin, it was divided to two separated parts and turned into a city which sat isolated alone, and at its central heart – a high wall.

✦ ✦ ✦

Like two heavyweight boxers in the ring, each one as massive as a mountain, their only ambition to bring the other to his knees, to smash his limbs and cause him to lose consciousness, make mincemeat of him, fight a bloody battle face to face, until one of them overcomes his opponent and is declared the victor; when this winner can hardly stand on his own feet after the cruel battle he has fought, one eye closed from a direct punch to it, the black eye darkening half his face, his body pierced with the pain of fractured bones, his nose broken and blood oozing from the corners of his mouth. On the other hand, his loyal trainer, overcome with excitement, takes hold of the hand of the winner and raises it to the enthusiastic crowd, the winner himself barely able to relate to his achievement while allowing his trainer to raise his hand at will – this was how Europe looked in 1945 at the end of the war: Torn and broken, as did the victorious soldiers in this war; as did the Jews who had survived the Holocaust, on that day in May 1945 when victory in Europe was declared.

Little by little, the Jews who remained lying on their bunks at the very edge of life in the barracks of the concentration camps managed to summon up the energy to lift themselves up from their bunks; and the Jews who had hidden in cellars, barns, attics, ditches and bunkers deep in the forests, came out of their hiding places, straightened their spines from the cramped holes they had bent themselves double in, their eyes blinking in the dazzling light which suddenly lit up the darkness of the lives they had lived for so long in fear, suffer, dread and humiliation. They were now free. Freedom – that was the word which swelled up in their hearts, and was trumpeted out of the mouths of millions of people all over the world.

These scenes were repeated over and over again until they became familiar. One after another, the exterminations camps in Europe were gradually liberated, and the prisoners set free; broken human beings, ghostly, walking skeletons but the breath of life was still present in their bodies even though the human spirit in their hearts and souls had long been snuffed out and buried deep in the ashes of the tragedy that had befallen them. They survived the Holocaust, but the Holocaust survived in their hearts and souls for many years to come. Even after they had apparently overcome the terrors they had experienced, returned to themselves, as it were, established a new family to replace the one which had perished before their eyes, it still gnawed away at their hearts, and the horrific nightmare never left them as long as they lived.

Like ants when they emerge from their nest deep in the ground and rush into a long line going back and forth, back and forth aimlessly, as if they have no idea where they are going, they go from the mouth of the nest, then they come out again, then back again, trying all the time to find a broken piece of straw which will serve to support them in a time of shortage, so in fact they do have a purpose going round and round the mulberry bush – this is how the liberated Jews of Europe would scurry along the roads, along the highways and byways, in towns and villages, in their search for any survivor or refugee from their family, a friend or even an acquaintance from those days before the abyss, to know whether anyone had survived, even though the chances were overwhelmingly against that happening. Still, they would at least return to the place they had lived in before and try to get back the property which had been robbed from them. But even that was denied them. They learned very quickly that everything had been requisitioned by the government, or simply grabbed by some covetous family. There was no chance either of a return, or of having anything returned to them.

And so they wandered, drifting here and there, and their eyes turned towards their sole objective: to get to their homeland, to Eretz Yisrael, in the direction of whose capital, Jerusalem, Jews had prayed for hundreds and hundreds of years, vowing that if they forget Jerusalem, may their right hand wither and wish their tongue cleave to their palate if they won't remember the Holy City.

Now, at last, they were able to fulfill that ancient oath which, between the sparks of the flames and the debris of all that was left, began to take shape and become more than a remote, impossible dream. They started to realize that it was not the homeland of their birth they were abandoning, which in fact had already abandoned them, but the Diaspora itself they were throwing overboard. This lodging they regarded as a temporary dwelling even though they had lived in it for centuries while waiting for the Redemption to come. And here it was, not trumpeted forth with thunder and lightning or on eagles' wings, but emerging from the ruins and from the mass graves of millions of dead bodies. Their eyes were now fixed on the future, on a future which would be lived in the East.

A great migration of the remnants of European Jewry, the survivors of a people who in four years had lost six million of its sons and daughters, began to take place. To the East, to Eretz Yisrael, to Jerusalem. Men and women who had been uprooted from their houses, torn from their families, from the country in which they had been born and grown up, which had vomited them out of it, who had been ejected from it with a kick of a hobnailed boot, gathered in vast displaced persons' camps which had been set up all over central Europe so that from there they could be brought to the Promised Land.

Two thousand years of exile came to an end in the most tragic way. But those who believed that the years of Exile were now behind them, found that there were still many obstacles which stood in their way before they could reach their cherished homeland. They had been deprived of exile, but the gates of their historic homeland were still closed to them. The wandering Jew would wander all his life, to and fro, wandering about always on shaky ground, with no place to put a pillow under his head, and always faced with towering fortifications blocking his way. So he had to pluck up all his courage and keep the passionate vision in his heart in the forefront of his mind in order to break through the gates of his homeland – until he finally succeeded. Until the door would be opened unto him.

# 14
# The Kielce Pogrom

Yudele was well hidden away during the last months of the war in Alina's house. Since they lived together as lovers, he received the news that war had ended with mixed feelings. What would he do now? Stay here with Alina all his life, or selfishly take himself away, leaving her on her own? Alina tried to convince him to stay, but she knew in her heart that living there with her would not be the right thing for him, nor for her either. The countrymen, her neighbors, would suddenly find out that she had hidden a Jew in her house, and even if they would not kill her, they would certainly drive her out. They would not forgive her. The war had ended, but the hatred of Jews still remained. Not to speak of what they might do to Yuda, her lover. She understood perfectly that he could not stay there with her.

You can come with me, if you want, Yuda suggested to her courteously, although he knew that his suggestion was quite absurd. Where indeed would she go with him? To whom she would leave her house and property? Where would he take her, this Christian woman, older by a good few years than he was, and he a Jew who had no idea where he himself was heading?

Another thing – in the strong bright light of the freedom which had suddenly returned to his life, Yudele was able to see the differences between them in so many aspects which had until now not been apparent. No, he would not uproot her from her land, from her religion, from her country. They each arrived at the same conclusion that there was nothing for them to do but to part. He would leave her house, her village, her body, her soul, her love, and disappear.

They held each other close for a long time before Yudele set out. Then Alina detached herself from his embrace, as if she had remembered something, and hastened to the dresser. She opened a concealed drawer, which only she knew existed, and took a document out from it. This is my husband's official identification made out more than 20 years ago, when he was about your age. You look quite similar. Take it. You will be able to move about on the roads freely and get to where you are going more easily. Alina even put into his hand an envelope she had prepared in advance, filled with money. Take this as well. You deserve to be paid for all the work you have done for me, she whispered, her voice trembling. Yudele did not know how to thank this wonderful, selfless woman. He hugged her tightly and could not hold back his tears, tears which suddenly filled his eyes, *davka* now, just when it seemed that his suffering was beginning to wane and perhaps even vanish altogether from his life.

*Suffering, presumably, blocks tears from streaming out of the eyes, as if it were a rigid, inflexible barrier which does not allow emotions to be expressed or be shown; while when one is moved by joy and gratitude, all the inhibiting barriers break down and tears may burst out and flow freely and unashamedly, releasing all the distress which has built up in the soul and mind for long time.*

When Yuda regained his self-control, he put the document and the money Alina gave him into his pocket, got up purposefully from his place, picked up his rucksack, and set off.
But where to? Where should he head for? The road to freedom might be as fearsome and threatening as going down to a dark cellar or even to a bunker deep underground.
All kinds of considerations and uncertainties ran around in his mind. His instincts urged him to leave the area of eastern Poland before he became trapped in the web of the Soviets, who had blanketed their control over Poland and the other

countries they annexed, so they could impose Communism there and bar people from going out of the country. This made Yuda want to get away from this place as fast as possible. But on the other hand, in spite of his anxiety, he felt a powerful longing to see his house, and the city where he was born. He also felt the need to take possession, or at the very least to make the effort to do so, of his parents' house, and even go back to live there. He therefore quickly made up his mind that he would indeed return to Warsaw, in spite of the danger he might expose himself to. He also nurtured the secret hope that the house might also draw back to it the rest of his family, and that his parents and brothers might gather there, who could tell?

At that time, Yuda had no idea at all what had happened to them. He only knew that his fervent hope that the family would be reunited made him determined to reach their house, at least to try his luck at doing so.

Warsaw received him looking as battered as someone who had suffered an alarming accident, or like a crushed and bruised woman after she had been stripped of her clothes and raped cruelly. The buildings were in ruins, the bridges blown to bits, the roads were full of pot holes, gardens destroyed, public buildings collapsed, people crouched over, walking in the streets with their faces turned towards the broken, unstable flagstones of the sidewalks.

Yuda found his parents' house without difficulty, the house where he was born and grew up and which, with unbelievable good fortune, had escaped almost unscathed, apart from minor damage when the city had been bombed, and its foundations were intact.

Yuda's heart pounded with excitement as he knocked at the door. He did not know what to expect. In his naivety, he expected that he would be greeted warmly, they would be happy to put him up their for a few days or even weeks, during which he would negotiate with them for his share of his parents' house, and the property he was entitled to inherit from his family. But the scowling face of an elderly woman, whose heavy make-up did not cover her wrinkles, soon let the air out of the balloon of his restless mind. What do you want, she asked, a mixture of irritation and anxiety in her voice, as if she had guessed why he come. When he said that this was the house where he was born and grew up, her eyes suddenly widened as if in alarm; she looked as if an evil spirit was standing in front of her and, in a shrill, threatening voice trembling with anger said: This is NOT your house. Get away from here before I call the police. Her voice was full of hatred, and she slummed the door in his face, as if he was a burglar who had come to steal from her.

Yuda was taken aback by the intensity of her hostility, from the hatred combined with the fear of the Jewish owners of the property who had survived, and would now come and demand that their houses and other property be returned to them.

Huh, under what a tragic illusion those Jews were living; what a sweet illusion they nurtured in their hearts, that became as bitter as wormwood. What did they think they were playing at, that natural justice would shine to them out of the blue? How could they think that the minute they appeared on the doorstep of the house stolen from them, they would get back everything which belonged to them, that they were forced to leave behind? It does not work like that, they would soon find out for themselves. Nobody intends to return anything to them. There will be no apologies and nobody will show any sympathy for them. The contrary.

Yuda stood for a long time by the door that had been slammed in his face, still stunned by the words, get away from here or I will call the police, which continued to ring in his ears until the new reality seeped into his brain and he realized that there was nothing for him to stay for. Feeling quite distressed, but at the same time determined, Yuda turned his back on his parents' house, and on the city that had betrayed him and kicked him out of it. To hell with Warsaw, he murmured to himself and began to leave the city by any means he could, on foot, by tram, with any vehicle that stopped for him, going southwards.

One day, during his wanderings, Yuda came across a large group of Jewish families and individuals, each loaded down with his own hardships. There were about 200 people clustered together, those who had crept out of their hiding places in forests and ditches, in attics and sewers, and those who had been liberated from concentration camps when the Allied Forces reached them. The one thing they all had in common was that they were all from the town of Kielce, in central Poland. They had all been born and grew up there. Generations upon generations of their families had lived there, and now they wanted to go back and live in Kielce. The faith and the passion which radiated from these Jews and their dream of recapturing the good days they had enjoyed before the war, returning to the houses they had been forced to abandon, and which would now be returned to them, after all, those houses were their legal property. Some of them were longing for their wide pastures and for the thick forests around the town. All their longings for Kielce and the way they described the town gave Yuda the rosy idealized image of ease and pleasantness, and he was tempted to ask them if he could join their group.

Do you think I could come with you and live there, in your town, he asked, and they replied, of course, there is no question about it. We will be happy to have you with us. You are a Jew, you are our brother, we will easily find you somewhere nice to live, for most of the Jews from Kielce were murdered by the Nazis – may their names be blotted out – so there must be lots of vacant houses there. Kielce is not Warsaw. And so they traveled onwards, and even though they were tired out, their hearts were full of hope that they were on their way to reclaim their inheritance, and in a short time they would arrive at their longed-for destination.

Out of the 24,000 Jews who had lived in Kielce before the war, only 200 survived the Holocaust, and now the small group of survivors wanted with all their heart and soul to go back to their beloved town. Yuda was happy when they invited him to go with them. He would no longer have to drift about on his own, wherever his legs would carry him. No more loneliness and uncertainty and depressed feelings. Now he felt his luck had changed for the better, for he was among fellow-Jews, close to his new companions. Fate had treated them harshly, being left shocked and damaged; these long-suffering young people. Their hardships showed in the deep lines entrenched into their faces, which made them look much older than their years.

Yuda joined them with a sense of relief, but to his amazement, the horrors he had until now been ignorant of gradually became known to him. With this knowledge, he realized that he had in fact not known nor heard nor seen anything of what the Jews of Poland had experienced during the war. He thus began to feel somewhat guilty that, relatively speaking, he had not suffered from starvation or torments and had not been exposed to the danger of extermination like the others in the group, who had returned out of the hellholes of the extermination camps. The period when he had fought with the partisans in the forests now suddenly seemed to him relatively bearable, in comparison with the terrors he had now learned about.

Horrified and aghast, Yuda listened to the stories of the members of the group and the torments they had gone through. His attention was particularly drawn by one sturdy, distinguished looking man, whose shoulders were slumped with fatigue, and heartache and suffering etched onto his face. Yuda noticed that all the while the members of the group described their hardships, he was silent, wrapped up in himself; he listened, but said nothing. Yuda however realized that there was something out of the ordinary about him, a kind of boldness, which raised him head and shoulders above the others. One time when nobody was talking, Yuda approached the man diffidently, and began to draw him out with the curiosity of a friend to tell him about himself, of what had happened to him during the war.

He was called Mendel. With a shrug, Mendel reluctantly agreed, and began to relate his remarkable story. The further he got into his story, the stronger his voice became and the passion with which he told it. Everyone grasped that he had gone through exceptionally tortuous hardships when it became clear that he was one of the few survivors of the Sobibor death camp.

I was one of the initiators of the great escape of prisoners from the camp, and also one of those who took part in it, he said. It is hard to describe the breakout from there. It was just like in a movie, maybe they'll make a movie about it one day, chuckled Mendel with a wry face. What a daring escape that was! I would not call it a heroic adventure; it was simply the only chance for people to try to save their lives. In a place where certain death is just waiting to pounce on you, you have not anything to lose by risking an escape that might, just might – for the chance of success was tiny – save your life.

We were not the first ones who tried to escape from there. Even before I myself came to the camp, from the time it was set up, in March 1942, north of Lublin, prisoners tried to escape from the Sobibor camp. However, each time they failed, and those trying to run away were put to death with other prisoners who had not joined in the breakout, as a warning to all potential runaways that they should be aware that not only would they be killed but they would also be the cause of other prisoners losing their lives. But that did not stop prisoners trying to escape again and again. The Germans tried to stop further breakouts by laying a lot of mines around the fences of the Sobibor camp so that the prisoners would not be able to get too far. The prisoners' response to the laying of mines was to dig a long tunnel to bypass the mines and bring them out as far as the nearby forest. But the Germans found about the tunnel, and a lot of the prisoners paid for this with their lives.

All this time the death machine in the camp was going at full speed, non-stop. Ukrainians who were working in it voluntarily together with the SS men brought the people on the transports from the trains straight to the gas chambers. They deceived them, reassuring them that they would be taken to the disinfectant showers and after that they would be sent to a work camp in the Ukraine.

Come into this room, take off your clothes and you will have a haircut. Obviously you will not have your clothes on when you walk on that path over there to the showers, because we do not take a shower in our clothes, do we? And so, believing every word of this, tens of thousands of people went to the gas chambers. Mendel's listeners were even more shocked to hear that at Sobibor the Nazis did not use the Zyklon B gas which was emitted from the shower heads in other death camps, and which killed people within twenty minutes, but that the gas chambers in Sobibor were connected to engines from old Soviet tanks standing outside the walls of the death cells, whose thick pipes pumped in poisonous fumes from the exhaust and that people were struggling, gasping for breath for much longer than twenty minutes during which they suffered excruciatingly.

For the next stage of the process, Mendel continued, the Germans needed Zundercomandos, strong Jews who would take out the bodies of the victims from the death chambers and throw them into immense burial pits which had been dug close by. They would pour quicklime on them. The quicklime eats away at the flesh and the bones and makes the bodies evaporate until there is nothing left. After a few months, when the extermination machine at Sobibor became more sophisticated, the bodies were thrown from the gas chambers into huge fires which burned them completely. By the way, in the same wing where the Jewish Zundercomandos were housed, there were also some of the Ukrainians who guarded the fences around the camp. Also under the same roof were the Nazi workers whose job it was to take out the gold-filled teeth from the victims, whom the prisoners called, with real gallows humor, the dentists.

One day, in June 1943, Mendel went on, a transport of 100 Jewish prisoners from the Belzec death camp had arrived. That was after the Germans had finished dismantling that camp and destroying the crematoria there. Obviously they had to get rid very quickly of the last remaining prisoners. They realized that if they were left alive they could be a real danger for them, because they would be witnesses to the terrible things that the Nazis had done in that camp. On their way to Sobibor, those prisoners, who knew first-hand the atrocities carried out in the camp, wrote down on scraps of paper all the horrific things they had witnessed in Belzec to alert those who might find the notes in their clothes in advance, and thus help them to be on their guard. And so it turned out, men who were pulled out of the transports for forced labor rather than being put to death immediately, found the notes the Belzec prisoners had written, when they were sorting through the clothes.

When those 100 prisoners from Belzec reached Sobibor, they were clearly not going to go willingly to the gas chambers, having been told that they were only going to be disinfected. They were already aware of that monstrous, cynical deception, of shower heads filled, not with disinfectant, but with a deadly gas. They should not insult their intelligence with this nonsense. They decided that they would not wait, and would not walk naked to those deathly showers, to be so-called disinfected as they had been reassured. The shadow of imminent, certain death lay heavy on them. It was worth trying to survive, even if they only had a chance in a thousand of succeeding. Even if they did not succeed, it was better to die a hero's death than to be brought to the death chambers like a flock of unsuspecting fools. And so, determined on rebellion, they revolted against the guards as soon as they got to Sobibor, and rushed, bellowing at the top of their voices, towards the gates and the fences. But they had no luck. They were shot and killed, and the ones who survived were all put to death. All the hundred of prisoners from Belzec perished at Sobibor, but the notes they left in their work clothes did help. The notes found by the forced laborers in the clothes of the prisoners from Belzec who had been put to death, alerted others of what the Nazis were doing to all those arriving on the transports. It is not work! It is murder! Save yourselves! Do not believe those crooks! They read the notes, and took in the message.

Immediately, some leaders came to the fore in the camp and decided to rebel and free all the prisoners. The plan to escape was obviously prepared in great secrecy, but each time it was turned down, and did not get off the ground.

Mendel repeated saying that during that period, he himself was not yet at the camp. I reached Sobibor only in September 1943, with a group of 600 Jewish prisoners who had served in the Soviet Army and, unfortunately for us, had been taken prisoner by the Germans. From June 1942, we were in the penal camp for Jewish prisoners in Minsk. One day in September, some prisoners arrived in our camp, one of them had been a lieutenant in the Russian Army, Sasha Pachersky, who had tried to escape from another prison camp but had been caught. What happened to him was a bit of bad luck, because during a routine medical examination it appeared that he was a Jew, something he had tried to hide for a long time. It is true, quite a lot of men survived by hiding their Jewishness when they served their country faithfully, but Sasha Pachersky had no luck. Just a routine medical examination – and his dangerous origins were discovered, so he was immediately transferred to the penal camp for Jews where we were imprisoned, and stayed with us until they decided soon to close down that camp in Minsk and we were all then sent to Sobibor.

Out of the 600 people on the train which brought us to that most horrendous death camp, only 80 men were chosen at a rigorous selection for the forced labor battalion.

Pachersky and I were among the lucky ones who were selected to work and not sent on the pretense – as I told you before – to the showers, that is, to our deaths. All the rest were sent the same day to be executed. That is exactly how it was. Whoever resisted was cruelly tortured. The guards and warders in Sobibor were notorious for being the most brutal, and during the short time we were in the camp, we saw the horrors the Ukrainians and Germans inflicted. They just got some perverse pleasure out of savagely abusing prisoners. They would slice off the breasts of young women just before they were shoved into the gas chambers, and smash the skulls of little children. They snickered and bared their teeth while brains burst out of skulls and blood splattered all around. Like retarded children pulling the arms and legs off their dolls and toy animals, the cruelest abuse they could inflict was their entertainment. What made them do it – family men, husbands, fathers – such hatred, bubbling up and bursting out of their souls?

If you ask me, it was not only hatred, those men were mentally deranged, crazy, they had the minds of criminals, Mendel added reflectively.

We soon made contact with the leaders of the prisoners in the Sobibor camp, and Pachersky, who had been a superior officer in the army, decided together with the leaders on a mass breakout of everyone in the camp, and in fact became the leader of the revolt.

The day fixed for the revolt was October 14, 1943, as we knew that the commander of the camp and his deputy would be away then. So, at 4 o'clock in the afternoon the revolt broke out. At the first step, we killed an SS officer, and when other officers came to see what was going on, the prisoners killed another ten SS men and three Ukrainians, and then everyone – 600 out of the 1,000 prisoners in the camp – broke out of the gate and began to run in all directions over the fences surrounding the camp, running, running, wherever their legs carried them.

All they wanted was to get far away and reach the forest, their final aim, that hopefully was supposed to save their lives. Many of them did not manage to get far enough away to be able to save themselves, because the Germans started to shoot at them and swat at them like flies in a fly-trap; and those who were wounded or trapped were killed afterwards; a lot of others who had avoided being shot, had trampled on one of the land mines the Nazis had dispersed outside the fence, and were killed or injured. And at last, when some of the prisoners had managed to get to the forest and hide there, they still did not get their freedom but were imprisoned again because the local people who had found them, exposed them and handed them over to the Germans.

Mendel took a deep breath. That is it, only 60 prisoners out of the 600 who made a run for it, managed to get over all these obstacles and reach the forest, without being exposed by the damned locals, including me and Pachersky.

We joined up with groups of Russian partisans and carried on fighting the Germans and striking at them from there, until victory was declared.

Mendel was silent for some time, and then added: All the years of the war, I never forgot the town I loved, Kielce, where I was born and grew up, and where in a terrible *action* the Germans took my whole family to be killed; my parents and brothers and sisters, my uncles and aunts and my grandparents. I was the only one who had left the house before the *actions*, and so I was left on my own, without any family. Now I want to salvage what I can from my house. I was sure that if I came out of that Gehinnom, that hell, alive, I would go back to Kielce. That is what we are all doing, all of us from Kielce here. Our hearts are broken, but we want to try to pick up the pieces of our lives, and put ourselves together again, look to the future, and hope that it will be as good as it was before the war, May God will it.

All Mendel's listeners, who had avidly hung on his every word, nodded their heads and said heartily, Amen and Amen.

The bitter reality stroked them in their face. When they returned to Kielce they found, to their great surprise, that all their houses were being occupied by the local residents who glared at them and drove them away with curses and snarls as if they were stray dogs. But the returning Jews of Kielce did not despair even though they could see that it was not only that their houses were being lived in by strangers, but that every trace of Jewish life had been erased in the town. Nothing remained of the schools, the colleges, the large yeshiva, the synagogues, the study halls. It was as if they had never existed.

Despite their disappointment and shock, they did not give in, and did not leave the town. They still had the hope that they could build everything afresh, to restore what had been destroyed or converted to a Christian institution, and renew Jewish life in the town. That is the way they thought, in their innocence. Or to be more accurate, in their ignorance. They had no idea of the present realities of life, that property belonging to Jews deported to the ghetto or the death camps had long ago been requisitioned by the State Treasury, and their houses given over to thousands of Poles without a roof over their heads due to the economic depression in Poland before the war. Laws had been passed to deprive deported Jews of the rights of ownership of their houses and their property. It was a monstrous paradox, to lose the right legally to something which was vested in them legally, and so it was quite natural that the lawsuit which the returning Jews brought against those who were occupying their houses ran into a brick wall and was strongly opposed.

One way or another, the leaders of the returning Jews looked for some temporary solution to their housing problem, and found a large building in the town with a lot of vacant apartments to rent. So they decided to live there for the time being, to the chagrin and dismay of the local Polish citizens.

Yuda sensed that the hostility the citizens of Kielce felt towards the Jews who had come back there boded no good. He was the first of all of them to feel the ground shaking under their feet, and immediately wanted to leave the place and continue on his way. Kielce was not his town, their battle was not his. He was only a casual visitor. What was he to them, really, there was nothing for him to do there. Yuda was already getting ready to leave them when he received a generous offer, quite out of the blue, which changed his mind, and his destiny.

Before the war, Eliyahu Leibowitz had been the owner of a large store selling sweets and confectionery in the center of the town. He was a wealthy and respected merchant, always accompanied by his wife and his daughter, Ahuva. Now he suggested to Yuda that he join and live with them in their apartment in the building which housed all the Jews who had come back to Kielce. This was an offer which, from the moment he had met them, Yuda had secretly hoped would come his way, although he himself would not have thought of initiating a close relationship with the family. And now he had received it on a silver platter, as it were, and without thinking twice, he agreed to stay with them, whatever happened.

One thing and one thing only persuaded him to stay. He yearned for Leibowitz's daughter, Ahuva, who from their first meeting had stolen his heart. Her huge black eyes, her tiny upturned nose and her cherry lips, made his heart flutter. Her clear skin and slim, shapely body aroused in Yuda longings for a woman, specifically for this young woman, only 19, warmhearted, tender and innocent. Alina seemed to him suddenly distant, an older woman, different in so many ways from himself. Now that he had come to live with a Jewish family and was in the company of fellow-Jews whose fate he shared, he had the feeling of having being estranged from his own people for too long, and now thankfully he had returned to live with them. He decided that he would stay with the Leibowitz family, who had given him a small room off the living room; only a thin wall separated his room from that of Ahuva, whom he so desired.

Pressure of hard experiences need to find ways to burst out and living under the same roof gave them plenty of time to tell each other all about themselves. Yuda told them only about the hardships he had gone through after he escaped from the ghetto, hiding in the forests, fighting with the partisans, and running away from the forest after the horrifying operation the Nazis perpetrated, which buried whole families alive in the bunkers where they hoped to be saved but unfortunately became their grave. He told them nothing at all about being sheltered in Alina's house. Instead, he mentioned a Christian family in one of the villages who had been on friendly terms with his family and who had agreed to hide him in their cellar until the end of the war. His story rang true, and they accepted it unquestioningly.

For his part, Eliyahu Leibowitz went into great detail when he told Yuda how he had survived.

Leibowitz and his small family were not deported to an extermination camp. His instincts were very acute, he said, and from the time the Germans started to make life difficult for Jews in the town, and issued all kinds of restrictions like forbidding them to engage in business, or be employed by non-Jews, having to wear the yellow star, he decided not to wait until things got worse and Jewish property was requisitioned, but quickly sold his sweets shop before the Nazis would simply take it away from him.

He sold it for a good price, and decided that he would not stay in the town and wait until they came to force him to move out of his house. Leibowitz indeed had sharp instincts, and felt very strongly that the ground was shaking beneath his feet. He began to act quickly making all kinds of enquiries and plans to ensure the safety of his family. Straight after he wound up his business and sold the shop, he traveled to the farm of a Christian farmer in one of the villages fairly near to Kielce. He had a good relationship with the farmer. They had done some business together and become friendly, and Leibowitz asked him to let him take shelter in his house, in a storeroom or attic, anywhere he could hide out. After all, he had sold his shop and was quite prepared to give the farmer a large amount of cash in return for hiding his family in his house. The farmer agreed. For such a huge sum it was worth his while to accept Leibowitz' proposal and also, he was a decent man and was not so caten up with anti-Semitism that he would turn Jews in to the Nazis. And so, with the utmost secrecy, in the dead of night, the Leibowitz family moved into the house of the farmer, and hid themselves away in the attic, which was camouflaged so well that none of the neighbors saw, or heard, or suspected anything. When the Germans burst into the Jews' houses in Kielce and dragged them to the trucks which took them to the railway cars whose destination was the death camps, the Leibowitz family was hidden in the house of the farmer, where they spent all the years of the war – and survived.

That village was one of the very many small villages scattered all over Galicia, surrounded by forests, in which for hundreds of years Jews and *goyim* had lived in them. A road separated the two rows of houses of the villagers, on one side lived the Jews, and on the other – the Catholics. Everyone worked on his land or in his small business, or in workshops. Everyone had his small farm, but the separation was crystal-clear. There were no shared social or cultural activities, each side kept to his own religion, beliefs and manners. Relationships with their neighbors were just civil, bearable. Until the poisonous thoughts in the Poles' hearts towards their Jewish neighbors had been allowed by the horrible circumstances to bubble up to the surface, exposing their ugliness.

Leibowitz did not want to stay hidden for a long time with his wife and daughter in the attic, so he convinced the farmer to let his neighbors know that one of his relatives was coming to stay with him in his house, an unmarried man of 41, who had come from another town to help him with the work on his farm. So that he would look the part, Leibowitz shaved off his sidelocks and beard, took off his yarmulke and went bareheaded, wore the clothes typical of Polish farmers, and looked just like one of them. However, Leibowitz did not abandon his faith or his religion; it was only for the sake of his personal liberty that he forsook the outward signs which were the hallmark of a religious Jew. He also changed his name: from Leibowitz to Breinitz. None of the neighbors suspected for a moment that Breinitz's origins were not genuine, and he was welcomed into their circle as the farmer's relative, exactly as he had presented himself. With this identity, he was able to go about the village freely, while his wife and daughter did not feel the warmth of the sun on their faces for four years of the war, and could only hear the birds twittering through the walls which hid them from view. They busied themselves with sewing and knitting and other handicrafts which they were able to do in their hideout, until they were liberated.

A short time after the family came to the village to hide themselves away in the house of the farmer, Leibowitz, who was able to go out and about in the village quite freely, saw with his own eyes a raid the Germans made on the Jews there. In the early hours of the morning, he awoke to the sound of trucks clattering and the screech of brakes as they came to a sudden stop. He peered out of the window and saw leaping off the trucks like a troupe of acrobats SS soldiers, polished and starched, the asphalt crumbling under the impact of their hobnailed boots.

Immediately there began to be heard cries of outrage and pain as people were being dragged along the other side of the street, where the Jewish homes were. Many of the Christian villagers looked out of the doors or windows of their houses, some out of curiosity, some with horror, and some with approval to see how whole families of Jews, men, women and children of all ages, were being pulled out of their houses in their thin clothes, and, huddled together like a herd of sheep, were ordered to walk out of the village towards the nearby forest.

You have nothing to worry about, there is not a lot of walking, it is not far away, they heard the reassuring words, and the column of walkers trembled with fear, some of them finding it difficult to walk and stumbling, and those who stopped to catch their breath were immediately goaded on by a whip or a cane wielded by those wild dogs, their fangs bared, in the guise of SS soldiers, who simply saw themselves as carrying out their work with devotion, swinging their clubs and bringing them down hard on the heads of the slow-footed, the threat of a gun pointed at them, the butt against their backs, this wretched group of people walking out of the village and gradually disappearing into the dark, tangled trees in the forest.

After a few days, one by one, a few men and boys returned. They looked like ghosts, haunted by what they had witnessed.

These Jews had managed to escape from the killing site in the forest and get back to their houses in the village, and the tales they told were hair-raising. Leibowitz-Breinitz would go out to meet them and urge them to tell him what they had seen.

From what he heard from the eyewitnesses, he put together the following appalling picture: Everyone taken out of the village in the *action* was made to walk to a large clearing in the forest. The men were given shovels, and ordered to dig long trenches, as deep as they could. Meanwhile the women and children and the old were ordered to sit down under the trees and wait – without knowing what they were waiting for. The men, who had begun to dig the ground, also did not know why they were doing it, or what purpose it would serve, perhaps hard, pointless labor just to make them suffer, to mistreat them for the sake of mistreating them. The real purpose of digging the trenches, they could not have pictured in their most pessimistic imaginings, or the enormity of the horror which was about to take place in front of them and which would be pierced into their flesh.

When the trenches had been dug, all the people – including the women and children and elderly sitting waiting on the ground under the trees – were ordered to undress.

Take off our clothes? Mothers in front of their children, women in front of men, strangers? Why, here in a clearing in the forest the excuse of disinfection, of showers, was ludicrous, it did not make sense. They were scared stiff, but with the butts of rifles threatening them, nobody dared utter a word.

Take your clothes off!

Ten people each time would line up on the edge of the trench, and bend down, with their faces towards the hole, and after them the next ten, each time a group of ten was lined up like this, and scores of people walked forward in turn, naked, and bent down to the open trench, and a line of SS soldiers, guns in their hands, stood behind them and when the command was given they would raise their guns and aim them and shoot the victims in the back so that they would fall straight into the hole. One group of ten after another, and another, and another, were brought forward in turn, shot and fell into the hole, and those whose turn had not yet come stood at the side and saw the horror and knew that very soon it would be their turn to be killed. All that they could hope for from those Nazi slaughterers would be for them to be good shots and kill them outright, not just to leave them injured, for they could hear terrible cries from inside the holes from those who had not been killed, but had only been wounded. The Nazis had no choice but to go down into the hole and shoot in the heads those still drowning in their own blood between life and death, and the soldiers kept shooting like robots, shooting and splitting heads open, and those waiting at the side for their own turn saw how the clothes of the murderers were stained with the blood and the fragments of brains spilled all over them. The soldiers were unmoved, indifferent as to what was happening, looking forward to finishing their work and going home to the bosom of their families in the evening.

Here and there somebody managed to get away unnoticed. A youth, who saw his parents shot and fall into the hole, managed to get away; an older man who took advantage of the turmoil and in a split second dodged out of eyesight of his captors; but very few escaped from under the very noses of the murderers and succeeded in dragging themselves back to their homes in the village to tell the tale of what they had seen. They did not escape the net for long. Those who escaped had not much hope of surviving, for the Nazis did not allow any Jew to slip through their fingers, and they came back time after time to the village and pulled the fugitives out of their hiding places, and did not lose any time before splitting their skulls.

The holes and trenches in the clearings of the forests filled up with human flesh, became mass graves, and in every place the Nazis tried to dig they came across bodies which had recently been buried there, Jewish victims from other villages in the region.

The few who succeeded in fleeing and hiding in the thick forests, survived to testify about the killings and atrocities perpetrated against the Jewish population, generations of Orthodox Jews who had worked their land in good faith, and who, one day, were brought like sheep to the slaughter with the most horrific cruelty. Lightning did not blind the eyes of the murderers nor did the earth open its mouth to swallow them deep inside its echo.

✦ ✦ ✦

Like many of those returning to Kielce, Leibowitz also had nurtured in his heart the illusion that it would be possible to cultivate normal relations with the Catholic residents there, and hoped that they would accept the Jews' presence and acknowledge their right to live in the town with them as equal citizens. However, hatred of the returning Jews on the part of the citizens had not only not vanished, but had actually grown and intensified. The evil and the crimes that the Nazis had carried out against the Jews not only did not arouse their compassion or soften their hearts, but made the citizens even more hard-hearted towards them. The message transmitted to those Jews who returned was clear and sharp as a razor: You are not wanted here. Stay out of our neighborhoods – we certainly have no intention of giving you back your property.

The hostile attitude from their former neighbors did not deter the Jews who had returned to the town and, despite of the loathing which the villagers conveyed towards them, they insisted on settling in Kielce, no matter what. It was their right to do so, for Kielce was their town, too. However, this right, as it were, did not ward off the evil spirits which had seized the hearts of the local residents of the town against the new-old settlers, whose presence in the town disturbed their peace.

It did not take too long, therefore, before the match was lit and fanned the flame of hatred and caused a great fire to burn.

One day, a boy of nine years old decided to go and visit a friend of his who lived in the next village, without telling his parents, and stayed with him for two whole days. His worried parents looked everywhere for him, and became more and more anxious until he came home of his own accord after being missing for two days. In order to persuade his parents not to be angry with him, he innocuously told them a lie that a child wanting to avoid being punished would tell, namely that a Jew from Kielce had locked him up in his cellar for two days, and he had only just managed to escape from it. His parents were shocked to hear this, and without looking into the matter or even asking who the alleged man was, and where exactly the boy had been locked up, went straight to the police to lodge a complaint that a Jew had kidnapped their son, had kept him locked up in his cellar until the boy had managed to break loose and run away from him. The rumor quickly flew all around the town, and the shocking incident of a Christian boy's imprisonment at the hands of a Jew gained even more shocking details with each retelling until it became like the false incitements of the past, that Jews snatch and murder Christian boys in order to butcher them and squeeze the blood out of their bodies to use it for ritual services and they intended to do the same thing with this boy, from our own town.

The Christian residents of Kielce could not claim any originality in inventing this wicked plot to discredit the Jews of their town, for the pages of history are full to overflowing with the vile blood libels the *goyim* had invented over hundreds of years as a pretext to blacken the Jews' names, and stoke up passions against them to justify their torture, murder, and expulsion in their hundreds and thousands.

The blood libels began in England at the beginning of the Middle Ages and spread to France, Germany and Switzerland, continuing until the beginning of the twentieth century, with the blood libel in Russia against Mendel Beilis: The basis for this dark lie, which ran through the centuries, was that Jews had the custom of murdering a Christian child before the Passover holiday, in order to drain the blood from his body, dilute it with water, and sell it to their fellow-Jews on the eve of Passover for the production of matzah, the unleavened bread eaten on Passover. It was a plot thought up by twisted minds and spurred on by hateful prejudice.

All the arguments that the leaders of the Jewish communities had aroused before them, could not refute these plots. Neither the argument that murder is one of the most preliminary, essential, prohibitions in the Ten Commandments, sacred to Jews, helped to convince them. Or that the Jewish holy rules in the Bible, in the Torah, according to which the eating of the blood of animals – even of those Kosher animals it is permitted to eat – is strictly forbidden; how much more is forbidden therefore, where human blood is concerned!

But nothing helped, because those vicious libels were just an excuse. Nobody, deep in his heart, really believed in them, they were just a symptom of brain-wash and prejudice to justify the criminal destruction of the Jews.

Therefore, it would be enough if someone were crazy or wicked, or just plain anti-Semitic to make up a plot about an innocent Jew who killed a Christian child, so that they would torture the Jew until he was more dead than alive, and whoever could not suffer the pain of the terrible tortures – they would succeed in getting him to admit that he in fact did kill the Christian child, which gave them the pretext for taking off the gloves and attacking not only that unfortunate

Jew, but all the Jews in their town, and torturing and killing them, destroying them and expelling them so that they would not ever be able to return to their houses.

One of the aims of the blood libels was to try to convert Jews to Christianity, but the accusers did not often succeed in this – for most Jews chose to die the death of martyrs and be burned at the stake, for the sanctification of God's name, rather than be forced to convert from their Jewish religion to the Christian one. True that there were also some Jews who did convert to Christianity in order to save their lives, to save their skins from the atrocities, such as the cutting off of limbs, disemboweling while they were still alive, hanging in public, burning when they were tied to a stake in the middle of a pile of twigs set alight, and all kinds of other cruelties. Satanic blood libels, bizarre myths, dark, malicious lies, in which there was never a grain of truth, crying out the injustice of it all from the heavens.

But what would Jew-haters not use as a pretext to start a pogrom? True, from time to time there was a Pope who denied the accusations and forbade the harming of Jews, but the authority of the Church was not sufficiently strong to stop the hatred; and there were kings who banned the killing of Jews. However, in most cases, the authorities and the kings and the law courts worked together, hand in hand, conspiring to blame and judge and find guilty and sentence the innocents to a cruel death.

And as a continuation of the same abominable tradition, Kielce experienced its own blood libel, which took place on July 4, 1946. A Jew snatched a Christian child and if he had not run away from his abductor he would have been killed and his blood diluted with water and shared out between the Jews who had now come back to Kielce from the concentration camps, so that they could quench their thirst with Christian blood.

Those rumors were enough to incite the population,

who came out of their houses wielding clubs and axes, and surrounded the building where the survivors of the newcomer Jews were living. They were enough for most of the population of the town to crowd themselves together at the doors of the building and call out insults to the occupants, accusing them of attempted murder; and it was enough for the officers at the police station to hear the accusation, for the loyal force responsible for defending innocent citizens – without investigating and ascertaining the truth of the complaint – to break into the apartments of the Jews in the building where they all lived, going from one apartment to the next apartment, breaking down the doors, and with guns cocked and using live ammunition, began to shoot indiscriminately in all directions, and the Jews fell where they stood, dead or injured, and others, stunned out of their wits, and terrified, began to flee for their lives in panic and went out of the building to dodge the bullets of the police, but the mob gathered in the doorways fell on the fleeing Jews and slaughtered them mercilessly.

Thus, in the pogrom in Kielce, which took place on the 4th of July 1946, 47 Jews were killed and 80 wounded.

As soon as Yuda heard the policemen firing from the other side of the building, he realized that they were coming dangerously close, and quickly calculated what he should do to keep himself safe. He watched through the window and saw the angry mob surrounding the doorways, wielding axes and knives and clubs. It was clear to him that he would not get out of the building alive. He suggested to Leibowitz and his wife and daughter, Ahuvaleh, that they should hide themselves under the beds or inside the closets, because the police were firing only at the people they saw. They would not waste time on searching for victims in hidden places. But the Leibowitz couple got into a terrible panic when they heard the shots coming nearer and louder, and when they saw most of the occupants of their floor fleeing for their lives, rushing down the stairs and out of the building, they ran out of their apartment down the back stairs, calling to Ahuva to come with them. Yuda could not stop them.

On their way down the stairs, Leibowitz and his wife were shocked to see Mendel's bullet-ridden body whom the police had shot. Mendel, a true hero, who had survived all the horrors of the war, even the Sobibor death camp, met his death in this perverse attack, as he ran out of his room, trying to flee, but fell into the trap of the armed policeman suddenly standing in front of him. Leibowitz and his wife could not linger for even a minute as they tried to dodge the bullets which were zipping all around them in the building – and ran straight into the enraged mob waiting for them with their axes and clubs.

In spite of hearing her father's urgent calls to her, Ahuva did not want to listen to him. She much preferred to listen to Yuda. During the time they had lived in the same apartment, she had grown to admire him and was even secretly in love with him, and now she had the opportunity to listen to him, and be by his side, just the two of them. So, they hid themselves under her parents' large bed, and that saved their lives, for when the police burst into the apartment baying for blood they did not see a soul, and concluded that the occupants had fled the building. So the policemen left the apartment, much to the relief of the two hidden under the bed. They could not then know how lucky they were, but when the pogrom ended, after the police and the murderous mob left the area of the building and went back to their homes, Yuda and Ahuva dared to go down the stairs to go out of the building, full of concern as to what had happened to Ahuva's parents. They looked for them among the survivors and asked if they had been seen after they had rushed away out of the building, but their enquiries came to nothing, and very soon they discovered that both Ahuva's father and her mother were among the dead.

There was nothing for Yuda to do except to try to soothe Ahuva when she came upon the bodies of her parents lying at her feet, and burst into heartrending cries. Suddenly she was left all alone in the world, after having lost her close family in the death camps, her aunts and uncles, cousins, nephews, and grandparents, who had all been pushed into the gas chambers and now she was bereaved of both her parents in this terrible pogrom. What would she do, orphaned and on her own in this cruel world, and Yuda, while stroking her tousled hair, promised her that she must not think she would be alone. He would not leave her. He would stay with her and protect her. The idea of sharing her life with Yuda comforted her immensely and she gradually became calmer; she was still sobbing, but through the sea of her tears, the hope that she had found the love of her life began to make its way into her heart.

Yuda did not want to take advantage of Ahuva's vulnerable position and, even though he was greatly attracted to her, behaved towards her as if he were a loyal cousin, helping her make all the arrangements so that the two of them would be able to leave that accursed place as soon as they had buried her parents, together with Mendel and all the others murdered in the pogrom.

Yuda and Ahuva were not the only ones who made up their minds to leave. News of the brutal pogrom in Kielce spread like wildfire through all the towns and villages in Poland where Jews had lived before the war, and had returned to after the Holocaust, trying to take up their lives there again. But they learned both from the slaughter which took place in Kielce, and from the feeling, ever since they had returned after the Holocaust, that the ground was burning under their feet. They were no longer under the illusion that they could ever be safe in Poland, and they decided to leave. They left in droves, 150,000 of them, whole families of Jews left the towns and villages where they had tried to start their lives anew after the catastrophe of the Holocaust. They left everything behind, and put their best foot forward, to the one and only goal which put hope into their hearts: To reach the shores of the Mediterranean Sea, to make their way to Palestine-Eretz Yisrael, their historical homeland.

# 15
# Traumatic Uprooting

The Jewish family which returned to live in Zamosc was received with mixed feelings. Within a short time, all sorts of people began to remember Reizele, one of Rabbi Reznik's daughters, the young girl who had run off four years ago with some soldier – Russian, Uzbek, Kazakh – nobody knew exactly, but the rumors flew around at the time not only amongst the Jews, but also among the *goyim* in Zamosc. And here she was again, doing her shopping in the market, buying provisions for some man and a child, and an older woman. What is she doing here? They were flabbergasted, and what is more, she has the nerve to come back and ask to be lodged in what used to be her parents' house! The whispering and the evil eye and the slanderous gossip made Reizele feel as if she was an uninvited guest, unwelcome intruder in her own home town. It was clear to her and to her new family that they could not stay there for long, and she was just waiting to see how things would turn out, as fate would direct it.

It was Yuzhi who set off the spark which grew into a fireball, which threw the grenade straight at the doorway of their house and put an end to her indecision. One day, Yuzhi came home weeping and crying, bruised and beaten. Between sobs, he told his mother that he was playing football in the yard with their hosts' children, as he often did, and he happened to kick the ball over the fence. Suddenly, the oldest of the children, a boy of eight, started to shout at him very angrily, what are you doing, you dirty Jew-boy. I don't want to play with you anymore. Our teacher told us today that the dirty Jews killed Jesus our Lord, so I'm not going to play with you anymore. We don't want killers living here with us. You're a dirty Jew! His two younger brothers took in what he let fly from his mouth and they also started to shout at him the same insult, dirty Jew, dirty Jew. Yuzhi, who did not understand the implications of this at all, but felt the hatred and hostility towards him by their tone of voice, took it deeply into his heart, as if terrible curses were thrown in his face. Their nasty, hurtful voices made him enraged, so instinctively he punched the biggest boy in the stomach while crying, I'm not dirty, I'm not dirty, I wash myself every day, and I did not kill anyone. The eight-year-old boy who had gotten a thump from the almost four-year-old boy hit him back, and the two other children who had been playing with him so nicely until then, sprang to their big brother's defense because what he said made them, too, not want this Jewish boy there anymore, and they also began to rain blows on him, which sent him to the ground where they kicked him in his stomach, all the time chanting in a singsong, dirty Jew, dirty Jew.

All the while this was going on, the lady of the house, the mother of these children, stood at the kitchen window in silence, listening to the shouts of the children in the yard. She saw perfectly well what was happening there. Her face could not be seen behind the curtain, but it bore an expression of deep satisfaction. She kept on staring at them, but did not lift a finger to stop her children from attacking the little boy and when they came into the house, she pretended that she had no idea what had been going on, even though they were quite grubby and bruised from the ruckus, and their faces hot and red with exertion. She simply ignored their disheveled appearance, nor did she ask them what had happened, but merely asked them to hurry up and wash their hands and faces before sitting down to eat. The meal was already on the table and the children, for their part, as if they had already spoken about it together, did not tell their mother anything at all about the scuffle. Were they embarrassed? Did they feel that they had behaved badly towards their small neighbor, who was also a guest in their house? No. Not at all. They were very hungry.

As for Yuzhi, those two words thrown in his face with such viciousness – dirty Jew – were so harrowing that they became engraved into his subconscious so firmly that they accounted for two traits in his character and attitudes which would stay with him for the rest of his life. The word dirty, which was easy to understand, Yuzhi translated immediately to a compelling need to be always clean. With this always in the forefront of his mind, it developed into a constant obsession about cleanliness, frequently washing his hands and demanding that his mother scrub his body from head to toe every day. The last thing he wanted was to be dirty. He would do anything so that nobody would point the finger at him and call him nasty names as if he were not clean. He would show everybody how fastidious he was. Nobody would ever again call him dirty, and when he grew up he would wash himself several times a day. It would not only be his body that he was concerned would be clean, but everything around him; the dishes, the clothes, the floors, everything around him must be kept spotless and shiny. He had an irresistible urge not to leave even one speck of dust anywhere. His compulsive cleanliness oppressed him, took over his life, caused not only Yuzhi to suffer, but anybody and everybody who unfortunately happened to live close to him.

The concept of being dirty, which Yuzhi immediately grasped, was only half the poisoned arrow aimed at him. The concept of being a Jew, to which the children had attached the adjective dirty and related to him as if he were, Yuzhi did not understand at all, so he insisted on asking his mother what does it mean, Jew? Why did the children call me Jew, I'm not. I'm not, said the four-year-old child, who had never in his life heard about the Sabbath, had never heard the word synagogue, was ignorant of the Holydays and Jewish customs. Yuzhi stamped his feet crying bitterly, and sobbing, tell me, tell me Mom, I'm not a Jew. I'm not dirty, I'm not.

I'm not, and all his family stood around him astonished at his outburst, and it was very difficult to repair the mistake that had been made, that they had hidden from Yuzhi his real identity, so that he knew only about the church and Christmas. All had been calm regarding his religious identity until now, but in a flash, the truth had hit him between the eyes, not in a positive way which would fill him with pride and faith when learning about his true religion, but in a very negative way, as if someone had flung a handful of mud at him which stuck to his face and clothes, and which he had to shake himself free of in case it would stick to him forever and befoul his whole personality.

When Reizele began, awkwardly, to explain to Yuzhi the essence of Judaism – and Gittel also took it upon herself to talk to him about it – Yuzhi stamped his feet harder, getting himself into such a tantrum that they decided to leave the subject aside. From that time on, Yuzhi refused to listen to anything connected to religion, any religion. He grew up as a declared atheist, even though he was painstaking about telling anyone and everyone that his father was a Jew. As an adult, he even developed rather logical theories about the destruction and wars that religions had brought upon the world, and that there was practically no war in the whole of history in which religion had not been the cause and which had not broken out in the name of religion or for its sake. Again and again, he would preach about the cruel and superfluous losses wrought on mankind by religion.

Yuzhi felt he had to keep well away from the neighbors' children in case they continued to curse and mock him and treat him with scorn. This was a warning light to Reizele and Ruvke which made it clear to them that there was no point of them continuing to stay either in that house, or in fact in that country. It was fortunate that before long the news that the Allies had won the war over the Germans reached Zamosc. However, in spite of their misgivings, Reizele and Ruvke had to wait there for some time, until Sergei was able to gain his release from the army and receive permission from the authorities to let him leave the borders of the Soviet Union. As a Russian citizen, it was not so simple for him to leave, but Sergei arranged everything so that he could join Gittel, his beloved, with whom he wanted to tie up his fate and spend the rest of his life with her, so everyone in the family waited for him. When he came, they packed all the bags and headed for their sole aim – which was also the only choice they had – to immigrate to Palestine.

✦✦✦

They had to travel a long and hard road before they could reach their destination. All over Europe, when war finally came to an end, and in particular in Germany, Austria and Italy, were set up tens of camps to absorb all the Jews who had survived the Holocaust, but had lost everything dear to them; their entire families who had perished, their houses and all their property. The Displaced Persons' camps were for people who had been torn from their roots, like an uprooted plant whose roots fluttered in the wind, whether it was a hot wind from the desert, or a freezing wind from the north. Roots of people who had been severed from the earth which had once secured them, and now they were left shaking in the wind, with no solid ground beneath their feet.

Displaced and uprooted, these were camps for the long-suffering Jews with centuries of experience of displacement, from the earliest days of Jewish history and in each generation ever since.

Being uprooted began for the Jews with the Babylonian exile, after Nebuchadnezzar – Nabuko – King of Babylon, conquered Jerusalem and destroyed the magnificent First Temple, which had been built by King Solomon, after a long reign of an outstanding dynasty of kings ruled from Jerusalem over Judah and Israel, for over 450 years.

Four hundred fifty years stood the glorified Temple in the independent kingdom of Israel and Judah, in Jerusalem. Many years of Jewish independence ruled by kings since King Saul and King David, had come to an end. The Jews were exiled from their Land, and were devastated suddenly to find themselves in the *Galut* – the Diaspora.

An amazing historical narrative, which begins with the siege which Nebuchadnezzar – Nabuko – imposed on Jerusalem and which lasted for two years when he burst into the city and set the Temple on fire and destroyed it. That happened in the days of King Zidkiahu, the last of the Kings of Israel, a weak and indecisive king, controlled by his ministers and advisers, who accepted their advice and decided to rise up against Nebuchadnezzar.

He did not take heed of the prophet Yermiyahu, who warned him against rebelling in order to maintain the integrity of the People of Israel in its land. Yermiyahu prophesied that the chance of success in a war against the Babylonians would be very small, and advised reconciliation and surrender so as to prevent a catastrophe which would bring on a disastrous war. But King Zidkiahu didn't want to listen to the awareness of the prophet and did indeed rebel against Nebuchadnezzar, and declared war against him and Yermiyahu the prophet was thrown into a pit by the kings' ministers.

So, in the year 586 BCE after Jerusalem had been besieged for two years, Nebuchadnezzar broke through the walls and captured the city. As soon as the wall was breached, Zidkiahu and his escorts flew out via the southern outskirts of Jerusalem in order to escape over the Jordan River, but he was ambushed and captured and taken prisoner in the plains of Jericho and brought to Nebuchadnezzar's headquarters.

There exists a different version of his escape. According to an Arab legend, Zidkiahu escaped via a deep cave which bears his name, carved into the bedrock by human hands, which was used as a quarry for supplying building needs for the city of Jerusalem at the time of the First Temple. It was a huge cave with a fresh-water spring flowing beneath it, which can be found today under the Muslim Quarter in the Old City of Jerusalem, east of Damascus Gate.

However, King Zidkiahu did not succeed in getting away and was captured. Nebuchadnezzar ordered him to be brought before him to be sentenced by him, and as a single judge, he accused him of rebelling against him and gave the king a terrible verdict, to see his sons killed in front of his face. Nabuko butchered Zidkiahu's three sons as he was forced to look on the horrific sight, the worst thing for a father to see, but more than that, this horrific spectacle was in fact the last thing those eyes would see, for immediately afterwards King Nabuko ordered both of Zidkiahu's eyes to be plucked out. His heart did not miss a beat to hear the king's cries of pain, either to watch the streaming tears that shed from the blinded king's eyes like rivers; and a legend says, that the spring in the Cave of Zidkiahu comes from the tears shed by the eyes of the last king of Israel, who was afterwards deported, blind, to the exile of Babylon.

The wall surrounding the city of Jerusalem was breached and came tumbling down. Nebuchadnezzar destroyed the holy Temple, which had stood intact in all its glory for four hundred and fifty years, and ordered into exile to his country, Babylon, the Jewish citizens, in particular philosophers and intellectuals and the *Cohanim* and *Levites,* who served in the holy Temple, and all the upper- and middle-class Jews living in Zion. Only the poor people remained in their homeland.

Weeping and bereft, the Jews were driven from their land, and by the rivers in Babylon they sat and wept, when they remembered Zion. They hung up their silent harps, and song no longer filled their mouths. Only the longings of their hearts took wings and flew to the mountains and the valleys of their homeland, to Zion, their beloved homeland.

The exile to Babylon lasted for seventy years, relatively a short time of exile. During that period the Jews prospered. Their cultural lives flourished, and the Babylonian Talmud began to be written and developed at this time.

Then Cyrus the Great, King of Persia, conquered Babylon and decreed that the Jews forced into exile could return to their land; he also allowed them to worship their God according to their own faith.

When Jews returned from Babylon to Zion, they were like dreamers, and joyful song then filled their mouths and all the nations around said, their Lord has made them great salvation, they were like dreamers.

Under the leadership of Ezra and Nehemiah, they returned to Zion, their homeland, and became an autonomous people once again. They were free to practice their religion, established a thriving economy, and they built the second holy Temple in 516 BCE, ~~built by King Herod~~, which served as a focus for pilgrims from all over the country, to come to Jerusalem, three times a year on the High Holydays. It was not only a religious holy place but also a social and national focus for another six hundred years!

During the period of the Second Temple, the Hashmonain dynasty flourished. This was a vibrant period of self-rule and military strength, a period when the Jewish people and their culture bloomed, and the economy expanded, thanks both to the reduction of taxes which had to be paid to foreign states, and to the extension of the borders of the kingdom of Zion, including seaports and trade routes.

Jewish self-rule came to an end when the Romans invaded the land of Zion in the year 63 BCE. The conquerors imposed onerous taxes on the inhabitants, and their rule over them was so tyrannical that the Jews felt that they could no longer suffer the rule of an alien invader over their lands; hence they twice revolted against the Romans, in order to throw off the yoke.

Both the yoke of the oppressive taxes, which was robbery by another name, and the yoke of humiliation, the cruelty and barbarism the Roman rulers dealt out towards the Jews. Both revolts failed, and brought about the destruction and ruin of the Jews in Israel.

When the first revolt broke out, naturally, the Romans did not want their rule to slip out of their hands, and in response to the revolt they besieged Jerusalem for a period of two years, thus holding the Jews captive within the city walls, withheld food and drink from the inhabitants, leaving them starved and feeble. Disease was rampant and death common in those conditions, until they no longer had the strength to fight the enemy. When the time was ripe, the Romans breached the walls of the city and invaded Jerusalem, under the command of Titus, son of the Emperor Vespasian. The Romans killed the inhabitants and the leaders of the revolt, under Shimon Bar-Giora, set on fire the city, and destroyed the holy Temple in Jerusalem.

Only one wall of the outer wall of the Temple remained – the Western Wall, which has become a sacred symbol for generations upon generations of the Jewish people, wherever they lived around the world, a wailing wall, a place to pray, a place to mourn the destruction the holy place, of the glorified past of the independent Jewish kingdoms in Zion, and mourn the loss of Jewish existence in the country, for more than two thousand years.

The second revolt against the Romans broke out under the leadership of Shimon Bar-Kochba, with the support of Rabbi Akiva, sixty-three years after the first revolt had been put down, which led to the destruction of the holy Temple.

When the Jews had reached the limits of their endurance of being ill-treated by the Romans, both physically and from the effects of the draconian taxes they were forced to pay, Shimon Bar-Kochba came to the fore and led the revolt, firmly convinced that the Jews could only regain their national independence by rising up against the foreign invaders. But this revolt, too, was doomed to fail. Jerusalem was destroyed, and most of the inhabitants were exiled in chains to Rome, where they were sold as slaves for the highest price.

Not all the Jews were exiled to Rome in the wake of the Bar-Kochba revolt, however. There still remained large Jewish communities in Eretz Yisrael, and the center of Jewish spiritual life, which had formerly been in Jerusalem, before the destruction, moved to the city of Yavne, and afterwards moved to Usha, and centers of Jewish population spread out towards Galilee, to Tiberias, Safed and Zippori, where the Jews established flourishing communities and also worked the land. In that period, work was something highly prized, and thus Jews lived in Eretz Yisrael for many hundreds of years after the destruction of the holy Temple and the exile to Rome, and continued to live there also after the fall of the Roman Empire, when the land was conquered by the Byzantines. Under their rule, too, Jews thrived and prospered, and the land of Eretz Yisrael since, was called Palestine ... until a desert storm arose, and Eretz Yisrael was invaded by the new Islamic rulers, in the seventh and eighth centuries of the Common Era, when the rule of Islam put an end to Jewish settlement in Eretz Yisrael.

The religion of Islam that was established by Mohammed in Saudi Arabia in the sixth century of the Common Era was a religion which aspired to rule according to the Islamic religious laws not only in the country in which it was founded, Saudi Arabia, but also aimed to dominate, by force, all the countries of the world. Thus, immediately after the death of Mohammed, his faithful supporters began to invade as many countries as they could, one after another in quick succession, and wasted not a moment in trying to achieve their ambition to conquer the whole world and rule it according to their religious precepts.

Islam invaded Eretz Yisrael in the seventh century of the Common Era, by means of Beduin tribes from the Arabian Peninsula, who stormed northwards with great force. Wave after wave of Beduins invaded the country from Saudi Arabia, and came up there with their herds, their swords in their hands; during the period when the land was under Byzantine rule, and Jews and Christians lived there amicably and together built a highly developed society.

But the desert tribes who invaded Eretz Yisrael from Saudi Arabia sought to destroy it, and by the might of the sword they succeeded to conquer the land from the ruling Byzantines – and destroyed the Land until it became a desolate wilderness.

Over a period of hundreds of years, Arabs never settled in Palestine. They were not interested to settle in Eretz Yisrael for they preferred to advance to new territories with their avowed holy purpose of bringing the Islamic religion to all corners of the world. So they reached far-distant regions such as Anatolia, Armenia, Persia and Egypt. The sons of the desert galloped on their horses with their swords drawn, towards North Africa – Libya, Tunisia, Algeria, and Morocco – and by the cruel sword they imposed their religion on all the peoples of these lands. Whoever opposed them was killed. In Morocco, the Muslim invaders met with fierce and violent opposition, for the Berber inhabitants were fervent believers in their own religion, and did not want to take upon themselves an alien, new religion. They resisted the Muslims bravely and resolutely until in the end they had to surrender to the religion forcibly imposed upon them and accept the Muslim religion in their country.

From North Africa the Muslim invaders turned towards the countries of Christian Europe and there, too, the Christians were forced to bend the knee to the religion of the Muslim conquerors. Thus they conquered large tracts of Spain, and for 400 years the Khalifs held sway there until they were ousted by the Christians. By that time, the Muslims continued galloping to the East, and conquered, by using cruel force, all the countries of the eastern Mediterranean – Turkey, Syria, Iraq, Persia, and Lebanon – from where they penetrated into Asia; Pakistan and Afghanistan and many other countries in southern Europe, in the Balkan, which were later annexed to the Soviet Union, until they reached far-off Indonesia and great parts of Mongolia.

In all these countries the inhabitants were forced to adopt the Islamic religion. Country after country fell under the sword of the Muslim religion like a house of cards. Those idol worshippers, who at the start, strongly opposed it, were reluctantly convinced to accept the religion, by the violent tactics used against them by the Muslim conquerors.

But not among the Jews, who had lived until then, in relative tranquility in their land, Eretz Yisrael. When the Muslim invaders began to impose their Muslim religion on them and forced them to convert, quite naturally they met with strong resistance from the Jews, who were adamantly opposed to conversion, for they were not pagan idol-worshippers who Islam fitted them like a glove to their hand. They were people whose religious faith was planted deep within them, and no new religion would uproot them from it.

In response to the Jews' opposition to conversion, heavy taxes were imposed upon them which they found impossible to pay; this was in addition to the persecution and harsh decrees inflicted on the Jews until their physical and emotional suffering was so great that they had no strength left to remain to work their lands or remain in their homeland. Having no other choice, some of them fled to other countries while they were still able to do so, and the Jews who did not succeed in fleeing, or who did not want to abandon their houses – the Muslims completely eliminated. They killed and murdered each and every male, and as for the women, now widowed, they converted them by force to Islam by taking them as wives. Their children, who were born Jews, were forcibly converted to the Muslim religion, and all the children born after to the Jewish women from their Muslim husbands, were Muslim from birth. Thus, because of the forced conversion of Jewish women and their children at that period, the situation arose that the majority of Palestinians born since then in Palestine are the descendants of those Jewish women and their children.

Thus did Islam succeed by force in expelling and killing and exiling all of the Jewish inhabitants of Eretz Yisrael from their land for many hundreds of years.

Hence Eretz Yisrael was almost completely emptied of its Jews in the wake of the Muslim conquest, and there began hundreds of years of exile for the Jews in Europe and North Africa and the Middle East.

But not completely. Jews still remained living in Peki'in, in Tiberias and Safed, and during the years, little by little, there were Jews coming back to their Land. In the 13th century and the 16th century the *Chasidei-Chabad* came, and in the 18th century the *Talmidei HaGara* came and settled in Eretz Yisrael.

Concerning the Arabs, for hundreds of years Palestine was left for the most part, uninhabited and desolate. Thorns and thistles and worms covered the land. The Beduin tribes who had penetrated northwards did not intend to settle and work the barren land to make it fruitful. They preferred to be traders and used the area as a conduit for trade between Egypt and Damascus. The Beduin invaders from Saudi Arabia controlled the passage of travelers with an iron hand, and exacted high taxes from all those who passed through the region. The situation continued to be similar during the period of the Mameluke rule when the Egyptians invaded both Eretz Yisrael and Syria. Even then, the Beduin were the dominant force who ruled by the sword and cast terror all around them. In the 16th century, with the invention of gunpowder, the Beduin could use guns and would threaten travelers in the region with these, and demand from each traveler a toll, which was called kahari toll. The same emptiness was true also after the land was conquered by the Turks in 1517. The Muslims did not settle the land and did nothing to cultivate it, so it remained a barren desert.

As far as the Muslims were concerned, it provided a convenient springboard to conduct wars of conquest in Europe and the Far East and to spread the Islamic religion to as more countries as possible and all this time they regarded Eretz Yisrael as a land merely to pass through.

In the late nineteenth century, Mark Twain, the celebrated American writer, described his experiences when visiting Palestine. He wrote in 1867 – only 15 years before the start of the First Aliyah of Jews to Eretz Yisrael, his book "Innocents Abroad", in which he wrote with some sarcasm about his Great Pleasure Excursion to the Holy Land.

In colorful language and sharp as a razor, Mark Twain depicts in his book the pleasures of his journey:

> A desolate country whose soil is rich enough, but is given over wholly to weeds ... a silent mournful expanse ... a desolation that even the imagination cannot give living beauty to ... We reached Tabor safely. We did not see a human being on the whole route ... hardly a tree or shrub anywhere. Even the olive tree and the cactus, those fast friends of a worthless soil, had almost deserted the country ... Palestine sits in sackcloth and ashes, desolate and unlovely ... Over it broods the spell of a curse that has withered its fields and fettered its energies ... Palestine is not part of this workaday world ... It is sacred to poetry and tradition, a dream-land ... Nazareth desolate ... Jericho cursed ... Jerusalem – a derelict, oppressed village.

The emptiness of Palestine at that period is not only described in the literary sphere, as in Mark Twain's chronicles of his travels. There was also a scientific aspect. A map of vast proportions prepared by a British survey expedition to Palestine, between the years 1871 and 1887, attests to it, too.

A well-known map collector, Dan Yardeni, purchased this map from an antique bookseller's store in London, at a bargain price. This colossal map – the size of a room – was drawn up by a team of British cartographers of the first rank, on a scale of 1:63000, after they taken meticulous measurements of the settlements then existing in Palestine. Thus, for example, they assessed the size of Haifa as a town of 400 x 90 meters; of Nazareth as 180 x 90 meters; of Tiberias as 600 x 60 meters; Sheik Munis, a small village, as 180 x 90 meters; Jaffa, a small town, as 180 x 90 meters; and even Jerusalem – which in that period was still confined between its walls – measured 1000 x 1000 meters, when the majority of whose inhabitants, as always, till then, were Jews.

During the period of the second half of the 19th century, the Arab population of all these centers together combined was around 100,000. The Israeli researcher, Professor Moshe Maoz, indicates in his wide-ranging study on the subject, that in spite of the fact that in the period of Ottoman rule which began in the 16th century, there lived in Palestine at that time close to 500,000 Muslims, as a result both of harsh measures carried out by the Ottoman rulers and the poor sanitation existing at the time, the population was in constant decline. Thus, for hundreds of years, the numbers of Arabs living in Palestine decreased and amounted to only 100,000 until Jews began to emigrate there, beginning with the First Aliyah, when they began to fill the almost total vacuum which existed.

The Jews of the First Aliyah, who returned to their historic homeland, found Eretz Yisrael almost completely uninhabited, apart from small Arab communities here and there. The

Jews began to fill the land with settlements and towns and kibbutzim. Jewish pioneers labored to coax the earth back to its previous fertility, and thus they returned to themselves their full rights to this Land, which had belonged to them since time immemorial, and in this way they represented the fulfillment of the Zionist vision:

> People without a Land.
> For a Land without People.
> A Land without People.
> For People without a Land.

It is an ironic coincidence that only then, around 120 – 130 years ago, the Arabs began to wake up from their long-standing sloth and lethargy, when they saw the Jews returning and coming to settle and work on the land, the First Aliyah and the Second Aliyah and the Third Aliyah, waves upon waves of Jews, mainly from Eastern Europe, who came to the Land, fuelled by Zionist and Socialist ideologies; and the Jews who came from North Africa, for the most part from Morocco, because of religious and nationalistic reasons, fuelled by the rich historical feelings of belonging.

The Arabs did not understand what was happening at all, and it aroused in them fierce opposition. Their response to the Jewish immigration to Palestine was to begin to gather people to live in Palestine from all corners of the Arab world, with the aim of demonstrating their presence there. At the beginning of the 20th century, there was suddenly a deluge of immigrants from neighboring Arab countries to Palestine: Egyptian citizens, who moved to live in Gaza; Jordanians, who penetrated into the center of the country to live in Nablus and Jennin; and Syrian citizens who flooded Galilee and established Arab villages there.

At the same time as they were massing in Palestine, the

opposition of the Arabs to the settlement of Jews who had returned to their Land, took a violent turn. Riots and the murder of Jews became an everyday occurrence, and the policy of the British Mandate gave them support and encouragement with the issuing of the White Paper, which severely limited the numbers of Jews allowed to enter their homeland.

This, then, was the situation in Palestine at the end of the Second World War, when hundreds of thousands of Holocaust survivors waited to emigrate there. Out of longings for a country of their own, out of religious yearnings, as the only choice for refugees, of feelings of historic belonging to the Jewish Homeland. For all – or any – of these reasons, these remnants of the devastated Jewish communities of Europe, were knocking at the doors of Eretz Yisrael/Palestine and begging to open to them the gates of their homeland and be allowed in.

# 16
# Dramatic Encounters

Miraculously, without either knowing of the existence of the other, albeit only a short distance one from the other, the two brothers, Ruvke and Yuda and their partners, were traipsing and trundling around almost in parallel, climbing onto trucks filled with refugees, crossing borders, aided by Jewish organizations which provided refugees with food and basic necessities. Ruvke was ahead of his brother Yuda by only a few days, traveling southwards, to the north of Italy, waiting for the smell of the salty sea, the Mediterranean Sea, which would take them on its waves to their destination – to their homeland country.

Until they reached the end of this stage of their exhausting journey, to the Displaced Persons' camp in northern Italy.

The camp had been set up by the Joint, the Jewish Agency, and other Jewish organizations such as the Jewish Brigade and the organization for illegal Aliyah, in order to aid Jews left after the war without a roof over their heads, and provide them with food and shelter there. They took care of arranging their passage on a boat which would one day take them to Eretz Yisrael.

Ruvke, Reizele, and Yuzhi, together with Gittel and Sergei, were tired but optimistic when they reached the Displaced Persons' camp, where they found a large assortment of refugees. These were the survivors of the concentrations camps and death marches, fighters, with the partisans and in the ghettos, Jews who had emerged from their hideouts, Jews who had been evacuated from anywhere, such a hodgepodge of everything there. The overcrowding was insufferable, a turbulent river of refugees overflowing its banks in all directions, sanitation left much to be desired. Each family received its own small space in a barracks, a tent, or a room in one of the buildings. However, the knowledge that these conditions were only temporary, a waiting-period until their turn came to embark on the boat which would take them to their homeland eased these difficulties.

What upset Gittel most, was the fact that she and Sergei were registered in the DP camp as single persons – each of them in fact widowed – that is, their connection and commitment to each other was not recognized by any official authority. They were unable, therefore, and in those circumstances they did not wish to have intimate relations. However, they were forced to live at some distance from each other, and this frustrated them greatly. Ruvke slept at Reizele's side, but Gittel slept with Yuzhi, and Sergei found a corner for himself somewhere. This situation, together with the knowledge that they would soon be setting sail and the boat would be even more overcrowded than the camp, made Ruvke think that *davka* now, when they were among their Jewish brethren and with Jewish leadership, the time was ripe to make their connection official, and he determined to do something about it.

The next morning, when they had finished breakfast, he said to Reizele and his mother and Sergei: Last night I came to a decision. We cannot go on like this. We have to make our relationships official, even today, let's get on with it. I want to marry Reizele. What about you, Mother, Sergei, do you want to get married? Ruvke's question was like sweet music to their ears, and Sergei and Gittel's faces were flushed with emotion. Yes, yes, they answered in chorus, we want to be husband and wife.

Reizele for her part turned to Ruvke and kissed and hugged him, saying that those words were the ones she had been longing to hear from the very first moment when she saw him holding his violin and playing in the prisoners' orchestra in the concentration camp. The only question was, if it is possible for a marriage ceremony to be conducted legally in the DP camp.

Ruvke had no doubt at all that it was possible. Among soldiers in the Jewish Brigade who had recently been demobilized from serving in the British Army, there were Rabbis who had been Jewish chaplains, and they, as far as he knew, were authorized to conduct marriage ceremonies. And so, later that same morning, his heart beating fast with excitement, Ruvke made his way to the hut of the camp administration in order to find out whether a double wedding could take place as soon as possible in the DP camp.

When he set out, he could not have imagined in his wildest dreams that, within a very short space of time, the original question he had intended to ask about having a double wedding performed, would be transformed into having a triple wedding ceremony.

While still on his way, deep in thought, to the offices of the administration, he passed by a young couple who had just arrived at the camp, trying to find the room they had just been told about where they would be able to stay. An ordinary couple, like all the overburdened couples living in that huge camp, and Ruvke passed them without taking any particular notice of them. Although, when he had gone another few paces, a sudden thought flashed into his mind, and he did a double take. There was something about the face of the man which looked familiar to him.

Good grief, how could I not have recognized him. The thought struck him like a blow, and he stopped dead in his tracks, and turned his head around, asking himself, Just a second, isn't that my brother? He was overcome by a wave of intense emotion, and he turned on his heels and broke into a run. He caught up with the couple from behind, and without a second's thought – perhaps he had made a mistake – tapped the man on the shoulder, who turned his head towards him with a dismissive, rather resentful, expression, which immediately turned into one of joy when he realized who the other man was. Yuda could hardly believe his eyes, seeing his younger brother, Ruvke, standing in front of him. The two brothers fell into each other's arms wordlessly, only the tears which filled their eyes were evidence of the joy in their hearts at this completely unexpected meeting. Ahuva was moved and thrilled as she stood to the side, looking on at the emotional scene. She grasped immediately that she was witnessing the reunion of two close relatives, and when Yuda introduced her to Ruvke as a friend he had come to the camp with, Ruvke hugged them both, and said excitingly, come with me, you have no idea, Yudele, who you are going to see here, and when Gittel saw her elder son coming towards her, she put her hands to her face in disbelief. She fell on his neck and burst into tears of happiness. Look, two of my sons have come back to me, she stammered, still hardly able to believe it. As for Ahuva, Gittel treated her lovingly as her son's partner, and made room for her second son, Yuda, and his Ahuva in their own cramped space and, in the difficult, crowded living conditions of the camp, nobody thought anything of it, other than as an astonishing family reunion.

They sat together for hours on end that day, recounting what had happened to them. Ruvke grasped that in fact Ahuva was Yuda's fiancée and that although she had at first clung to him in the wake of tragic events, he for his part had chosen her out of love, and Ruvke was happy to tell the couple that when they had met that morning, he was on his way to the offices of the administration of the camp to ask if someone could officiate at wedding ceremonies for two couples there in the DP camp. Do you also want to take part in the wedding ceremony? Do you want to get married, as the third couple, under the same wedding canopy as us, Ruvke asked them with a hint of a smile. Yuda and Ahuva blushed with pleasure, and nodded their heads in agreement and great happiness, for soon the prohibition on any physical contact between them which they were so eager for but had abstained from, would be lifted and they would become husband and wife and thus have the status, according to Jewish law, to enjoy loving marital relations.

✦✦✦

Ruvke's request was received with great enthusiasm in the offices of the camp administration. A triple wedding? Whoever heard of such a thing? Yes, absolutely yes. The Rabbi of the DP camp will marry you according to the Jewish laws but your marriage certificates will be issued only when you reach Eretz Yisrael. But after the wedding ceremony you will be properly married couples.

When Ruvke returned with that good news, the three brides embraced each other and energetically and excitedly prepared to get themselves ready for their weddings, which would take place in only a few days' time. They washed and scrubbed and perfumed themselves, and even though there was no *mikveh* for the purpose of purification before the wedding, they showered themselves as thoroughly as they could, given the circumstances in the camp.

In the evening before the day of the wedding ceremony, Ruvke brought out his violin from the pile of his belongings, the violin which had never been out of his hand during all the years of the war and its tribulations. He began to play, as if he were playing to himself, soothing music, traditional Jewish tunes, music from prayer services, songs of Eretz Yisrael which they were already familiar with in the Diaspora, and his family and those who lived with them in the same barracks, slowly gathered round, one by one, and a hush of silence came over them, broken only by occasional soft humming, as they listened for a long time to the tunes played on the magical strings of Ruvke's violin.

The three brides dressed the next day in the best clothes they possessed, straightened out the creases with their hands, combed their hair and made up their faces, hugged and kissed each other and walked together towards the hut which had been prepared for the triple wedding ceremony.

Behind them, trailing in silence, there walked Yuzhi, with an expression on his face of someone who, for lack of any other option, had reconciled himself to an evil decree.

Many of the inhabitants of the DP camp had gathered around the wedding canopy, which was made from a white sheet tied to four poles, which four muscular men held firmly in their strong arms, and under it stood Ruvke and Reizele, Gittel and Sergei, and Yuda and Ahuva. Although the canopy was only made from a big white sheet, it gave them the same wondrous feeling as if it were made from the richest purple brocade, and the officiating Rabbi sang all the seven blessings of the wedding ceremony, to which all those present said, Amen. He even gave a short speech remarking on the wonders performed by the Creator of the world who brings couples together at such a difficult period as their own, and how out of the ashes left by the flames of war and the Holocaust, He still makes it possible for love to bloom and hope to flourish, so that life can continue.

After the *Hakafot*, and each of the women had sipped from the glass of wine held to her lips, and each of the bridegrooms had put on the finger of his bride a makeshift ring of which he was the owner.

And then came the traditional breaking of the glass. Each groom in turn stomped on a tiny glass which was put on the floor next to his foot, powerfully so that it broke into fragments, in memory of the destruction of the holy Temple in Jerusalem, hundreds of years ago, never to forget.

After the legal part of the ceremony was over, everyone who was present applauded, and the sound of clapping echoed all around, and more than a few tears were furtively shed.

Quite spontaneously, someone began to play the accordion, and a few couples hesitantly got up to dance, and the dancing gathered momentum with spirited Chassidic circles, and also Israeli folk dances which they remembered learning in the youth movements before the war and even in their time in the ghetto. The bridegrooms were hoisted up one by one onto the shoulders of people who only the day before they had never met. Yuda, Ruvke, and Sergei were lifted up, raised high in the air, while their brides modestly looked on, standing at the side and laughing with unrestrained pleasure, and at the end of the proceedings, the hugs and kisses continued, and happiness shone over everyone.

Except for one small boy who remained standing, bewildered, at the side, without the hint of a smile on his lips. Nobody took the slightest notice of him, nobody held out a hand to him. Yuzhi was dumbfounded as he watched the ceremony, his face red with rage. He understood the situation very well and, to put it mildly, he did not at all like the rejoicing and merriment taking place in front of him. What Yuzhi understood most acutely was that a large share of his mother's love for him was being stolen from him at those very moments – forever.

The days at the Displaced Persons' camp were full of organized activities. Soldiers of the Jewish Brigade who had participated in the battles to liberate northern Italy remained in Europe to help with the absorption of the hundreds of thousands of refugees. Together with emissaries of the Zionist movements from Eretz Yisrael, they did sterling work in rehabilitating the refugees and in preparing and giving them practical guidelines regarding their immigration. They even gave them military training towards the struggles which they anticipated would break out in Eretz Yisrael. These people in the camp accepted all activities very eagerly, since they knew that all the bridges which connected them to their former lives had been burned behind them. They were now prepared to put up with all the hardships that they knew there would be on the cramped immigrant ships just as long as they could reach Eretz Yisrael, their hearts' desire.

Before long, Yuda and Ruvke were given the task of helping the instructors prepare the refugees for immigration, and while they were becoming familiar with the camp leadership, it fell to them to allot places for the immigrants on the ship which was shortly due to set sail from the port of La Spezia for Haifa.

In the middle of one night, 38 army trucks full of aspiring immigrants, driven by soldiers from the Jewish Brigade, clandestinely set out from the DP camp for the port in northwest Italy, where they would board the ship, the Af-Al-Pi-Chen, which was waiting to set sail on the open sea, towards the east, to Eretz Yisrael.

The trucks traveled slowly in the dead of night, carrying hundreds of passengers of all ages. The Kirgelik family was among them, excited and on edge about the voyage. Even though they realized that it would hardly be a pleasure cruise, they could not imagine the obstacles which would be placed in their path to prevent them from reaching their destination. The first of these was, when they arrived at the port and the convoy of the trucks was ordered to stop by Italian soldiers, who suspected them of hiding Italian Fascists trying to get out of Italy. However, the Jewish guides persuaded the Italians that they were not carrying Fascists, but Jewish refugees, that the most appropriate place for them to hide was on a boat waiting in the harbor to spirit them away. The Italians searched the trucks and were finally convinced that there were no Italian fugitives to be found but indeed only Jewish refugees, and agreed to let them go on their way to the ship.

In a calm and orderly fashion, the illegal immigrants silently got down from the trucks in total darkness, and climbed one after another up onto the deck, which was already occupied partly by refugees who had been brought to it from Italy itself. They were allocated small cabins, and everyone could already visualize himself sailing out to sea in a very short time.

Their hopes of a pleasant and speedy voyage, of looking out on silver-tipped waves or at the reflection on the sea of the golden sunsets or the silvery moonlight; to spot fish darting about; to gasp in wonder at the spectacular scenery of the islands they would pass – these were quickly dashed on the rock of murky reality and heroism at one and the same time.

The British Mandate authorities were subject to the laws laid out in the White Paper of 1939 in which Britain restricted immigration to Palestine, and therefore did not allow ships which had Jewish illegal immigrants on board to set sail from ports on the Mediterranean Sea. The reason behind this restriction was ostensibly economic, assuming that too many residents in Palestine would, Heaven forbid, topple the economy and cause those already in the country difficulty in finding work. This alleged reason was, essentially, only an excuse. The real reason was black politics, black like the oil supplied by the Arab countries to Great Britain. That is why the British were so stubbornly blocking the country's shores – just to support the Arab position against Jewish immigration.

The ship, Af-Al-Pi-Chen, a name which means Although, Against All Risks, was ready to raise anchor and try to leave the port without being detected, but the British grasped immediately the nature of the passengers the boat was carrying and closely surrounded it with their destroyers, blocking it from going out of the port. In its desperate situation, the ship behaved in accordance with the meaning of its name: although the doors of Palestine were closed to it; and although the British sent warships in order to stop them from leaving the port, and ordered them to disembark from the ship, the refugees did not give up, refused to move an inch, and declared a hunger strike.

At this time, when the hunger strikers were refusing all food and only allowing themselves a daily ration of a meager amount of water, something extraordinary happened within the Kirgelik family, who were still thrilled by their completely unexpected reunion with Yuda. This additional bonus filled their hearts to overflowing with joy.

One day, Sergei and Ruvke were sitting on deck playing chess; Reizele and Gittel sat not far from them patching up some of their worn-out clothes which until now they had not had time to mend, and now they had time in abundance; and Yuda and Ahuva, who had taken it upon themselves to assist refugees who were all alone without anyone to attend to their most basic needs, were helping a lame old man, his face wrenched in pain, find a place to sit on the crowded deck – *and then it happened.*

Yuda and Ahuva were standing talking to the old man, trying to figure out how he, who in their eyes was extremely old – around 70 – had gotten himself onto the boat bound for Palestine, and were interested to know how his leg had gotten injured. When they asked him, the old man began to tell them his life story, but became somewhat confused, and it was clear that he was quite taken aback by the situation he found himself in. He gradually calmed down and began to tell them that only a few days ago, he had had no idea what on earth he was going to do. He was desperate and, as he was absentmindedly wandering along a street in Milan, he collided with a large stone mushroom-shaped barrier, on a cracked curb, which he had not noticed, and fell flat on the street. As he fell, his leg buckled under him, and he probably dislocated his kneecap. He was very fortunate that his leg was not broken, but it hurt terribly. His greater stroke of good luck was, that when he fell, a soldier ran to help him get up. When the soldier heard that he was Jewish, one of the survivors of the Jewish community in Rome, and that he had lost all his family in the Holocaust, he suggested to him that he should get on this immigration ship, which was what he was intending to do himself. If it had not been for this soldier – Anshel, if I'm not mistaken – yes, his name is Anshel, I don't know what would have happened to me. He saved my life, and put me on this boat. I will never forget what he did for me. Thanks to him I will get to sail for my homeland. I have distant relatives in Haifa and they will be happy to have me with them. If it wouldn't have been for that soldier, that what's his name, Anshel, I would have been left there in the street like a lost dog. Anshel put me on the ship, and I will never forget his kindness.

Yuda listened intently to the old man's tale, and was quite riveted when he suddenly heard the name, what a coincidence, his brother's name, Anshel, his younger brother by a year! The last time he had seen him was when the two of them had decided to flee from the Warsaw Ghetto. Since then, they had gone their separate ways, and it was as if they had been separated for an eternity, an eternity of time and of distance.

When Yuda had gotten himself together again after the shock of hearing the name of his brother, he tried to get the old man to describe the soldier as best he could. The old man was just beginning to give Yuda some details about him, when a broad smile suddenly spread over his lined face, the smile of a man who had seen someone he was pleased to see, for, at that same moment, a young man, full of energy, came up to him. The young man was wearing the uniform of an army Yuda found hard to identify. It was certainly not the uniform of the Jewish Brigade. The soldier cried cheerfully to the old man, Hi, Roberto, how are you. I can see you have already found yourself people who can help you, and when he saw the trembling finger of the old man, pointing to the couple standing behind him and stuttering with excitement that they had just been asking about the soldier, Anshel turned towards the couple – and remained standing rooted to the spot.

Seconds passed in silence while the brothers stood facing

one another, until they were able to whisper the other's name, tentatively questioning: Anshel? Yuda? And then, they gave a cry of delight, and fell into each other's arms, hardly knowing if it was a dream or reality.

At that moment, Ruvke had just managed to take off the chessboard the knight which had been attacking him, and Sergei was holding his head in his hands, wondering how he had made such a stupid move. Suddenly Ruvke heard loud voices coming from behind him and wondered how on earth any of the hunger strikers, their stomachs rumbling from severe hunger had the energy to utter more than a squeak. He turned his head, and saw Yuda hugging a man dressed in a scruffy army uniform. His interest was aroused, impossible thoughts began to fill his mind, and his heart began to beat faster. He stood up, and began to walk hesitantly towards them. He recognized Anshel immediately, and hurried to his brothers, still locked in an embrace, and hugged the two of them in his long, muscular arms. They stood there, the three brothers, for a long time, holding each other close, too happy for words, oblivious to the stares of everyone, open-mouthed, around them, who were moved to tears by this miraculous reunion.

When Gittel saw that her two sons who were with her on the ship, were embracing another man, she slowly got up from her chair, and went towards them, full of curiosity, her heart pounding away as if it suspected that something very much out of the ordinary was taking place. When she saw Anshel, she almost fainted, and Ruvke had to hold her in case she fell. He comforted her, and watched with emotion as his mother held the son she had just been reunited with. They held each other close in a long embrace, their tears falling freely, until someone found them somewhere to sit and Anshel could tell them all everything that had befallen him during the war, which he had come through safely, with God's help. He told them about his escape from the ghetto; about his change of identity after finding identity papers in the clothes of a dead man; about his wondrous time with the small boy, Lova; about his joining the Anders Army and taking part in the battle for Monte Cassino, and the battles for Bologna and the Po Valley; and about going to Milan for a short time when the war ended and he joined up with the Jewish Brigade, who had also fought in the invasion of northern Italy, until it finally surrendered, and whose mission now was to aid Italian Jewish refugees who had survived the *actions* and the transports to the Nazi concentration camps. That was how he had come across Roberto, the old man, whom he had seen fall in a street in Milan, when he happened to be walking along, and ran towards him to help him. As he found out that Roberto was a Jewish refugee, and was in dire straits, he took Roberto under his wing and saw to all the procedures which had to be taken care of to arrange for Roberto to embark on the same ship that he himself had chosen to immigrate on.

The only thing he deliberately kept from them were the difficult events in the Italian village in the Caccuri region – the gang rapes of the Moroccaniata, and the rape he was personally subjected to by that woman Silvana. He just did not want them to know he was involved in all those events.

Immediately after the war ended and he was released from Anders Army, Anshel got rid of the identity card he had carried with him which he had taken from the body of the dead man he had come across after he had fled from the ghetto. It had been an alien identity, although one which had helped him greatly in his hour of need. However, he no longer needed it. He was now a proud, bold, Jewish immigrant.

*Get away from me, Milush Grybacz, he said to himself, go away, Milush, don't come near me again, go far away from here, Milush, and don't come back anymore. No more Milush, No more Grybacz.*

Anshel tore the identity papers into tiny pieces and threw them away, together with all the forms he had had to fill in bearing his adopted name. He breathed deeply, feeling the fresh air of freedom fill his lungs, with his return to his own name, the name that would leave no room to doubt that he was a Jew, and proud to be one – Anshel Kirgelik.

✦ ✦ ✦

The Af-Al-Pi-Chen spent a long time at anchor in the port of La Spezia, but in spite of the constant hunger the passengers experienced, no one protested or complained. Everyone was determined to show that their faith in their basic right to free the ship and sail off eastwards, would bear fruit. In that time of waiting, the Kirgelik family adopted Roberto, and he became almost one of the family, and the warmth they showed towards him gradually encouraged him to open his heart to them, and he agreed to tell them what he had gone through during the war. Was the Holocaust in northern Italy similar to the Holocaust for other European Jews? You would think they were living in two different worlds, except that Jewish destiny is the link between victims whatever their geographic region; the only difference was that in Italy, the Holocaust began later.

The Kirgeliks were open-mouthed from the start, when they heard that Roberto had been a professor of history at the University of Rome. His ancestors had reached the Italian capital with the Jews the Romans had exiled after the Bar-Kochba rebellion in the first century of the Common Era, when the cream of Jewish society in Eretz Yisrael was expelled from its land. Dumbfounded, shamefaced, uprooted from their land and their homes, they were exiled to Rome and sold there as slaves. Roberto was a descendant of one of these ancient exiled families, which had deep roots going back hundreds of years in Italy; he was a law-abiding and fiercely loyal citizen, and left no stone unturned at that time – the 1920s – during

Mussolini's rule, to prove his devotion to Il Duce and his patriotism. Like many Jews, he served in the Italian Army for a long period, and even joined the ruling Fascist party. Yes, that's right, we didn't see any conflict between our Judaism and the ideology of Italian Fascists, Roberto was quick to add when he saw the amazement on the faces of his listeners. At that time, Mussolini was good to the Jews, and they felt politically and economically secure during the 1920s and the early years of the thirties.

Things became significantly worse for Jews when Mussolini joined Hitler and in 1938 allowed the Nuremberg Race Laws to apply to Italy, too. However, it was only in 1940 that they began to be put into operation, and then the Fascist ideology slapped us in the face, and we began to understand the connection between Fascism and racism and anti-Semitism.

What was typical about the Racial Laws was the discriminatory decrees that were passed, for instance, the heavy taxes Jews had to pay, the ban on Jews owning land, the requisitioning of property, things like that. The Jews who suffered most were those who held jobs in government offices, and in academic and educational institutions; lecturers, teachers, and clerks. Overnight, they all lost their jobs. They simply came to me and said, we're sorry, but we aren't allowed to employ you any longer at the university. Your position is closed to Jews now, we're sorry, Roberto said – his face red from the humiliation that still burned inside him – and I was forced to leave the position I'd worked in for decades.

No one organized a farewell party in my honor. I did not get any compensation for being dismissed. They sent me away in disgrace. But I didn't give up, and I didn't go into a depression like others who were dismissed. The shock helped me become active in helping members of the Jewish community who were having a hard time, mainly students who had been expelled from their schools and colleges. I put my heart and soul into the work. We set up independent educational institutions of all kinds for these young Jews; schools, centers for Torah study, music courses, and so on, and we hoped that the bad times we were going through would soon be over once the war ended.

But we were mistaken. When Mussolini surrendered to the Allies who had invaded southern Italy, he was deposed, and the leaders of the Italian Socialist Republic that was established, immediately issued orders calling for the Jews to come and report to their local police station and bring with them their belongings. All the naive, compliant, obedient Jews packed their suitcases, and off they went to the police station. And what did they get for being so trusting? They were sent off to a concentration camp, and later to a death camp. Only the young ones, those who were healthy and strong, were sent to a forced labor camp. The Jews who had better instincts and were less easily deceived, ignored the orders, and many of them began to leave their houses and hide themselves in villages round about, and in monasteries. Whoever was able to and had more sense, left the country and fled to Switzerland. Did I flee abroad? No, I did not. In fact, it never entered my head. My wife and I carried on living in our large apartment on the outskirts of Rome, where we had brought up our two daughters. They were married now, each of them with two children of their own. When the decrees began to take effect, and they were left alone with their children after their husbands had been taken to do forced labor or to Heaven knows where, my wife urged them to come and live in our house, assuming it was better protected than theirs. I'll never forgive myself that I let them come to us, although of course it never crossed our minds that the worst was still to come.

Suddenly, one autumn morning, September 5, 1943, the Germans invaded the whole of the north of Italy and reached Rome, where they immediately began to persecute the Jews.

They summoned the leaders of the Jewish community to the

German Embassy there and, without any attempt at civility, began to hurl at them harsh allegations in the most chilling manner, akin to an iceberg causing the sinking of a ship: We regard you Jews as enemies, the Nazis thundered at them, their faces on fire with rage, while the Rabbis stood shaking with fear. You Jews pose a special danger to the Third Reich. However, they added, if you manage to collect 50 kilograms of gold within the next 36 hours for the German war effort, nothing bad will happen to you or to your community.

Roberto held his head in his hands, as if to hide from what ensued after that impudent scheme was put to the Rabbis. Good grief, how stupid we were, but I immediately sensed that this was a plot. While the heads of the community were at the German Embassy, I was in the offices of the Jewish community, and when I heard the proposal that had been put to them, I warned them not to believe the Nazis. Nothing good would come out of it. They are lying to you! I shouted out to them, but they nodded their heads wearily and shrugged their shoulders, as if to say, do we have any choice? The Germans look upon us as dangerous enemies, they threatened us! So, we mustered up every shred of hope we had, for the slightest chance they will leave us alone if we come up with the gold.

We all rushed off, everyone who was active in community business, to collect whatever gold the Jews of Rome possessed. We went from house to house, everyone understood what was at stake, saving lives is more important than gold, as long as they will leave us in peace, they said, and unclasped their necklaces, took off their rings, opened chests and drawers and pulled out all their treasures, jewels which had been passed on for generations from grandmother to granddaughter.

Those who had hidden away gold bars didn't hesitate for a second to bring them out and hand them over to us. Some people were against giving up their precious gold, protested, and at first refused to part from it, but we convinced them that their lives were more precious than gold, and in the end they agreed. I actually thought in my heart that I was lying not only to them, but also to myself, but I prayed that I was wrong and that the gold would indeed save us from those coming to annihilate us, for we had heard what the Germans did to Jews in the countries they invaded, so should we believe them when they said that no harm would befall on us if we bring them the gold? I was in two minds and struggled with myself all the time I was doing what I could to collect the gold for the German *Moloch*, but I was more and more skeptical, and I'm sorry to say that my instincts proved to be right. In the 36 hours they gave us to come up with the gold, we collected 30 kilograms more than the 50 kilograms the Germans had demanded. We gave them 50 and the 30 that were left, we locked away in the safe of the community offices for future needs. In our innocence, we thought, we can relax. We have nothing to be afraid of, now that we have paid our pound of flesh. But it didn't take long before we realized how greatly we had been deceived, and it hit us like a bolt of lightning in our head. For the Germans' behavior to us after they had received our gold became harsher and harsher. It reminded me of the extortion of the kidnappers towards the rich parents of children they had snatched; they demanded a ransom for the child, and when they receive it, as soon as the money was in their hands, it turned out that the child they had kidnapped, had already been killed.

Yes, Adolf Eichmann, who was in charge of the extermination of the Jews, did not lose much time from the minute our gold was turned over to them and transferred to the treasury of the German Reich. In October 1944, he sent one of his people to Rome, and immediately afterwards, special security forces were sent there from Germany and started hunting down Jews. The Germans divided Rome into sections according to where the Jews lived – the Jews' addresses were already known to them – and gathered the Jews together in *actions,* when they were imprisoned, and later sent to concentration camps or death camps.

Roberto almost choked on his words when he came to the hardest part of all, but he made a great effort, and continued with his story: On the same day as the *action,* which was carried out as a secret military operation, I went out of my house at crack of dawn to meet up with others active in the Jewish community so that we could go to the homes of Jews and help them get organized and find somewhere to hide. That was after I had arranged an excellent hiding place in the attic of the building where we were living for my own family, and we had taken provisions up there which would last us for quite some time. Our Catholic neighbor lent me his ladder and helped me get everyone up there; my wife, our daughters and grandchildren. So with an easy mind I went out to do my sacred work, to help lot of other Jews to hide or to flee, but when I came home late that evening, no one was there. The attic was empty. It had been turned upside down, and there were signs of a struggle, of things, or people being dragged along. I was scared stiff that the worst had happened, and ran screaming to my neighbors, who just stared at me glassy-eyed, open-mouthed. I could not tell if they were silent because they were shocked and upset, or because they felt ashamed and guilty. They could hardly bring themselves to say that the Germans had come and dragged out of the attic everyone they found there, and loaded them onto the trucks waiting in the street. They said they recognized my wife and my two daughters and some of the children. The Germans knew where to look, perhaps somebody informed on us, that's what they said, and I went crazy with fear and worry. I just rushed outside like a madman, until I got myself together and realized that I was putting myself in danger, too, and made up my mind that I would not let them take me as well. I still had a smidgen of hope that somehow I could rescue my family out of the jaws of danger, perhaps they were imprisoned in some camp and there was still a chance of getting them released. However, I very quickly realized that I would have to go underground otherwise I would fall into the clutches of that devil, Eichmann. I also knew that I could not put my trust in any of my Catholic neighbors anymore, because it was as clear as daylight that one of them had informed on me and my family. I dismissed the possibility to stay in my apartment, since I knew the Nazis would come for me straightaway and drag me out of there, so the only thing left for me to do was to leave my house, which was no longer my fortress, and go into hiding in the safest place I knew – inside the church. Only with the neighborhood priest I knew I would find a place of shelter, and that is what I did. The priest, who knew me well, opened the doors of his church to me and hid me in a tiny storeroom next to his room until things calmed down.

All Roberto's listeners sat listening to his story as if they were hypnotized, when out of the silence the voice of Anshel exclaimed loudly: But Roberto, the Church was silent! The Pope has not to this day said a word against the murder of Jews by Germans, so what happened? – Well, yes, you are quite right, Roberto answered him quietly. Pope Pius XII kept silent, all the time the Germans invaded one country after another in Europe and took control of them all, but by the end of 1944, it was clear to him that the Germans were being defeated and would lose the war. He was certain of this, and changed his policy, telling the priests and heads of the monasteries to help Jews and shelter them, and that saved a lot of Jews from being taken to the death camps.

Roberto was not the only one who was saved, thanks to the Church. About 4,000 Jews were hidden in churches and monasteries in and around Rome, and their lives were thus saved. However, thousands of others were trapped in *actions* and transported to Auschwitz, including all of Roberto's family. Together with other doomed Jews hunted down and ensnared in other Italian cities, in particular Florence and Milan, the number of Italian Jews sent to the gas chambers in the death camps of Germany and Poland was more than 7,000.

The dramatic story of how the Chief Rabbi of Rome, Israel Zolli, was hidden became known later. When the Germans invaded Rome and started their persecution of the Jews, he found refuge in the Vatican. The Chief Rabbi spent several months under the protection of the sheltering wings of the Bishops in the Vatican, until the Allies liberated Rome in July 1944. However, when he wanted to return to the office of the Chief Rabbinate and take up his position again as Chief Rabbi of the city, the Council of Rabbis refused to let him do so, and held some sort of short trial, a show trial, where it was alleged that he had betrayed his Jewish flock in the city by handing over lists of the Jews to the German regime when the Nazis invaded Rome. He denied it, but because of solid, proven evidence against him, Rabbi Zolli was dismissed from the throne of the Rabbinate and, in reaction to his ignominious removal, he converted to Christianity!

Converted? The Chief Rabbi of the Jews of Rome during the war became a Christian? What came over him? Was he baptized? Did he kneel during Mass? Did he make the sign of the cross when he saw a statue of the holy mother and her son? Opened his mouth to receive the communion wafer on his tongue? What did a man like him feel in his heart of hearts while doing all these acts?

Something else was bothering Reizele. How and why did Roberto reach Milan, where Anshel came across him? Why, *davka*, Milan, when his home was in Rome? Roberto's glance fell on her. He had a far away look in his eyes, which had misted over as if he was not seeing the people in whose company he was, but the events themselves, which he had just described to them so vividly that the Kirgelik family had hung on his every word.

The priest who had hidden me for all those months in the

storeroom next to his room came to me one day in May 1945, said Roberto, and told me that the war was over, the Allies had won. He said that I didn't have to hide myself away any longer. I was free to go out into the world again. I felt relief and anxiety at the same time, for I knew that things would never be the same as they were before the war. While I was in hiding, I felt that all my worries and sorrow about the loss of my family, and the fact that I had not been able to do anything to save them, had aged me. From being an active and energetic man, I was now a wreck. Even though my physical health was good, I was in very low spirits, and a man whose world has fallen apart neglects himself and becomes weak and frail, a shadow of what he used to be. I thanked the priest for everything he had done to save poor souls like me, and went out into the glare of the sunshine. All around me in the streets were people whose reactions to the end of the war, to the victory of the Allies, were similar to mine. They too felt a mixture of joy and relief, and sorrow, stunned at being free again, overwhelmed by what they had lost, by the devastation, and by all the destruction the war had brought about.

On a pendulum which swung incessantly between hope and gloom, Roberto, who for months had hardly had room to move his legs in the confined space that had been his hiding place in the church, put his best foot forward and set out to walk towards his house. He had decided that he would go back to his large, spacious apartment on the outskirts of the city, and try to rebuild his life. But when he got there, he was met by the glaring faces of strangers. A family with many children had settled themselves in his former home, and behaved as if they owned it.

We are sorry, but the apartment is ours now. We came by it legally; and without bothering to explain further, the door was slammed in Roberto's face. He realized that there was no one to talk to there, and full of rage, set out for the offices of the municipality to protest that his apartment had blatantly been taken over by strangers. They informed him politely but firmly that all his property had been requisitioned, and that ownership of his apartment had been handed over, legally, to the family now living there. We are sorry, but that is how it is.

In desperation, Robert now turned to the offices of the Jewish community, for which he had put in so much work, and met up there with many other Jews whose property had also been seized. After a great deal of effort, they eventually found him a place he could stay in for the time being with a Jewish family who had managed to go back to their former home. Everyone was resentful and bitter about the Holocaust, which had fallen on them like a ton of bricks, but determined to get over it and do their best to recover from it. The Jewish community held elections to choose a new Chief Rabbi to replace the deposed Rabbi Zolli, and the new Chief Rabbi worked tirelessly in helping to rehabilitate those Jews who had survived the horrors of the war, the deportations and the transports to the death camps.

Gradually, Roberto came to the decision to leave Rome. He felt in every fiber of his being that he had made the right decision, for he realized that he was sick and tired of the city which had taken his dearest family from him to slaughter them; the city which had robbed him of all his property; which had left him without a roof over his head and made him dependant on the mercy of others. He was given a modest sum of money for his expenses from the administrators of the Jewish community for all the work he had done for it, and set out for Milan, which after the war became the main artery for Jews from all over Europe, wanting to immigrate to Palestine. Roberto even nurtured the hope that he would meet some of his distant relatives who had lived in Milan for years, and that they would offer to put him up until he got back on his feet. When he reached Milan – that magnificent city where

12,000 Jews lived before the war, and of whom only a few thousand were left, all the others having been exterminated – he did in fact meet there one of his distant cousins, somewhat older than himself. His cousin described to him the *actions* committed in Milan, in which his wife and children had been taken cruelly away, when he was absent of home, so he was left on his own, like Roberto himself, except for one of his sons who had survived, and he wanted to be with him and stay in Milan.

Roberto, who was lucky to find a place for himself with his cousins, had spent the days wandering around the city, and his heart ached to see the terrible destruction suffered by the Great Synagogue, when the Allies had bombed Milan in a bid to force the Germans surrender and leave the city. The synagogue that had a glorious past, filled to capacity, and now stood silent in the rubble, as if in mourning for all the congregants who had thronged there on Sabbaths and Festivals; a magnificent synagogue tear-stained, as it were, from weeping for the congregants who had most of them been murdered, a once-impressive synagogue at the sight of whose crumbling walls every Jew who passed by, shed a tear.

One fateful day, walking as usual through the city, Roberto did not see a barrier put up on the street, stumbled over it, and fell down, unable to move. Luckily, a young man in uniform rushed over to him and helped him get up, and sat him on a bench, and began to talk to him. What a fantastic chain of events his stumbling in the street produced: truly miraculous, for Anshel suggested that he come with him and get on the boat waiting to sail for Eretz Yisrael. And, as he had relatives in Haifa, he decided that he would do that. He would go to them when the ship arrived. He was sure they would be happy to have him, and here I am, telling you the story of my life.

Fatigue suddenly came over the Kirgelik family, and they looked exhausted. The constant hunger and thirst they battled against had not worn them out as much as Roberto's story;

it had shocked them all, in spite of the fact that each one of them had suffered in the Holocaust, and each had been scarred by it. They fully empathized with Roberto, but now they were very tired and closed their eyes to rest a little, after they had received some water to relieve their thirst.

✦ ✦ ✦

The hunger strike staged on the ship, the Af-Al-Pi-Chen, made news all over the world. Radio and newspaper reports told of the cries of the would-be immigrants languishing from hunger and thirst, and the unsanitary conditions on the ship, and emphasized that the hunger strikers had survived the Holocaust and had suffered indescribable torments during the war. The media strongly criticized the indifference and inhumane insensitivity of the British, until the British were forced to give in to public pressure and withdrew the warships blocking the ship from setting sail and allowed the ship to raise the anchor and leave the port for its destination.

The passengers on this ship were remarkably fortunate. The British allowed the Af-Al-Pi-Chen to anchor in Haifa port and its passengers to disembark. However in return for this, the British subtracted the numbers of people on the Af-Al-Pi-Chen whom they permitted to set foot on the shores of Palestine, from the quota of immigration certificates they would issue to future immigrants.

Not every immigrant ship was so fortunate. Other ships, organized by Aliyah Bet emissaries, who by subterfuge of one kind or another succeeding in having them set sail from ports in Italy and France, were captured on the high seas, and British warships would immediately stick to the sides of the boats like leeches and, like on the dodgem cars, would push the immigrant ship on to its side, swinging all its passengers in all directions, while firing cannon shells at it, disregarding the severe damage they inflicted which would cause the ship to sink and all its passengers to be hurled into the sea.

Don't think we will allow you to bring more Jews to live in Palestine! It will not happen at any price! the British stated emphatically. We shall not endanger the black gold, oil, that the Arab countries supply to us, to fulfill your needs.

So, it came to the surface that the refusal to let Jews immigrate was not because of an economic situation which might arise, but just a political decision based on the pro-Arab leanings of the British, who abandoned the generous Lord Balfour Declaration of 1917, which granted the establishment of a national home in Palestine for the Jewish people; and preferred Arab rule there, subject to the recommendations set out in the White Paper of 1929, which imposed restrictions on Jewish immigration to Palestine. Based on this policy, the British sent destroyers to ram ships carrying immigrants and blockade the shores of Palestine, lest the immigrant ships somehow succeed in reaching them. They related to the immigrant ships, full to the brim with wretched and weak human beings, as if they were enemy battleships. If any of the immigrant ships managed, after a voyage beset with many dangers and having been attacked from all directions, to reach the shores of Eretz Yisrael, British soldiers would lose no time in barricading the approaches to the shores, push their way onto the ship, and force the passengers to disembark. They would then be taken to the Atlit Detention Camp along the coast, as if they were criminals, surrounded by barbed wire and watchtowers.

For months on end, people were kept imprisoned there, without trial, and when the detention camp at Atlit was full, the immigrants were brought on board, immediately on reaching the shores. British warships which stood waiting to fulfill their mission; the would-be immigrants were taken, as if they were damaged goods, to crowded, fetid detention camps in Cyprus, in which disease and epidemics spread like wildfire in the appalling conditions there.

This situation persisted for more than two years after the end of the Second World War, and during this time the *Yishuv* in Eretz Yisrael revolted against the British authorities, blew up and destroyed and shot and struggled with the British in order to force them to leave the country. All the Underground movements, the Haganah, and the Etzel, and the Lehi, even with so many opposing viewpoints and fierce arguments amongst themselves, united against the British Mandatory rule which was so blatantly biased, in order to force them to leave Palestine and put an end to their rule.

And then, after the British were pushed out of Palestine, in a dazzling, historic moment, full of faith, and taking his courage in both hands, the leader of the *Yishuv*, David Ben-Gurion, announced the establishment of the State of Israel. No calculations regarding the economy or employment for new immigrants stood in the way of the urgent need to rescue all those prospective new immigrants being made to drift about on the stormy seas, or face the dangers of being smuggled via alien mountains and valleys from the Eastern countries like Syria and Iraq, on their way to Eretz Yisrael. Now the doors of the State of Israel were wide open to them. The Law of Return was passed legally in 1950, and all the refugees languishing in detention camps, and all Jews anywhere in the world who desired to immigrate to Israel – became citizens of the State immediately on setting foot in the Land.

# 17
# With The Abandoned Child

Within a short time after they had disembarked from the ship in Haifa, the Kirgelik family knew where they were headed. They first of all took care of Roberto's needs, and made sure that the immigration authorities in the port located his relatives in Haifa and that they would come to get him and take him to their home. They bade farewell to their dear Roberto, after assuring each other that they would certainly meet in the future.

The Kirgeliks were of one mind regarding their own first steps in their new country. The story of Anshel's coming across the abandoned child, Lova, and taking it upon himself to look after him, had touched them greatly, and when they saw how Anshel was eager to set off to see the boy, they all agreed that they would go with him. So, they asked the immigration authorities to look after all the formalities to make the necessary arrangements for them to stay on the kibbutz for an unspecified period. Only after they recovered from the traumatic journey, and got to know the place and the way of life a little, would each couple be able to decide where they wanted to make their permanent home. Even at this stage, however, Gittel said that she had no intention of living on kibbutz. She needed her privacy, her independence. She did not want the members of the kibbutz secretariat dictating to her how to live her life, and where she had to work. She did not fancy the way of life of a cooperative agricultural settlement. No, no, that was not for her. As for Sergei, he strongly agreed with Gittel. From what I have heard, he said, the kibbutz way of life reminds me too much of the collective Kolkhoz in the Soviet Union which I ran away from. I want to be free of all forms of the collective way of life the regime imposes on its citizens.

Ruvke and Reizele had their own reasons for agreeing with Sergei. We are not going to stay on the kibbutz. We are going to live in the city, because only in a city will Ruvke be able to find an orchestra of a high enough standard so that he will be able to make a living playing his violin. But for the time being, let's all go to the kibbutz. It will be a good opportunity for us to live close together for a little longer, and enjoy being with our wonderful, supportive family.

When the Kirgeliks put their suggestion to the Jewish Agency team responsible for new immigrants' first steps on landing in Eretz Yisrael, they immediately agreed and, within only a few hours, the formalities had been settled and the Kirgeliks were on their way to the kibbutz. There they were allocated three small huts, each furnished sparsely but adequately, where they would be able to rest and relax, and recover from all the rigors and hardships of the journey.

As to contribute their share for their keep, they had to do kitchen duty, and work wherever the work manager sent them. It was quite clear to them that in the kibbutz, if you wanted to eat, you had to work, and it made no difference if you were a guest or a member. As soon as new immigrants arrived at a kibbutz they were thought of as potential members whose commitment to work was taken for granted. None of the Kirgelik family considered this a problem. On the contrary.

After resting for a couple of days and seeing to various things for the family, Anshel asked at the kibbutz secretariat office where Lova's adoptive family lived. They had already been told of the turns and twists of fortune which had brought Lova to them, and late in the afternoon, after the parents had completed their work for the day, and the children were brought from the children's house to their parents' home for their daily visit, Anshel made his way along the paths of the kibbutz to meet Lova. His heart was pounding and he was tense and nervous. The secretariat of the kibbutz told Lova's adoptive parents that Anshel was coming, and they decided to wait for him in their modest home, but they did not tell Lova in advance that Anshel would be visiting them, for they wanted to see with their own eyes what Lova's unprompted reaction would be when he saw Anshel – so unexpectedly – again. Would he remember him? Perhaps he had forgotten all about him. Who knows? Only a surprise encounter, completely unplanned, would enlighten them as to Lova's feelings about the man, who deep down they had the feeling that he had come to claim his own adoptive paternal rights to Lova.

Anshel knocked nervously at the door of the house, and a middle-aged woman opened it, asking him quietly, Are you Anshel? He nodded, and she beckoned him to come inside. Sit here, in the armchair she whispered to him and then she turned towards the child who sat in the corner frowning with concentration as he played with his toy cars, and called over to him, Lior, you have a visitor. Come and say Shalom to him. Lova lifted his head, not too interested to see who the visitor sitting in the armchair might be, who was looking at him so intently. It took about a second for his indifference to vanish and for his eyes to shine with happiness. A glimmer of joy spread over Lova's face, and he leapt up like a frog in pursuit of a dragonfly, from where he had been sitting on the rug, and ran straight into Anshel's arms, saying with excitement, papa Milush, papa Milush, and hugged him as if they had not been separated for three whole years, but only for three days. For his part, Anshel put his arms around the child and gave him a strong loving hug. Lova, my dear Lova, I've come back to you now, as I promised you, and Lova, even while being embraced, protested, I'm not Lova anymore, I'm Lior, and I go to school and I know how to read! Hebrew words streamed from his mouth, which Anshel, the new immigrant, could not make head or tail of, but it was enough for him to see Lova approach, to grasp that the child was genuinely thrilled and excited to see him again.

So that they could carry on a proper conversation, Anshel began to speak to Lova in Polish. The child understood, and asked Anshel how long he intended to stay there, and if he would come to live with him. Anshel replied that he hoped to stay there for a long time, but still didn't know for exactly how long, for he suddenly realized instinctively that the child had become the adopted son, though not yet legally adopted, of the middle-aged couple sitting across from him, their incredulous eyes following the dramatic scene of the encounter between Anshel and the child.

Anshel had no idea how they were all to manage their lives, and he kept on hugging his beloved child, and said, Lior is a lovely name. Then a thought entered his mind that he should change his name, too, for here, in the Hebrew spoken country, the name Anshel is not really appropriate.

Anshel and Lior's adoptive parents sat and had a cup of tea together, the couple still startled by the emotional reunion they had witnessed, at Lior clinging to Anshel, not wanting to let him go. They had never imagined that Lova-Lior had, during all this long period of separation, hung on to the hope, that Anshel would come back to him. It was simply incredible since he had never asked about him, he just waited with endless patience, so it seemed, completely certain that Anshel would keep his promise and return to be with him.

Anshel and his hosts talked pleasantly amongst themselves for a while, and although the conversation was accompanied by smiling and joviality, there were undertones of tension caused by the fact that each side wanted very much to bring up Lova-Lior as his son. Lova sensed the tension in the air, without understanding its cause, and pressed Anshel to go outside with him so that they could go for a walk. Anshel was happy to get away from the oppressive atmosphere that had arisen in his hosts' house, and he and Lova quickly went out, and happily ran and played hide and seek on the grass.

They played until the time came when Anshel had to take Lova back to his family, as one of his adoptive parents was due to go back with him to the children's house. However, Lova refused to leave Anshel, and pleaded with him, pulling at his arm, to come with him when they went back to the children's house. Anshel hesitated. He felt uneasy that, already in this first visit, it would look as if he were trying to replace Lova's adoptive parents by taking the child back to the children's house, but in the end he gave in to Lova, and they went back together to the house, happily walking hand in hand.

Instead of finding the couple being there, Anshel was surprised to see a young woman standing in the living room. She was slim and wearing shorts and sandals, her black wavy hair flowing onto her white neck, and her pretty face, wore no make-up. Anshel quickly realized that she was the only daughter of the couple. Hi, Lior, she smiled brightly at the child. I have been waiting to take you back to the children's house, and added apologetically that her parents had asked her to take Lior back there, as they had urgently to go to visit a friend who was very sick. Lior said to her, I'm glad you came, Nina, but I want Anshel to take me back as well, and Anshel patted his shoulder as if to say that this was fine with him as long as Nina had no objection, and what objection could Nina possibly have, to see this good-looking, well-built young man appearing from nowhere and striding into her parents' house as natural as anything?

They shook hands and introduced themselves, and fortunately Nina spoke good Russian, and Anshel had enough basic Russian to get by, so they were able to talk to each other. They walked along, with Lior in the middle, holding each of them by the hand, towards the children's house.

Nina said to Anshel that she knew that he was coming to visit them, and she straightaway began to tell him how Lior had curled up inside himself, as it were, in his first weeks with them, not wanting to speak to anyone, and the poor boy could not understand a word of what anybody said to him. He played with the children, but did not join in much, certainly did not make any friendships, and did not utter a word, until suddenly, all at once, he began to chatter away to everybody in fluent Hebrew!

He had learned the language and stored it all up in his head until he felt completely confident of speaking it without making mistakes, said Nina, and Anshel, who had been looking at Lova affectionately, suddenly found himself bringing to the children's house a child he regarded as his son, and walking with a stunning young woman he had been talking to as if they had been close friends for years. When they handed Lova over to the capable hands of the child care worker, the two of them walked together to where Nina lived and went their separate ways, having arranged that they would meet the next day to take Lova from the children's house at the usual time, and would both spend time with Lova while he was at her parents' house.

If Anshel had previously had any doubts about whether he wanted to settle down in the Kibbutz, they all disappeared into thin air. He came back to his cabin, then went in to see his mother and brothers and said, his eyes shining: Well, my darlings, I'm staying here. I intend staying to become a member on the kibbutz, because today I have found here not only my son, but also a woman to love.

A month after their arrival at the kibbutz, and after they had begun to take part in the work roster and begun to get to know members of the kibbutz socially, the Kirgelik family decided to contact the Interior Ministry – through the good offices of the kibbutz secretariat – in order to change their names to Hebrew, as their present names did not feel right now that they were living in their homeland. They had left the *Galut* behind them, and they wanted to do similarly with their names and change them into Hebrew names. After a brief discussion, they decided to change their surname from Kirgelik to Kidron; Anshel would be called Aharon; Gittel chose the name Geula, and Sergei, who changed his forename to Shmuel, took on his wife's surname and also became Kidron; Yuda was registered as Yehuda on his identity card; Ruvke was from now on Reuven, Reizele became Rivkah, and Yuzhi – as for Yuzhi, he became Yossi.

This was also a vital opportunity to legalize Yuzhi's status as a citizen, so, at the same time as his name was changed, he also received his birth certificate, according to the details his mother, Reizele, gave the clerk at the Population Registry of the Interior Ministry. Yuzhi was born in Poland, on June 22, 1941, she declared to the clerk. His father's name? Does his father's name also have to be recorded? Fine, no problem, his father's name is Mordechai, Mottele everybody called him, Mottele the son of Berele. No, of course I haven't got his father's birth certificate, nor my marriage certificate. My son was born during the war. We fled from there with just the clothes on our backs, don't you understand? We are Holocaust survivors. We have no papers. Everything was burned, destroyed, especially since my husband was killed on the same day my son was born, and my name is Rivkah, daughter of Yechiel Reznik, who was a rabbi, and he was murdered in a death camp in Poland with all my family!

In this way, Yuzhi's birth certificate was issued according to the details Reizele furnished, without her heart missing even one beat as she gave the authorities inaccurate, or to be more precise, wrong information. The main idea was not to leave any gaps on the birth certificate, and Mottele is certainly a more acceptable name for the father than Arkadi. Better to have a fictitious name than a problematic, obviously *goyish* one, or leaving a blank in the space for "Father's name" on the birth certificate, which would blind her son with the brilliant white space of its omission every day of his life.

The week after Yuzhi became Yossi, he was circumcised.

This was not done by a ritual circumciser in a religious ceremony with prayers and the customary feast, but by a surgeon in the hospital, because Yuzhi was already a boy of five. His foreskin had not been removed eight days after his birth but, better late than never to enter into the Covenant of Abraham. Now Yuzhi had at long last been circumcised. He was a Jew, according to religious law, and the law of the country that demanded being a son of a Jewish mother.

For six months, all the family stayed on the kibbutz together, learning the Hebrew language diligently in the *Ulpan*, the special intensive language study program, and working at all the tasks required of them. They were content, even though they knew that they would not be there for much longer.

Two months after their arrival at the kibbutz, they all joined in the celebrating the marriage of Anshel and Nina.

At the wedding ceremony, held in the Cultural Hall, Anshel and Nina were married, and Lior and Yossi, the two pageboys, accompanied them to the wedding canopy. The face of one of the pageboys, Lior, was suffused with smiles the whole day, while that of the other, Yossi, revealed his anger and unhappiness; for everything that could be said to increase the happiness of the family as a unit, Yossi experienced as having the effect of decreasing his own well-being, and he felt discarded, sidelined, his heart was as heavy as a stone.

After the wedding night, Anshel and Nina moved Lior from her parents' house to live with them in their new home, and made all arrangements to become his legal adoptive parents, while Nina's parents, who had adopted him until now, became his grandparents. Lior was as happy as a dog with two tails, he had a mother and a father and also a grandmother and a grandfather, and the tensions that there had been at the first meeting between Anshel and Lova's adoptive parents disappeared completely. They all rejoiced at this perfect solution to what could have been a problematic situation, a solution which seemed to have come from on high in such amazing circumstances, so that it was as if there had been heavenly intervention to arrange matters to have them all stay together, closely involved in bringing up that enchanting boy. Lior, despite all the hellish traumas of his past, was, at the core of his being, both emotionally and physically healthy. This enabled him to develop a joy in life and a deep insight, so that he became a capable, hardworking person, succeeding in whatever he put his mind to.

After they had spent six months together on the kibbutz in Galilee, the Kidron family said their farewells and went their separate ways, rather like a pod whose seeds the wind scatters in different directions. Anshel of course stayed on as a member of the kibbutz with his wife, Nina, and his adopted son, Lior; Gittel and Sergei went to live in a rented apartment in the Florentine neighborhood in South Tel-Aviv, which bordered Jaffa, a small town surrounded by orchards, where Arabs and Jews coexisted, not too harmoniously.

Sergei proved to have a good head for business. His years-long experience as quartermaster – responsible for supplying food and uniforms for the units in the Soviet Army in which he served – stood him in good stead now, and he began to engage in trade, making a living by buying and selling. He had been a reluctant communist, and now, out of the blue, he found himself free of all the pseudo-ideological restraints of communism and rose up and tore them to shreds and ground them to dust. But not those of the slaves and the starving did he throw off, rather the shackles of communism that had hampered him all his life which he rejoiced to break free of. The period he had spent on the kibbutz, which he regarded as a miniature Soviet kolkhoz, opened his eyes, and it was clear to him that this kind of life was contrary to the way people were meant to live. As soon as he realized that the communal life was not for him, he determined to go it alone, and by his own efforts build his life the way he felt was best for him.

As for Gittel, she had been as happy as a songbird ever since she had come to Eretz Yisrael, and was full of gratitude each day for her good fortune. She was overjoyed to have met and to be living with such a wonderful man as Sergei, who was generous and hardworking, a man she could rely on, with a good sense of humor, pleasant to be with, and helpful to everyone he came in contact with, and was so charmed by him that she lovingly accepted their challenging living conditions, for she felt that with Sergei by her side, she lacked nothing. Even though these were difficult times, beset with the anxiety and fear of what the future might bring, she did not let things get her down. After all the horrors and traumas she had gone through in Poland, nothing could frighten her. The life of wealth and happiness she had enjoyed before the war now seemed far removed from her; it was all water under the bridge now.

Yuda and Ahuva chose to go to live in the old-established village of Hartuv in the Judean Hills, and after the village had to be abandoned, went to live in Bet Shemesh which was established next to it. In those days, it was in its infancy, but grew to become a large town.

Ruvke and Reizele, with Reizele's son, Yuzhi, went to live in the capital city itself, Jerusalem. The little money they had at their disposal, together with an allowance for new immigrants from the immigration authorities, enabled them to live in a two-room key-money apartment in the center of the city, and they hoped that it would not take long for Ruvke to be accepted to play in the Voice of Jerusalem Symphony Orchestra and develop the musical career he so longed for.

*But the pages of history never stop turning themselves over, not asking anyone when to speed up events and when to slow down. Time is indifferent to the events and needs of man, and does not adopt itself to circumstances. It has been unfailingly accurate for millions of years and thus has never disappointed. Because of this, it does not hesitate to demonstrate its superiority without a trace of false modesty, knowing that everything is subordinate to it, whether willingly or unwillingly.*

The pages of history turn, and those who only recently were freed from the dark abyss of the Holocaust in the lands of their birth, now found themselves trapped by a bitter, ruthless enemy, the Arabs, demanding that they give up their freedom, their religion, their homeland, and their lives – and this after they had at long last gotten to the Land of their Forefathers. This was the reality that greeted the new immigrants, and the Kirgelik family found themselves driven to volunteer and enlist in the fledgling forces to fight for their lives and the lives of their own people, the Jews, in the land for which they had yearned for hundreds and hundreds of years.

Each couple in the Kirgelik-Kidron family made for a different area of the country, as if a virtual work manager directed them to their destinations, a higher power that the Minister of History forced upon them without their being able to resist; an inner urge which took them to the places they were assigned to, far away from the peace and quiet they were hoping to find.

Instead of joining the orchestra, Ruvke joined the Underground. Underground organizations were not alien to him ever since he had participated in the Warsaw Ghetto revolt against the Nazis. Now he presented himself at one of the stations of the Irgun, which were located in private, out-of-the-way apartments, in the city, in order to volunteer. The commitment to rebel against the enemy who – also here, in his new homeland – wanted to exterminate him, appealed to him. In addition to the Jews' specific enemy, the Arabs, the British had made common cause with them and were trying with all their might to aid the Arabs in their black and dark desires to obliterate the Jews.

It is unbelievable, Ruvke said to his wife, Reizele, the British are always portrayed as being gentlemen and believing in fair play, in equity, and here they are, knowing full well that the Arabs have more than twenty states where they speak the same language, have the same religion, the same culture and customs, and some of these states are a vast distance from here, and *davka* here, in the very land which is considered to be the historic homeland of the Jewish people, and is the only place this people can find shelter, for they have no other country – *davka* this tiny country they are intent on pulling away from us like a carpet from under our feet?

Ruvke eloquently and passionately inveighed against what he felt was a blatant lack of justice, and this feeling impelled him to volunteer with the Etzel Irgun. He took part in a number of operations whose aim was to get the British out from Palestine, which they were holding onto by their fingertips even though they knew that their days as holders of the Mandate were numbered and that they would be departing from Palestine very soon.

Yuda, the eldest brother, enlisted in the Haganah organization. His experience in fighting with the partisans in the forests of Poland led him to the most well-established organization in the country.

Anshel, for his part, had had the best military training and had fought under the command and supervision of General Anders, and as one who had participated in battles against the Nazis in the Second World War, was given command of the Galilee region and of the Haganah fighters serving there.

Thus, in the spring of 1948, the Jews in Palestine were involved not only in armed struggle, but in a struggle to make sure that daily life was able to continue, and in making a supreme effort to rid the country of the British, whose rule under the Mandate was very far from impartial. And at this time of turmoil and turbulence, with each and every one of the Jews in Eretz Yisrael determined not to let the opportunity for autonomy slip between their fingers, came the historic declaration of David Ben-Gurion of the establishment of the State of Israel.

A few months earlier, on the evening of the vote on the future of Palestine by the United Nations, half a world away, in New York, the whole of the *Yishuv* was sitting biting their fingernails listening to the live radio broadcast. Will we have a State? One by one, members of the General Assembly voted, and the *Yishuv* held its collective breath. YES! YES! It was unbelievable, yet for all the hundreds of years which had gone by since Jewish self-rule in Eretz Yisrael, when a variety of foreign rulers had conquered and reigned and fallen so many times, and had slipped in and out of the land, stamping on it and battering it with disdain and neglect – a state would arise!

On November 29, 1947, a large majority in the United Nations voted in favor of the establishment of a Jewish State. Such excitement, such delight, such cries of joy!

But all the tide of heartfelt rejoicing and the circles of happy dancers and all the celebrations which filled the streets, could not dispel the anxiety and concern about what the future would hold.

Now that the world, in the guise of the UN, had given legality to the proposal to establish a Jewish state, this was the signal for the Arab countries to declare war on the infant state. Their culture of aggressive conquests – they always said *No* to any suggestion of sharing the Land, and always opposed and deprived any hint of compromised agreement – drove them to rush over the emerging Jewish state, to conquer it, to destroy it and to exterminate all the Jews living in it. There would be no Jewish state in this region, they announced. There will only be Muslims here.

The desolation and neglect which had prevailed for hundreds of years in the land which would now become a state, and the fact that only a hundred years ago they started to inhabit it, were of no interest to them and enough to justify their lust for possessing the country, even if remaining deserted and neglected as it was these days with meager and small, lousy, poor Arabic settlements. The main thing was that the Muslim religion would subjugate the Jewish one, and that the land would be ruled by Arabs.

And what about the Jews living here? In war, it is permitted to kill, and even if not, no nation in the world would utter a word against seven Arabic countries, supported by other fifteen Muslim countries. Anyway, any of the Jews who survive, would convert to Islam and whoever is unwilling to convert, would leave. Or – at the best – stay here as a dispossessed minority.

In the all-out war which the Arabs waged on the nascent state, they were defeated. Justice was the winner, natural justice, and moral justice, resulting in justice for humanity. The Arabs lost most of the battles and, finally lost the war itself, and Israel became and has continued to be a sovereign state since 1948.

However, the Arabs did have some significant successes in the War of Independence. Eighteen settlements in Israel fell and were conquered by the Arabs, and by a strange – and perhaps symbolic – coincidence, each man from the Kirgelik-Kidron family took part, separately, in these fierce encounters. Ruvke fought in the battle for the Old City of Jerusalem, while Yuda fought at Latrun, two battles which ended in defeat; Anshel fought for the liberation of Western Galilee, and Sergei took part in the conquest of Jaffa, two clashes that only a hair's breadth separated the eventual victory – after sustaining setbacks and losses – from failure and defeat, and each of the Kirgelik-Kidron men had a hand in the victories which were achieved.

# 18
# Battles Of Independence

Passion, rebellion, mutiny, the readiness for sacrifice, the desire to fight in defense of the homeland; heroic feelings mixed with dense clouds of anxiety and concern, like an intruder gripping their throats – fired the entire *Yishuv* in Eretz Yisrael in those fateful days.

The days of the British Mandate were nearing their end, but like the spasms of a dying man in his death throes who summons up every ounce of energy in his struggle to get some air to breathe, the British made it their policy to sabotage and delay and thwart with all their power and cunning, the achievement of the independence of the Jews in their own state; in contrast to their enthusiastic efforts to aid the Arabs to undermine and block every possible step to advance the Zionist enterprise.

Ruvke did not manage to play his violin much after he came to live in Jerusalem. He preferred to join the underground movement and took part in some of the most daring operations intended to expel the British from Palestine. When the War of Independence broke out, he was enlisted in the defense of the Old City of Jerusalem. In opened eyes he joined in the battle, which went down in the history books as the worst and most searing failure suffered by Israel in the War of Independence.

In the Old City of Jerusalem, Jews had lived for 1,700 years without a break. In the year 1836, synagogues and study halls and some *Yeshiva* schools were built in the Jewish Quarter, and the cultural life inside the walls was rich and vibrant – until the War of 1948 had broken out and the Jewish Quarter was captured by the Jordanians, destroyed, razed, and lost to the Jews.

In the thick of desperate combat, what was especially frustrating and painful about that battle, in retrospect, was that the fall of the Old City could have been prevented; and the defeat and surrender were not supposed to have happened, which would have changed forever the whole picture regarding the historic rights to ownership of that bitterly disputed area of unique significance.

But in that campaign were errors of strategy, flawed evaluations, unreliable intelligence reports and general confusion. Consequently, at a certain stage of the fighting, the situation arose in which Jordanian soldiers of the Arab Legion discovered to their great amazement, that the Jaffa Gate, which soldiers of the Israeli Palmach had broken through earlier, had been deserted and was not booby-trapped or fortified and therefore posed no danger to their soldiers. So, when they realized that their chances of advancing through the Jaffa Gate were high, due to the Israeli oversight to secure it, they immediately called for and received large reinforcements of fighters, blocked the open gate, and sealed it up completely, and began a fierce attack on the Jewish Quarter. For seven consecutive days, from May 19 to 25, soldiers of the Jordanian Arab Legion, bombed and shelled and fired into the Jewish Quarter, advancing right inside it, and the Israeli soldiers defending it, most of them still inexperienced in battle, trapped inside the Walls without being able to get any enforcement from the outside because of the sealed gates, founded themselves facing a situation which sentenced them to either be killed or injured.

Dead or injured, which sustained them in that immortal honor and privilege of fighting and dying for the sake of Jerusalem, the eternal.

For death has a life of its own. In death there is eternal life after death. The kind of death and the circumstances of the death dictate what kind of memory a man bequeaths to future generations. To die in battle, in a war for the defense of the homeland, and especially the defense of Jerusalem, is a most honorable death and one to be envied, which fills the hearts of the warrior's descendants with pride.

*Death has a life of its own. To die for the sake of your belief, such as the martyrdom of those who perished in the Holocaust; to die for the sanctification of the Holy Name; to die for the sake of a humane ideology, for the sake of mankind, for a noble cause; to die while saving someone from death or danger; to die for reasons such as these leave the hearts of succeeding generations and descendants overflowing with pride. Death does indeed have a life of its own.*

Ruvke fought valiantly to defend the Old City of Jerusalem. In the mayhem of the assault by the Jordanian Legion, he saw his commander fall wounded at his side at their post, and without loosing a moment, he immediately took command and together with his soldiers, kept firing relentlessly at the enemy, even though, deep down, he felt that they were fighting a losing battle. The few soldiers whose strength held out enough to continue firing at the Arab invaders, managed to kill many of them as they rushed forward further into the Jewish Quarter. Even though they put up a brave stand, they were too few to withstand the surge of Arab forces as they burst right inside the Jewish Quarter, where they blew up and destroyed synagogues and study halls, and the houses where Jews lived. Every building the Arabs captured, they severely damaged immediately in order to make it impossible for the Jews to return to them.

All what was left after the Arabs' orgy of destruction was the smell of the scorched earth and clouds of smoke which covered the ruined Jewish Quarter. All the inhabitants were forced to flee from their houses, and took refuge in the Shelter Houses which absorbed them in droves.

When the officers of the Quarter grasped how desperate the

situation was, and that most of the defenders had been killed or wounded, and that those who remained at their posts – of whom Ruvke was one of the ones who survived – were left without sufficient ammunition to block or halt the onslaught, the decision was made at the military and political levels – to surrender.

The commander of the victorious Arab Legion, Abdullah El-Tal, dictated the terms of the surrender: It is stipulated and agreed that the Israeli soldiers will dismantle their weapons and hand them over to the Jordanians; that the residents of the Quarter, the old, the women, the children, and the severely wounded, will be transferred to Jewish-held West Jerusalem; and that the surviving fighters will be taken to Jordan as captives, and that the Jordanian Legion will be recognized and declared as the conquerors of the Jewish Quarter of the Old City.

In fact, the conquest of the Old City of Jerusalem by the Arabs began many years before 1948. Little by little, the Arabs pushed the Jews out of the walled city, from which the Tower of David proudly rises. In the middle of the 19th century, Jews constituted 52 percents (!) of the total population. To put it another way, more than half the residents of the Old City were Jews! But in the course of the following century, and in particular at the height of the Great Arab Revolt of 1936-1939, rampaging Arabs began violent riots against the Jews who lived in the Old City – attacking and killing them or driving them out of their houses, and the Jews were gradually forced to leave the areas where they had lived side by side with Arabs for hundreds of years, and to confine themselves to live in the small Jewish Quarter.

However, the threats and the riots and the looting on the part of the Arabs, even drove the Jews out of the cramped Jewish Quarter, and many of them fled to the western part of the city, so that the Jewish community in the Old City was gradually depleted until on the eve of the War of Independence it amounted to only six percent of the total of residents there. The Jews, then, were expelled little by little over many years, until the final crushing blow was inflicted on them – the *coup de grace* – which led to the bitter signing of the terms of surrender.

According to those terms, it was decreed that everybody still living in the Jewish Quarter would be forcibly expelled from their houses; the women, the children, and the old and given one hour to pack and leave. Each one clutched a bundle of his belongings, leaving behind ruins and destruction, burning houses, and the mass of graves of the tens of fighters hastily buried there, who gave their lives in defending the Jewish Quarter.

Against a backdrop of cheering and wild enthusiasm from the Arabs, as they were frenziedly burning, smashing, and grinding to dust hundreds of years of Jewish life in the Old City of Jerusalem, whose stones bore witness to all the historic events that had taken place there in the alley-ways and squares, the Jewish residents made their way out of the Quarter. Two by two the refugees passed through the Zion Gate and began to walk the 500 meters which separated the Zion Gate from Jewish-held western Jerusalem, numb with the shock of being uprooted from the place they and their ancestors had lived in for hundreds of years, which had been the symbol of the Jewish people, and was now devastated... And the weeping which would last for generations, began.

For 19 years, the Jewish Quarter in the Old City was left in a state of destruction and abandonment. Here and there ruins and mounds of rubble were piled up in the streets, and the smell of cinders and ash from the huge fire permeated the air, and wafted into the nostrils like a bitter drug. The ruins were left where they were. No attempt was made at reconstruction, no new buildings were erected. Nothing at all was done. The

Quarter remained desolate, in ruins, and in mourning, as if it waited throughout those 19 years for the Children of Israel to come and set it free from its devastation. And they indeed returned to it, in 1967, when they overpowered the Arabs who had foisted war on them, and in a war waged at the speed of lightning in only six days, the Old City and the Jewish Quarter were returned to them. They renovated the ruins, constructed new synagogues and study halls, and built in the Jewish Quarter homes where they settled Jewish families, and by that they restored to it the glory of its dignified past.

Ruvke was one of the soldiers who, according to the terms of surrender, was condemned to be taken into Jordanian captivity, so he did not return to his home immediately after the end of the battle and the surrender of the Jewish Quarter.

Dazed and downhearted, he found himself being put onto a Jordanian Army truck, together with the rest of the soldiers taken captive – captives from all the places which had fallen into the hands of the Jordanians, such as the Etzion Bloc, Atarot and Gezer Tedium – which began making its way toward the eastern border, to Jordan. On their way, the prisoners passed Arab villages, where at each place they halted, the local Arabs cursed and swore at them and mocked them with the arrogance of the victor.

For two whole days the trucks taking the soldiers into captivity journeyed until they reached the prison camp in the heart of the Jordanian desert. A camp in the heart of the desert, yet another camp in which Ruvke was doomed to spend a period of his life. They were imprisoned, with watchtowers on the perimeter of the camp, suffering from the freezing cold and burning heat of the desert; from the mosquitoes and the fleas and the dust; the dreariness and boredom and depression, which weighed them down and pierced their bodies and minds.

The days turned into weeks, the weeks into months, and

the captives could track only from rumors and news leaks the progress of the fighting and the outcome of the battles; their faces would fall to hear that Israeli settlements had been overrun, or would be wreathed in smiles on the victories the Israelis gained in other areas under attack. And so the time passed, until the day came when the commander of the Legion got all the prisoners together and informed them that a decision had been made at the political level to carry out a prisoner exchange. Even the faces of their Jordanian guards lit up to hear this news. You are released, they told the captives happily, and we will get our captives back, *Inshallah*.

Release of the captives was to be implemented in three stages, with a three-week gap between the delivery of one group of captives and another. A lottery was held to determine which captives would be included in the first round, and Ruvke was lucky enough to be one of them.

The very next morning, trucks driven by Jordanians arrived at the prison camp and drove them to a certain spot on the border with Israel, where they were transferred to Israeli buses driven by Israeli drivers. They journeyed on for another few hours, until they reached an army camp. From there, they all went their separate ways. Each set out for his home, and Ruvke returned at last to his wife and their son.

✦ ✦ ✦

Yuda, with his background as a fighter with the partisans, was caught up in a battle not far away. Jerusalem, West Jerusalem, with its only Jewish population, had been put under siege by seven Arab armies from seven Arab countries, which had entrenched themselves on the hills overlooking the outskirts of the city; and from the opposite side, the Jordanians opened fire with mortars from all the positions they held on the wall surrounding the Old City, in the direction of the western, Israeli, part of the city. Not only the Old City, the whole of Jerusalem the Arabs desired, as well as the whole of the Jewish country which had been just re-established.

As for the British, they went out of their way to give the Jordanians all possible back-up in their attacks, and placed at the side of the statue of a lion, located on the roof of the Generali Building on Princess Mary Street, an exceptional vantage point overlooking the whole of the center of the city, a fortified position with mortars and guns, from where soldiers of His Majesty fired at innocent people passing by on the sidewalks.

The threat of these snipers, in addition to the shells fired by the Jordanians, forced Jerusalemites to shut themselves up in their houses. Everyone was afraid to go out into the street because of the shells and sniping and the bullets which would whistle in the ears of anyone who had to go outside to collect water from a standpipe or on some other urgent errand, and no one knew where the next shell would fall or whether they would be hit by a sniper's bullet. The hospitals were full of the wounded – ordinary citizens, innocent people. People went out of their houses for a few minutes to do some essential errand, and paid for it with their lives or were badly wounded.

As well as all the murderous attacks, which created a threatening and fearful atmosphere in the city, the main artery bringing in supplies to the city was blockaded. The only approach to the city from the west, the entrance to Jerusalem from the coastal plain, was impassable from Latrun onwards, and the Arabs besieging the city did not allow convoys carrying food and medicines – the most basic humanitarian aid to the citizens under siege – to enter Jerusalem. The terrible danger that hovered over the residents of the capital and of the entire State, and the struggle to break the siege of Jerusalem, prompted Yuda to fight in the battles at Latrun, the weak point which barred the only road to the capital, in order for the Jewish inhabitants to starve to death, or to surrender and give up their holy city. To their enemies; To loose their renewed Independence; to give up their Liberty and Freedom.

Latrun was of the utmost strategic importance, commanding the only one entrance road from the coastal plain to Jerusalem, and the Arabs who controlled it, prevented Israeli armored convoys from bringing food and medical supplies to the besieged citizens. So, the convoy trucks, full of food and medicines were ambushed, shelled, and blown up; the soldiers driving them were killed; and the skeletal frames of the armored vehicles wrecked in these murderous attacks, were left at the side of the road leading up to the city, in commemoration since then, forever.

The Arabs decided to starve an entire population into submission, not one slice of bread would they allow to be brought into Jerusalem. They based their decision on the assumption that the Israeli soldiers would have no more strength to defend the city and would raise their arms in surrender, and then Jewish Jerusalem would fall under Arab control.

This hope of the Arab commander was actually not so far-fetched. Latrun seemed impossible to conquer, and hundreds of Jewish soldiers who were charged with its capture had fallen in battle. Three assaults on Latrun had already been attempted, and had failed, one after the other. Yuda, who at the time of the first battle had been enlisted as a common soldier to serve in the Alexandroni Brigade sent to reinforce the 7th Armored Brigade with the aim of attacking and taking Latrun, took part in all the battles and assaults on the heavily fortified position – but in vain. Latrun stood firm in the face of the assaults, an unassailable fortress. The battles for Latrun exacted a heavy toll in human losses, hundreds killed and wounded, and Yuda, who had fought in all of the battles had been incredibly lucky to have gotten away with hardly a scratch.

Doubtless, when Yuda and the vast majority of soldiers in the Brigade took up their gun or grenade or sub-machine gun to attack and capture the police fortress at Latrun, they knew nothing of the battles which had been fought in that same place over the whole course of history. The region was known as being a site of battles as far back as the 13th century BCE, when the army of Joshua Bin-Nun defeated the Amorites in the area of Beit Horon-Latrun; and in the year 163 BCE Yehudah Ha'Maccabee defeated the Greeks at Ammeus, in the same region; and in the period of the Crusades many battles were fought between the Christians and the Muslims. The Templers even built a large fortress there, which was later abandoned and destroyed by the Muslim invaders, only traces remaining of it for future generations. In 1840, a Trappist monastery was built at Latrun – where the heavy silence could even raise the dead – by an Order of Trappist monks, where in the vast gardens the silent monks grew grapes and olives.

In the First World War, Latrun was captured from the Turks by the British and units of the Australian cavalry, wearing their slouch hat with the upturned brim, which lent distinction to their appearance. The joint forces surrounded Turkish positions and took them by storm all the way from Latrun right up to Jerusalem itself.

Following the Great Arab Revolt of 1936-1939, the British Mandatory rulers, built, close to the Trappist Monastery in Latrun, a fortified police station, which controlled the road from Tel Aviv to Jerusalem. To the Israelis' deep anxiety and frustration, this police fortress was handed over by the British to the Arabs, one day before the War of Independence broke out, that is, the day after the United Nations formally recognized the State of Israel. Why did the British do this? What impelled them to stick such a sharp knife in the Israeli's throat? – Only politics. Ugly and dirty politics that knows nothing of compassion or righteousness.

There is no bread in Jerusalem for people to eat? So they

won't eat cakes either, until they give in.

The siege in Jerusalem grew tighter, conditions worsened as day and night shells rained down on the western part of the city. People could not go out of their homes. Only minimal amounts of bread and water could be obtained. Food was more strictly rationed, and the failure of the many attempts to take Latrun was one of the most searing and painful failures of the War of Independence.

But amid the distress and hardships and dangers surrounding them, there happened an unexpected miracle: One day, Israeli soldiers on a routine patrol of the area discovered a thin track, an alternative route to Jerusalem from the coastal plain, a passageway which was located between the Jordanian forces in Latrun and the Egyptian troops stationed south of Jerusalem, a route which neither the Jordanians nor the Egyptians could control.

Thus, in a rapid operation of superb daring, the Israeli leaders managed to make the narrow road fit for convoys to use, and within a very few days, the road winding its way through the steep hills was constructed. The primeval landscape was as if shocked into splitting itself open by the force of bulldozers, steamrollers and compressors, all intent on creating a new road between the rocks and boulders, which would bypass Latrun. As soon as the road, which became known as Burma Road, could be used, the first convoy of armored trucks set out, bringing to the besieged city of Jerusalem food and medicines and other essential supplies. Thus Jerusalem was saved from falling into the hands of the Arab predators.

A collective sigh of relief could be heard all over Jerusalem when the siege was lifted. No need now to spill anymore blood over Latrun. To hell with Latrun! The way to Jerusalem was opened, food and ammunition flowed into the city, which had been cut off for months from the rest of the country, and its brave defenders fought like lions and defeated the Arab invading forces, which retreated to the borders of their own countries. A cease fire agreement was drafted and drawn up, and signed by Abdullah El-Tal of Jordan and Moshe Dayan of Israel. Jewish Jerusalem was declared again the capital of the Jewish Nation, but the Latrun road remained blocked by the Jordanians for another 19 years, until it was reopened in the Six Day war.

✦ ✦ ✦

Anshel-Aharon sustained a heavy setback in the area of combat to which he was sent, whose aim was to secure Western Galilee from the threat of the Syrians, who were intent on capturing it. Only a hair's breadth separated success from failure in this mission. The whole of this beautiful region in northern Israel could almost equally stand or fall and, in particular, Kibbutz Yehiam, which had been founded at the foot of the impressive ruins of a Crusader fortress.

The first attack on Yehiam was in January 1948 by hundreds of Arabs who entrenched themselves in Giv'at-Ha'Etz (the Hill's Tree), and from there shelled bombs on the kibbutz continuously for days on end, until after two months of attacks all access roads to the kibbutz were blocked and all communications between Nahariya and all the settlements in Western Galilee were completely cut off, and the Arab troops placed them under siege, which led to dire shortages of food and water. Yehiam, as an isolated settlement surrounded by Arab villages, was in an especially vulnerable and bleak situation. Food reserves on the kibbutz were dwindling rapidly, so it was vital to break the siege by any possible means – primarily by means of convoys of armored trucks – so as to get food to the kibbutz members.

The first convoy of trucks was crammed with items of food for other kibbutzim in the area – Hanita and Matsuba, which were also completely cut off – set off, driven by courageous volunteers who successfully carried out their mission and returned back to their starting point, Nahariya, the same day.

Encouraged by the success of the operation, they prepared to go out again the next morning, this time to Yehiam. Seven armored trucks laden with foodstuffs, and accompanied by 89 soldiers, made their preparations to set out in the morning. At the side of the trucks they said their farewells to their wives and children, fathers and mothers, who had come to see them off. The faces of their families showed anxiety and fear, but the soldiers cheerfully reassured them: What are you worried about? We will be back home this evening. The families waved them off ostensibly in good spirits, but with the lines of worry on their faces betrayed their true feelings.

Cautiously, the convoy began to move off towards the narrow, winding road leading to Yehiam, but it managed to go only a short distance, when at the Kabri Junction, the drivers found their way blocked by a barrier which stretched across the whole width of the road. They were forced to stop and get out of the vehicles in order to remove the barrier, but then, all of a sudden, fighting soldiers of the Syrian general Al-Kabri, ambushed them, fell on them like a pack of wolves, with cocked guns and rifles that fired wildly at them. Only one armored truck out of the seven in the convoy managed to keep going and arrive at Yehiam. All of the other six trucks were stuck, because their wheels were trapped under the barrier, and the Arabs just kept shooting at them with their rifles and guns, slaughtering and killing 47 of the Israeli soldiers on the convoy, who were ensnared in a fire trap which caught them by surprise. The remaining soldiers, only 42, fought back and showered a hail of bullets at the Arabs, killing many of them, and by the end of the fighting they had forced the Arab soldiers to flee towards the Syrian border. What befell the convoy on its way to Yehiam was an almost unbearable calamity, both because of the loss of human life and because the siege in Galilee was not lifted.

For another seven weeks after that calamity, Yehiam remained under total siege. They were immensely fortunate that some friendly Druze from the villages round about, supplied them with food which, even if it was not enough for everybody, at least it prevented them from dying of starvation. There were also occasional airdrops of food to the besieged kibbutzniks, which helped them to hold out.

The whole *Yishuv* was hoping against hope that they would not crumble. Meanwhile, a plan began to take shape for a major military operation to break the siege and release the settlements in Western Galilee from its stranglehold and from Arab control.

Anshel, full of fighting spirit and patriotism, was commander of a platoon in this operation. It was not only that he was determined to play his part in relieving the distress of the kibbutzim, he also loved and was captivated by that area, and in particular the Crusader castle perched at the top of the hill which looked down proudly at the fascinating view all around. He was deeply concerned that Galilee would fall to the Arabs, who were attacking it ferociously in order to invade it, and the very real fear that this might happen made him resolve to defend Galilee to his very last drop of blood.

The besieged members of Kibbutz Yehiam waited impatiently and with mounting anxiety to be rescued from the stranglehold of the Arab blockade, which threatened their lives and also the future of their young kibbutz, until at last help arrived.

In a well-planned and wide-ranging military operation which was launched – Operation Ben-Ami – Israeli soldiers charged the Arab armies holding the settlements in Western Galilee under siege, and the soldiers led by the Syrian General Shishakli were taken by surprise, for they had not expected such a fierce attack, but managed to fight back with all their strength. After heavy exchanges of fire which caused many fatalities on both sides, the Arabs retreated to the north, hotly pursued by Israeli soldiers, who thrust them back towards the borders of Syria and Lebanon.

The retreat of the Arab armies brought relief to the Galilee settlements, in particular to the besieged members of Kibbutz Yehiam, who were rescued literally at the eleventh hour. They survived. At last they could breathe the freedom.

It was a matter of pride for Anshel-Aharon Kidron for the rest of his life that he had taken part in the operation to liberate Western Galilee, to help ensure that it would remain an important region on the map of the State of Israel.

✦ ✦ ✦

Because Sergei had been busy with his business affairs, he had not managed to do much to fix up his house since he and Gittel had come to live in the Florentine neighborhood, which was then one of the most southern in Tel Aviv, and very close to Jaffa, that was notable for its mixed population of Jews and Arabs.

Jaffa, a picturesque town with an Oriental character situated on a fine beach, had at that time the only port in the country, and ships and boats which anchored there, provided the lifeline of commerce and tourism. It connected Israel to the ports of neighboring countries in the Mediterranean, and was a source of income and business to all the residents, Jews and Arabs alike. On the wide expanses of land surrounding the town, orange groves were planted, and the scent of their flowers wafted in the air. The Arab and the Jewish citrus-growers came to an amicable agreement to set up a joint association to sell their luscious produce – oranges, which made a name for themselves as Jaffa Orange, and became a trademark for quality, sought after and appreciated all over the world by people of discernment.

This was not the atmosphere which prevailed in Jaffa, when the Turks ruled the country. At the end of the 19th century and the beginning of the 20th century, Jaffa was then neglected and bleak. When Theodor Ze'ev Herzl, the visionary of the Zionist State, came to Palestine in 1898, in order to meet with the German Kaiser who was visiting the country, he recorded in his novel, Altneuland, his impressions of Jaffa after he had arrived there by boat:

*The town was in a state of extreme decay. Landing was difficult in the forsaken harbor. The alleys were dirty, neglected, full of vile odors. Everywhere lay misery in bright Oriental rags; poor Turks, dirty Arabs, timid Jews lounged about – indolent, beggarly, hopeless. A peculiar tomb-like odor of mold caught one's breath.*

Jaffa began to shake itself out of its misery when Jews immigrated in the First Aliyah to Palestine, and in the subsequent waves of Aliyah which followed. At the end of the First World War, when the Turks were expelled from the country by the British, it seemed likely that the amicable social and economic relations between the Arab and Jewish residents of the town would continue in the future, and that all would stand to benefit from the profits the beautiful orange groves brought to everyone, Jews and Arabs alike.

However, the Arabs of Jaffa woke up with a start, under heavy pressure from the propaganda directed at them by more militant, politically – in the worst sense of the word – motivated Arabs, and went back on cooperating with their Jewish neighbors regarding joint control of the mixed town, and on jointly selling the Jaffa oranges. So, over the years, they began to engage in competition in the most hostile manner with the Jews, as the seed of animosity planted by their Arab hostile leaders took root in their hearts; the atmosphere became more and more charged, and hostile rivalry turned into physical attacks on their Jewish neighbors, until they came to be a routine, everyday occurrence.

Towards the end of the 1920s, bloody disturbances broke out in Jaffa in which Arabs attacked and murdered Jews to compel the Jews in Jaffa to leave. A high proportion of them were indeed forced to flee from their houses in fear and panic, and went to live in Tel- Aviv, where they built a new neighborhood, the Shapira neighborhood. The Jews remaining in Jaffa suffered blows and hatred on the part of the Arab residents, who created all kinds of difficulties for them, especially rivalry over selling oranges, which grew and became more bitter, accompanied by antagonism and hatred and physical attacks. Difficulties of this kind continued until the Great Arab Revolt of 1936-1939, in which the Arabs of Jaffa fell on the Jews of the town and murdered them in droves, and forced most of those remaining to flee from their houses. The situation there worsened until it became impossible, and economic relations between Jaffa and Tel Aviv, which had previously been flourishing, reached a crisis point.

When, in the year 1936, a strike broke out at Jaffa Port, and Arab workers walked off their jobs, it was not possible to use the only port then in the country for exporting goods and products by ship to foreign countries. However, every cloud has its silver lining. The political situation, which brought about the economic crisis, made it essential, as a matter of urgency, to establish a new port in Tel Aviv. The leaders of the British Mandate administration gave the Tel Aviv municipality permission to construct the port – a generous gesture for which the Arabs have not forgiven the British to this day – and building the port got under way with an immense rejoicing by the *Yishuv*. All hands were on deck, as it were, between the blue sky above and the blue sea below, every able-bodied man was put to work on this important project, and that was how the independent, sovereign Tel Aviv Port was constructed, and the whole *Yishuv* gloried in it and reveled in the feeling that now they would be the ones to decide when ships could sail away from it, and they would no longer have to rely on the vagaries and goodwill of Arab port workers in Jaffa who could strike at a moment's notice, leaving their oranges to rot, and their economy to collapse.

Continued hatred and aggression on the side of the Arabs of Jaffa towards their Jewish neighbors led to renewed hostilities between the two communities, which reached their peak in November 1947, with the agreement of the United Nations to the establishment of a state for the Jews in Palestine. In the eyes of the Arabs of Jaffa, this was no less than declaring that Tel Aviv was officially registered in the land registry of the Nations of the world in the name of the Jewish residents. This, the Arabs were not willing to accept under any circumstances, and they angrily rejected the UN plan. The Jewish city of Tel Aviv was like a bone stuck in their throats. They refused to recognize its existence or the right of its Jewish residents to live there. They were incensed by the Declaration of Independence, and not only incited each other to lash out at the Jews with curses and fiery rhetoric, but put their words into practice by sniping relentlessly at the Jews still living in Jaffa itself.

The Jews living in the southern neighborhoods of Tel Aviv were also subjected to bullets constantly being shot at them, and many Jewish residents of south Tel Aviv left their houses and fled for their lives in fear and panic. In this way, the Arabs succeeded in silencing large parts of the first Jewish city, Tel Aviv. During the first five months after the UN Plan to set up the State for the Jews, which was later called *Israel,* dozens of Jews were killed and hundreds wounded, and thousands of Jews who had lived in the town of Jaffa itself for a very long time, were forced to leave their houses out of the very real fear that their Arab neighbors would attack them and murder them. Terrorized and apprehensive, they fled from their town and overnight turned into refugees, being billeted in Tel Aviv in schools and public buildings in cramped and difficult conditions.

Sergei and Gittel, who were living within earshot of the gunshots being fired from the direction of Jaffa, decided that they would not move out of their apartment, not only because they didn't have anywhere to flee to, but to flee was, in their eyes, leaving a vacuum, an empty space which the enemy would simply take for himself and which they would not be able to reclaim. Rightly or wrongly, they felt that leaving their house would be a kind of surrender, even if it was justified by the circumstances of a war going on around them. But to forgo their home might mean that the other side would take it for himself, and that would be a point of no return.

It did not occur to Gittel and Sergei for a moment to leave the civilian campaign. On the contrary, Gittel harnessed all her energies to help the hundreds of Jewish refugees who had fled from Jaffa and now crowded into Tel Aviv. She did not flinch from bombs and explosions. She was not the woman to be alarmed so quickly by them, for she had already experienced the very worst things of all that life could throw at her. Gittel volunteered several days a week to help organizations which had taken it upon themselves to absorb the refugees and to aid the injured get to the hospitals or clinics in the center of the city.

Sergei, in spite of his years, felt that he could not just stand idly by with the threat of the rifle and the submachine gun hovering over him, and knowing that in the event of an Arab attack on Tel Aviv, he and his wife would be among the first to be hit by the barrage of fire.

So, as he had a great deal of experience in fighting, he decided that he should do what he could do in defense of the city. It did not matter to him which organization was in charge of taking precautions to defend Tel Aviv, for him it was all the same if it was the Irgun Etzel or the Haganah. So, indifferently, his legs brought him purely by chance to the Irgun headquarters next to the Alliance School in Jaffa, (which today is the Suzanne Dallal Center for Dance and Theater). Sergei made an excellent impression on his listeners, and after they had heard that he had extensive experience in combat, he was accepted with open arms into the team at Irgun operational headquarters in Jaffa.

The defense organizations and politicians feared that with the imminent departure of the British from the country, Egypt would join the front against the nascent Jewish State, and that Jaffa, which was designed by the Arabs for use as a base for naval actions for the Egyptian Army, would bring the war right into the center of Tel Aviv.

Prevention is better than cure, as they say, so, with the aim of defending Jaffa, the Irgun headquarters prepared a plan to encircle the town by occupying the Arab villages to the south of it – Abu Kabir, Jabaliya, and Tel Arish – assuming that the encirclement would lead to the surrender of Jaffa without a shot having to be fired. However, this plan was not, in the end, carried out because the fact that the Egyptian Army, being able to sail right up to the port in Jaffa, could still penetrate into the country through the sea, which would negate the effects of a land blockade.

The team at Irgun headquarters, with Sergei taking an active role in the decision, made its mind up therefore that they had no choice other than to march into Jaffa even before the British left the country, in order to conquer it with its port, and annex the town to the new Jewish State and prevent its political independence.

For their part, the British, as they were in the habit of doing, left a significant military force in Jaffa, which they intended to hand the town over to the Arabs leaders when the time was ripe. Just like that. Their goal was to tie the Jewish population up in a stranglehold in the center of the country and then gun them down.

In order to prevent such a threatening situation from arising, the decision was taken to carry out a major operation. On Saturday, April 24, 1948, 600 Irgun fighters assembled at the Dov Camp in Ramat Gan, and after weapons were distributed to them, rifles and machine guns and mortars as well as four armored cars, the fighters lined up on parade, and Menachem Begin, the Irgun Etzel Commander, stood in front of them and proclaimed dramatically: You are setting out on one of the most decisive battles in the struggle for our independence. Remember who you have left behind. You face a cruel foe, who wishes to destroy us. Strike at the foe! Aim well! Do not waste ammunition! In this battle, show no mercy to the enemy, but spare the life of anyone who raises his hands in surrender. He is your captive. Do not harm him.

In this spirit of fighting a justified battle for their right to live, the fighters set out to attack the enemy. They were led by Amichai Feiglin, who had been appointed commander of the operation, that began at 05.00 on April 25.

The mortar gunners started by a heavy bombardment of the center of Jaffa and the port area, and shortly afterwards two companies set out, one towards the railways tracks and the other towards the sea. The two forces met with heavy fire from Arab fighters, who were well entrenched in the houses, and after bitter fighting, in which the Arabs had superior firing power, the two companies retreated to their base.

At operational headquarters, where Sergei was part of the team, they acknowledged that their assessment of the size and the strength of the Arab forces had not been correct. They decided to send sappers to blow up enemy positions where Arabs were entrenched, after which an infantry unit would take them over and occupy them. Thus, the next morning the units set out, but this time too they were unsuccessful because they encountered heavy machine-gun fire, and even anti-tank weapons brought in by the British. The sappers, in spite of being attacked, succeeded in blowing up a number of positions held by the Arabs, but the infantry units failed to occupy them.

In the meantime, shelling of the Arab positions continued and the earth-shattering noise it made, caused tremendous havoc and fear among the Arab inhabitants, and in the panic it aroused, there was a stampede to flee however they could, by land or sea, on wheels or on foot. For their part, the Jewish fighters suffered heavy casualties, as a direct result of the intervention of the British Army, who contributed tanks and machine-guns to the battle in order to destroy the Jewish force.

In light of the large number of casualties and wounded, a discussion was held whether to continue the operation. The situation was reassessed, and it was decided to halt the attack, withdraw the rest of the units from the front, and only continue to strengthen what had already been occupied; at the same time leaving a strong vanguard force to be prepared for whatever the next few days would bring. However, the commander of the operation, Amichai Feiglin, and others, including Sergei, were against the proposal to halt the onslaught and withdraw. Feiglin argued that the enemy was about to collapse and that fighting should continue. The discussions continued, and in the end his opinion was accepted, and the green light was given to continue to fight.

On the third day of fighting, Feiglin had a brilliant idea as to how the fighters could protect themselves from being fired on by Arab snipers without exposing themselves to this danger in the open roads and alleys of the town. Feiglin gave the order to blow up the walls of the houses vacated by their inhabitants, to enter the houses and advance towards their objective, concealed and protected between the walls from the eyes of the Arab attackers. He also ordered the blowing up of large buildings to thwart the advance of the British soldiers who had joined the combat and were putting all their efforts and their considerable firepower into hounding and bombarding the Jewish force.

In order to carry out the mission, drills and pick-axes were brought to break down the walls of the emptied houses, and the fighters, who had made their way inside the houses after breaching the walls, were protected now behind the walls and the mortar gunners launched a heavy bombardment in order to start the battle again in a better position.

In the afternoon the onslaught began. The fighting lasted all day and night, the objective being to cross the Arab quarter of Manshiyeh and cut it off from the rest of Jaffa. Thus all the Arab positions, one after another, were captured in the onslaught. Now only one objective remained – to capture the Manshiyeh police station and, once it fell to the fighters, Arab resistance collapsed and it seemed that the fighting was in its last stages.

However, the Irgun fighters were stunned to see that the British were trying to thwart their advance. This intervention by the British took them by surprise, but they continued their advance within Manshiyeh and by 7:00 in the next morning the first fighters reached the sea. This, to all intents and purposes, was the end of the battle to take Manshiyeh.

Meanwhile, total chaos ruled throughout Jaffa and the Arab inhabitants continued to run away, full of fear, both by sea and by land, trying to escape over the borders of the country and enter the neighboring Arab states. They fled of their own free will, certainly no one forced them to do so, and the British Army was shocked to see this mass exodus, and took it upon itself to take full responsibility for the defense of Jaffa in case it fell to the Jewish fighters.

Reinforcements of British soldiers based in Cyprus and Malta, who had been alerted beforehand, at the start of the operation, arrived to swell the ranks, and British ships were waiting at the ready off the shore of Tel Aviv. The British then issued an ultimatum: The British governor of the Lydda district informed the Mayor of Tel Aviv, Israel Rokach, that if the Irgun did not stop the attack on Jaffa, the city would be shelled by tanks on land and bombarded by ships offshore and by Royal Air Force planes.

This was a real and frightening threat, but the ultimatum

was audaciously ignored by the Irgun command: What damned business is it of theirs? To hell with them! In response, the next morning the British began to shell the Alliance School area, where the Irgun headquarters were located.

At the same time, British tanks and armored cars moved towards Manshiyeh, and opened heavy fire on the newly-occupied area. This was the first time that the Irgun fought the British directly and despite the superiority of the British artillery and armor, the Irgun fighters battled courageously and refused to retreat. Senior commanders went into battle at the head of their troops, and halted the British armored force by blowing up big houses and scattering the debris on the roads and alleys. While the battle was raging and grew more intense, the Irgun command announced to the British that if they did not stop shelling them, the Irgun mortar gunners would fire on the British Army camp in the German colony on the borders of Jaffa and would inflict heavy casualties on the British on the eve of their departure from the country. The British took this threat seriously, and no longer insisted on the total evacuation of the whole of Manshiyeh, but demanded that the Irgun evacuate the police station they were occupying and return it to them. If you hand over the police building to us, we will stop bombarding you, the British said.

The Irgun command delayed responding to this demand and, after a brief discussion, surprised the British by their willingness to return the police building to them. They would indeed do as asked, but as to the condition the building would be in when it was handed over, no commitment had been said about. So the Irgun used the time before returning it, to play a bit of a trick on the British. Yes, They will be glad to give them the police station, without making any difficulties, so please if they don't mind waiting a little.

In that little time, the Irgun sappers set out clandestinely to blow up the police station in Manshiyeh, using such massive quantities of explosives that the whole building collapsed into a heap of rubble. Here you are, take the police building, they said to the stunning British. You wanted it, you have got it! Here it is! The Irgun commanders were hardly able to keep from grinning from ear to ear, when they informed that to the humiliated British commandments.

The sappers also blew up blocks of houses, and the resulting debris fell into the street and formed barricades, obstructing the British from reaching Tel Aviv.

During the battles, an agreement was signed between the Etzel and the Haganah that Irgun forces would be replaced by those of the Haganah and, after the fall of Manshiyeh, the Irgun handed all its positions over to the Haganah forces. Early Tuesday morning, at 3:00 am, the Haganah girded their loins and launched Operation Hametz, with the objective of occupying villages south of Jaffa. It was an extremely difficult mission, for the Arabs put up strong resistance and in Tel Arish counter-attacked, resulting in heavy losses for the Jewish fighters of 19 dead and tens of wounded, and forced them to retreat from the village. The following day, however, Haganah fighters returned to the fray, joined by Irgun men, and together they managed to occupy Tel Arish and the village of Salameh.

After that, the Arabs of Jaffa had reached the point of surrender. On May 12, 1948, a deputation of Arab notables who had not fled from Jaffa, came to Haganah headquarters and, after negotiations, signed a surrender agreement.

Overwhelmed from that step, in the early hours of the following morning, a long convoy of jeeps and armored trucks, like a centipede on the crawl, the British troops left Jaffa, without a backward glance, without a farewell word.

This was not the only convoy which made its way through the streets of Jaffa after the end of the battles. On the following day, a big convoy of Irgun and Haganah fighters, all the officers and men who had contributed in any way to the mission, of whom an emotional Sergei was one, had marched in the streets of the town, led by an armored car requisitioned from the British, in the presence of Arab notables, Martial Law was proclaimed in Jaffa, and a joint Haganah-Irgun command was established.

Later, Jaffa was incorporated into the unified city of Tel Aviv, and Jews and Arabs live there in close proximity to each other. Even if the ideal of neighborly peace and harmony are as far off as ever, at the very least, co-existence has been achieved and has been sustained for decades, with smiles that might not be seen as friendly as they were on the surface; also the baring of teeth to each other are not as hostile as they were.

The battle for Jaffa was not fought to conquer and occupy that town, but with the sole objective of defending the Jewish city Tel Aviv, and to thwart and avoid Egypt to invade the country as a whole, from the sea, through Jaffa port. From the moment the go-ahead was given, in November 1947, for a Jewish state in part of Palestine, the Arabs saw this as an excuse for waging war on the Jews, to conquer the whole Palestine for themselves only. But they failed. Thus the National Fate had determined. Thus History had dictated.

Few days after the surrender of the Arabs of Jaffa, and the day of victory came over for the Jews, Sergei's heart was bursting with conflicting emotions. On the one hand, the joy and relief he felt that Tel Aviv had been liberated from the danger of occupation and even total destruction, and the pride he felt that Jaffa would be included within the area of the newly-established State of Israel; but on the other, the scenes of the people of Jaffa, women and children, and old people, fleeing from their houses in panic, leaving behind them everything, their homes, their furniture, their memories, their past, their present, their everyday routines, fleeing towards a future in which the only certainty was uncertainty – all this preyed on Sergei's conscience.

However, Gittel did not allow him to sink into depression. She even protested passionately. What are you talking about? For five months before the UN declared that we could have a state of our own, we have suffered attacks every day. The Jews of Jaffa have been expelled from their houses, injured and murdered, when the Arabs made up their minds to wipe out the Jews living in Tel Aviv. I put my heart and soul into looking after them. There were terrible injuries, you know that. So how much longer could we have just stood by and done nothing? Until they would have drained out our last drop of blood? Or fight and defend ourselves until our last drop of blood? And another thing: We did not drive them out, the people of Jaffa took it into their heads to run away even though we had not done anything to hurt them. I also feel sorry for the children and women and all the people who had to leave their homes, but we did not harm them. It was the people ***of their own side*** who caused them their calamity; they were the victims of the connivance and violence of their leaders, who decided to eliminate the Jewish community in the country and in Tel Aviv, their neighbors, in particular! The only people the refugees from Jaffa can come to with their complaints, are the leaders of all the Arabic countries who foisted war on us.

Gittel continued in the same vein: Just imagine what would have happened if the Arabs of Jaffa, helped every step of the way by the British, would have beaten us and taken control of Tel Aviv. What would have happened, do you think? They wouldn't only have destroyed all the houses, they would have had a field day, killing everyone along the way. Yes, you and me as well, because we have nowhere to flee as they are lucky to have. Only towards the sea, to drown in its deep waters. They would have terrorized and crushed anybody who had not managed to escape or be killed, and taken away all our basic human rights and our national rights to build up this country and make it our home. Don't forget that for a long time before the war had broken out, the Arabs kept declaring quite openly that their goal was to annihilate us and I'm sure they will keep declaring it in the future and no country in this world, full of hypocrisy, will not even blink. To our great luck, they failed. They were defeated, but I'm afraid they will use this defeat as a weapon against us in the coming days. They will weep and wail about the disaster that befell them, which has made them refugees and will blame us for that, just you wait and see. I wouldn't be a bit surprised if, with all the Arab states backing them up, they will want to come back to their houses and get everything back, with the hope to get another chance to throw us into the sea.

Not everything's going to be clear sailing now. I feel it in my bones that there is a lot of trouble ahead of us.

Sergei sat and listened in admiring silence to his wife's impassioned words, grateful for the privilege of having a wife as determined as Gittel, who believed with all her heart every word she had spoken. Perhaps she is right, he said to himself, and he did not argue with her, for deep down he actually agreed with her.

Sergei got up slowly from his chair and approached Gittel with reverence, as though she were a sacred object. He slowly lifted her from her seat, hugged her close, and it was hard for him to speak. All he could say, over and over again, was thank you, thank you for everything, you have managed to get rid of any doubts I had; you have made things clearer. I don't feel guilty anymore. Gittel, so tiny and fragile that it seemed that she could be crushed by Sergei's large frame, stood reveling in the warmth of his embrace for a long time.

That night, as they lay in bed, they confided to each other that more than anything, they would love to have a child together. Gittel, at the age of 45, was still fertile, she was still able to have a baby; many women at that age did so. She had already born four children, three of whom were alive and living quite near her. Sergei had had two daughters but had lost them, and was left without a child of his own, and he wanted to have a child with his adored wife. Yes, *davka* now, the night of the convincing victory over the enemy, the night when hostilities ceased, as if to make up for the killing and the loss, Sergei wanted to give himself some protection from whatever difficulties the future might hold, by bringing into the world a son belonging to the two of them.

And I am longing for a daughter, Gittel thought, as she lay in her husband's arms. I will call her Naomi, my Naomi, she'll replace the daughter who was taken from me at the start of the War, when Warsaw was bombed by the Germans, and the synagogue roof collapsed on her head and killed her, and I was left without a scratch. I will have Naomi back again, my beautiful Naomi, she determined in her heart, as she devoted herself with passion among her husband's arms.

# 19
# Wheel Of Fortune

When the War of Independence came to an end; when the guns fell silent and the sound of carnage ceased – a silver platter overloaded with seven thousand fatalities was presented to the Jewish people in the State of Israel – a silver platter full with pain and mourning. More than one per cent of the population then living in Israel fell in the battles. A heavy price to pay. Heavy price in blood to pay, seven thousand young men who died in the bitter battles; but from the historical perspective, the sacrifice was worthwhile: The Jews got, at last, their own State. The Jews got back their historical State.

Gittel's sons returned home after the war, their heads filled with all kinds of experiences; suffering and pain, triumph and victory jostled together in their hearts, all of them determined to start new life.

Amazingly, without saying a word to each other, but as if they had come to a joint agreement, each made up his mind at the same time as the others, to bring a child into the world. Perhaps the new life would provide them with some compensation both for the loss they had suffered in the horrors of the Holocaust, which had left an open wound in their hearts, and for the loss of their brave fellow soldiers in the War of Independence whose deaths ensured a State to its citizens.

Thus, within less than a year from the end of the War of Independence, Gittel gave birth to a daughter, her longed-for Naomi. The birth was uneventful, and could not even have been called a medical miracle at her age. Her determination overcame any physical constraints of a woman in her mid-forties, and Gittel's strength of mind and good sense helped her recover well from the pregnancy and the birth. Gittel-

Geula now had a daughter, Naomi, a sister for her three sons, and during the same month, only a few days apart, a baby was also born to each of her sons, making her, in the space of one month, a grandmother, three times over: Yuda and Ahuva had a son; Anshel and Nina a daughter – a sister for Lior, who was as happy as a lark when he held his baby sister for the first time; and Ruvke, who only a short time after he returned from the Jordanian captivity was accepted to play with the Voice of Jerusalem orchestra, had a son. They called him Nachum, after his father. The next year, a second son was born to them, and they called him Yechiel, after Reizele's father. It was rather like a fairy tale, each couple established a fine family, and made a success of their lives; even yet, the horrors of the Holocaust cast a dark shadow over their lives and they did not forget for even one day how their families had been taken from them so cruelly. Time could never erase the memories of their terrible past, but still, they overcame their deep injuries and built a healthy life.

Only Yuzhi's fate remained problematic, as if it had been ordained to be so from the moment he emerged into the world. Only Yuzhi felt rejected and alienated all his life. During the three years that followed, after the births of Nachum and Yechiel, two more sons were born to Reizele and Ruvke. Four sons, four new brothers who thrust themselves, uninvited and unannounced, into Yuzhi's world, without even any cautionary word from his mother to warn him of their arrival. Each infant who set out to his private world, was like a ball thrown straight at his chest with savage intensity and he felt hurt, insulted, and full with envy.

Yuzhi felt that his mother had betrayed him, deserted him – he wanted his mother all to himself! He did not want any competition! It was bad enough that she had gotten married and had to devote herself to her husband, and here she was adding fuel to the flames of his envy by giving birth to more children!

He reacted to the birth of each of his brothers, from the time his first brother was born, by sticking to his mother like glue, more and more, with the hope and the unconscious assumption that perhaps in that way he might prevent her from bringing more children, more brothers for him. After the birth of each additional son, he hardly left her alone, trying to get her undivided attention once more, and trying to wean his mother away from this new wailing infant, but the more he attached himself to her, the more he felt that his mother was losing patience with him and he was rejected by her even more.

Enviously, Yuzhi saw how his mother lovingly devoted most of her time and energies to caring for his new brothers, explaining to him that he was already a big boy, and they were little, so she has to devote most of her time to take care of them. However, this explanation caused a red light to flicker in his brain which told him that it was not the real reason. The pounding of his heart told him that it was all nonsense. It was only an excuse to stop him from objecting to his decreased importance in his mother's life, and that the real reason for his brothers being preferred to him was that they were the sons of her husband, Ruvke, whom she loved and admired with all her heart, while he, Yuzhi, was the son of a father he was not sure who he was, so he had become an unbearable burden to her.

For his part, Ruvke tried his utmost to make no distinction between the way he treated Yuzhi and the way he treated his own children, but Yuzhi still interpreted his approach in his jealous eyes, that the children who were born to him and his mother, were his true sons and that he, Yuzhi, was the son of a different father, a father whose exact identity he, Yuzhi, still was not sure about. What he did know, however, was that Ruvke was not the father who had sired him, but his step-father only. Hence his envy of his brothers grew and gathered momentum all the time, and when they had all grown up, he felt ambivalent feelings towards them. He both loved and hated them at one and the same time, thinking they were condescending towards him, although they really did not intend to be, a kind of humiliation he could not forgive them for.

Yuzhi dropped out of high school. He was not one for book-learning, but picked other things up quickly. He knew a little about a lot, as it were. He also developed a style of talking – fast, loud, garrulous, over-confident, argumentative – which people found hard to tolerate, so he came to be a rather solitary figure, left to himself, not only by his family, so it seemed to him, but also by everyone who came into contact with him.

Not only did Yuzhi drop out of studying, but he refused to learn any kind of profession or work which could provide him with a living, or at least cover his few expenses, so that he would have some money in his pocket. Reizele was afraid that he would be a financial burden on her all his life, and she comforted herself with the thought that Yuzhi would soon be 18 and be drafted into the army; he would not be at home, buzzing around her like an irritating fly all the time, wearing her out.

However, all too soon, her hopes collapsed like a balloon punctured by a pin, which is what happens to most fondly held hopes: It only needs the smallest pin to puncture both the balloon and the hope altogether.

This balloon collapsed the day Yuzhi declared to her and her husband Ruvke, that he had no interest and no intention of being drafted into the army. There is nothing for me there, he said, and what good will I be for the army? What, *me* a fighter, a gun in my hand? Shoot someone? Or just be a clerk? Or stand in a little *butke*, a guard post, waving people through the gate of an army base in the middle of nowhere? No, no, no, the army is not for me. I am not going to any boot camp with all that grueling training. What, do you think I haven't anything better to do than crawl under fences and jump over obstacles? No, they do not need the likes of me in the army. I am not built for it.

With that attitude, Yuzhi appeared in front of the Exemptions Board and babbled on about his past. He was an orphan; he never knew his father because his father was killed by a bomb the day he was born during the Second World War, that terrible war, and he was hidden away and lived in a dark cellar until he was three, at the end of the war. He is a Holocaust survivor, he cannot do it, he doesn't function properly as it is. He jabbered on and on trying to convince them that he was not capable of joining the army, until what he was saying became gibberish, nonsense. The members of the Exemptions Board grasped that, indeed, he was not all there, and gave him his desired exemption on the basis of mental disability.

What do I care, Yuzhi would say, if my CV shows that I did not serve in the army for some reason? O.K., right, it is recorded that I was exempted from being drafted because of mental instability, so what? It does not bother me if they have written that I am as mad as a hatter, a crackpot. I have no intention anyway of applying for any kind of job with a government body or public institution. Anyhow, I am not interested in learning any profession. Working every day from 8 until 5 is not for me. The thought of having to stamp a card every morning to record the time I got to work sends shivers down my spine. So punish me, put me in jail, kill me; I really couldn't care less.

When Yuzhi received his exemption from being drafted into the army, Ruvke had to think of some way to help him earn a living. So he sent him to one of his colleagues in the orchestra who would teach him to play the French horn, not a difficult instrument to learn. Yuzhi was found to be quite talented musically, so after he took some lessons on that instrument, he managed to earn a living with a local band playing light music for the public, even though the band itself was not particularly well regarded. Yuzhi was proud of his own musical ability, and he presented himself as if he were at least as talented as Dizzy Gillespie or James Galway.

He could only handle the icy reactions to his presence emanating from his brothers and his parents by exaggerated behavior, and he was obsessively caught up in the details of his own family drama. My father was a Jew who was killed in the bombing the day I was born, the same day the Germans invaded Russia. Such heroism, such pride, such nobility, he would say, as if the words themselves would cover the isolation and uncertainty he always felt as he would sink into the shifting sands of his parentage.

Yuzhi grew up without roots. The roots of his family and those of his own personality were not firmly planted, and were carried away on the wind, whether from the hot east or the freezing north. He never married, and never fathered a child. He wandered alone through his own illusory world, and while all his family struck deep roots in their new-old homeland, throwing off their Polish mother language and speaking fluent Hebrew, Yuzhi, *davka*, did not want to perfect his Hebrew. He spoke Hebrew fluently but with many grammatical mistakes, and his writing was full of spelling errors, and that was the way he rattled on in several languages, just as he did in Hebrew, a bit of Polish, some Russian, some English, which he learned in school. He didn't really have any Mother language.

Yuzhi was damaged by the childhood trauma whose presence still made itself felt in his subconscious, when the curse flung at him – dirty Jew – made him depart himself from all religious rituals and symbols. He was not opposed to religion after investigating and studying it in depth. His opposition came rather from ignorance and the lack of any basic knowledge. He was adamant that he did not want to know or to listen to anything about any religion whatsoever.

In Bible lessons in school, he put his fingers in his ears; he would not read from it or do the homework. Paradoxically, the fact that he would collar anyone and everyone he came across and insist on telling them that his father was a Jew, so important for him to emphasize this point, would have suggested the opposite:

*Like a man who swears morning, noon, and night that he only tells the truth, that he has never told a lie in his life, an incredible statement which immediately gives rise to the suspicion that such a declaration has no basis in fact, and is only made to conceal and deceive and allay people with the constant stream of lies and fictions spewed out of his mouth from dawn to dusk.*

Over the next few years, Yuzhi began to have an uncontrollable compulsion to look into and expose and analyze all the events of the Holocaust. Not so much the extermination of the Jews itself, but more the course of the war and the personalities of those who devised the whole apparatus of the extermination. A sort of compulsion drove him to study the theory of Nazism, to read about the personalities of the leaders, and primarily to analyze the personality of Hitler and the steps he took at each stage of the war. Why are you wasting your time *davka* on that monster, was the question Yuzhi would be asked by everyone in the vicinity. As to the answer, he would simply shrug his shoulders for, truth to tell, he found that monster Hitler a fascinating study, and even though history would condemn him, it would never be able to forget him. I am sure that many more books will be written about him. Look, he would say, Hitler really wanted to study art because he was a gifted painter, but the director of the academy of art – a Jew – refused to accept him. He said he was not good enough. Hitler applied again to the academy of art, but his application was again rejected on the grounds that the only subjects he was good at were landscapes and buildings, and that was not enough to be accepted. I think that the director of the academy had a large part to play in pushing that arch-criminal into politics and, indirectly, in causing the Holocaust.

By the time he reached the age of 25, Yuzhi felt so browbeaten by all those living with him in his mother's and step-father's house, that he could not take it any longer.

The humiliation and sense of deprivation he felt deep inside himself made him, in his own eyes, into the black sheep of the family, and they reached such a pitch that he could no longer bear it, and one day he picked himself up, left his home in Jerusalem, and rented a one-room apartment in Tel Aviv.

For a source of income, he managed to get accepted into a small orchestra which accompanied singers at family celebrations, like weddings and bar mitzvahs, and the pittance he was paid was enough to cover his modest expenses. He received reparations from Germany after he was recognized as a Holocaust survivor – through the good offices of Renate at the Finance Ministry – and these supplemented his small salary to take care of his expenses, more or less. He did not want a second job.

He needed more free time for himself, especially to be able to tell the story of the day of his birth to anyone and everyone he met in the street, shopkeepers, optician, or a bored neighbor he was helping carry her bags home from the supermarket.

Yuzhi would prattle on to her about his unusual start in life and she would give him all her attention, not because she was particularly interested in what he was saying, but out of politeness, to thank him for helping her carry her bags.

One day, when nothing unexpected was expected to occur, the wheel of fortune suddenly turned for Yuzhi in a completely unforeseen direction. For the first time in his life, he wallowed in the subject of the Holocaust from a completely different angle, which he had never in his life envisioned. He certainly had not expected to find himself burrowing into it and busying himself with it so diligently and with a passion that was so unfamiliar to him.

The same neighbor whose bags he had carried, mentioned casually to him that she was going to try to take part in a seminar, really rather a special one, a seminar about astrology. The presenter of the seminar was giving a free introductory lecture, and she would be glad if he would come along with her. As somebody who had no particular interest in anything except for digging into the subject of the Holocaust and the course of the war, and in spite of the fact that the concept of astrology did not mean anything to him, Yuzhi agreed to accept the invitation and go with his neighbor, just to fill an hour of his time, rather than wasting it, idling about, as he usually did.

Yuzhi went along to hear the lecture not expecting to be interested in the subject, certainly not imagining for a moment that, for the first time in his life, a whole new, mysterious world would open its doors to him and that he would be beguiled by its magic. A universe studded with radiant, glittering oracles which beckoned to him. From the presenter's very first sentences, Yuzhi felt as if the whole universe had opened its wide mouth to him and that the vapor emanating from it enveloped him in the dust of the stars and constellations, which could predict what would happen in the future to human beings, countries, peoples and their leaders, everything dependant on the timing at which things occur, a really amazing concept.

Suddenly, he became aware of the planets predicting the success or the failure of people's actions. It all depended on which angle the planets stood in their courses, this one in relation to that one. Yes, it really was worthwhile starting to make your plans according to the timing of where the benign forces – those that bring good luck – were in the heavens, and if you have made sure that the timing is right to go ahead, then do not stop, everything is set up to go well. On the other hand, you have to watch out that you do not find yourself in a negative cosmic situation, because then nothing will help you – neither your wisdom nor your intelligence nor your initiative, and all your efforts will be doomed to failure.

Yuzhi had heard of Venus, the planet of love, and of the planet Pluto, but what had he heard until now of all the other planets surrounding the sun, like our planet, Earth, for instance? Nothing. And here he was suddenly finding himself reciting the celestial names of Pluto and Uranus, of Mercury and Jupiter and the planet of justice, and the luminaries, the moon and the sun, in all, 12 signs of the zodiac and 11 planets navigating our lives and to know, when each one is set in its course, that each one alters its position at a different time and at a different angle. The moon alters its position once every two hours, while the sun alters its position once every day by only one degree. Uranus changes its position after an entire year. Neptune moves itself once every twelve years, and the most lethargic of all, Pluto, alters its position once in every twenty years, on average.

Once Yuzhi became aware that it was possible to predict his future and that of other people at any given moment in their lives, and even the fate of countries, according to the stars, the idea completely bowled him over. He was swept away by the subject as iron filings are attracted to a magnet, and continued to delve into it with every fiber of his being. So, without much hesitation, he decided to use his savings to pay for courses in astrology run by the eminent astrologist. For the first time in his life, Yuzhi felt happy. Completely out of the blue, he had found purpose to his life. He spent all his time studying birth charts, according to which it was possible to examine the cosmic system of the universe, the stars and planets in the heavens, while relating to the position of each planet towards the other planets, which generate different angles, and change, in effect, from hour to hour.

It was with a certain amount of both fascination and wonder that Yuzhi looked at his birth chart, the day of June 22, 1941, the worst possible day on which to be born. Despite the fact that he did not know the exact hour of his birth, he understood that he was born during the morning. A few hours before, Hitler had begun his surprise attack on the vast Soviet Union in order to secure it for himself and his people, an additional territory for their expansion. Yuzhi wondered for which of the two of them the date was worse, for without a doubt, it was not only for him that the day was catastrophic. That same day, the Fuhrer himself went blindly on, in his obstinacy colliding with a wall which took the form of the endless snowy expanses of Russia.

The moment of a quick flash of intuition electrified Yuzhi, he knew he would be able to trace step by step the moves made by the Nazi leader in that bloody war he was so fascinated by, at what angles the planets were arranged on the day of his birth, and also on the days on which he successfully invaded countries, and on those on which he met with defeat, if it would have been possible to change the outcome of the war for good or bad if the fateful moves had been carried out on a different day or at a different hour. Yuzhi was convinced that, indeed, that was the way things would turn out.

How did King Solomon – from whom wisdom flowed out of his every word – put it in Ecclesiastes?

*To everything there is a season, and a time for every purpose under heaven.*

And here we are, the time of his birth, Yuzhi could not have changed, the worst thing of all had already happened, for on the same day war broke out in the east, and his father was killed by a bomb. However, there was a crumb of comfort for him, for that day began the start of Hitler's downfall. Yuzhi feverishly searched through history books and the motions of the planets to see how such a failure could have happened. To his great surprise, he discovered that the date that had been fixed for Operation Barbarossa to begin, was in fact May 15, 1941, and only because Hitler ran into difficulties in Yugoslavia, was the invasion of Russia delayed by a month and a half. So, as they say, ultimately, it all comes down to luck. If Hitler had attacked Russia on May 15, the whole course of the war would have been different and gone in his favor. He would not have been up to his knees in the mud and snow of the Russian winter; and apart from that, the main thing is that the aspects of the planets then were much more favorable for him, but fate, or Lady Luck, decreed otherwise. To make matters worse, the plan for Germany to invade Britain broke down, after the British bombed the ports, sank German ships and caused severe damage to their supplies of food and ammunition that they were counting on. A combination of all these reasons made the Germans delay their invasion of the British Isles to some future, unspecified date, and they had to be satisfied with massive air bombardments on London, which the Londoners faced with stoicism and courage. Instead of invading Britain, Hitler had to send his army to Yugoslavia, after the Italian Army's performance there under Mussolini had been highly unsuccessful and had greatly disappointed the Nazi dictator. He therefore decided that his army would mount a fierce attack on Yugoslavia, which counter-attacked with equal force, but finally had to surrender unconditionally after the devastation it suffered.

The operation in Yugoslavia caused Hitler to delay Operation Barbarossa until June 22, a day when the planetary aspects were negative. Yuzhi made his calculations, and found that out of the 25 cosmic aspects projected on to the birth chart of Hitler on that day, around more than half of them were negative, while the planet Mercury, which supplies the energies for analysis and communication, was in the descendant. This was a very bad position, because Mercury in the descendant causes plans to go wrong, brings confusion to thoughts and ideas, and disrupts communication. The planet which could – literally – have saved the day for him would have been Neptune, whose special energies were in the fields of creativity, esthetics and inspiration and, at the same time had a positive influence on dreams and ambitions. On that fateful day, Neptune was to be found as conjunct to the Moon – which strongly affects domestic and emotional life and influences the pattern of ocean tides, which in turn exert their influence on the human body; also conjunct to the Moon was the planet Uranus – whose effects are often seen in revolutionary changes, and act as a harbinger for sudden and unpredictable events; and so to the planet Jupiter, the planet of luck, which rules the areas of philosophy, generosity and the expansion of horizons, and so *davka* this confluence of planets caused Hitler to lose clarity of thought, make inaccurate assessments of the facts on the ground, be blind to difficulties which would arise, and make unwise, ill-considered decisions. So, when all is said and done, Yuzhi would smile knowingly, there is nothing to wonder about, after all and above all, Hitler had only the rank of a Corporal....

No one in Yuzhi's family wanted him to prepare a birth chart for them. His half-brothers regarded him as eccentric and obsessive, and dismissed his astrological analyses with a contemptuous flick of the hand. His preoccupation with Hitler turned them against him and distanced them from him even more, and Reizele, his mother, begged him over and over again not to mention the name of that swine in her hearing.

She was adamant that she was not interested in hearing about the position of the planets which influenced the shared fate, so to speak, of her son and of the machinations of the enemy on that day. Once, Reizele even added sarcastically that at least Hitler had plenty of successes to his credit before that day, but he, her son Yuzhi, was born straight into failure.

At any rate, I am not to blame that on the day you were born, the attack in the east began and your father was killed.

His mother's words were as welcome to Yuzhi as if he had been told that he had won the jackpot in a gambling casino. His preoccupation with astrology opened his eyes, and he suddenly felt an intense need to know the exact identity of his father. Enough!

From now on, he would not let her get away with not giving him the exact details about his true father. Yuzhi's new passion had given him self-confidence, which made him decisive and fearless. I want you to sit down with me and tell me the whole truth, and answer all my questions, he said firmly to his mother the next time he visited his parents in Jerusalem, which he did once or twice a month. I have the feeling that all these years you have run away from talking about it. I want to know exactly who he was. What was his family like? What was his background? You must tell me!

Reizele still kept her silence, and weeks went by – until, under the pressure of his nagging, she broke down. The veil of secrecy was lifted.

This did not happen all at once but, little by little, thin cracks began to be visible in the impregnable wall she had built for herself over the years. Her voice became less strident, her movements less sure, her stomach churned day and night because of her anxiety that Yuzhi would not forgive her for lying to him. Anyhow, she already understood that Yuzhi had begun to doubt what she had told him about his father and that he suspected more and more that she had shied away from telling him the truth, that she was hiding away from him vitally important facts about his origins. His niggling suspicions became severe doubts which plagued him day and night. Then, out of the blue, as if he and his mother had coordinated the timing between themselves in advance, the moment of truth arrived.

Reizele felt that the true story, which she had tried to bury deep within her, was elbowing its way out, coming nearer and nearer to the surface and then surging forth like lava from a volcano. Enough of lying, she simply could not be silent any longer.

Perhaps it was also the aspects of the planets on a particular day which made Reizele want to release herself from the heavy burden of the anguish she felt, and which made Yuzhi, for his part, take his courage in both hands and demand that she finally break her silence. He clutched the hem of her dress as if he wanted to tear it from her in his frustration and despair.

Enough of all this, Mother, stop trying to appease me with evasions and lies, tell me the truth at last! I want to know everything! I want to know about you and your first husband, my true father. Tell me the truth! I cannot continue to live like this, with so many questions unanswered, so many blanks about my father – it is impossible for me! I am eating myself up about it! I am in shreds! Tell me the truth!

Yuzhi's voice grew louder and louder until in the end he was almost shrieking. Reizele began to tremble uncontrollably all over. She felt that the moment of truth was indeed rising out of the depths of her consciousness, like the steam of a pressure cooker which builds up and suddenly escapes in a tremendous hiss. Yes, she will speak about it, she will tell him. But not only him. The false impression she created for herself and carefully cultivated for so many years did not affect only her son, Yuzhi, but also affected her whole family, including her husband and her four other sons, her two brothers-in-law, Yuda and Anshel and their wives, and Gittel, her mother-in-law, and Gittel's husband, Sergei. She will tell all of them the whole truth; together they will hear a completely unexpected, dramatic, account of the circumstances of the birth of Yuzhi, her first-born son.

# 20
# Exposing The Truth

This was a golden opportunity to gather all the family together for lunch on the Sabbath, for a get-together which promised to be quite out of the ordinary. This time everyone was asked to come to the spacious new house Reizele and Ruvke had bought in the Talpiot neighborhood of Jerusalem, a nice place where they had moved to not long ago. Reizele had specified in the invitation that they should come without the children. I have got something to tell you and I need to do it without the little ones bothering us. She hinted that this would not be the usual kind of family gathering, but one at which she would have significant information to reveal to them.

Reizele was under some strain, which showed on her face as she welcomed her guests. Anshel had come with Nina from their kibbutz in the Galilee; Yuda and Ahuva had come from Bet Shemesh, Gittel and Sergei from Jaffa, where they had moved to live in a large house with a panoramic view of the sea. Everyone felt the heaviness in the atmosphere but none of them had the slightest idea what awaited them, apart from Yuzhi, who was tense with anticipation. The smiles and hugs and kisses they all exchanged were more perfunctory than at their usual get-togethers, but everyone enjoyed the delicious buffet and helped themselves freely before sitting down with full plates on one of the many chairs or sofas in the spacious room whose large windows looked out onto the well-kept garden.

Everyone, quite by chance, formed a semicircle and began to eat. When they had finished, Reizele took her chair and sat herself across from her family. After a long, tensed silence, she began to speak. She told them that she had a confession to make to them, something she had kept to herself for many years. It had been troubling her for some time, and not only her, but Yuzhi, too, and she felt she had to open her heart both to Yuzhi and to all the family and reveal the whole story to them. She turned to Ruvke with a forced smile and added, it is quite possible that my dearest husband, Ruvke, will be very surprised indeed to hear the real details of my past, not the imaginary story I have told him.

Reizele bit her lip nervously, building up her courage to begin. Everybody sat on the edge of their chairs, tensely waiting to hear what was so vital for her to tell them, and which she was having such difficulty in finding the words to express.

And then, without any preamble, Reizele fired the opening shot: First of all, I want you all to know – and it is certainly time you knew – that Yuzhi's father was not a Jew, as I have always deceived you, and as I also misled Yuzhi, my son.

Immediately after saying this, Reizele fell silent, and gazed at one member of her family after another sitting across from her, and actually enjoyed seeing the expression of astonishment on their faces which her declaration had triggered. I lied to Yuzhi, and I lied to you all, too, she continued.

The yeshiva *bochur* I ostensibly married, Mottele, never existed. He was a figment of my imagination.

In the deep silence which followed her revelation, Reizele related everything that had happened to her from her first meeting with Arkadi in the open vegetable market in Zamosc, how he had taken her away from her father's house on the very day that the war broke out, and traveled with her to the house of distant relatives of his in Belzec, thus saving her from the *action* and persecution which forced all her family into the ghetto and from there to the extermination camp, which was established, ironically, in the same town where she was living.

Reizele continued with her story. She spread before them

all the dreadful things which had happened to her, but with great restraint, giving them an almost dry and matter-of-fact account, so that she would not be overcome by emotion and tearfulness. It was not the time or the place for that. What she had to do now was just to present the facts, including the horrible scene how she and her father exchanged glances as she came out of the church and saw her family and people from her town she had known, standing shivering, their eyes full of fear, in the wide square, surrounded by wolves exposing sharp teeth against them, that after a short time they were being driven by cruel marshals to their deaths like sheep to the slaughter.

You came out of the church? What did you do in the church? It was Ahuva who was mostly shocked by Reizele's confession, asking the question.

I needed my freedom, Reizele almost whispered her words as if she was defending herself. That was my protest against evil decrees, not to shackle myself in a dark basement for months. Of course I did not convert my religion. It was a facade, pretending with forged documents.

At that moment Ahuva felt she almost swallowed her tongue. Yes! Now I realize and understand the situation! she called out surprisingly. My father too survived by so-called converting, and he did not mean it. He only changed his religion because of the war – it was a time of danger.

For some moments there was hamming-babbling around this subject, everybody said his opinion about, and finally all of them justified that kind of urgent necessity, if needed to save one's life.

I was not married to Arkadi, Reizele continued after all her guests got in silence. In fact, we did not have the time we needed to become true soul mates. He was serving in the army, and could hardly manage to come home, and even when I was pregnant I didn't see much of him. The day I gave birth to Yuzhi, he came to take me out of the hospital, which was in danger of collapsing after one of the wings of the hospital had been bombed, and was in ruins. When we got outside, making our way home – remember, it was the day the Germans invaded the Soviet Union, June 22, 1941 – a whole formation of German planes began raining down bombs, throwing around death and destruction. Yuzhi and I were very lucky not to be injured, but Arkadi, who had gone on in front to clear a way for us among the masses of people fleeing for their lives, was hit and killed instantly, with so many others. It was really a miracle that my baby son and I were not injured. We fell because of the strength of the blast.

Reizele continued to tell her family about their lives with that wonderful couple, Katya and Piotr Polski, who hid her and Yuzhi in their house, and looked after them devotedly until a spiteful neighbor discovered that she was a Jew and told the Gestapo, so the day that she went by train, traveling with false papers, to Lublin, to visit relatives of the Polskis, she was caught and sent to the Majdanek concentration camp. She met Gittel there, and through her, Ruvke too, and walked with him on the death march which they manage to survive, and since then … well, you all know everything that has happened to me since then.

Stunned from the odd and unexpected revealing story, there was a long silence. No one said a word, and Reizele turned her head to Yuzhi and said, sadly: My dear Yuzhi, I'm sorry. You will have to come to terms with the fact that your father was not Jewish. The one I told you about did not exist, and your true father was not my husband. Where was he from? He was born in Kazakhstan, don't make such a distorted face. He was originally from Russia. His parents went from Russia by force, to live there, so you can relax. He was really Russian, Pravoslave by religion, that is not so awful, is it? My life had been saved because he was not Jewish, but he was a good man, so calm down. As you can imagine, I did not manage to meet any of his family, apart from Piotr and Katya, and they were outstanding people.

Reizele did not say a word about Arkadi's mother. There is no point in adding fuel to the flames of his fears and frustrations, she thought. Or perhaps she was mistaken? If Yuzhi knew about his Turkish-Mongolian roots on his grandmother's side, he might begin to take a peculiar pride in them, *davka* because they were so rare! He would start to trumpet to anybody and everybody the fact that he had Jewish-Turkish-Mongolian-Russian blood flowing through his veins. No, no, she wouldn't be the one to provide him with these grounds for dubious pride or depression. Let him be satisfied or horrified with what he now knows.

Reizele was very quiet, contained within herself as if all her memories – which were hers alone – had wrapped themselves around her in layers. Her listeners had also gone into their shells, each one enveloped in the details of the horrendous events they had suffered. Memories which would not be divulged, of an intimacy which each had experienced, also rose to the surface of their consciousness.

Yuda thought of loyal, passionate, Alina, who saved him from being trapped both by the Nazis and by the Polish gangs who were hunting down Jews; Anshel could not stop himself from remembering the appalling evening of the rapes in the Italian village he was sheltered in. An image of Silvana came into his mind; Silvana, who forced herself on him in a fit of passion he did not share. Gittel was remembering her first husband, Nachum, who was murdered after blood-curdling torture, his body thrown on a pile of corpses as if it was the carcass of an animal; and Reizele's other sons, all only youths, listened open-mouthed to the story of what had happened to their mother during the war and how she had somehow managed to survive it. What they had heard about Yuzhi's father's origins gave them something to think about, too. They now looked at their oldest brother in a different light, and could better understand why he was such an odd person, after all he had gone through.

The family continued to sit, subdued, for some time, each with his private memories, until they heard out of the silence, a trembling voice uttered from Yuzhi's throat: Is that all? Is that all of the story you have hidden from me all these years? That my father was not a Jew? That you ran away with him from your home, from your town and by that you had saved your life? In response, Reizele shrugged her shoulders like a little girl who admits she had done something she should be ashamed about, but did not say a word.

Listening to Yuzhi's reaction, the atmosphere lightened at once and everyone could breathe more easily once the tension was released. It was rather like after a heavy meal when the buckle of a tight belt is released a notch. Then Ruvke got up slowly from his chair, and walked over to his wife. He kissed her gently, and looked into her eyes as lovingly as if he were seeing her for the first time. *Davka,* her confession had strengthened his love for her, this brave woman. He was intensely proud of her, and now they all fully relaxed after the prolonged tension, and grasped that the skeleton let out from the closet was not such an awful creature after all. Smiles of relief began to appear on their faces. So he was a *goy* they all said, so what of it? The main thing is that he saved Rcizele from being killed!

Yuzhi still felt uncomfortable. Oh, well, yes, it could have been worse. But even that, what his mother had revealed fell on his head like a heavy boulder. He felt he could not join the smiles of everybody around and without a word, he got up from his place to try to unwind and get some air into his lungs.

Everyone followed him with their eyes, concerned as to how he was taking the news, and wanting to reassure him that he should not take it to heart. The important thing was that he had survived the Holocaust, nothing terrible would happen to him now that his origins had come to light, when you come to think of it. In fact, they had no need to give any words of comfort to Yuzhi at all, because when he came back to his seat, he was grinning from ear to ear, as if he had received the most sought-after pedigree from his father. Never mind. One does not have to be planted deep within the earth to be able to stand up straight on firm ground. There is no reason to worry, he will survive. Yuzhi smiled wryly at each one in turn, as if he were resigned to the truth of the matter of his personal status, which his mother had revealed that day. Whatever would be would be, everything was now out in the open. His roots on his father's side were exposed and flapping in the wind, whether a desert wind from the east or a freezing wind from the north. To hell with the genes he had inherited from his father, he would never know whether they were good genes or bad ones.

As if they had decided in unison, everyone began to shake themselves free of their memories, and now started to enjoy themselves at the family gathering, eating and drinking, chatting and laughing, in a pleasant and happy atmosphere in Reizele and Ruvke's new home. It was hard to grasp that barely an hour ago the atmosphere in the same room was as dull and grey as if a volcano had spewed its ash into it.

Apparently, at least on the outside, Yuzhi was calmer. His mother's confession seemed to have released him to a large extent from his compulsion to tell everyone he chanced to meet about his origins and the circumstances of his birth. And another thing: Now that he knew how to interpret the significance of the stars in their courses, he could go far, with his new powers he could discover the deep dark secrets of men, of countries, peoples and leaders. He would be omniscient and all-powerful. Everyone would beat a path to his door to ask him to predict their future. Women would beseech him to predict who their future husband would be and from where he would come, from Afula or Hadera, from Bet-Alfa or

Tiberias, and they would pay him well for his expertise. There was a good living to be made in this line of work, there is nothing wrong with that. His luck had changed for the better, the angles of the planets were working in his favor, and the story of his birth was as exciting as ever. He was born on the first day of the Operation Barbarossa offensive, and his father was killed by a bomb only a few hours after he came into the world. He was now careful to omit the word Jew, which until then he had always included in his description of his father, and decided that as his father's religious affiliation was no business of anybody else, he would not enlighten them about it.

Yuzhi removed the matter of his problematic origin from his consciousness and suppressed it in the deepest reaches of his being. He continued to chart the movements of the planets relating to the leaders during the period of the war, and in particular those of the leader of the German enemy, and so Yuzhi continued to make his predictions according to the position of the planets and the stars twinkling away above, drawing detailed birth charts of everyone who sought him out to forecast what their fate would be, as written in the stars.

And what about his own fortune? Yuzhi shrugged his shoulders. Whatever would be, would be. He would accept the fact that his father barely existed, not only in his own life, but also in that of his mother. So he had no choice but to come to terms with the fact that the only his inheritance from his father were the man's genes, and he had no way of knowing – and would never know – what kind of genes they were, and perhaps it was better that way.

# 21
# Monuments

A blow from an iron fist inflicted on the concrete blocks of the Berlin Wall; an iron fist that was driven by the strength of ideological, social, psychological, personal, historical truth – caused the massive checkpoint in the center of Berlin to crumble.

Since 1961, Checkpoint Charlie, a barricade made of barbed-wire, had divided the city into the two parts of East and West Berlin. The fall of the Berlin Wall had brought in its wake the fall of the Iron Curtain, which had blocked and sealed off almost hermetically the countries of Eastern Europe for more than 40 years – No entry, no exit. This man-made wall of separation divided the members of one nation into two, like identical twins separated from one another because of unfortunate circumstances for many years. One brother flourished and became wealthy, while the other remained poor and deprived, his heart heavy, his eyes looking longingly over at how his twin brother succeeded and prospered because of the thriving household he was privileged to grow up in, while he was prevented from getting on in life because of the rigidity and strictness of the household he grew up in, which depressed him and blocked all his initiative and thoughts about how he could improve his situation in life, and tied him to outmoded ideologies, and social and economic norms which had become obsolete.

The getaway began when one East German policeman was at his post one day, and mustered up all his courage to run in the direction of the barbed-wire wall which divided the city into two, even he knew very well that this could cost him his life. He bent down to evade the shots of the policemen who were trying to stop him from escaping, but he managed to crawl nimbly through the barbed-wire, and with the assistance of policemen from the Western side of the city, who welcomed him with open arms, he became the first refugee to cross the border to the West, successfully.

Following his bold step, a small window of opportunity opened for others to try to flee. These attempts became increasingly frequent, more and more people tried to cross the wall, not all of them as fortunate as others, and many of them were killed by East German guards sniping at them, which turned them into instant, although dead, heroes. Even the comparatively high rate of deaths did not deter the wave of those who were determined to achieve their freedom, and this resolve led to many from Soviet-dominated East Germany, countless brave men and women, to break through the dividing wall, to find a foothold on a ledge to hoist themselves over, to jump from high up on the wall to the other side, desperate to get to the West, whatever the physical and psychological cost – until the wall came tumbling down.

Naturally, the political atmosphere was a factor in the collapse of the wall. When the trickle of people fleeing to the western side became a strong surge, the then president of the Soviet Union, Mikhail Gorbachev, who initiated *perestroika*, reached the momentous, historic decision to allow whoever wanted to, to go to the western part of the city, with one condition, that he would not be allowed to return to the east. That is, it would be a one-way ticket, with no chance of returning. What irony! The leaders of the Soviet Union did not, at that stage, expect or imagine that the Berlin Wall would be dismantled, and did not dream that its being ripped apart would lead to the complete collapse of the communist regime.

Following President Gorbachev's fateful decision to cancel all restrictions on emigration from the East to the West, and of removing all the barriers and roadblocks, within one day, a mass of Germans from the East rushed in the direction of the open gate to the West as if a dam had been opened, or like wildfire which spread out of control, or a sandstorm violently swirling around, wave upon wave of people, suddenly free and reveling in their unfamiliar freedom, roaring triumphantly, breaking through and running into the western part of the city where they were greeted with shouts of joy by the hordes of Westerners, like twin brothers who had been separated for years and had become reunited, overcome with emotion, ecstatic, flowing and streaming towards the long-desired lack of restriction, until the complete breakthrough had been achieved, and a huge hole opened up in the center of the wall, until the wall came down altogether, resulting in the fusion of the two parts of Berlin. And like a line of dominoes falling in quick succession one on top of the other, Communist regimes collapsed one after the other in the whole of the Soviet bloc, and soon became independent states.

Gradually, one after another, for all kinds of reasons, Israelis began in their multitudes to travel to the countries of Eastern Europe whose doors were now open after so many years, and to look around and seek and wonder, and remember. They did not go back there in a quest to find their roots, for these no longer existed. They had all been ground to ashes in the hellfire which had devoured them without leaving even a trace, except for the very few Jews who had survived, and were as smoldering embers floundering in the cinders.

Those who went back, went out of curiosity, driven by an urge to see what remained and what had changed. They found that nothing was left and everything had changed. On the ruins of its destruction, Europe rebuilt itself with energy and determination, and restored all its historic and public and private sites.

Within the space of a very few years, it was no longer evident in Europe that such a cruel war had slashed her throat, leaving her gravely wounded. Everything returned to what it had formerly been, and in fact in many ways it was even better than it had ever been.

*Like a beautiful woman whose face has been injured in an accident and has successfully undergone plastic surgery to repair the scars, remove the blemishes, and flatten out the wrinkles – yet at the same time the expression, her inner personality, has been erased from her face.*

Europe was completely empty of Jews, it had struck them out. It had a sublime, but expressionless beauty. It lacked vitality. Nothing remained from Jewish lives. Only monuments, memorials to those who were cruelly murdered. Here and there synagogues still stood, cleared of worshippers. Restored after the damage done to them, they became museums and tourist sites people paid to enter, to see their past glory which was now withered on the bough, sterile and bare of all content. Monuments that sprung up in the places where Jews had once lived, a memory of times gone by, a dry historical chronicle of a group of people that an evil regime decided they would be massacred, and had been massacred.

Reizele was the first of her family who felt impelled to return to those blighted places she had been born in and where she had lived during the war. Something extraordinary which had happened to her some years before inspired the impulse, which bubbled up and grew in her during those same years, until she gave into it and made up her mind to go to its real source, which she had long been physically cut off from but which remained vivid in her memory.

This extraordinary happening was her chance meeting with a hospital doctor, at the time of the Second Intifada, terrorist attacks carried out on Jews in Israel when Arab Palestinian suicide bombers would blow themselves up – together with all the other passengers – on crowded buses; would detonate the bomb in a belt around their waist in coffee shops and restaurants; would place explosive charges in markets or on streets thronged with people, ordinary citizens going about their business or eating in a restaurant, in the middle of a sentence, or their fork raised to their lips. A bomb would fall on them, sowing destruction and inflicting disaster of all kinds, physical, emotional, wounds, shell shock, death.

Arab suicide terrorists were incited to murder innocent people in exchange for their being recognized as Shaheeds, holy martyrs. They would achieve holiness, if they would carry out wanton murders. A red carpet to Paradise – for a hideous crimes.

One day, during those nerve-wracking years of the intifada, Reizele heard on the radio news that there had been a devastating explosion in a restaurant on Jaffa Road, in the center of Jerusalem. She was by then used to the screeching of the alarms, as she volunteered on a regular basis at the hospitals where victims wounded in these murderous terrorist attacks were brought.

On that day, on her way to the hospital, she passed by the place of the explosion, and was shocked to see that the restaurant building and all its contents was reduced to a heap of wreckage with some of the wounded still trapped within, being taken out by ambulance men. Pools of blood of those killed and wounded stained the sidewalk. It was almost impossible to get through because barriers had been set up on the main roads, to prevent non-essential cars from driving along them, so that the wounded could be taken to the hospitals as fast as possible.

Reizele reached the hospital as some of the wounded were already being taken on stretchers to different departments, and yet others were still overflowing the corridors. Reizele went straight to the pediatric department where she volunteered each week, to help the medical team. In the corridor on her way there, she almost collided with a stretcher which was being brought to the department. A young girl of about 15 was lying on it, her head bandaged, blood seeping through it. Reizele walked at the side of the stretcher, and when they came into the department, helped the nurses transfer the wounded girl from the stretcher onto a bed.

She murmured words of encouragement to the girl and stroked her hand to calm her a little. As she did so, a middle-aged woman in a white coat walked across the room to the bed, the stethoscope around her neck signifying that she was a doctor. The doctor put the two ear pieces of the stethoscope in her ears, and gently put her fingers on the girl's wrist to measure her pulse, quite oblivious to the elderly woman standing opposite her on the other side of the bed. While the doctor was absorbed in examining the girl's pulse rate, Reizele could not take her eyes off her. She had the oddest feeling that grew stronger the more she looked at her, almost hypnotized, and her heart began to throb vibrantly.

Where does she know this woman from? She remembers meeting her, oh, years and years ago, a face like this you never forget! Reizele strained to remember, pressed hard upon her brain until the gray cells creaked with the effort, and then the glimmer of a memory began dancing its way before her eyes, that of an expensive fur coat which had been stripped from a young woman with the most remarkable eyes, the distance between them giving her face a unique expression; the secret whispered to her just before she was taken to the gas chamber, that hidden in a deep pocket in the coat which was stolen from her by force was ... oh, dear God, Reizele thought she would burst with the realization, recognizing that the woman standing only a meter away from her, was the baby snatched from her mother's belonging! She also estimated that the doctor was the age that same baby would have been!

It was all now as clear as daylight to her. Reizele was

completely sure in her assumption, and when the doctor finished examining the girl and prepared to leave, Reizele hurried over to her. She looked her full in the face and said without any preamble: Excuse me, I know who you are, I have no doubt about it. I can tell you your life story, and you can tell me if I am right or not. Were you born in Poland? In Lublin? Though not really in Lublin. A Christian woman brought you up, and you discovered that she was not your real mother? That is what happened to you, isn't it? The doctor, who had been cool and calm when she was taking care of the wounded, now, all the color left her face. The shock of this surprise revelation had thrown her into a state of confusion.

Who are you? she asked in a shaky voice. How do you know all these details about me when we have never met? Reizele took her hand and pulled her to the side, so that she could tell her how she came about the information.

I met your mother when we were brought to the Majdanek concentration camp, she said to her in a voice full of emotion. We walked together from the train station in Lublin to Majdanek. Your mother carried you in a deep pocket of her coat, an expensive fur coat, thinking that she would be able to save you from being found by the Nazis, when they came to her house looking for Jews in the *action*; but two Polish women attacked her on the way, and tried to strip her coat off her, and I came over to her and helped her push those robbers away. They had more strength than we did and managed to get the coat away from your mother, and ran off with it. When we reached the concentration camp and stood in front of the Nazis carrying out the *selection,* I saw your mother being sent to where all those intended for the gas chambers were sent. But before it was your mother's turn to step forward at the *selection*, she turned to me and told me how happy she was that those Polish women had stolen her coat from her, because she had hidden her baby in the coat, her month-old baby. You can be sure that if the coat had not been stolen from your mother, you would have been found in it and would have died along with her.

The doctor was very moved by the story, and asked, but how did you recognize who I was after all these years! After all, I am not my mother! – You look exactly like your mother, as alike as two drops of a tear, Reizele answered. You have the same eyes, the same distance between them, a face like that you never forget, and all your features are like your mother's. You have no idea how moved I am to see you. I would love to hear what happened to you before you immigrated to Israel.

The doctor took Reizele's hands in both of hers and said, it is a long and quite amazing story, but I really have to get back to work now. Thank you, thank you a thousand times for telling me what you did about my mother. You are a very special woman to me, because you are the last one who spoke to my mother, and remembers her.

When the doctor had turned to go out, all of a sudden, an elderly distinguished-looking man burst into the department, distractedly asking if his granddaughter, a girl of fifteen, had been brought there. He had to find her. She was sitting with him in the restaurant when it was bombed and he saw her being taken out of there wounded. He himself had not received a scratch. When he was asked his granddaughter's name, he was so shocked and confused that he could not remember it, but he asked to identify her by the gold necklace she always wore. His eyes searched back and forth in all directions, and came to rest on the young girl the doctor was examining, and went over to her bed, beaming. The doctor suddenly became irritable and restless. She came close to the old man and challenged him: Where is the necklace that that young girl wears, can you show it to me, so that we can identify your granddaughter? Of course I can, he replied. He kissed the young girl on the cheek, and gently pulled out from around her neck a gold necklace with a pendant on which was engraved, in Hebrew letters, a woman's name. The doctor almost jumped out of her skin when she saw the gold necklace with the pendant on the neck of the girl. She was so shocked that she demanded to know from the grandfather where the girl had gotten the necklace, and who had given it to her, and where was it possible to buy a necklace just like it. Proudly and firmly, the old man replied: You cannot buy a necklace like this anywhere in the world. I designed and made this necklace with my own hands. It is my profession. I only designed two necklaces like this, for my two daughters. One of my daughters is the mother of this young girl, and my other daughter, the elder one, died in the Holocaust, wearing the necklace which she never took off.

Reizele had to hold the doctor steady in case she collapsed on hearing the grandfather's words. But the doctor immediately recovered herself and asked the old man to look closely at the necklace she herself wore which. With trembling hands, she pulled it out from under the neck of her blouse The doctor held out the pendant, on which was engraved a name in Hebrew letters, and asked: Did you design this necklace for your daughter who died? Is the name of the daughter who died, the same as the name engraved on this pendant? The old man was astonished. His eyes, like steel pins, fixed on the pendant dangling in front of him. It took him a short time to understand the implications of what the doctor had said, and then he began to stutter, Wh-wh-where did you get this n-n-n-necklace? Who did you get it from? How did it come to you? It is indeed the name of my daughter who died in the Holocaust! And that *is* the pendant I designed and made for her with my own hands!

In a flash of understanding, the doctor grasped her relationship with the man standing next to her, and smiled a bitter-sweet smile of sadness and joy. She took a deep breath, and said quietly, and with restraint: Shalom, my dear grandfather. I am also your granddaughter. I am the daughter of your other daughter, the one who died in the Holocaust.

My mother did not go to her death with the necklace you made for her. She put it around the neck of her baby, who was saved. I was that baby, grandfather.

Reizele, who was a witness to the drama unfolding before her eyes, began to weep tears of happiness and emotion, when two people, grandfather and granddaughter, who only a few minutes before had each been unaware of the existence of the other, now stood crying and hugging each other.

People in the vicinity did not grasp exactly what happened, obviously some strange kind of emotional encounter, but not especially out of the ordinary, as far as they could gather. Cries of agony and cries of relief were part of the everyday life of a hospital. It was not all that unusual. Only Reizele understood the extraordinary sequence and the timing of events she had just witnessed, and marveled at the wonder of the chance meeting between granddaughter and grandfather. And then, feeling that they deserved some privacy, she slowly moved away from them, and left the two of them to rejoice together in their family reunion, while she went to another department to help tend to others injured in the horrendous terrorist attack on the restaurant.

This dramatic reunion remained in Reizele's mind for years, long after it happened.

✦✦✦

When she herself became a grandmother, her face lined and her hair gray, but still full of energy and vitality, Reizele made a suggestion to her eldest son, Yuzhi, to accompany her on a trip to find their roots, which she wanted to do in Poland. It was as if she was seized by a strong urge to pick at a wound which the skin had closed over, but which had not healed. She was not going to make the journey with her husband nor with her other sons, who were born in Israel. Only with Yuzhi, who held a unique significance to that period in her life. Come with me, she urged him. Let's go to the country where you were born but which you have never seen, have no memories of, and Yuzhi, who was almost overcome with emotion because of the possibility of spending a week or two alone with his mother, was happy to agree to her proposal.

Their first stop was Lublin. They landed at Warsaw Airport and straightaway set off to travel by train to Lublin. When they got off the train and went by cab on the main roads of the city, on their way to the hotel, they found a grey, dismal, somber city, and felt as if tears erupted from the walls of the buildings, a city weeping for its children, the Jews, who had made their homes in it for hundreds of years and now where no more existed.

Lublin was of vital importance in Jewish history. Hundreds of years of Jewish culture unsurpassed in its variety and vibrancy, synagogues, study halls, and yeshivas filled the city. Already in the year 1530 the first Jewish court, the *Beit Din*, was established, and the most important institution of Eastern European Jewry, known as the Jewish Council of Four Lands, was held each year in Lublin for 200 years, when issues of importance to Jewish communities were discussed and decided upon. By the year 1557, books in Hebrew were being printed in Lublin, and the city enjoyed unparalleled status in the Jewish world as a city renowned both for its Talmudic learning and for its generosity towards those in need. Before the Holocaust, 40,000 Jews were living in Lublin out of a total population of 122,000.

Now, as Reizele and Yuzhi went around the town, they saw the curved gate leading to the lanes of the old, historic part of the city which was now a popular tourist site; they saw restaurants and coffee houses, and well-stocked, fashionable shops; the view from all directions was remarkable; but in the narrow alleys, the old houses, crowded together, were empty and sealed up, and the alleys themselves were silent, as if in continual mourning for the glorious past of the Jews of the city which had vanished for all time.

In September 1939, Lublin was occupied by the army of Nazi Germany, and immediately one quarter of the Jewish inhabitants were evicted from the city and sent to small towns nearby. In 1941, a ghetto was established in the city, and all the remaining Jews were forced to enter it. After a few months, in March-April 1942, there took place a mass deportation of Jews from the ghetto to the Belzec extermination camp. In addition, hundreds of Jews were gunned down in the forests on the outskirts of the town, and the few thousand Jews still living in the ghetto after most had been deported to Belzec, were sent to a small ghetto set up in an outlying suburb of the city, where the conditions were extremely severe. Within a short time, transports of Jews were sent to Majdanek and they were put to death, until not one Jew was left.

The intrinsic beauty of the city combined with the gloom that had settled like a shroud upon it, bore down on Reizele. Even the old, vaulted buildings where small cafes had opened and where they enjoyed delicious hot soups, failed to gladden Reizele's heart, and she continued to go back *davka* to the old Jewish cemetery in Lublin.

This cemetery was established in 1555 when the Polish authorities allotted three plots of land to the Jews, two of which the Jews would have to pay an annual tax and an annual sum for candle wax tallow. In this majestic cemetery are the graves of many famous rabbis from the golden ages of Lublin, Rav Tzadok Hacohen, Rav Azriel Horowitz, and Rav Shalom Shachna. There are also graves of Jews murdered in 1655, after Cossack troops attacked and captured Lublin, looted and plundered, and murdered tens of thousands of Jews. In the midst of the carnage, an amazing tragic drama began to unfold. Across from the Cossacks, whose blood lust was still not sated, appeared a large group of Jews wrapped in prayer shawls, that came nearer and nearer to the Cossacks, after having seen their families murdered in front of their eyes and knowing that they would themselves very shortly be killed, implored the Cossacks not to slaughter them but to bury them alive. Don't lay your hands on us, they begged. If you want to destroy us, please bury us alive. The Cossacks acceded to this strange and hideous request, to kill them without shedding their blood, and so, among the graves lie the bones of Jews who preferred to be buried alive rather than have their bodies bloodied and thus defiled by the sword.

The next day, Reizele and Yuzhi sat in a cab driving them to the Majdanek concentration camp, a very short distance from Lublin. Many years earlier, Reizele had covered the same route on foot, except that then, instead of the wide highways jammed with the most recent models of automobiles, there were open fields and unpaved roads. So many memories of that place were evoked that she felt herself opening up. She found she wanted to tell Yuzhi what had happened to her in that place, at that time. All the details poured out of her mouth in a fast torrent of words, how the Nazis had trapped her at the train station in Lublin after a neighbor had informed on her being a Jew; about the dreadful journey on foot she was forced to make to the concentration camp; she also told him how she had gotten to know Gittel, and through her, Ruvke, when fate had put them together on the gruelling death march. All of a sudden the images and the memories came to the surface of her awareness and her emotions, and she talked on and on, describing those events, hidden deep inside her for so many decades. Yuzhi, who was generally an incorrigible chatterer, hardly stopping to take a breath, sat in silence and listened to his mother without uttering a word.

When they were still quite a distance from the entrance to the Majdanek camp, it was already possible to see the sinister outlines of the watchtowers from the side of the main road leading in to the camp. Reizele was surprised to see a massive dark brown monument, standing at the edge of a steep concrete path, pockmarked by bullet holes on both sides. Reizele and Yuzhi stood reflectively at the monument for a long time, before continuing on their way into the camp. The Germans had not had enough time to pull it down before they abandoned it, and the Polish regimes turned it into a tourist site, on display to all who wished to visit the camp. Look, there are the barracks, only a few of them remain standing, all the rest of the huge area has been left bare, fenced in with barbed wire, with watchtowers on the perimeter whose searchlights would be trained on anyone who moved anywhere in the whole area. Reizele remembered that well. They went into the barracks, some of them still had bunks crammed together in rows, just the way they were, to show the grossly overcrowded conditions the prisoners slept in. And here are the barracks, ostensibly containing showers, but the shower heads emitted gas; and next to them the crematorium with its chimney, smoke rising from it when the bodies were burned after the victims had been gassed.

Not far off stands a mushroom-like-shaped monument with a wide stretch of white concrete round it, on the frieze of which was something inscribed in Polish. Reizele slowly walked around the monument in order to the read the words, which were in the nature of being both a warning and a threat:

*Let our fate be a warning to you.*

This memorial stands on a mound of ashes, Reizele explained to Yuzhi. Under this dome lie the sacred ashes of the murdered Jews, collected from the crematoria. Yuzhi nodded his head, and was silent, for there were no words which could be an adequate response to such a warning. He continued to walk towards the barracks, looking at the objects placed around the wooden walls, as if he were at an exhibition. In one barracks were showcases containing piles of shoes of the murdered men, women and children. 30,000 pairs of shoes, only a small fraction of the total number of shoes which had been worn by the 300,000 people put to death there. In another barracks were displayed forms which had been found in the camp, which the Nazis had not managed to destroy before they fled in haste. On a huge table, fenced off, lay a topographical model of the camp as it had operated at the time of the Holocaust, and on the walls hung photographs of the camp as it had looked then.

What shocked Yuzhi most of all, out of all the deplorable exhibits he had seen in the camp, was the barracks of the showers, which were not connected to water pipes, but through which deadly gas was channeled, which put an end to the lives of millions of human beings, most of them Jews. He stood in the middle of the gas chamber, and tried to imagine the mass of people huddled there naked, waiting for the warm water they had been soothingly promised would cleanse their bodies to come down from the shower head, when from outlets in the ceiling a stream of poisonous gas filled the room which suffocated them to death. Yuzhi kept staring at those seemingly innocent shower heads, until his eyes were full of images which had built, one by one, a mosaic never to be erased from his mind.

All right, Mother, I've seen everything now. Come, Mother, let's get out of here, I've got the point, it's too terrible for words, but let's go back to the hotel now.

The next day they caught the train to Zamosc, the town where Reizele was born, now such a large, spacious town that Reizele could barely recognize. Wide streets, modern houses, whole new neighborhoods, shops, industrial areas. Only the main square of the old town remained as it was. The magnificent town hall, the immense church with its priceless treasures, whose golden dome dominated the entire area, and at the front, set on a wide grassy area, stood the statue of the founder of the town, Jan Zamoyski, still seated upon his horse.

Reizele was very moved to find that there was a museum in the spacious square, which she had not known existed, and which chronicles the development of the town and extols the praises of the family of Prince Zamoyski. The three floors of the museum contained splendid portraits, landscapes, exhibits of traditional dress worn by noble families and the fine china they used, as well as Christian symbols, giving an atmosphere of sanctity, which permeated the extensive collections of archeology, ethnography and history. Each floor was reached by wooden staircases, and it was possible to examine the culture of the old town of Zamosc which, in the process of giving way to the new, had lost what had made it so special.

As far as she knew, no Jew lived in the new Zamosc. Reizele did not look for the site of the ghetto which had been established in Zamosc in order to concentrate there all the Jews expelled from their houses, among whom were her parents and the rest of her family. She was in no doubt that a new neighborhood had been built on its ruins. It did not even enter her mind to go to see the house where she had been born, and where she had lived for some time with Yuzhi, Ruvke and Gittel after the war. She did not want to come face to face with the family who had usurped her family's rights to the house, if in fact any of that Polish family was still alive and living there. The thought of Zalman suddenly came into her mind, the Jew from whom she had first heard the heartbreaking testimony of the sufferings of the Jews of Zamosc. Two Jews that met by chance and wept together at the fate of their fellow Jews from Zamosc, and now again brought tears to Reizele's eyes.

Reizele wanted them to get to Belzec as quickly as possible, for she was very keen to visit Katya and Piotr. After all these years, who knew if they were still alive; if they were, they would be very old indeed, but with any luck it would be better late than never. She felt she simply had to make every effort to see them, mainly because she wanted to repay a debt she had owed them since she had last seen them, so many years ago.

The next morning, Reizele and Yuzhi traveled by bus to Belzec, 40 kilometers south of Zamosc. Reizele had to think hard to remember exactly where Katya's house was, but the cab which brought them from the station found the address quite easily. Her heart pounding, Reizele knocked on the front door, still so familiar to her after all the time that had elapsed. An old, white-haired woman, her face very wrinkled, her body thin and bent, opened the door to them and Reizele immediately recognized the remarkable woman who had been so good to her. Katya looked at her as if she were not quite sure who she was, and Reizele immediately came straight to the point, saying, I'm Reizele, do you remember me? I have come to see you with my son, the one you kept hidden away here in your house for three years. This is Yuzhi, look how tall and strong he is, putting her arm round Yuzhi with pride. A spark of memory flashed into Katya's mind, and her eyes showed the emotion she felt, for she was too overcome to speak, and just beckoned them to come inside. She clung to Reizele, and wept until her eyes were red with the surprise and emotion of seeing her again.

Yuzhi stood a little to the side, not quite knowing what to do as the two women, each of them overwhelmed by emotion and memory, wept copiously and tried to find the words to express what they felt. All Yuzhi wanted was to see the cellar where he had been hidden from prying eyes for three years, during such a crucial period of his life.

He left the two women together, and went down the stairs to the cellar, to the room which had been his hideout, where the whole period of his infancy had been lived in the shadowy dark, and the warmth and the light of the sun never crossed its threshold.

Next to the wall, there was a child's bed on which was a mattress and a flowered coverlet. A dresser with drawers stood next to it, and a small table and two chairs located at the center.

The room had been left exactly as it was when he and his mother had lived there. Katya had not changed a thing. It was as if she had made of this isolated room a memorial, a small sanctuary for the child she had had for a short time, and who had been taken from her.

Yuzhi returned to the others, and the three of them sat around the kitchen table having something to eat and drink. Katya could not stop herself from looking at Yuzhi in wonder, and saying, Goodness, how he has grown! She told them sadly, that her husband, Piotr, had died few years ago. It was his kidneys, you know, he suffered for a long time. Her evil-hearted neighbor, Mrs. Ohlenburg, the one who had denounced Reizele to the Gestapo, had died too; she had never been allowed over Katya's doorstep again once Katya knew what she had done. So you see, I live on my own now. Please sleep here tonight, she begged them. But Reizele explained that they could not stay on, as their travel schedule was very full and there were several other places in Poland they had to see before going back to Jerusalem.

This was only partly true; the real reason for Reizele's unwillingness to stay there even overnight was the memory of the trauma she had suffered from being denounced by the neighbor – which resulted in her being sent to the extermination camp. I am sorry, she said. We would really like to be with you longer, but we have to keep to the schedule arranged for us here in Poland.

When they stood up to go, Reizele took out of her bag an envelope containing a considerable amount of zlotys which she had prepared in advance, before coming to see Katya, and put it on the table. This is a fraction of a fraction of what I owe you for everything you did for me, she said quietly. Katya looked at the envelope, quite taken aback, and expressed her gratitude, without even bothering to pretend that she had no need of the money. Thank you, thank you, she mumbled. Each of the women in turn thanked the other and hugged and kissed at this, their final parting, but also gave a sigh of relief as if they had discharged the heavy debt that had been hanging over them for a long time.

After a short visit to the site of the extermination camp in Belzec, where they stood in silence opposite to the solitary monument that stood there, with wreaths of flowers at its foot, Yuzhi was beginning to show signs of emotional exhaustion from everything he had seen and heard. His intense interest in the subject of the Holocaust, which had obsessed him for years, had not demanded that he look its horrors in the eye. He took satisfaction in analyzing the events of the Holocaust from an academic or astrological point of view, but what he saw with his own eyes hindered the theories that his delusions harbored.

Let's go back to the hotel, there is no point in seeing any more of this kind of thing, he begged his mother, but Reizele obstinately replied: We are going to stick to our itinerary. Tomorrow we are going to Krakow. I was born in Poland, and all of a sudden I realize that I have hardly seen anything of the most important cities in the country. In fact, I have hardly seen Poland at all. Apart from Zamosc and Belzec, two quite small cities, I have scarcely been anywhere in the country I was born in. We will go to Krakow tomorrow. They say it is a magnificent city. Let's look for the beauty, but I'm sure that we will also feel sad at seeing what has been lost. Indeed, beauty and loss walk side by side, almost tangibly, in that spectacular city in the south of Poland, in particular in the Old Town and the Jewish Quarter, the neighborhoods which held special appeal for them.

First they met the striking beauty of the medieval wall

that surrounds the whole area of the Old Town of Krakow. A pedestrian mall with exclusive shops on both sides with all kinds of luxury items and artistic window displays that are a feast for the eyes. The mall leads to the wide Town Square, which extends as far as a vast, magnificent cathedral church which is full of worshippers every hour of the day taking part in a Mass or other religious service held several times each day. On the opposite side of the square, stretching from one end to the other, is a wide walkway where hundreds of stalls sell all kinds of artwork, jewelry, handicrafts, and pretty mementos; vibrant colors filled the eye. Outside, next to a row of coffee shops and restaurants, stood garlanded horse-drawn carriages waiting for tourists eager to take a turn in them, to see the area of the Old Town, and to gallop through the narrow streets on both sides of which are picturesque houses and massive, baroque-style buildings, luxury hotels, high-class stores, and superb restaurants and coffee houses.

They even found time to visit the Krakow Art Museum, where are exhibited the treasures of the kings of Poland, an extraordinary experience, to see all the wealth and beauty displayed there – the history, the art, the genius, to let oneself take pleasure for a while in the glorious past, which was in fact steeped in poverty, wars, blood and tears.

On the next day, the tram brought them from the Old Town to another neighborhood, to the Jewish Quarter, which was an antithesis to the splendor they had feasted their eyes on until now. On the map of the city, the Jewish Quarter appeared with the name Kazimir, as it was called by the name of King Kazimierz, who ruled Poland in the 14th century and established a new town adjoining Krakow, which bore his name. To this new town came many Jews fleeing persecution in other countries, in particular Jews who had been exiled from Spain after the Expulsion of the Jews, refugees who were educated and highly experienced merchants and traders, so the king invited them to establish in his new town the urban foundations for the development of the country as a whole. For hundreds of years, Kazimierz prospered in spite of the fact that even then the Jews were hated and suffered from the invasions of foreign nations, but they managed to stand firm.

Until the 15th century Jews also lived in Krakow itself; but *davka*, because they were so successful and talented and prospered, they aroused the hate and envy of the Polish residents of the town, who imposed on them heavy economic, educational, and residential restrictions until, at the end of the 15th century all the Jews were expelled from Krakow to Kazimierz. They added considerably to the numbers of Jews already living there, and built beautiful synagogues and established yeshivas and talmudic academies and study halls, and opened businesses and shops.

The Jewish Quarter still stands. Over the years, Krakow grew and expanded its boundaries, and merged with Kazimierz, which became a neighborhood within Krakow itself. At the end of the war, in 1945, the Jewish Quarter became a Jewish Quarter without Jews. The remains of the city wall weep, the cobbled streets cry, the houses which generations of Jews lived in them, stood there naked without any living, breathing Jew, anywhere in the vicinity.

Continuing their depressing and grief-laden itinerary, with the map of the Quarter in their hands, Reizele and Yuhzi passed through the Temple Synagogue, built only in the 19th century. It is exquisite, let's go inside. The guard at the entrance told them there was a fee to enter; payment goes towards the upkeep of the building. No, there are no prayer services, only some kinds of Jewish happenings, very rarely.

They went into the large, ornate prayer hall, gazing with awe and marveling at the intricately embroidered crimson curtain covering the Torah Ark. They stood on the *bimah*, a square stage in the middle of the prayer hall, looked up at the impressive crystal chandeliers hanging from the wide ceiling; peered at the women's gallery with its latticed railing high up on both sides of the central nave of the prayer hall. They looked all around them and breathed in the beauty and grandeur of the synagogue.

Reizele and Yuzhi continued to walk along the narrow streets of Kazimierz until they found themselves outside the oldest synagogue in Poland, built in the 14th century. The building of the Old Synagogue is divided into two wings, and supported by two pillars; the synagogue holds a valuable collection of Jewish ritual art and relics, historic documents and photographs, and its walls are decorated with oil paintings of the renowned artist Maurycy Gottlieb. The synagogue and its contents were destroyed by the Nazis, but was restored and reconstructed after the war. It is one of the few synagogues to be restored, and is now a museum of Jewish life in Poland, an enduring monument of centuries of a vibrant Jewish presence in that country.

From the old Synagogue, Reizele and Yuzhi strolled towards the synagogue of the 16th century, located next to the ancient cemetery of the Jews of Krakow and called after the Rama, Rabbi Moshe Isserles, the head of the yeshiva in Kazimierz, who wrote commentaries and additions on the *Shulchan Aruch*, the book which contains all the Jewish laws, written by Rabbi Yoseph Karo.

Like all Jewish-owned property, the synagogue, Jewish community buildings, and dwelling houses, were nationalized after the war and became the property of the State. It took many years of constant effort to have this property of the former Jewish community returned to them. At last, the communal property was returned to their management and became museums, monuments, and tourist attractions, while houses owned by Jews remained the property of the State of Poland, and were allocated to Poles almost free of charge.

The Jewish Quarter without Jews. For hundred years before the Second World War broke out, Jews had been allowed to live wherever they wished outside of the Jewish Quarter of Kazimierz, and enjoyed full equality, bloomed in their emancipation and were granted the freedom to work in any profession and employment they chose.

Until Germany invaded Poland, and with a kick of its hobnailed boot put an end to the idyll of the Jews of Krakow. At the beginning of December 1939, the first *action* was carried out, and one quarter of the Jews living in Krakow were deported and sent to villages round about. In March 1941, a decree was issued which ordered all the remaining Jews to leave their houses and move to the Podgorze neighborhood, a run-down area of Krakow in which the ghetto for the Jews of Krakow was set up. The Poles who lived there were ordered to leave, and because they were unwilling to do so, they were forced, with the Church's intervention, to vacate their houses, in order that the thousands of Jews expelled from other parts of Krakow could be crammed into them.

The borders of the Podgorze Ghetto were closed and surrounded by a wall which looked as if it had been made by using Jewish tombstones. The houses whose sides faced out of the ghetto also constituted part of the wall, and the windows of these houses were bricked up and darkened the world of all those packed into the tiny rooms. The Krakow Ghetto comprised only 21 streets, 320 houses, most of which were damp and with untiled floors; on average, four people to a room, two meters living space for each person, three people to a window, including the kitchen, which was also used to accommodate people. A year of suffering in the squalid ghetto, a year of life. No more, even of such a life. In March 1942, the transports began from the ghetto to the death camps. In the beginning, the Jews were taken to Belzec; afterwards, until March 1943, they were closely packed into sealed freight cars that made their way to Auschwitz, where all those who survived the horrific journey, were exterminated.

Only a few Jews from the Podgorze Ghetto succeeded to

escape the deportations, and they organized themselves into an underground cell and were in contact with the Warsaw Ghetto. They were helped by Tadeusz Pankiewicz, a Polish Christian, the owner of the Eagle Pharmacy, who was willing to allow the Jewish resistance to use his pharmacy as a cover for their activities, and he even allowed them to improvise and store there sabotage devices, as well as forging identity papers and maintaining contact with their counterparts in the Warsaw Ghetto. But all their superhuman efforts to survive were of little avail. Most of them were caught by the Nazis and were murdered. Only a very few of the Jews of Krakow survived the war.

What remains – and here in the desolate Jewish Quarter, which today is a popular tourist attraction – is the pharmacy, which Reizele and Yuzhi made their way to, and which commemorates the Jews of Kazimierz, thanks to a brave Pole who allowed it to be used by the few Jews comprising the resistance in Krakow. In appreciation of his bold acts, Pankiewicz was awarded the title of Righteous among the Nations.

Before they left Krakow, Reizele insisted that they go to the small town of Kazimierz Dolny, on the banks of the river Vistula, especially to see the monument made up of Jewish gravestones. The local guide explained that the Nazis took the gravestones from the Jewish cemetery in the town and ordered the Jews to pave roads with them for the Nazis to drive on. The Jews in the forced labor unit that were ordered to carry out this degrading task, decided to honor the dead as best they could in the circumstances, by placing the side with the inscription facing downwards, buried, as it were, in the ground, so that the vehicles driven by the Nazis, would not ride over the side with the inscription, but on the reverse, blank, side. After the war, all the gravestones were dug up and, amazingly, the inscriptions were still intact and clear enough to be read easily. The salvaged gravestones were arranged and embedded to construct a huge monument in the form of a wall. The architect who designed the monument left the center open, and on both sides of it fragments of broken gravestones protrude.

A colossal fissure in the wall of gravestones represents the massive fracture in the heart of European Judaism after the destruction inflicted by the Holocaust.

The next morning, Reizele raised an issue to Yuzhi which had been bothering her: Do they want to go to visit Auschwitz, which is only about an hour away from Krakow?

Every day, the tourist office in Krakow was full of people, tourists from all over the world, arranging to go on a tour of the death camp which has become a symbol of the Holocaust. What, go and see Auschwitz? Yuzhi made a face at his mother's idea. What, to look at another heap of shoes in a glass showcase? What, more piles of crutches and spectacles? I have already heard about the wall of death where people stood facing the wall and were shot in the back or the head by firing squads. That was much slower and more primitive, before the Nazis began with the gas. I know all the stories. The iron gateway, as well. I have a mental picture of it. I have seen it so often in films, leading to the camp with the inscription over it, Work Brings Freedom. That is the most cynical thing I have ever heard. You have to get that into your head, really understand it, not just see the words. Work brings freedom? From such work only death frees you. And how many times have we seen the films they show on Holocaust Day of the barracks in Birkenau, Jews crammed together on wooden bunks, eight men on a bunk of three tiers. How could they sleep there, good grief, if they slept at all. And the row of latrines in the same barracks, men had to sit with their backs touching another man's when they needed to relieve themselves. Horrendous, who can imagine it, the right to the most basic privacy was trampled into the dust. And the backbreaking work they had to do? We know the Nazis would make the men, and the women too, haul heavy loads, like pails of boulders, from one side of a field to the other side, and back again, again and again, just to break their spirit, not only their bodies. And in fact, only a few managed to keep going. But how they organized things there, the efficiency, perfect, right down to the last detail.

The first thing that every single person who was doomed to go through that gateway was forced to hold his arm out, to have a number tattooed on it. That was what they did with animals, tattoo a number on sheep and cows. It is still hard for me to see all those people in Israel going about with a bluey-green number tattooed on their arm, their skin is wrinkled now, the nib of a special pen, red-hot from the fire, pierced their skin to have that number engraved in it. Instead of their name, they became that number. The Nazis took their name from them, they became nameless, they lost their identity, their individuality, the essence of themselves. And in the end they were practically all sent to the gas chambers. Only a few of them had survived, and they were saved by the American soldiers who liberated Auschwitz.

I know all that, Mother, so what do you want us to go and see there. I really think it won't do you any good, Mother, you have been through all that yourself in a death camp. I suggest that we give up the idea.

All right, I agree, Reizele replied to Yuzhi. I am tired. I think we have done Krakow, so tomorrow we will take the train to Warsaw. Warsaw? Yuzhi said he had had enough. He already wanted to go home. I have the hang of it, he said. Reizele was annoyed with him. What do you mean, you have the hang of it? In any event, we have to go to Warsaw to fly home from there, so if we are already there, there is no way we are going to miss the chance of a tour through the city. I have heard Warsaw has become one of the most lively and most beautiful cities in Europe. It is unbelievable just to think how the fall of communism has benefited those countries under the Soviet regime. Also, I feel I must see the city where Ruvke was born. Let's see what is left of the Warsaw Ghetto, where Ruvke lived and fought in the uprising. Let's see what the Poles remember of their Jewish citizens.

What they remember? It is not altogether clear what they remember, but at least they commemorate the fact that Jews once lived there. Reizele and Yossi went from one monument to another, from one stone on which were engraved the names of those murdered to another. Memory lies only in stone. Poland has really gone out of its way to commemorate the Jews killed on its soil. More monuments, more memorial tablets, more mounds of stones in everlasting remembrance.

The most prominent among them being the small hill at 18 Mila Street under which lie the bodies of the heroes of the Warsaw Ghetto Uprising under the leadership of Mordechai Anielewicz, who put an end to their own lives in a bunker deep in the ground, after a month of engaging the vastly better equipped Nazis in fierce fighting. For the leaders of the uprising, holed up in the bunker, there was no choice. The Germans had sent for reinforcements and issued the fighters an ultimatum which sounded too good to be true to the embattled fighters, that they should come out with their arms raised and thus their lives would be saved. Naturally the leaders of the uprising did not believe this inducement for a minute, and were not tempted to do as the Germans proposed, but when the Nazis threw canisters of tear gas into the bunker so as to force them to come out of it, they chose to commit suicide rather than have their blood spilled by the bullets of the enemy.

And there, in that spot, on a mound of rubble, on a black memorial stone, was engraved the names of the Jewish heroes who are buried beneath it. Heroes who died in sanctification of their nation and their faith.

They continued walking around sites of Jewish significance and came to a massive park, with trees and lawns, flowers, benches, with a huge monument created by the sculptor Nathan Rappaport, a wall made of grey marble within its center a large raised section depicting several of the resistance fighters in the Warsaw Ghetto, led by Anielewicz. A drop of courage among deep oceans of weakness, inability, innocence, unknowing, unbelieving,

From the heroism of the uprising, they went to observe the humiliation of the transportations towards extermination: To the *Umshlagplatz*, the large square from where 300,000 Jews from the Warsaw Ghetto were sent by trains to the death camps. Reizele and Yuzhi stood in silence for a long time looking at the wall with its blocks of marble and their inscriptions, a large fissure indicating the break, the relentless, forced disappearance of people, screaming out wordlessly to an unhearing world. It was not hard for them to imagine the thousands upon thousands of people pushed roughly and violently into the box cars of the freight train which were crammed full to capacity of human cargo, and in which Ruvke and his mother Gittel had also been pushed into, and were taken, to their great luck, to Majdanek, where they got the chance to survive, and not to Treblinka, to a certain death.

When Reizele and Yuzhi went away from there, they were so mentally and emotionally exhausted that they had no strength left for any more monuments.

Enough! Now let's go and look around the new Warsaw, suggested Reizele, and they went to walk through the Old Town of Warsaw. The Old Town that had been masterfully restored and reconstructed on the ruins and heaps of rubble caused by the bombs dropped on it by the Nazis when they invaded Poland and by the Allies when they liberated it. Incredible, authentic, and artistic restoration returned to the city its past glory.

They strolled in the spring sunshine, in the wide city square, then they made their way along the narrow, picturesque lanes lined with small, exquisite, shops; and gasped to see the red walls surrounding the area as if they had been there since the Middle Ages, like in a fairy tale, and went on to see a farmers' market, with all kinds of foodstuffs for sale, lots of people bustling about, filling their baskets with treats and tidbits, in particular mouth-watering sausages of every shape and size. Reizele did not want to sample any of the meats, as she felt rather revolted by them, but Yuzhi had no such inhibitions and licked his fingers with gusto, sucking the delicious red juice which dripped onto them. They wandered around leisurely, at their ease in the relaxing atmosphere, such enviable tranquility, which made Reizele at the same time, see again in her mind's eye the monuments and the difficult emotions they aroused.

She could not help wondering how all the commemoration of the cruelties which had been perpetrated throughout all the six years of the war fit in with the fact that everything took place in full view of the parents or grandparents of the people walking next to them, watching the atrocities of the Jews take place in their city and in their neighborhood – how they saw everything, and remained silent.

Many of the Poles gave a sigh of relief, while many others said good riddance, because they all only profited from the Jews being thrown out: They received the Jews' houses, their businesses, their jobs, their property, and could buy the contents of the Jews' houses at public auctions organized by the authorities very cheap. So, from their point of view, they really had good reason not to offer their help or to shed a tear, or to protest about the treatment of their Jewish neighbors.

When Reizele expressed her thoughts to Yuzhi, he gave her an odd look and asked her, casually: Be honest, Mother, what would you have done if you had been in their position? Reizele pursed her lips angrily at her son's unfair and provocative question, and did not answer.

They had one day left in Warsaw before returning home. Ironically, Yuzhi was the one who suggested to his mother that they should go to visit the house of Janusz Korczak, whose book King Matt the First he had read as a child and had been very impressed by. Just think, he said to his mother, a boy king, ten years old, who tries to free the children of his state from being controlled by adults who conduct a policy of lies and intrigues, and the boy king works to transfer power to the children. It is a wonderful book. I want to pay tribute to Korczak. He taught me a lot about the freedom which should be given to children, about teaching them to be independent, about the clear way they think things out, without the agendas adults have. I want to know more about him. *Davka,* because I grew up without freedom, and for almost a year even without a mother, I hardly spoke, admit it, Mother, of course I am not blaming you, but that is what my life was like as a child, wasn't it, Mother? So let's go and see Korczak's house. Imagine, instead of saving his own skin, which the Nazis even said they would let him do, he chose to go with the children from his orphanage to Treblinka, where he and all of them were killed. He was a great man, Yuzhi added, admiringly.

Poland did indeed give considerable honor to Korczak's memory. A huge statue in his image presides over a wide plaza in front of the Korczak house in the center of Warsaw, where his writings and other mementos of his life's work are displayed. Reizele and Yuzhi walked through the rooms, and learned much about the children's doctor from Warsaw, a Jew who grew up in an assimilated family, who, after seeing what orphaned children had to suffer in orphanage institutions, where the atmosphere of fear and threats was caused by the policy of the domineering adults in charge of them, constantly humiliating and punishing the children, as well as by the lies and malicious gossip bandied about – was persuaded to establish his own orphanage, with a completely different educational policy.

In order to achieve this goal, Korczak brought together 200 children who went through a rigorous screening process, and the orphanage was founded on the principles of mutual understanding between children and adults, and education for democracy. He let the children rule themselves, encouraged them to develop their inner worlds, and set up for them institutions which they governed themselves such as a court, and a committee to pass laws, a sports committee, a newspaper, and so on. Korczak also made sure that there would be plenty of opportunities simply to relax and enjoy themselves. He created a games corners, formed an orchestra, and made sure that the atmosphere in the orphanage was always cheerful and loving. Korczak ran his orphanage from 1911 until the Germans invaded Poland in 1939, which marked the beginning of the end for his revolutionary educational enterprise, even though it was still able to function, at least for the time being.

In 1940, like all the other Jews in Warsaw, the children of the Korczak orphanage were ordered to move into the ghetto. All the contents of the orphanage, beds and mattresses and pots and pans and clothes and books, were all piled onto horse-drawn wagons, which slowly straggled through the streets of Warsaw until they arrived at the gates of the ghetto. The orphanage was allotted a regular school building. 200 girls and boys settled themselves in two vast halls, which were crammed with beds from one end to the other. One hall was for the boys, the other for the girls, and Korczak continued teaching and educating his children – for so he regarded the children of his boarding school. To him, they were his own children – and continued to instill into their minds and hearts the principles of the social convention that he had compiled, and which was his and his alone, and which incorporated the basic rights to which every child was entitled. This convention was compiled many years before the United

Nations convention on the Rights of the Child, a convention which states the child's right to be loved, to be respected, and to have the best possible conditions in which to grow and develop; the right to be true to himself, to make mistakes, and to fail, to be related to with the seriousness due to him, to be valued for what he is, to expect that his property will be respected, to receive an education and to be able to refuse to be educated in a way that runs contrary to his worldview; the possibility of protesting against injustice and to receive a fair hearing; the right to communicate with God, and the right to die prematurely.

It was as if Korczak prophesied what had entered nobody else's head. In the most cynical and cruel way imaginable, this right to die prematurely was given to him and all the children from his orphanage, his educators and workers, without much delay. After living in the ghetto for two years, in harsh conditions of constant hunger and cold, in August 1942, German troops came to the school in order to transport everybody in the orphanage to the Treblinka extermination camp.

The Nazis recognized Korczak's renown and were acquainted with his life's work in education, for his books had also been translated into German and were highly valued, so they offered Korczak the chance to save his life and stay in the ghetto and not go with the children. But no. Korczak rejected the proposal without any hesitation and went of his own free will with the children to face death together. No, he would not abandon his children and save his own skin. Korczak joined his children but hid from them the nature of the place they were going to. That was the first and the only lie Korczak had told them, so as not to frighten them.

The children walked four to a row, and in front of them all, so that they could all see him, their teacher, Dr. Korczak, standing upright and proud, holding the green flag of their educational institute. They walked innocently, enjoying the journey, from the ghetto to the *Umshlagplatz*, where they were loaded onto the train waiting to take them to Treblinka, the death camp where every single one of them was annihilated.

Reizele and Yuzhi stood silent, wonderstruck at the sight of the green flag which Korczak had held high as he marched at the head of the rows of children. The flag had miraculously been found intact at the death camp, and was now displayed in the museum as the key exhibit in memory of Korczak. On the one hand, the flag screamed out the injustice, the wrong done to human beings; on the other, it served to praise the man who had held it in his hand, whose humanity was such that he chose to die with his children rather than live without them.

Yuzhi could not help wondering out loud what would have happened if Korczak would have chosen to stay in the ghetto, as the Nazis, with a generous dollop of hypocrisy, had suggested to him, rather than going with his children to their deaths. Would he have survived the transports of all the remaining Jews in the ghetto after that? There is no doubt that he would not have survived. He would certainly have been taken on one of the other transports to the death camp after the uprising was suppressed. No, he would not have survived. And thus Janusz Korczak died showing unsurpassed moral courage and selflessness.

Yuzhi suddenly felt sorry that the trip was at an end. He found that he wanted to go to visit more places, more monuments. But everything has to come to an end. He would have to be satisfied with what he had seen. When he and his mother sat on the plane on the flight back to Israel, his mother saw him deep in thought and, for the first time in his life, during all the hours of the flight, Yuzhi hardly uttered a word.

✦✦✦

Gittel and Sergei were not willing to consider even for a

minute the idea of going to visit Poland or Germany. They would never set foot on that tainted earth, they said vehemently. We would rather go and see other places, America, the Far East, thank goodness, the world is a big place, even if they acknowledged that, for them, there is no other continent that can equal Europe for beauty, culture and history. However, they could not forget, and would not forgive.

Gittel was even among the group of Holocaust survivors who, in the 1960s, refused to accept monetary compensation from the Germans that was offered to everyone who had been harmed by the crimes of the Nazi regime. Reparations from Germany? No thanks. She would not touch their filthy money with a barge pole. Gittel kept up her adamant refusal for many years, until she finally succumbed and could be convinced that in return for her suffering, she could be compensated in only two ways: asking for forgiveness – and money. In the end, Gittel agreed to accept the money but flatly rejected the Germans' request to be forgiven. She would never forget and not forgive.

Ruvke, for his part, did not feel like that. Time sharpens the memories but also blunts the intensity of past horrors. After he had listened to all the experiences Reizele and Yuzhi had had on their trip, he decided that he would also go. Alone. Not to Poland, but to Germany. Yes, *davka*, to Germany, the source of all the catastrophes. Now he had plenty of time at his disposal. Since he had become a pensioner from the orchestra, his time was his own to do with what he wanted, and the memories that were embedded in his heart were like a locked box whose key to the secret contents was in his pocket, waiting for the right time for it to be used to open the box. He really had a strong desire to travel, *davka*, to Germany. To himself he admitted that a scrap of paper on which was written a certain address in Berlin, which he had kept all this years in his desk drawer, had set his mind on fire with its implications and possibilities. At this time, when his hair had turned to silver and wrinkles of age were etched onto his face, the spark of youth still shone in his eyes and he was still full of vigor, he wanted to go there. To see the place, have a look around, and also try to meet the man whose experiences which he had related to him during his own incarceration, still had the power to intrigue him. In light of a strong impulse, he suddenly felt he must see him. Yes, he would try to meet Gregor Wolfgang once again.

After he parted from Reizele, his children, and the many grandchildren that had been born to them over the years, Ruvke flew off to Berlin. He settled into the hotel he had chosen because of its proximity to the address he intended to go to, and when he felt he was ready, he took a cab and told the driver to take him to that address. Ruvke had taken into account the fact that he might well not find anyone there, for that was the address of Gregor's parents, and he had most probably married, with children and grandchildren, and had gone to live somewhere else. But perhaps one of the neighbors would know what had happened to him, and where he was living now. There was also another, better, possibility, that Gregor's parents – who had doubtless died – had bequeathed him their house, and that he had gone to live there.

Ruvke did not remember, and perhaps had never known, if Gregor had had any siblings, but what did it matter? The cab drew up at a large building in an exclusive area in the center of Berlin, a building which had obviously undergone extensive renovation after being severely damaged in the massive bombardments that the Allies had rained down upon the city during the war. Ruvke's finger shook as he pressed the bell of the apartment listed, as he had hoped, in the name of Wolfgang. The voice of an elderly woman asked, who is it, and Ruvke answered, a friend of Gregor. The woman's voice said, Sixth Floor, and with a buzzing sound, the outer door opened. Ruvke went up in the elevator, and as soon as he pressed the bell of the apartment, and, as if someone had been waiting there for him to arrive, the door opened.

A man of about his own height, thicker set than he was himself, his head balding but with a small goatee beard, welcomed him inside. His pleasant face and the way his eyes looked at him – in spite of all the changes brought by his advanced age – could not hide the man's identity, and Ruvke was certain that the man standing opposite him was Gregor Wolfgang. They shook hands warmly, and smiled at each other trying to contain their excitement at the joy of this completely unexpected meeting. Please come in, said Gregor. I had a feeling that it would be you. For many years I have waited for you to come and visit, and here you are, at last.

Gregor introduced Ruvke to his wife, Helga, a pleasant-looking woman with brilliant white hair, who immediately held out her hand to shake Ruvke's, and said that Gregor had told her so many times about their wonderful friendship and that he hoped that one day they would meet, so she was not surprised that it had actually come to pass now.

After refreshments had been brought in, and they had settled themselves comfortably in the antique armchairs, Ruvke looked around the room with interest. He thought to himself, well, at least this exquisite antique furniture was not damaged when a bomb fell on the building – it looks as if time has stood still here.

I suppose that you inherited the apartment from your parents with all the contents, Ruvke said to his host. Gregor nodded, his glass in his hand. Yes, there was not too much damage inside the building, it was all on the outside, the whole of the left wing of the building was wrecked. When I came back from the prisoner-of-war camp, I found my mother living here completely on her own. The whole district, and in fact the entire city, was just a pile of rubble. My mother was very lucky that I returned, because my only brother was killed in the war, and my father was executed before the end of that damned war.

Executed? Ruvke exclaimed, his eyes opening wide in disbelief. Your father, who was a senior officer in the Wehrmacht, who berated you for running away like a coward, as he put it, from the killing fields of Babi Yar, and said he was ashamed of you for it, he was executed? By whom? And what for? Gregor smiled proudly, and put his cup down on the table as if he were ready and willing to tell the fantastic story.

Well, yes, it seems that what my father was up to in the war was just a façade, a pretense, for what he was really involved in, at the same time he was following the Fuhrer with blind obedience, he was active in the resistance with other Wehrmacht officers planning to assassinate Hitler. My father was a close friend of Count Claus von Stauffenberg, who was chief of staff of General Friedrich Fromm, head of the German Reserves Army. Von Stauffenberg masterminded the plot to assassinate Hitler. After a number of unsuccessful attempts to assassinate him, Operation Valkyrie was meticulously planned, down to the last detail. To this end, they put the units of the Reserves Army on standby, so that at the critical moment they would capture key positions in the city and control government offices and communications systems. Operation Valkyrie was planned to go into action on June 20, 1944, and because von Stauffenberg, who had lost an eye, his right hand, and two fingers from his left hand in the war, was the only one of the conspirators with direct access to Hitler, he was the one chosen to carry out the assassination.

Ruvke shook his head in amazement, but nodded knowingly when Gregor gave details of the assassination attempt. This was what happened, Gregor said: During one of the daily briefing sessions of the High Command headed by Hitler, which took place in the headquarters in the small town of Rastenburg, Eastern Prussia, known as the Wolf's Lair, hundreds of miles from Berlin, von Stauffenberg placed a bomb, with a timing device, into his briefcase. The bomb was timed to explode within ten minutes from the time the mechanism was activated. All the officers stood around the table, which was covered in maps of the Russian front, discussing the situation of the German troops which were close to collapse, and von Stauffenberg placed the briefcase literally at the Fuhrer's feet, with the bomb hidden inside it which would kill him ten minutes after being activated. Von Stauffenberg then surreptitiously set the timing device, and left the room, on the pretext of waiting to receive an urgent telephone call.

Unfortunately, however, just as he had gone out of the room, one of the officers standing next to Hitler, found that the briefcase was getting in the way of him leaning over the map he was studying, and he bent down and moved the briefcase a few centimeters away from him and propped it against the thick wooden board which kept the briefcase a bit away from where Hitler stood. And so, when the bomb was detonated in the briefcase, the thick wooden board absorbed most of the force of the bomb.

Von Stauffenberg stood outside the building for a few minutes until he heard the sound of the blast he had been waiting for, and was convinced that Hitler had been killed, together with all the other officers in the conference room. He then set off by car and drove to the airport with his aide, who had been waiting for him, and the two of them flew in a light airplane to Berlin so that they could get things in motion for gaining control of the army of Nazi Germany.

For several hours the conspirators succeeded in taking control of government offices. They issued orders, made arrests, replaced a large number of soldiers with men from General Fromm's Reserves Army. However, they did not have enough time to take over the channels of communication, including the radio. When rumors began to circulate that Hitler had not been killed, von Stauffenberg did not believe them. He could not imagine that, after such a powerful bomb as the one he had himself planted, Hitler was not badly wounded. It also did not enter his mind that anyone would move the briefcase with the bomb and put it at a distance from where Hitler was standing and thereby cause the assassination attempt to fail.

The broad consequences of the planned assassination of Hitler were to put an end to the evil regime and to effect a revolution, with the involvement of the army who, according to the plan, would take control of the Nazi apparatus and commandeer the radio stations in order to announce to the German people that a new era had begun in the life of the nation.

Instead of that announcement of deliverance from evil, that very same evening the radio broadcast Hitler making a speech in which he proved that the rumor about his death was false, and informed the nation that he had only received surface burns, and swore that he would suppress the rebellion and liquidate the conspirators who planned to murder him.

Immediately after the broadcast, Hitler's closest loyal followers, scattered in all directions like leaves in a whirlwind, to find all the conspirators, and in the same evening many of the officers who had taken part in the revolt, including the perpetrator of the planned assassination, von Stauffenberg, were shot one after the other by firing squads, by the light of the headlights of a truck.

And what happened to your father? How did they find him, what did they do to him? Ruvke was very curious to know all the details.

Gregor lowered his eyes while he answered Ruvke. My father, who was one of the conspirators, was caught with many others. He was interrogated and tortured by the Gestapo. They all stood trial, which was more like a circus than a court, conducted by a single judge who saw his role more as a prosecutor than a judge. He sentenced all of them to death. My father was fortunate in that he was sentenced to death by shooting. Many of the other plotters, after their torture and trial, were put to death by a very cruel method. They were strung up on butchers' hooks, which are usually used for hanging the carcasses of cows and sheep, but instead of using a rope, the Nazis took their revenge on them, and used piano wire which they tied around their necks so they had an excruciatingly painful, slow death. You can just imagine it.

The Nazis didn't even spare General Rommel, who had been idolized earlier in the war, after his involvement in the attempted revolution. He was still recovering from his injuries at home, when the Gestapo burst in, but instead of shooting him themselves, they handed him a gun so that he could commit suicide. Rommel did as he had been ordered – placed the gun to his temple and pulled the trigger. The Nazis did not tell the public about his suicide, but informed them that General Rommel died from his wounds. For the sake of appearance only, they gave the general, who had been so admired by the people, a state funeral, as befitting his heroic exploits during the war. Only after the war did they tell the public the real circumstances of General Rommel's death.

Ruvke and Gregor were deep in reflection for some time, trying to absorb everything that they had discussed, until Ruvke roused himself to ask, Just a minute, if the plot to murder Hitler was on July 20, 1944, that means that it was not long after Sergei and I came to see you in the prisoner-of-war camp! Do you remember? Gregor smiled at the recollection. Of course I do. I was so taken up with worrying about myself, as a prisoner of the Russians, that I did not even think about my father's situation in Berlin. I had no idea what was going on with him. But when I was told he had been put to death, and the reasons for that, when instead of grieving over him, I was as proud as I could be! I was happy! It was suddenly clear to me that my father was not one of those monsters who sat in the Reichstag and hatched a plan to inflict a Holocaust on the peoples of Europe ... Ruvke cut him short at this point and added ... and how to continue to murder as many Jews still left in Europe. If that villain had been killed then, it might have been possible to save the last of the victims from being gassed in Auschwitz-Birkenau. Gregor nodded his head in agreement, and muttered, exactly, but that did not happen. What a missed opportunity!

But what happened to you in the prisoner-of-war camp? Tell me how it was for you there, Ruvke urged Gregor, who nodded his head in consent, and said, Well, think about this: In the same prisoner-of-war camp, there were quite a lot of Jewish prisoners from Hungary who were brought there from forced labor camps in the Soviet Union, where they were taken from Hungary at the beginning of the war. They were very lucky they were not kept in Hungary, otherwise they would have been sent to Birkenau with all the other Hungarian Jews that were transported there almost at the end of the war. They survived, but the Russians related to them in the most appalling way! In spite of the fact that they were actually citizens who were taken to do forced labor in work camps and not soldiers who had enlisted to fight the Russians, they were regarded as prisoners-of-war and they were treated worse than the German prisoners!

Ruvke interrupted Gregor here, and asked quickly, because he was most curious: But what happened to you there, in the Russian camp? Did you get any special privileges after Sergei and I recommended to the camp commander that you deserve better treatment? Gregor answered him glumly: First of all, I want to thank you again from the bottom of my heart for all your efforts to come to look after me and asking the commander to give me better treatment than the others, and for trying to have me released. I did receive excellent treatment – my living quarters were much more comfortable. I received better food, and they generally tried to let me have whatever I asked for. However, release was out of the question, and the better conditions I received lasted only for a short time, because the commander of the camp, Druyanov, your friend Sergei's friend, was transferred somewhere else, I don't know, maybe he was discharged from his post, or even from the army altogether. He could have been arrested, or killed, and on the other hand perhaps he was promoted. I have no idea, but he was replaced by a tough Russian commander and he, with one fell swoop, did away with all the special privileges I had been getting, and I went back to being a punching bag like all the other prisoners of war, with harsh conditions, but I was strong and managed to survive. I cannot grumble. I was also lucky to be one of the first to be released at the end of the war. A lot of others were kept in the camp for months or even a year or two, after the war ended, especially the Hungarian Jews, because those in charge of the camp regarded them as citizens of one of Germany's allies in the war against Russia.

When Ruvke asked Gregor what he did after the war, Gregor again told him about how he had come back home, to this apartment, the whole city in ruins, and found his mother on her own after being in the bomb shelter for weeks because bombs were falling all around. She had not only been widowed, but had also lost a son who had been killed in the war, my only brother, younger than me by a year. As a bereaved mother, she received a generous pension from the state, and later on was also awarded a pension as the widow of an officer who was opposed to Nazism and executed for his beliefs. They gave her a lot of respect, and compensated her well. But that was quite a number of years after the war. It took the Germans years to grasp the nature of the revolt and the planned assassination. Only after that period, the public saw those involved in it as heroes who were intent on overthrowing the Nazi regime.

Anyway, my mother was left on her own, grieving and frail, mentally and physically, and I came back to live with her. When Helga and I got married, we stayed here and have lived in this apartment ever since. With an expression of great sadness, Gregor said, my mother found things very difficult, and only a few years after the war ended she became ill, and died a few years later. We have two sons and four grandchildren. I set up a business importing Japanese and French cars. The business did very well. My elder son manages it now, so I have a lot of time on my hands, and I have no complaints or worries, except for that terrible period which still haunts me every day, but it gives me a good feeling to know that my father was not really a part of the Nazi set-up but opposed it, and even took part in the revolt against it.

Gregor, Helga and Ruvke remained sitting for a good while, talking and chatting, listening to the unfolding of the sequence of events.

Ruvke told Gregor and Helga of meeting in Majdanek the woman who would become his wife, about escaping from the death march, of the astonishing reunion of his family on the way to the boat which brought them to their homeland, of the hardships on that illegal immigrant ship to Palestine, of fighting in the battle for the Old City of Jerusalem and being taken into captivity in Jordan, and of his violin, which had become the source of his livelihood for the many years he had performed with the Jerusalem Symphony Orchestra. He told them, with obvious happiness and gratitude, of his life with his wife and children and their many grandchildren. They sat on and on, relaxed in each other's company, until Helga looked at her watch, and said, Oh, dear, I am sorry, but we have to go out very soon. We arranged to meet friends. Ruvke could not hide his disappointment, for he had wanted to have Gregor and Helga tell him about Berlin, and recommend sites they thought he would be interested in going to.

Seeing Ruvke's downcast face, Gregor suggested that he would be happy to be Ruvke's guide in Berlin and take him each day both to the tourist spots in the city and also to the monuments in memory of the Jews.

Gregor was as good as his word, and on each of the next five days, he would collect Ruvke from his hotel each morning and go with him all over Berlin. Now, not only had the two parts of the city of Berlin been reunited, but the two parts of Germany – East and West – had become one state again.

✦✦✦

It took East Germany quite a few years to rehabilitate itself and to recover from the economic damage which the communist regime had caused its citizens in the more than 40 years since it had imposed its rule upon them. West Germany took it upon itself to restructure the East German economy, and was amazed to see commercial companies with such low rates of growth, outdated equipment in factories, inefficient work methods, agricultural and industrial backwardness, and the poverty and shortages, all of which the communist regime had caused and which, now, had fallen upon the West Germans like a ton of bricks. They came to the conclusion that the best thing they could do with all the government companies, the public enterprises and in fact all the factories and workshops still in operation, was to close them down, throw them into the garbage dumpster, and start everything completely from scratch.

As Gregor and Ruvke went around the city, the wealth and liveliness of the Western part of the city was still very marked, in contrast to the miserable grayness of the Eastern neighborhoods. Only the magnificent Pergamon Museum sparkled like a diamond in the dull Eastern side of the city, and Gregor suggested that they go inside before they begin to visit the sites in memory of the Jews who perished.

I am sure you'll be interested in seeing this museum, said Gregor, because all its exhibits were excavated and collected in the Middle East, a whole culture of ancient kingdoms which came to Germany in the years between 1910 and 1930, after a German engineer uncovered them in the 19th century in the excavations of the ancient city of Pergamon, in Turkey.

Naturally, Ruvke agreed with enthusiasm, and while they were walking the length and breadth of the huge museum, he had the feeling that he was living in the fabled world of 3,000 years ago.

They went through the market gate of Miltos, from the Roman era, and through the Ishtar Gate and the Pergamon Altar dating from the second century BCE; looked at the outstanding collections of Greek and Roman antiquities, and the artifacts and Islamic art brought to the museum from Iraq, statues of immense size and unequalled beauty, whole rooms from Sancherib's palace in Assyria, and a street of the processions of Babylon, all within short reach of Eretz Yisrael.

During their tour of the museum, Gregor explained to Ruvke that all these treasures were moved about several times during the war. The museum building itself was hit in the battle for Berlin, although the management was wise enough to store most of these priceless artifacts in shelters, in advance, in case they might be damaged. The vast ancient structures, such as the Pergamon Altar and the Ishtar Gate, were covered by a protective wall so none of collections of the museum was damaged in any way.

But then what happened? At the end of the war, when East Berlin came under the control of the Soviet Union, the Red Army meticulously collected together all the artifacts, and transferred them to their country, and they were displayed in the Pushkin Museum in Moscow and at the Hermitage Museum in St. Petersburg. Some of the exhibits were returned to East Germany in 1958, but the majority of them remained in the Soviet Union.

The irony, Gregor continued, is that according to the Agreement signed in 2003 between Germany and Russia, Russia undertook to return the artifacts to Berlin, but nothing was done about this, on the grounds that the agreement contradicted Russian legislation, which forbids taking archeological exhibits out of the country.

Ruvke chuckled to hear this abstruse reasoning, and blurted out, Oh, for goodness sake, just see where all this political funny business leads us in to. Do you think that when the Russians signed the agreement to returning the artifacts they didn't know that their own law made it illegal to take them out of the country?

Robbers, it is just robbery, mumbled Gregor and added: The greatest robbers in the world are governments. All kinds of governments. First they rob their citizens and if they can – they rob other countries…

Ruvke agreed and by the way hinted that Iraq, on the other hand, had complained against Germany that it took its archeological artifacts from her land and claims them back and Germany does not respond to it. Gregor nodded his head and said: You see? As I have said before, governments are the biggest robbers in the world. Both of them laughed heartily.

The next day, Gregor and Ruvke began going around the sites of Jewish memorials. Ruvke said he would like to visit Platform 17 at Grunewald, the train station from where the Jews of Berlin were assembled after they had been forced out of their houses and were sent to their deaths. Gregor suggested that they go there by train, as it was quite far away from the center of the city.

They came off the train, and went down the steps to the tunnel linking the platforms. The arched tunnel was neglected, pale lightened, looked as if it was hiding a dark past of the one track it concealed. Attached to the wall of the shadowy, depressing tunnel, next to the steps leading to Platform 17, was a sign indicating that this was Platform 17. No other explanation.

What would this sign mean to someone who had no idea

what happened on Platform 17? Nothing. There is not the slightest hint that from that platform the Jews of Berlin were transported to the death camps. A disused platform, deathly quiet now. A platform which has become a memorial. 186 large metal plates lie along the floor of the platform, and along the edge of each plate are engraved the date of deportation, the number of people deported from there to their deaths, and the destination of that train. Most transports of Berlin Jews went to Theresienstadt, as a transit camp for Auschwitz and Treblinka.

Ruvke walked slowly along the platform, his eyes looking downwards to the metal plates. He glanced from one to another, read the date on each plate. Trains left from there, one after another, only a few days apart. On that platform clustered thousands of people trying to calm their infants and children, while they themselves were trembling with fear and cold, not knowing and not suspecting for a minute what kind of hell they were being taken to.

Out of a population of 170,000 Jews who lived in Berlin before the outbreak of the war, only 8,000 were left when it ended. A third of all German Jews had lived in Berlin, and they had been taken from this platform to their deaths. Gregor walked slowly behind Ruvke, sympathetic to the profound sorrow his guest felt which was written all over his face. Gregor did not utter a word, and Ruvke was grateful for his silence. At the edge of the track, where Jews had been loaded onto the train, hung a metal sign, which also had a Hebrew inscription commemorating the Holocaust, and on the concrete fence along the whole length of the railway tracks were placed black stones, between which memorial candles had been put so that visitors could light them in memory of the Jews who had been taken from that spot, Platform 17 at Grunewald, to be killed. Trains and railway tracks have become symbols of the horrors carried out on the Jewish people during the Holocaust.

On their way from Platform 17, Ruvke and Gregor got off the train at the *Potsdamer Platz,* and made their way on foot to the Holocaust Memorial for the Murdered Jews of Europe, which was designed by the Jewish-American architect, Peter Eisenman. This tremendous vast monument, spread out over an area of 19,000 square meters, was not just for looking at. In order to understand its impact and implications, the visitor needs to give himself a long time to wander, to get lost in, and lose himself in the maze of its stones. With some trepidation, Ruvke started to walk within the thickness of the walls surrounding him on every side, 2711 concrete slabs varying in height, slabs arranged in a grid pattern resembling graves, spread out on a sloping field, wave upon wave of stones of uneven height. Ruvke walked around, one moment he had the sensation of falling into an abyss, then he suddenly stood erect again, but all the time being pulled downwards, drifting into an unnerving disorientation between the corridors of massive stones streaked with a dark dull copper color as if they were made of cast iron. Ruvke felt the horror, the silence, the empathy with those in whose memory that unique monument had been erected. Back and forth he wandered between the slabs of the huge memorial as if he were being swallowed up by them, into them, into the graves they seemed to him to symbolize, conveying an uneasy atmosphere of confusion, of fear, until he absorbed the sensation, the sensation of a man who had indeed known first-hand the horrors of the Holocaust. This memorial reminded everyone who saw it, of graves, and more graves, graves stretching as far as the eye could see, so they should know and understand – so that they should remember and not allow a regime of terror to rise again in their country and return it to the darkness of the Second World War and the Holocaust.

Not far from the Memorial to the Murdered Jews of Europe, the glass dome of the Reichstag Building glinted in the sun and Gregor suggested that they stroll around the impressive parliament building and go to see the large glass-domed ceiling with its mirrors reflecting the people standing opposite it. But Ruvke made a face at Gregor, and shrugged. Actually, I have no wish to visit that building with its dome of mirrors. I really do appreciate the efforts that the Germany of today makes to commemorate the Holocaust. It is a new generation and all that, and it condemns with all its heart what was done in the past. But I would rather see whatever remains of the past, things which can never again be what they were. All the reconstruction in Germany generally, and particularly in Berlin, is tremendously impressive, but to be honest with you, I have mixed feelings all the time: I can admire the beauty of the buildings. I admire the new initiatives and industry of today's Germany, but I also feel that that is also tainted by mourning for what had existed and had perished away. I feel most intensely, the depressing reality of emptiness.

Gregor listened and understood what Ruvke was getting at, and only said, in a rather matter-of-fact way, Anyhow, the line to get into the Reichstag building is so long that we would probably have to wait two hours, so we can certainly give it a miss.

Instead, they strolled slowly along a small open area with well-kept houses a short distance away, which served as parking lot. At the edge of the square was a billboard with a drawing of twenty or so rooms; each had a number and the function of each was described – store room, clinic, situation room, office, living rooms, bedroom, guest rooms and so on and on, which had stood in that spot, built in the bowels of the earth: Hitler's bunker. Nothing remained of it. No trace at all. It required a great deal of imagination to conjure up in one's mind that in the spot where the small parking lot stands today, under Hitler's Chancellery, above the bunker dug under the earth where he and his evil cohorts stayed, a trench was excavated and the bodies of the despised Fuhrer and his wife were burnt, leaving only their foul ashes, which were scattered over the ruins of the city. Nothing remained. Only loathing.

Let's get away from here, said Ruvke, trying to shake himself free of the revulsion he felt, and they drove off to visit the old Jewish cemetery, established in the 17th and 18th centuries. As an antithesis to the memorial they had seen earlier, with its thousands of bewildering blocks, where imagination became reality, here in this old cemetery, reality became self-delusion. The burial ground consisted of a huge expanse of grass, with here and there tall poplar trees whose shadow rested on one tombstone, related to Moses Mendelssohn. The single monument still standing in that ancient Jewish cemetery, all the others having long vanished from their places, leaving no sign that they had ever existed. The Nazis had razed them all, except for that one modest, unassuming, solitary gravestone left standing in the center of the burial ground, on which was engraved the name Moses Mendelssohn, the Jewish philosopher from the period of the Enlightenment in Germany. Mendelssohn's gravestone had also been destroyed but, in contrast to all the other tombstones, his was restored thanks to the greatness of the man whose remains lie beneath it. Now it stands there alone, as if to represent all the others whose memorial stones were smashed and removed.

The only thing Ruvke knew about Moses Mendelssohn was that he was regarded as the spiritual leader of the Jewish Enlightenment in Germany in the 18th century, who preached liberalism and claimed that integration of the traditional Jewish world with the new, educated, non-Jewish secular world, was possible and even desirable. He believed, therefore, that a Jew should be a Jew in his home and a man in the outside world. Ruvke was aware that Mendelssohn translated the Pentateuch, the Five Books of the Torah, into German and wrote a book on philosophy entitled "Jerusalem".

Out of the blue, while they were still standing in silence next to Mendelssohn's gravestone, Gregor's voice was heard. Until then, he had been careful not to say anything at all when they were visiting memorial sites, to make it easier for Ruvke to internalize the experience without distraction. Ruvke was sure that Gregor had no idea who Moses Mendelssohn was, and to his great surprise discovered that Gregor knew a hundred times more than he did himself about the German-Jewish philosopher. In the framework of his philosophy studies at the university, when he took courses on the German philosophers, he learned about Mendelssohn's theories too. Gregor explained to him now that Mendelssohn was regarded as the Jewish Socrates, and that his views on religion were published in a letter he wrote to a Protestant priest, Johann Kaspar Lavater, who had been a friend of his for years, but who became antagonistic towards him. The priest demanded that Mendelssohn refute *the Christian truth* and if he could not succeed in doing so, then he should immediately convert to be a Christian! Mendelssohn answered him in an open letter, in which he wrote that he was as convinced of the truth of Judaism as Lavater was as convinced of the truth of his religion, and stated that he would never convert from Judaism, which was based on wisdom and authority, so he has no reason to become a baptized Christian.

When Gregor intended to continue to develop the rivalry of the priest and the philosopher, Ruvke made a gesture as if to stop this potentially dangerous slide into an argument about religion, and said to Gregor briskly, Come on, let's leave the subject of religion alone. In any event, nobody is given a free choice as to which religion he can take on from birth. To the contrary, from the minute everyone enters the world he finds himself bound and chained to the destiny that his religion imposes on him. Gregor chuckled, Yes, indeed, everyone is chained to the religion fate assigns to him. You are right. Dammit, said Ruvke, if only there could be some kind of universal agreement and recognition of live and let live, whatever someone believes in, leave him alone to live with whatever religion fate has decreed for him, without criticism or hatred, or coercion. That way, the world would be a better place to live in.

Ruvke and Gregor stood reflectively for some time at the modest gravestone of the great man, until it was time for them to go on their way, one to his home, the other to his hotel.

The following morning they drove off in Gregor's car to the Jewish Quarter. Or, more accurately, to what had once been the Jewish Quarter. Ruvke and Gregor strolled slowly along the narrow streets of the neighborhood which had once been a spirited place, full of life. Now new people had come to live there, actually not so new, who had opened small businesses. These new owners could never forget the previous ones who had lived there before they moved in, and had lived out their lives and run their businesses there, but who would never return to claim what was rightfully theirs.

The new owners would never forget, because the names of those no longer alive, were carved on the walls of the houses at eye level, and on the floors they walked on. When they looked down onto the sidewalks absentmindedly, here and there they came across a name glinting out at them from a gold-colored plaque: Onto these small plates, set into the sidewalk, were etched the names, and the dates and circumstances of deportation, and the deaths of the victims who had lived there.

The artist who had initiated and carried out this special project, the Berlin-born Gunter Deming, had received the details of the victims from Yad Vashem, the Museum of the Holocaust in Jerusalem. In order to read the names, you have to lower your head, thereby honoring the people whose names are inscribed into the stones of the sidewalk. These unpretentious memorials are there to remind passersby of the names of the victims of Nazism.

*For a person is erased from memory, when his name is erased. For every person has a name, and the Jews lived their lives like every human being, until they were turned into nameless shadows, by depraved villains. For a shadow of a person is not a person, and a shadow does not have a name. Only when the name of a person is wherever inscribed, it banishes the shadow and returns the person to memory.*

Where should we go today, Ruvke asked Gregor the next morning. Gregor answered, there is one more place I think we should visit, but you should know that it is one of the most challenging memorials, perhaps because of its ironical location. Let's drive to Villa Wannsee. It is right near Potsdam. Have you heard of it? Ruvke had most certainly heard of it and understood its significance, and told Gregor that from what he knows, Villa Wannsee was a guest house for the SS, and that it was where they made the despicable decision, the cruelest and most inhumane thing that human beings can think of doing. At Wannsee the decision was made about the Final Solution for the Jewish problem. Can you grasp the implication of a handful of people meeting one day to define a whole people, a people which has been in existence for close to 4000 years – as a problem? And that this problem had to be solved, and the best solution to this in their eyes is by annihilation, extermination, murder, wiping this people off the face of the earth – in short, the Final Solution?

Gregor shook his head. That is not exactly what was decided at Wannsee, he said. The decision on the Final Solution to the Jewish problem – as they put it – was taken before that at the highest levels of government. Reinhard Heydrick had been appointed to deal with the Final Solution even before the Wannsee Conference. The Conference met on January

20, 1942, and after that the extermination machine was put into top gear in all the death camps. When they met at Villa Wannsee it was to have the process of exterminating the Jews given full legislative and administrative authority. They also discussed how to coordinate implementing the killing process in different countries. On the agenda that same day was also the subject of racial purity, how to define who was a Jew for their purposes. They decreed that each of a person's four grandparents had to be Christian. If only one of them was not, then he was considered to be a Jew.

Gregor added that Adolf Eichmann was present at Wannsee that day. He had done his homework very thoroughly and laboriously, and presented those high-ranking Nazis there with the most up-to-date, detailed lists of the numbers of Jews living in the whole continent of Europe, both in the countries already under the Nazis' control, and those the Nazis yet had to invade. In all, there were 11 million Jews in Europe.

When they arrived at the place, Ruvke was taken aback by the dissonance between the splendor of the building, which stood in a large garden filled with trees and plants, and the topics on the agenda on that day in January 1942.

The Villa was built in the old style for a German industrialist, and had undergone various changes until the German Reich took it over and used it as a conference center and guest house for the SS. At the very top of the building were cynically placed four stone statues of happy, carefree, children in flight. On January 20, 1942, fourteen high-ranking officers of the SS met under the leadership of Heydrich, who was in charge of the extermination operations in Europe; next to him sat Adolf Eichmann, responsible for carrying out the Final Solution of the Jewish problem. (The Israel Supreme Court ruled, in his trial in Jerusalem, that he was responsible, among other things, for the murder of a million and a half Jewish children, during the War.)

Four stone statues of children flying high in front of the

building – they are the victors over the 1.5 million Jewish children suffocated to death by gas, as a result of the deliberations of the handful of senior Nazis at the Wannsee Conference.

Ruvke and Gregor walked in the same rooms as did the members of the Conference at Wannsee on that long-ago day; they leafed through and read with appalled interest some of the hundreds of documents on display in what had been the dining room. In all the rooms of the Villa the exhibits were devoted to the persecution of the Jews and the Holocaust, beginning with an analysis of the causes of anti-Semitism and documents detailing the restrictions forced on Jews at the beginning of the War, to the orders for transports to the death camps. The Nazis were punctilious about recording their crimes in every corner their jackboots strode throughout the length and breadth of Europe. Every single thing was documented and could be read, and Ruvke's eyes and heart registered all the shocking details of these most heinous crimes, with Gregor at his side murmuring repeatedly, I'm ashamed, I'm so ashamed.

So as to rid themselves of some of the difficult feelings their visit to Wannsee had left them with, Gregor proposed that they drive to Potsdam, only half an hour's drive from Wannsee. Potsdam has a lot of glorious palaces, and its own history is interesting, too. Let's go and have a look round there, he suggested, and drove Ruvke to the Cecilienhof Palace.

The palace was built to look like an English Tudor country house, with a white and beige brick and timber frame exterior in a zigzag pattern, which was both unusual and pleasing to the eye. The Cecilienhof Palace was the venue for the Potsdam Conference at the end of the Second World War, and Gregor told Ruvke of the tension between the participants on the day of the Conference.

Stalin entered the Great Hall from the eastern gate of the

Palace, and Truman and Churchill came into the Hall from the western side. There were no amicable handshakes, no genial smiles, no friendly pats on the shoulder; the atmosphere at the conference which split Germany into two was icy cold. Potsdam found itself, together with Leipzig and Dresden, in East Germany, under Soviet control. Straight after the Potsdam Conference, the period of the Cold War began between the superpowers, which led to the building of the wall, splitting Berlin by force into two, like twins who were separated for many years.

The next day they went to Checkpoint Charlie. The wall that divided the two halves of Berlin almost hermetically, and Checkpoint Charlie was the only point where foreigners could cross over to the east part of the city while West German citizens were prevented from doing so. Now, all that remained was a section of 1,500 meters with all kinds of graffiti scribbled on it and drawings of the stages of the wall as it finally came down, an open-air art gallery, if you like, which passersby could enjoy at their leisure.

They also did not miss visiting the Checkpoint Charlie Museum where, on each of its three levels, documents, pictures and memorabilia provided a striking description of how the wall was built and its eventual tearing down, against a historical background of events during the period of the Cold War. Stunning!

On his last full day in Berlin, Ruvke went alone to the new Jewish Museum which had opened recently. The uniqueness of the museum was not in the artifacts it contained. Anyone who wants to see Holocaust exhibitions could go to the Yad Vashem Museum in Jerusalem, or to the Holocaust Museum in Washington D.C. The Jewish Museum in Berlin is first and foremost an architectural gem, designed by the artist and architect Daniel Libeskind. The building takes the shape of a flash of lightning, and symbolizes the history of the Jews of

Germany from the flourishing of their community right up to their destruction. The many spaces integral to the structure represent the breaches left after the annihilation of the Jews, both their physical absence and the void they left in all the facets of German society they had contributed to. The museum was built as a work of art in itself, in the shape of a zigzag, an exceptional sculpture, without regard to the exhibits that would be displayed inside, whose aim was to embody the history and culture of German Jewry, sculptural art which suggests more the symbolism than the functional.

Ruvke wanted to see just one more thing before he left Berlin, the Great Synagogue, on Oranienburg Street. As soon as he emerged from the subway station which brought him there, he saw the synagogue, a huge impressive building, with its carved, golden dome in the shape of a crown and at its tip a gold Star of David. A most splendid synagogue, which was destroyed in the war but now restored – apart from the prayer hall which had not been rebuilt. Because of that, a strikingly glorious synagogue was not used for the purpose it had been built for, but was used merely as a museum documenting the life of the flourishing Jewish community in Berlin before the war.

Emptiness, deep disappointment, great frustration, filled Ruvke's heart while seeing the beautiful synagogue empty of its worshipers. He felt the floor begin to shake under his feet as he remembered with a feeling of intense happiness that in a very short space of time he would be back to his home and his family, his home in Jerusalem which he so loved.

That evening, before he left for the airport, Gregor and his wife invited him to go with them to a restaurant, which was also a nightclub and beer cellar. Ruvke thoroughly enjoyed all aspects of the evening – the somewhat erotic floor show, the music, and the gourmet food. He looked around him at all the people eating and drinking, laughing and cheerful having an evening out, Berliners who were used to dining out at the best restaurants, who had no financial worries and no political instability. Nobody was threatening to annihilate them as the people in his country were threatened, but Ruvke did not envy them. No, he would not be willing, or wish to live among them. He was happy in his soul that in a very few hours his feet would be touching the ground of his own country.

They had a parting embrace. A hug which gave and received the message that this was the last time they would meet. They were both too old to renew their bizarre friendship, rooted in the horrors of the very distant past, within the reality of their present-day lives. They would leave things as they stood, with unforgettable memories of a bond which was almost incomprehensible to outsiders, and gratitude for the wonderful few days they had spent together.

✦✦✦

When Yuzhi heard from Ruvke his impressions of his visit to Berlin, he twisted and turned here and there like a caterpillar, a feeling of depression came over him which gradually crept up the whole length of his spine. Something which had been sealed up in his heart and mind burst, and he was overcome by intense flares of anger and jealousy, which stabbed him like a thick needle piercing delicate silk fabric.

He swayed to this side and that in his chair, and began to criticize Ruvke:

Why did you need that German to go around with you, he himself doesn't believe a word of all his pretenses, he is a sham. Even if it is true that this Gregor's father was one of those involved in the plot to assassinate Hitler, the top and bottom of it is that he was a Nazi through and through. If the Germans had not been defeated in the war, his father would definitely have become a big shot in the Nazi apparatus they set up, so don't come to me with tales about Gregor being proud of his father. What it comes down to is that his father went whichever way the wind was blowing.

Gregor himself was not as pure as the driven snow. Remember, Yuzhi added crossly, he took part in *actions* when Jews were sent to the ghetto or to concentration camps, and was in one of the *selections* teams which sent people to their deaths without batting an eye, and even if he did save your mother's life – and I have not a clue why he did so – it is not enough. And he also participated in the massacre at Babi Yar, so why you are making a big fuss of this friendship. I do not understand at all, and even if he did not shoot the youth who was still alive in the pit there in that bloody ravine and let him get away from there, it is still not enough to make him a saint.

Ruvke listened to Yuzhi's remarks and did not react. In his heart of hearts, he agreed that there was a lot of truth in them, but he saw no point in taking up the argument, for what could he say? It was a question of emotion, not of logic, and he was not inclined to be drawn into any lengthy arguments. The matter touched on too private a note for him. His relationship with Gregor, the way he felt about him, even he himself could not fathom. So he settled for a somewhat terse response, shook his head, and continued to describe what he had seen on his trip to Berlin.

Yuzhi felt he had been dealt with rather contemptuously by Ruvke's lack of response. After all, his opinions were surely worthy of being reacted to, either angrily or by being opposed, or even defensively. The fact that they were more or less regarded as having no importance, was like a heavy weight that had come to rest on his heart, adding to the considerable distress which his visit to Poland had left him with.

Like a delayed reaction, it disturbed his sleep. It kept him awake; he had no rest from it and now Ruvke, back from his travels to Berlin, did not even react to his comments about his Nazi friend, which added fuel to the flames of his anguish and made him feel that a deep chasm had opened in his heart and shocked his mind into a frenzy, and created a kind of geological abyss in his world, which exposed a deep fracture in his soul.

He began to withdraw further and further into himself, and to be compulsively drawn to analyze the factors in the heavens which, in his opinion, predict fateful moves. The stars were dancing in front of his eyes and running across his brain. Mercury and Mars were on the descendant and caused disfunction in communications, and the retreat of Mars which stays in the sign of Leo is likely to bring about a war situation, and here is a cluster of planets which focus on the Sun – Venus, Mercury and Pluto – which create an aspect of disharmony to Saturn, indicating increasing aggressiveness, the danger is coming closer and closer, not to speak of the withdrawal of the planets whose influence extends over the economic situation and bring woe to business deals decided on at an inauspicious time. And here is Saturn radiating to Jupiter, and Neptune radiating to Mercury, which radiates towards the Moon, the orange Moon, which sometimes turns to black, and the Moon radiates to Neptune, and now you must beware, for you must not act when there is a ninety-degree aspect between Jupiter and Mercury.

Yuzhi saw negative aspects from all angles. There was no chance for him now. Even though it states in the Bible, in the Book of Judges, in the Song of Debora:

*The stars from their courses had fought Sissera.*

But that was in ancient times, in our days stars do not fight, they only use their lights to beam the positive or negative aspects on to the fate of human beings, and perhaps even control their destinies.

Yuzhi's depressive and precarious mental state deteriorated, and gradually not only those around him, but he himself, too, felt that he was losing his mind. There was a fire burning within him. The fears of his infancy, which he had spent in the shadowy cellar of Katya and Piotr's house in Belzec during the war now took control of him and darkened his whole world; as well, the anxiety and uncertainty concerning everything connected to his father's identity, which arose from the denial, the way his mother had consistently pulled the wool over his eyes, and even lied about his origins, had, when the truth was eventually been revealed to him, broken him into tiny pieces. His mind could not take it. And if that was not enough, he felt as if had taken a blow from a sledgehammer which cut his soul into fragments after the veil was lifted and his former world was exposed for him to see, during his traumatic visit to Poland.

The deceitful showerheads of the gas chambers in the death camps, retracing his steps in the dark cellar of his infancy in Katya's house in Belzec, all these images ran across his brain like cockroaches trapped inside a closed box, scrambling and climbing this way and that, and treading on each other in their desperate urge to get outside, but to no avail.

Hunched over and bent down, Yuzhi sat for days at a time in his rented room, eating and drinking little, sad and depressed, even the light of the sun bothered him.

One day, quite out of the blue, and for no good reason that anyone could figure out, Yuzhi went from the depths of despair in his self-imposed isolation, to the other extreme: A wave of joy, exhilaration, ecstasy swept over him, and in a wild celebration of extravagance, he began to spend his money on nonsense, buying jewelry and dresses for his mother, and lotions and after shave for each of his brothers in unreasonably huge quantities. For himself, he bought expensive clothes that were the height of fashion, and withdrew all his savings to pay for his excess of ridiculous generosity. He rode everywhere only by cabs, and was soon left with hardly a cent for his actual living expenses.

His anxious parents realized that his bizarre behavior was extreme, and that he was losing control of himself, and took him to a psychiatrist who examined him and pronounced that Yuzhi was mentally ill, suffering from manic psychosis, which presents itself with symptoms of schizophrenia and bipolar disorder and ordered him to be admitted to a psychiatric hospital.

When Ruvke came to drive him to the hospital, Yuzhi refused to go with him, and began to rant and rave. In the end he agreed, after he understood from Ruvke that if he would not go with him voluntarily, they would send hospital warders to come for him, and he would have to be put in a straitjacket they put loonies in, and be forcibly hospitalized. Yuzhi understood what would happen to him if he continued to resist, so reluctantly he went with Ruvke, his bowels turned ups and downs.

In the hospital, Yuzhi had to submit to all kinds of unpleasant and humiliating medical tests, and was brought a mountain of pills which the doctors ordered him to swallow to stabilize his mental state. Then he began to rebel, and in his anger threw all his tablets at the nurses and caregivers, and refused to swallow any of them. He shouted, and screamed insults, and rampaged all over the place, until the warders had to put restraints on him and indeed put him in a straitjacket so that his arms were kept close to his chest. Now that his movements were restricted, the caregivers succeeded in getting him to put the pills in his mouth, and swallow them.

The medications did calm him down, and after a few days he was allowed to be released from that awful straitjacket, and he stayed in the psychiatric hospital for a limited period, not for long, passive and obedient, until it was considered that his mental state had stabilized sufficiently for him to be discharged from the hospital to his home, to his room, that is, on condition that he would return to the hospital for frequent follow-ups to check his mental health.

After his discharge, it was suggested to Yuzhi that he should go back to live in his mother's house in Jerusalem, but he did not want to. He would manage on his own, thank you, he said, but he was by no means certain that in fact he would be able to. And in fact, he only lasted out for a short time, before he succumbed to the loneliness, and to his fears, and to the severe anxiety that if he became mentally ill again, he would have to go back to the psychiatric hospital – a panic thought he could not bear.

His condition seemed to be closing on him from all sides, he felt his situation was desperate, and as gloomy as a tunnel that no ray of light could enter, and he could see no light at the very end of the tunnel.

Because Yuzhi's intellectual faculties had not been affected by his psychiatric problems, he reached a decision one day that really began to burn him up inside – to put an end to his life. He very carefully made the practical preparations for carrying out his fateful decision. He planned everything with meticulous accuracy and even with an element of ceremony, as if it were a military operation. First of all, nobody must know or even suspect that his death was suicide. He must therefore leave not the faintest sign or shred of evidence that he died by his own hand. His death must appear to be entirely due to natural causes.

Just before Yuzhi went to bed on the night he had designated to be his last night on earth, he poured himself a large glass of water and put it on the night table next to the bed. Typically, for someone who is rigidly compulsive about cleanliness and neatness, Yuzhi painstakingly and ceremoniously arranged the large quantity of sleeping pills he had accumulated, which he had bought on the same day from several different pharmacies, so as not to arouse any suspicion in the pharmacists. He put on his pajamas, got into bed, and arranged his pillows, and took a look around his room to make sure that he had left no hint that his seemingly natural death was in fact suicide.

As he arranged his sleeping pills with precision – in rows, leaving exactly the same gap between each – for this austere ceremony of his suicide, Yuzhi started to talked to himself, making up excuses and pretexts to justify his decision to end his life by his own hands.

Why do I need to go on with my pointless life, I really cannot explain, there is no purpose to my life. I have no deep love for anyone, and even my own family can barely put up with me. My mother let me down, first of all when she married a man she loved more than me, and worse than that, when she began to bring more children into the world, those brothers of mine, they have always condescended to me, as if I am a strange wild bird invading their band of white swans and they do not know how to push me away from them; not to speak of the women I have met in the course of my life, not one of whom has even let me touch her. I would only just begin to try to put my hands on them and they would shy away from me, as if I was a leper, when in fact I look good. I take care of my body. I am certainly not fat, and I am not scrawny like a chicken either. I used to go every day to the pool. I would swim thirty lengths, and exercise a lot. I am in good shape. I always thought they should be grateful that I was even willing to look at them, those women, but each time I asked them for a kiss, they would back away and say, no thank you, and when I tried, like a vigorous man, to insist on giving them a kiss anyway, even if they had not agreed, and I forced myself on them a bit, it is what women really like, they would turn their heads away from me in disgust, and some of them would even yell, You sex maniac, don't you dare to touch me!

I told them everything I knew about music and history, especially the period of the war, but they were not impressed, and it did not make them more attracted to me, so I immediately let them go. So I am at this point, that I am now more than 60 years old and have never had a physical relationship with a woman. Not even a proper kiss.

I once met a woman who agreed to come and stay with me here, in my room, a German tourist, a Christian, not a great beauty but not bad-looking. I made a very good impression on her at the beginning, and when I invited her to come with me she was quite moved by the idea, even though I think that she agreed to come here only because she would not have to pay rent. She was an intelligent woman and we had interesting conversations, and I remember that instead of courting her and going out with her, maybe it would lead to love, from the first moment she came to live here, I began to bombard her with arguments about Hitler and all the wrong moves he had made in the war and all the terrible crimes he had committed against the Jews, and she, because she was German, started to feel that I was blaming her personally and holding her responsible for the Holocaust. Also, all my compulsive opinions began to irritate her so one day she just packed her bags and left. Got up and went without so much as saying goodbye.

So what have I got to look forward to, if I keep deteriorating like this. In no time at all I will be back in that psychiatric hospital and I will turn into a zombie with all the pills they will force down my throat. They will put me in a straitjacket again. No, no, no, they will not get the chance to do that to me again. I will show them. I will not give them the opportunity to keep mistreating me and stuffing me full of pills, for I will not do it anymore.

Quietly and peacefully, convinced that he was justified in doing what he was doing, Yuzhi picked up the glass of water and began taking the sleeping pills one by one. He held every pill in two of his fingers and placed it on his tongue, taking a sip from the glass and swallowing slowly, one pill after another. When he realized that this method of taking the pills was having no effect on him, he decided that it would be better for him to swallow a large number of them at the same time. If he did not do that, he would not achieve the result he longed for and he would never get to the end.

He therefore took a handful of the pills and crammed them into his mouth, a few handfuls one after another, swallowing them down hastily with a gulp of water until he had finished them all. Then, he put his cup down, and looked around his room for the last time to make sure he had not left any evidence which would give a hint of what he had planned so meticulously. When he saw that not one pill was left, he lay down on his bed, feeling strangely satisfied, lay his head on the pillow, snuggled up and made himself cozy in the blanket. He emptied his head of thoughts, and fell into a deep sleep, from which he never awoke.

The owner of the apartment discovered Yuzhi's body two days later, and informed his family in Jerusalem. The doctor who confirmed his death was not able to find the cause of death without carrying out an autopsy, but none of his family was willing to have that imposed on Yuzhi.

For heaven's sake, he has suffered enough without it, they justified their refusal, and they generally accepted that the reason for his death was from a heart attack while he was asleep. It had been a merciful death. He had not been in pain or had to live with a serious illness, we wish all of us will die like that, they unanimously agreed, and were able to comfort themselves with the thought.

For death has a life of its own, a kind of hierarchy defined by the kind of death that has occurred. The suicide of a member of one's family is ranked lowest of all on this strange ladder, so it is far better for death to be caused by an illness that suddenly puts an end to a someone's life, in order to preserve the honor of the family, rather than have them bowed down with guilt because one of their close relatives has put an end to his life. Anything but that. Yes, Yuzhi died from a heart attack, they pronounced confidently.

But deep in their hearts, each one of them knew that Yuzhi had committed suicide.

Despite the fact that he had not been a refugee or a survivor of a death camp, Yuzhi's life-long suffering was directly caused by the Holocaust. He was a victim who felt the ground consistently shifting under his feet, by the skin of his teeth he tried to hang on to whatever was dear to him, although in vain. All the memories going back to his infancy made him fearful and anxious, those early days spent hidden away in the darkness of a lonely cellar, sealed up to keep him from meddling eyes. His personality was formed then; climbing up on his way to thoughts of fire. A dense cloud of haze obscured his view and the clarity of his thought, and no manna fell from the heavens to quench his thirst, to allay his hunger, to repair the fragments of his fractured soul. The sands of time in his hourglass ran out, until they submerged all his dreams in the everlasting sleep he himself had chosen to sink into.

Only sparks of blazing fire, and dark cellars, and trenches dug, and smoke from the crematoria, exposed the roots of Yuzhi's miserable existence, until he ceased to exist ...